A Saint Comes Stumbling In

Bonnie McCune

Published by Inspired Romance Novels
ISBN-13: 978-0615642222 ISBN-10: 0615642225
First Edition, 2012
Published in the United States of America
Contact info: contact@inspiredromancenovels.com
http://www.inspiredromancenovels.com

DEDICATION

To the world's best critique group, members past and
present, who helped me never give up.

CHAPTER ONE

On Saturday, the doorbell chimes and for the first time in several months, I open the door with neither hope nor fear. For a heartbeat, I fail to recognize the man's back as he surveys the street instead of me. It should be as familiar to me as the lumpy overstuffed chair in the living room or the collection of family photos in the hall—its breadth, the slope of the shoulders, the ragged neck of the faded red t-shirt covering it.

When I realize the visitor is my husband James, the shock paralyzes my vocal chords. Why is he here? He removed all his portable belongings long before and the terms and division of property were hammered out several weeks ago. A thin tendril of hope struggles to force a way through the arid wasteland of my self-esteem, decimated after his desertion. Perhaps the twelve years of our marriage hadn't been ecstatic, but at least I'd found our marital bliss comfortable.

I'm now wary enough of another rejection not to invite him in. Instead, I step out to the small square of concrete that serves as a porch.

Some inconsequential chatter, an exchange of how-are-yous and nice-weather-we're-havings, leave me wondering why he's suddenly reappeared. Then James's voice turns resolute.

"Joan, I need to ask you a favor," he says with a stiff formality, as if we're strangers instead of a couple who have seen one another with drippy head colds or climaxing with animal moans and groans. "I know I told you there was no hurry to sell the house, but I'm pressed for money. Maureen and I need to get a place of our own. We've been squeezed into that tiny apartment too long."

"You mean you can't live on love?" My disappointment increases my inherent sarcasm, recently suppressed toward the finale of my marriage as I struggled to band-aid the relationship's incurable wounds. "When you left, you claimed you needed nothing else."

"Yeah, well, things change," he mutters and wipes curved fingers across his lips. "Love won't feed us and it won't pay the rent. This mortgage is strangling me. Our settlement calls for you and me splitting the house's value. So sell it or don't sell it, but I need to have my share soon."

My anger flares and I forget the house's expense and inconvenient location in a new middle-class enclave far from Denver's center. "You told me I could stay as long as I liked. I love this house. I spent nearly a year finding a place that we could afford in a style I liked."

James retreats hastily. "I'm not taking legal action, just asking you to think about putting this place on the market."

"I don't know a thing about realty. You do it." I cross my arms over my chest and feel my jaw tightening. I've had to learn to ignite the stove's pilot light, add oil to the car, even drag the ladder to the ceiling fixture in the hall to change the light bulb while standing on my toes. I've dealt with too many changes in too short a time—I shouldn't be obligated to deal with a real estate agent.

"You're living here. It makes more sense for you," James insists. "You can schedule appointments at your convenience, that sort of thing."

My temper turning to a slow but feverish burn, I object. "I can't guess the value. You run the ads and talk to prospective buyers. I don't have the background or training."

James snorts, a particularly unpleasant habit of his when he wants to act superior. "You're deliberately making the process complicated. What do you think we have real estate agents for? I've asked Kevin to contact you. See what he says."

"Kevin is *your* friend," I say between clenched teeth to control my volume. Even at eight on a Saturday morning, our neighbors have sharp ears and we're standing in the full glare of the sun on the front porch. Verbal brawls are definitely not allowed under the terms of the development's covenant, any more than painting an exterior bright purple. "You call him."

"Kevin is, was," James corrects, "*our* friend. "I haven't seen him since I moved out. When I called to tell him about our decision..." — *Your* decision, I interject in my mind — "I think he disapproved."

"Hmmm... I wonder why?" I purse my lips and hold my index finger over them. Damn, that irrepressible sarcasm again. Can't beat it down even when I realize I'm sabotaging my self-interest. But striking back at James alleviates my pain. "Not because twelve years of a marriage went down the drain?"

"Don't." James is clenching his teeth now. I can hear them grinding. "Be rational for once in your life, not emotional. Just call Kevin."

"Not because we were together all through school, when Kevin was part of our crowd?" I dig my sharp words deeper and I hit something, for James turns to flee. "Not because he's known about your little liaisons, your affairs, your peccadilloes, while I kept my head firmly in the sand?" I taunt and tag along.

"Drop the drama queen act! I'm not going to fight with you," he calls over his shoulder as he moves down the sidewalk. "I won't lower myself to your level."

"You mean you lack the balls," I respond and *not* in a lowered voice. "Maureen is welcome to you."

James reaches his new molten-gold Lexus, jumps in the driver's seat and locks the doors. I'm mere seconds behind, pounding on the window with both fists, neighbors and their reactions the last thing on my mind.

"That's right, you bastard. Hide in your fancy-schmantzy convertible. Won't do you any good! Lucky at cards, unlucky at love, isn't that what they say? I hope the car keeps you warm on winter nights after Maureen discovers what a worm you are and leaves."

James screeches away, tires smoking a burnt-rubber smell, his attention riveted on me in the rear-view mirror rather than the street ahead of him. Not once have I ridden in the white, smooth, leather-lined luxury of the new car. Pardon me, vehicle, for a Lexus is so much more than mere transportation. He bought it with his ill-gained earnings from the Powerball game, the two-hundred dollar thousand runner-up prize. This bonanza sprang loose the trap of our marriage, as he so kindly told me on his way out the door two months ago.

I never knew he'd been 'investing' several hundreds a pop in lotto tickets. Colorado's a common-property state, so I tried to claim half the windfall in the divorce settlement. That's when his lawyer most solemnly and officially told me the money was exempt because James purchased the ticket *after* he'd filed the initial divorce papers. Not that I knew he'd ever filed anything other than income tax.

I was equally an ignoramus about the other woman in James's life. No, make that *women*. Although this last one appears to have stuck, I've been uncovering evidence of his sundry infidelities—an unexplained motel charge here, a lipstick-stained hanky there.

So here I am, bewildered and betrayed, kicking dust in the gutter, staring after my soon-to-be-ex-husband in his fancy car, possessing nothing but a suburban house identical to its neighbors and destined to be sold from under my feet very shortly. No wonder I'm blue.

I'm at work, silently crying over my keyboard, thinking again of Saturday's confrontation.

Every minute or so I blink rapidly to keep the tears from falling into the electronics. I know what I owe my bosses, attorneys-at-law Horowitz, Trimble, Hawkins, & Jones, and it isn't shorting out this expensive equipment with sobs.

Didn't they take a chance on a nearly unskilled, displaced homemaker six short weeks prior? After I learned their routines, hadn't they upgraded both software and hardware so I could produce documents faster?

Yes and yes.

I wipe the tears from my face with the back of my hand. Nearly coffee break time. Then I'll flee to the restroom for a really good cry. In the meantime, concentrate on the document, I warn myself, and stop sniveling. Mustn't present a bad image of the law firm to the client sitting just on the other side of the room waiting to see Mr. Hawkins.

Kimberlee, the paralegal, glides into her chair at the next desk, the complete sophisticated professional. Batting her long lashes (real) and tossing her blonde curls (bleached), she nods to me to indicate her willingness to cover the phones. She isn't the type to add a pleasant word to someone lower on the office hierarchy ladder than she.

I stand and push an old navy-blue polyester skirt down from around my thighs where it habitually clings, like an especially annoying collection of cat hair. It was the first thing to hand in my closet this morning. Rather, the first piece of clothing that fits over the twenty or so pounds I've gained since my marriage turned sour. Kimberlee's eyes flicker over my form, then return to the law book in front of her.

Too bad, I think, lifting my chin. Just too bad you don't like my clothes, you anorexic witch. Not only are you skinny, even worse that you have to be intelligent and competent. Couldn't you have some flaws? Why do some women get all the advantages? Why isn't Mother Nature evenhanded when she distributes gifts at birth?

Down the hall I flee, barely reaching the restroom in time to seize a handful of tissue in which to stifle my sobs. Small, thin, smart, and charming versus tall, fat, dull, and depressed. Why does the same situation occur at work as at home? James's new sweetie is Kimberlee's double—I know from having been her "very bestest friend in the world"—as she crooned at me just after her own divorce and before she went after James, no holds barred. Unfair, unfair. I was doomed from the get-go to lose to the competition. I weep so hard my cries turned to hiccups.

That's how Dolores finds me a minute later, leaning on the sink and hiccupping, my nose shiny and red as a ripe cherry tomato, mascara smeared down my cheeks.

"*Hija*, little one, what's wrong? Here, have a pastry. It'll be all right." Dolores digs into her apron pocket and pulls out a napkin-wrapped, gooey, almond-encrusted bear claw left over from the breakfast rush. Dolores works in the building's cafeteria and believes with the totality of her own chubby strength that food, unlike men or even money, solves all problems.

"It's James," I answer, reaching for the pastry. "He came over Saturday and insisted I put the house on the market."

"Good riddance," spits Dolores. "Once you move, you'll be free of every reminder about that scum-ball."

"But I'm alone, all alone," I wail.

"You're sooooo emotional. Calm down. You have me," says Dolores as she puts her arm around my shoulders and offers a tissue. "We're *amigas*, aren't we?"

In the mirror over the sink, I see myself and Dolores reflected, two well upholstered female figures. One (me) has a face that looks like it has been in a collision with a truck or a brick wall, so marred and damaged are its makeup and expression. The other (Dolores) sports black hair bound under the hideous hairnet required by her job but also displays features softened with sympathy.

The sight is horrendous enough to dry up any waterfall of emotion. My lip quivers, but I mop up the final traces of tears. "Yeeees."

"Well, then? Men! Who needs 'em?" Dolores is just over her fifth live-in boyfriend. "Only to start the kids off."

Dolores abandoned marriage after her second steady liaison. Marriage laws cause more problems than they solve, she maintains with some credibility. Without legalities, Dolores can drop her boyfriends as soon as she discovers that the current one is as despicable as the previous. The causes of these partings range from lack of child support to other women. Yet she continues to search endlessly for romantic liaisons, much like a risky addiction she can't live without.

"You on break yet? When you didn't show, I hightailed it up here to find you. Come on down," Dolores urges, steering me by the shoulders.

We take the elevator to the second floor. Mid-afternoon is the slow time in the cafeteria, so Dolores joins me at a booth for coffee. Well, actually not for coffee—that's the euphemism covering the range of comfort food she totes—a package of corn chips, soft drinks, and the remains of the luncheon special, lasagna dripping with sauce and cheese.

"You need a new guy like a birthday needs a cake." Dolores plunks her generous derriere on the maroon plastic seat and continues the conversation from where we've left off. "Someone to take away the bad taste of that *James*." She purses her lips into a crumpled circle. "Someone *boing!* To get your juices going again."

I tear open the orange and red bag of snacks and pause to consider. "Who'd have me? My father left me years ago, now my husband takes off. I must be cursed."

From the wall of windows facing west, Dolores squints in the streaming sunlight to study me. "You're nice looking. Pleasantly plump. Many men prefer that. Gives them something to hold onto during the cold winter nights. My brother, for instance, he likes solid women."

With a wave of my hand, I dismiss Dolores's brother as a prospect. "Him? You've told me about his drinking and his four children and ex-wife. Not to mention his lack of a job. You can't complain about him all the time and then suddenly spring him on me as a suitable romance. Anyway, James was my one true love." I sigh from my toes up.

"Speaking from experience, one true loves come many times in a woman's life. If you're open to them."

"I'm terrified," I admit. I chew some chips slowly until they're ready to dissolve, then lick the salt off my fingers one by one. "Not just at the thought of being a single in a doubles' world. But of maybe never finding my soul mate."

"Hmmm. I don't believe in this soul mate babble," says Dolores. "But it sounds like you've decided to toss in the towel about James."

I open my mouth to deny this when the image of James standing on the porch, demanding that I sell the house, comes to mind. The infuriation I felt at his sudden decision, the desolation at my isolation, rebound, redouble, resolve into a blazing rage. "Yes," I say, "yes, I have."

"Good," replies Dolores with the self-satisfaction of a vindicated prophet. "Now all you need to do is practice taking some chances."

"I'm not a chance-taker," I respond, feeling myself shrink even as I think about dipping into that great squalid pool of people known as "singles." Sleek, well dressed, confident, flirting, chatting, petting, having sex. I turn my mind from that direction at once.

"What do you mean? Isn't your name Joan?" says Dolores.

"Yes. What's that got to do with anything?"

"Your patron saint is Joan of Arc. There was one lady *loco* enough to face being burned at the stake for what she believed. Surely you can follow her lead a little?"

"I'm not Catholic," I point out.

"But surely you know her story? She marched forward bravely, proudly, to show the world what she could do. Nothing phased her, nothing stopped her." Dolores holds her bag of chips in front of her like a shield.

The bell on the cafeteria door tinkles as someone enters. I'm facing the door and I freeze, chip-clutching hand mid-air, every nerve ending on full alert. My mouth drops.

"What's wrong?" Dolores asks.

"Him," I croak, breath fighting for territory with food. "That man."

Dolores swings in the booth to see what I'm watching. Gray, pin-striped suit, shoulders broader than Mr. America's, russet wavy hair, firm nose, all smoldering in one neat bundle like a package of dynamite, walks into the food line of the cafeteria. "Who's he?" she asks, turning back.

I possess the female skill of motionless verbal response like a ventriloquist, in which a tooth-baring smile provides cover for a *sotto voce* rejoinder. I murmur, "A new attorney in our suite. Scott. Not really part of the firm. He's sub-leasing an empty office." I maintain the smile until it feels frozen on my face, hoping and fearing the man will look in my direction.

"No soul," Dolores throws her instant judgment over her shoulder as she gets up to return to the cashier's station at the end of the food line.

I sit paralyzed where I am. Because the entire interior of the cafeteria lacks walls and is open to a wide-angle view, I can see the food preparation area, the metal counter beside which customers walk and slide their trays until they reach the cashier. The object of my fascination must believe a tray to be unnecessary, for he balances a container of yogurt and a banana in one hand and reaches for a coffee cup with the other. No soul? I wonder. With a face like an angel's? Or at least a Greek god's. Dolores is crazy. Well, maybe not so crazy. For a moment, every thought of my "one true love" has fled faster than soap bubbles burst in air.

The man exits from the cafeteria line and strides to a nearby table. His disinterested look sweeps over me, not even registering my presence, just as it passes over plastic booths, slate walls, signs advertising the special of the day. Well, what did I expect? My hand flies up to my hair, light reddish-brown, fine as cotton candy, slicked back into a scraggly ponytail. Since James split, I've lacked the energy to bother with curlers, blow drying, even hair cuts.

Dolores returns and catches me staring at the man as if he were a chocolate sundae and I haven't eaten in a month. Dolores claps her hands and I jump.

"I'm back. Now stop looking starved. Where were we? A boyfriend." She slides into the opposite side of the booth, her back to the man, and helps herself to one of my chips.

With the dignity of the innocent in a court of law, I speak. "Dolores, I appreciate what you're trying to do. But I have to go through the grieving process for my marriage before I start mixing with new men. You know — denial, acceptance, all that."

"The way you're eyeballing that guy, you're well on the road to recovery. Anyway, you read that self-help garbage in some women's magazine? Listen, girl, what you need is *fun!*" Dolores snaps the fingers of both hands high in the air and wriggles her torso in a gravity-defying shimmy. "You got tied down way too young. James was your first? And your only?"

"Ssssh," I hiss. "The world doesn't need to hear this." But then I nod, despite embarrassment about my lack of experience. "We were in high school together. Married right after graduation. Then three years in the service, in San Diego. Then back here to Denver. But we had a good marriage at first. And we did have fun," I insist.

"You *have to* believe because you don't want to face up to the facts. Was it fun to work as a waitress putting him through college?" demands Dolores. Her brown eyes flash a challenge, as if daring me to fib.

In my mind, many voices echo from the course of six years of waitressing, demanding instantaneous food service. "Not exactly," I say, remembering days that started at five a.m., the smell of ammonia-tinged cleaning water, the roughness of perpetually chapped hands.

"You're telling me. My feet feel like huge sores at the end of the day. And I never can get the smell of fried hamburgers out of my hair."

"I prefer to look at my glass as half-full, rather than half-empty, even a container as leaky as my marriage. There were good times," I continue. "We went to movies, bowling. I thought we were happy. My God, he should have been." I sit straight up abruptly. "His word was my command. I catered to him like royalty. Clean, ironed shirts organized in the closet by colors. Dinner on the table when he came home. Visits with his family every week. I thought that's what men want, to be the boss, to have the full support of their wives."

I get hot under the collar again just thinking about my marriage, the one-sided sacrifices, James's cowardly exit, and Dolores can tell, probably from the steam coming out my ears and the sputters issuing from my mouth as my voice rises. "That's right," she urges. "Get good and mad. But then, get even. What is it they say is the best revenge?"

"Living well. Living well is the best revenge."

"So go live well. Hot damn, you're named after most ballsy woman who ever lived. Joan of Arc. Didn't fear crap. Copy her. Get out there and raise hell for a while."

I throw my paper napkin down on the table. "Okay. You're making sense. That's just what I'll do." I leap to my feet like an eager grasshopper, rocking back and forth from the vigor of my response.

Dolores looks up at me with a trace of alarm on her face. "I didn't mean right this second. What are you up to now?"

"You'll see." I head straight for Scott's booth and he looks up at the sound of my approach, his absolutely blank expression changing second-by-second to one of bemused unease as I near his table. I stop, my insides shaking, but my exterior as erect and high-chinned as I can manage.

"Mr. Clark?"

"Yeeeess?" His response ends as a question. In his beautiful, sea-green eyes, shot through with shards of black, fringed by the darkest lashes, is not a glimmer of recognition or interest. I cast desperately around for some topic of conversation, some reason for approaching him.

"I'm Joan Nelson, the receptionist in your office," I babble. "I just wanted to welcome you and tell you that I'll route callers to your voice mail when you're not in."

"Thank you. Joan?" He says my name as a question, as if wondering if I exist. Those same sea-green eyes rake up and down my body, the one that's somehow, without my knowledge or consent, assumed the burden of twenty extra pounds over the last few years. Unable to think of anything else to say, I nod, whirl around, and return to my booth. I slide back in, shaking.

"Wow!" Dolores says, wide-eyed. "I'm impressed. When you make up your mind to something, you move right out there. What did you say? What did he say?"

CHAPTER TWO

I'm still trembling. "I told him I'd route his phone calls. Real brilliant. He, of course, said pretty much nothing. How could he respond to such a stupid statement?"

"At least you took a chance, said something. That took some guts, girl. You're on your way," says Dolores.

From the corner of my eye, I see Scott edge out of the cafeteria. "Yeah," I say and sigh, "and now he's on his way."

"Not important," Dolores insists. "It's putting yourself out there, taking chances that will eject you out of your rut."

"You sound like my mother," I say. "She keeps lecturing me about making changes. She compares my situation to hers. After my father left us, she became a woman's libber. From middle school on, she was yammering at me I should get an education, training in a career so I could support myself if I had to. Looks like she was right." I pick up the bag and chips and select one with careful thumb and forefinger, sure it is going to break into bits.

"Sounds like good advice to me," says Dolores.

"You would think that. You remind me of her. A good man is impossible to find...most of them are big babies...strong women can cope without a partner." I make my voice assume a monotonous, lecturing drone as I mouth the words I've heard so often.

"I'm no women's libber," Dolores objects stoutly. "I'm realistic. You can't depend on someone whose only thoughts are about a football game or the next good ass that wriggles by."

"Whatever. But I really thought I'd escaped my mom's fate. I felt James and I had everything, a perfect marriage. But then we tried for a child. Nothing happened. Except my marriage fell apart."

Dolores shakes her head. "You're crazy. Why are you blaming yourself? Men wander. They see something they want, they think is better, and they go after it like dogs on the loose. Missy Joan, most you can hope for is to train them. I don't especially care for you taking on a job like that right now. But you need to do something, start moving your feet to a new rhythm, or you're going to turn into stone."

"Maybe you're right." I pause to think. "I never thought I'd find a job, as unskilled as I am. But once I got out there and kept searching, this one came along. Speaking of jobs, oops, time's up. I've got to get back to the office."

I pry my thighs from the plastic seat where they've stuck and wave a good-bye to Dolores, still thinking about my mother. Barbara hadn't had an easy time of it. I consider for the first time the sense of failure that must have swept over my mom. Year after year she struggled to improve her homemaking skills only to run smack bang into an unsolvable problem—her husband's departure. Certain parallels exist now between me and Barbara. I'm not sure I want to pursue the comparison.

On the bus ride home after work, I'm pitted against other tired commuters for six-inches of space in the crowded aisles. A month's practice has taught me to keep my balance hanging on the overhead bar even while careening around corners and daydreaming during the ride. When James first left, I daydreamed about reuniting, about losing twenty, no *thirty!* pounds, bleaching my hair, somehow mysteriously enticing him back to me. Or him running home, full of regrets about abandoning my reliable and solid self for the shallow-if-sexy girl, my former friend, he's temporarily taken on.

Now the daydreams tend more toward the extravagant variety, in which I meet a rich old woman while grocery shopping at Whole Oats, show her how to evaluate organic produce, make friends with her over a cup of espresso, and finally accept her gift of a full scholarship to college. Or run into an attractive man, say the one from the cafeteria, who needs assistance in saving the office building occupants from a raging fire. I'm not sure if the change in fantasies indicates increasing acceptance of the end of my marriage or a decreasing grasp on reality.

An uncomfortable forty-five minutes later, I push the bell for my stop and struggle down the aisle to the back door exit through other immobilized riders, who are numb to or uncaring about the small courtesy of moving aside. Still several blocks to walk to home. I really should sell the house, I think, much as I hate to agree with James. It's so far from work and too expensive for me to make payments on by myself after the property's divided.

In fact, I hate this area, I suddenly realize, as I dodge the neighbor kid practicing moves on a skateboard who doesn't seem to realize a collision will injure him and me. But what's brought on this feeling of revulsion? I weave around balls, a bright red wagon, two miniature tricycles abandoned on the sidewalk in front of the home next to mine, and pause to pull out my key. Through the brightly lit window of nearby residences, I can see children watching television, pouring over homework, bugging mothers making dinner. And I realize every house has children except mine. The women who inhabit these pastel-colored houses that extend for miles on north, south, east, west, stay home to care for their families. Over the years, I've been constantly, if subconsciously, reminded of my failure, my lack. And now, I have no chance of changing the situation. That's why I loathe this house, this street, this community. Guess I'd better sell.

I unlock my front door and enter the compact suburban square. Just because I've surrendered to James's plea doesn't mean I'm instantaneously equipped to take action. My musings about real estate continue—what do I know about mortgages and points, liens, insurance, property appraisals? I have trouble figuring out checking accounts. And I won't even talk about the monetary settlement for the divorce! Let's just say I trust my attorney utterly.

Panicked at the idea of grappling with yet another complicated financial matter for which I've no experience, I swallow to control my apprehension as I pick up the mail in the hallway. One light burns in the living room, left on all day. Since James's abandonment, I can't bear to enter a dark structure. The setting brings back childhood nightmares—I imagine monsters with fangs dripping blood and huge curled claws ready to snatch me. Or maybe the dark is just the absence of safety, the pervasive feeling in my young mind when my father disappeared.

I flick on every light on my way to the living room. Thumbing through the mail, I note nothing but the regular bills and stacks of flimsy ads interspersed with offers for credit cards. Funny how money is. Even if you don't have much, someone is always eager to get you to spend more. Fortunately, I didn't have to plead with James or fight him in court for maintenance. He's been as equitable as he knows how, although rotten as a three-month-old egg. Only the vow "till death us do part" has been broken.

I'm lucky, too, that my job pays enough to cover essential expenses. Every day I collide with examples of other women's desperate straits as they dig in the bottom of their purses for bus fare or hold cardboard signs begging for handouts on street corners. Thank God. Divorce alone is humbling enough. A living, breathing manifestation of my failure as a wife.

A familiar hollowness balloons in my stomach. Dinnertime. Food for one, not much fun. A quick initial snack to take the edge off, along with a frozen dinner in the microwave, will suffice for now. I'm peanut-buttering some graham crackers when the doorbell rings.

Who could that be? I'm not expecting anyone. Barbara, who's taken to dropping by at odd hours to catch me in a pity party? James, usually circumspect lately about returning to his former home without approval, except for his recent visit? A teenager toting boxes of ancient candy and pitching a sale with "save a kid from the streets?" A robber? No, that type doesn't usually doesn't ring except to determine if an owner's home. The bell plays its tune again and I shake myself. I certainly won't find out by standing here in the kitchen, clutching a sticky knife in one hand and a dingy dishtowel in the other.

Checking through the curtains framing the door, I don't gain much more information. A man is standing there, his face in the shadows, a leather messenger bag hanging from his shoulder. He shifts from foot to foot as he waits. I'll have to answer. I've turned all the house lights on and their blaze makes my presence obvious to anyone outside.

The man turns into the light when I open the door, bracing the big toe of my left foot against the bottom of the door as a safeguard to prevent it breaching any further. Big-boned, almost bulky, comfortable body. Sandy blond hair shaggy and long enough to qualify for an immediate cut. Taller than I by some four inches. A face strong in its features and a smile surrounding square white teeth.

I throw the door wide. "Kevin!" I squeal before I remember this is the first time I've seen him since James skittered from the house shame-faced, lugging three large suitcases and dragging a duffel by a strap across his shoulder. I flutter my eyelids, throw my hands outward, palms up and repeat in a subdued tone. "Kevin. James isn't here. You know, right? About James and me?"

"Yes." For his part, he looks as embarrassed as I feel. "Jim asked me to come over."

Mortification threatens to swamp the fondness that normally anchors my contacts with Kevin. I recall that James said he'd asked Kevin to help. James's pal, chum, best buddy from high school, witness and perpetrator of the misdemeanors of passion and inexperience every teenaged boy goes through. At least every teenaged boy subjected to his body's flood of hormones and excess energy in a tiny agricultural community like Clear Fork, on the plains of eastern Colorado. There innocuous mischief-making simply made adults, even the sheriff, choke back a laugh rather than subject them to instant arrest. I accompanied James and Kevin on some adventures, like the tubing trip that went astray by several unplanned miles, down a creek swollen by a thunderstorm, forcing us to hitchhike back to the starting point.

Still, this *is* Kevin, my friend too, infrequent as our contacts have been over the past several years. Just the sight of his solid shoulders brings a sense of comfort and recently vanished stability. And, I remind myself, I have nothing to be ashamed of. I haven't made stupid excuses for my extended absences from home, nor become bored with my partner, nor walked out of the marriage with nary a guilt-tinged twinge or an embarrassed backward glance.

I step aside and nudge the rumpled entry rug with a stockinged toe. "Come in." I wave the grubby knife in a small circle as I lead Kevin to the kitchen. "Do you want coffee? Something to eat? I was just nuking dinner. I can get you some."

"Coffee's fine."

Although he's accepted the offer of hospitality, Kevin stands by the kitchen table, the messenger bag dangling awkwardly from one hand, rubbing the palm of the other hand along the side of his trousers. I wonder why he doesn't plop down in the side chair. He usually makes himself right at home. His appearance is different, too. No jeans and tee-shirt, but a blue blazer and tan slacks. His thick sun-streaked hair is neatly styled, comb-tracked left to right, not rumpled.

"What's wrong?" I ask as I hand him a mug of coffee. "You look weird in that jacket. And you're acting strange."

His brown eyes survey the room. "These are my go-to-work clothes. But I admit I feel strange. As if any second Jim will walk through the door."

"He won't," I say sharply as I dispose of the knife in the sink. "He's made that quite clear."

Kevin sets his bag on the table and steps toward me. "I haven't said how sorry I was to hear about the break-up. I never expected it between you and Jim."

"It was pretty bad at first." I concentrate on unwrapping the frozen Salisbury steak meal, peeling the plastic back from the corner of plaster-like mashed potatoes so they will heat properly. "You talk about a shock! I didn't have a clue. Of course, looking back, now I can see that things weren't quite right. I thought it was the baby. Or rather, the lack of a baby. You probably remember, we were trying to get pregnant. But thank God, I don't have that complicating factor. That's what I keep telling myself. It would have been hell to drag a child through this mess." I look up to see Kevin with that haunted look around the eyes people get when they're dreading a long recitation about someone's troubles. Stop babbling, I scold myself. How many times are you going to trot out this tired, whiny, boring rationalization about pregnancy troubles?

Shoving two plastic trays into the microwave, I switch on the timer, draw a deep breath and turn back to Kevin. "Enough about me. What about you?"

"Um, well, I thought you knew, Jim asked me to come over." Kevin unbuckles the leather bag and starts poking through papers and brochures.

"Oh, yeah. The house. But, you know, according to the financial settlement, the home is mine," I say. "I'm in no hurry to get rid of it."

"Just so there's no misunderstanding, Jim authorized me to proceed. Since you both hold title, either one of you has the ability to begin transactions as long as the other one signs the agreement later. Unless you've purchased his share?" Kevin's probing, trying to avoid hostility, I can tell.

He clears his throat and I look up at him. "Well, this is certainly embarrassing," I blurt, figuring the truth is easier and better to deal with than bluffing a false sophistication. Kevin's swishing his coffee around and around in the cup so violently some liquid spills on the table. "Guess you know I'm not in a financial position to do that."

"Yes," Kevin croaks. "But I thought Jim was going to be more up-front about his plans. Seems like I need to give you some time to adjust." He buckles up the leather bag and hoists it to his shoulder. "Let me know when is more convenient." Fishing in his pocket, he draws out a business card and hands it to me, touching my fingers with his as he does so. He pulls his hand back. "I'd better go. Another appointment. Across town."

I can hardly keep up with Kevin as he races for the door. "You didn't even finish your coffee," I manage to say by the time I catch up with him.

"No, that's okay." He pauses in the open doorway. "Listen, Joan. If you need anything, someone to talk to or whatever, go out for a beer or a walk, call me. Any time, day or night. Okay?"

Caught by surprise, I manage a subdued, "Thanks." Closing the door after him, I lean against the wall and look at the business card. "Kevin Bostwick, Realtor" it reads, along with a miniature photo and contact information.

The buzz of the microwave draws my attention back to dinner, such as it is. Kevin. Interesting. I've never discussed careers with him, had no occasion previously to find a real estate agent. But Kevin is in the business and fairly successful at that, even though he doesn't seem particularly hard-sell in his approach. And why has he agreed to take on this particular listing? Should I feel suspicious or thankful?

I've always supposed him to be more a friend of James than mine. In high school, a barrier existed between boys and girls that was crossed only for dating purposes. It was invisible but had actual dimensions and bulk. Boys here, girls there. Boys walked down the hall in gangs, girls in twos and threes. Seldom did the groups mingle. An expanse of two to four feet always existed between the genders. In the cafeteria, the sexes might have shared a table but not in alternating seats. Girls giggled and squealed in corners, boys guffawed and boomed. Girls hugged, boys punched. Girls blushed at natural functions like burping, boys drew attention to these.

Steady couples like James and me were exceptions to the rules. They hung out—and hung on—together. Each half of the duo had same-gender friends attached to him or her who functioned somewhat like foster brothers and sisters or a lamprey eel affixed to a whale. So at a dance, my friends felt no compunction in teasing

James to dance with them and a good pal like Kevin didn't mind my tagging along as he drove a crew of boys, including James, around town to indulge in minor devilry.

In particular, I recall a midnight run to t.p. a cheerleader's house. Kevin and James and I and miscellaneous others alternated flings of rounded rolls of the tissue over tree limbs and a susceptible chimney. Things got so loose that particular incident the boys had a contest on that very same lawn to see who could pee the farthest. Of course, James insisted that I turn my back and close my eyes.

Kevin. Big, blond, burnished most of the year with a tan, first from his boyhood chores on the family farm, then from outdoor sports. Taller than I, which is saying something, since I'm as tall as an average man. Dense bones, substantial bulk, but in no danger of flab since he excelled in tennis in high school, skiing in college, jogging since then. Chatty, sociable, knew what to say to everyone. An inconstant constant as he drifted in and out of relationships with women. He appeared for a dinner or a party with a new one on his arm, two months later reappeared alone.

His visits to James and me always signaled a temporary return to the comparatively carefree days of high school. We'd swill beer, watch football games, gobble potato chips, scramble eggs, read one another questions out of the *Playboy Advisor* column, create fantastic responses, fall asleep at three in the morning draped over the padded arms of the couch with the TV blaring an ancient horror film starring a headless woman.

Kevin. Just saying his name makes me feel more grounded, safer. A fragile warmth flowers behind my eyes as I remember his parting words. Is Kevin a friend? Yes, certainly. He suffered as a patient worker through the move of our furniture into this house. He held me with wordless comfort once as I sobbed my grief over another failed pregnancy. He wouldn't need to choose sides in the divorce to help me sell the house. I'll call him soon. Very very soon.

Making a decision always raises my spirits. It can be a decision to cut my hair, go for a walk, buy a car. A tiny surge of energy runs down my arms. I think about my conversation with Dolores, my friend's claim that any action would be better than no action. What am I, I ask myself, a mouse or a man? Well, not a man, a woman. A mouse or a woman? The comparison doesn't ring quite as true, but the challenge is the same. I walk to the telephone and prop Kevin's card next to it. At that precise moment, the instrument rings.

"I found a class we just have to take. Ceramics. Once a week at the recreation center." Dolores is on the line. With three children under the age of ten, Dolores is on a constant quest for "opportunities," as she labels them, whether physical, monetary, social or spiritual. I suspect Dolores is lonely for adult companionship of any type during non-work hours. But ceramics? I'm not the artsy type. I try to wriggle out of the situation.

"I don't think so, Dolores. I'm too busy."

"Busy doing what? I've been begging you to get out of your house for weeks."

"Well, then, I'm not ready. Emotionally. I can barely drag myself to work and back." As I speak, my vision of myself as Saint Joan fades. I find myself pulled back and down into an immense vortex of exhaustion, with obligations like my job, house-cleaning, and regular bathing circling like so many starving sharks ready to tear my tired body to pieces. Evidently, I've a way to go before I plunge back into *Life!* with a capital L and an exclamation point.

"The more you do, the more you *can* do and want to do. Try it. Please, Joan. I don't want to sign up by myself."

All I really want is my old existence back. An impossibility. I might as well start building a new life by sampling the ceramics class.

"Okay," I surrender. "Where shall I meet you?"

I accept Dolores's challenge. I've never been a coward, a pansy, a patsy before. Never have surrendered without a struggle. Maybe I have more in common with Saint Joan than I think. How about when Susie Rhodes wanted to cheat off my social studies test in sixth grade? I absolutely refused, despite her threats to spread a lie about my kissing her brother. Or the time I went back to the library to admit I'd simply dropped my overdue books in the return slot rather than paying the fines. Or when my dad left and I would not cry over it, not even when I was alone in the darkness of my bed.

I remember how determined I was to get married immediately after high school graduation. Barbara certainly hadn't favored that. But I was determined to walk my own walk. While I might now acknowledge that decision as a major mistake, instead I choose to view it as a courageous breaking away from childhood. Whether James and I resolve our differences—and the possibility looks fainter with each passing day—I have a life to live. Damned if I'm not going to! Starting with this class.

CHAPTER THREE

The registration line for all summer classes at the rec center meanders down the sidewalk, through a grassy section of Washington Park and out to the parking lot. I find Dolores in line and cut in to the disgust of those farther down, a collection in the main of mothers and fathers dressed for the summer heat in khaki shorts and plaid shirts. These (the parents, not the clothes) call with regularity to an assortment of children of varying heights, clothed in their uniforms of miniature khaki shorts and plaid shirts. The kids ignore their parents' cheery commands tinged with desperation, in favor of chasing one another over the lawn, screaming at high pitch.

"Sorry," I apologize to the woman directly behind me with two preschoolers hanging on her legs. The kids lick ice cream cones half-a-scoop too large for their mouths. "My space was being saved."

"Just listen," Dolores breaths out in awe. She reads from a newspaper-sized catalog of classes. *"Ceramics—a good introduction to the wonderful world of creativity. Express yourself! You'll choose from striking wall hangings, decorative statues, useful serving dishes. Make items for yourself or for gifts.* Doesn't that sound wonderful? I'm going to save mine for Christmas."

I'm dubious. "I'm not very artistic. I'd better keep my stuff. I won't be getting much for Christmas anyway, so I'd better build a cache of presents to myself."

Slowly as the toddlers' ice cream cones melt, the line moves forward. Minutes turn to half-hours turn to hours. An assortment of teens—male, female, or undecided—cling to one another's arms and shoulders as if unable to support their weight independently. They ricochet up and down the line as they sport friends spreading the rumor that the computer system has utterly crashed, that registration has to revert to the old-fashioned pencil and paper and clipboard system. People shuffle one-by-one to the registration table in a test of endurance under the beating sun. Periodically, a collective moan ripples down the line as word comes that a popular class has filled.

"Maybe we won't be able to get into ceramics," I say, suppressing a note of hope in my voice, springing from my disastrous attempts at self-expression during art classes from first grade onward. Even maternal affection couldn't inspire Barbara to enthusiasm to praise my efforts. One particularly stupendous failure started as the outline of a leaf in clay, only to achieve final form looking like a three-legged dog.

"We're almost to the front," Dolores points out. "Don't worry."

Finally, three hours after we met, Dolores and I reach our goal. Several perky, athletic girls in shorts and tee-shirts, looking hardly old enough to be in high school, let alone run recreation classes, sit behind mounds of official papers. Abandoned computers function simply as massive paperweights, so the rumors must be true.

"Do you have your forms?" asks one.

"Oh, yes," says Dolores. "Beginning ceramics." She presents her sheet with a flourish. I slide mine across the table.

"Sorry. Just closed," says the girl. "I can put you on a waiting list or you can sign up for another. *If* you see it on the list posted behind me. Otherwise, you'll have to get in another line."

Without hesitation Dolores picks. "We'll take Saturday morning exercise."

"What?" I shriek.

"Both of us," Dolores continues firmly. "There's room in that, I trust."

"Oh, yes. Exercise is held outside. We can add to it until the park's filled. Anyway, lots of people drop out." She throws a dubious glance in the direction of our plump figures.

"I agreed to ceramics. *Not* exercise," I protest.

"Calm down. It's only once a week. Besides, I've heard that class is a great place to meet men."

The girl endorses the forms before I can raise more fuss, shuffles the papers to the side, and motions to the next person, the weary mother of two, now bedraggled and sweaty from the effort of controlling her irritable youngsters. Dolores and I gain the best incentive to move on when the little boy threatens to go pee-pee right in line if his mommy won't take him to the potty.

Leaning earnestly to Dolores's ear, I continue my complaints as we walk away. "Ceramics. You said ceramics. I haven't exercised in years. I can't do it. I don't want to do it."

"You agreed to one class. Exercise is one class. You weren't that keen on ceramics anyway, were you?"

I shake my head.

"Won't hurt to try it. Both you and I could stand to firm up and lose a little."

"Enough, enough," I say in mock surrender. "Now, come on. Let's indulge ourselves with a bagel at the coffee shop. We'll have to face the music next Saturday."

A week later I pull on my oldest, baggiest slacks and a sweatshirt. Next come pristine running shoes, purchased several years ago and never worn. Last, a scarf to cover my entire head. I only wish I could cover my face, too. A merciless, all-exposing, early summer sun beats down, revealing every pore and incipient wrinkle.

I join Dolores under the shade of a huge cottonwood. Dolores has been shopping, I note, and is dressed in a new set of hot pink nylon shorts and tank top. I can't see decking yourself out in skimpy, form-hugging exercise clothes unless you have the shape for it. Dolores is better equipped than I, but she doesn't equal most of the hordes now surging toward us to occupy the open meadow where class is to be held.

Many of them boast near-perfect bodies. Skin-tight pants cropped at knee level, paired with teeny leotards that flaunt rounded rear ends, are the order of the day for women. Men are even more exposed. Most of them don't bother to cover their chests, which bulge with muscles and match their firmly defined thighs and calves.

A woman with the smallest, tightest outfit over the thinnest body prances to what appears to be the front of the group. She flicks on a portable CD player and shouts, "Are you ready?" over the blaring music. An enormous roar rolls back at her. "We're *ready!*" The leader immediately begins throwing her arms around and around, simultaneously gyrating her entire torso in a circle.

I'm not ready. I don't understand how these people can focus, let alone move, at eight o'clock on a Saturday morning. But Dolores has positioned herself at the back of the class and is turning in time to the music. Unless I want to collapse under the tree in full view of the group, I have to follow Dolores.

I join Dolores and try a few small swivels. I don't want to throw a joint out of whack. Just as I catch the beat, the leader switches to forward thrusts of the upper half of her body, held horizontal to the ground.

"Where are your smiles, ladies and gentlemen?" yells the leader. "This is *fun!*"

Around me, people grin and cheer. The unrelenting torture continues for an hour. Every muscle that can be stretched or twisted is. Each bone that can jolt or pound does. Heartbeats accelerate to eighty percent of maximum rates. Except mine, which must be accelerating to one hundred and twenty percent and feels like it's ready to burst.

"A few slow wrap-up moves, ladies and gentlemen. We don't want to shock our bodies," announces the skinny leader. With a dancer's grace, she flexes her knees, breathes deeply. In unison, everyone except me mimics her perfectly.

Shock is the wrong word, I think as I collapse on the grass. Paralysis is more like it. "You'll have to drag me home by my heels," I tell Dolores. "I can't even twitch."

Dolores prances with her head back. "I feel great. Exercise is so invigorating. And did you see the men? Some of 'emwere boing-bingo!"

Lifting my head from the ground, I fix a steely look on Dolores. "How could I? Sweat was pouring off my forehead."

"They were super, believe me. And you'll get used to this," Dolores promises.

I drag myself up. "Since I've been so good, let's go reward ourselves with a bagel."

I use exhaustion as an excuse to do almost nothing the rest of the day other than drive to the grocery store and poke through piles of limp celery and flaccid lettuce that resemble my physical state. I'm even too tired to pull dinner together and opt instead for a huge bowl of popcorn and a chocolate milkshake.

No wonder you're putting on weight, eating crap like that. A sigh of rebuke as if from a ghost pulses in my ear. A reprimand, an attitude frequently exhibited by James, familiar from the months before he split, when all he seemed able to do was criticize, criticize, criticize. Thank the powers that be, I don't need to heed such slights any more. I answer to no one about my food choices, whether good or bad. There are definite advantages to being alone.

Carrying my off-balance meal to the living room, I thumb through the television schedule. Hmmm. On the classic films channel, *Joan of Arc* with Ingrid Bergman is playing tonight. An easy way to discover what Dolores has been yammering about. My patron saint. Who'd have thought I had one? Deserved one? I settle down for a few hours of forgetfulness.

One hundred minutes later, my jaw snaps shut between the tracks of tears down my cheeks. It aches from hanging open so long while I soaked up the excitement, the challenge, the drama of a classically beautiful Swede acting like an impeccably clean French peasant who chats regularly with God. And who wears metal armor without sweating. And faces death by fire, a smile pinned on her radiant face. Wow! What a woman. That's definitely the way I want my life to be, where I'm the one in charge, and courage, if not a sense of self-preservation, is my creed. I stagger off to bed, still under the movie's spell.

The next morning I leap out of bed, ready to do battle with the world, just like Joan of Arc. My legs buckle from the aches of exercise class and my right shoulder feels wrenched. But I'm determined to view the class in retrospect as fun. Maybe the uniqueness of the experience colors my view. Or the pride I feel from simply surviving, the obvious physical differences between me and most of my fellow classmates notwithstanding. Soon I might come closer to their standards of fitness, I muse. Anything is possible with enough determination! Like Saint Joan. She was determined and she certainly was fit. She had to be to wear that heavy armor and lug around that humongous sword and shield. It's a wonder she ever was physically able to drag her way to the head of an army. I shake myself out of this train of thought. In any case, the resolve that possessed me after last night's film sustains me as I begin Sunday's housecleaning.

I'm tackling James's closet, or, rather, what used to be James's closet. I've put the task off far too long, dreading the memories sure to arise.

They don't. Without a man's suits, pants, shirts, ties, the closet is only an empty space that can be filled with whatever I choose. I sniff. Even his scent is gone or maybe I'm getting a head cold, brought on by too much exercise. No, that can't be—exercise helps you fight viruses. In any case, I waft disinfectant and spray cleaner with a vengeance, just on principles—anti-viral and anti-James. A cloud of perfume next, to convert the closet into woman's territory.

Storing winter clothes, I decide. The perfect use for the closet. I'm lugging two armfuls of seasonal dresses from the bedroom when the doorbell rings.

My mother stands at the door. Barbara only visits at times she thinks won't conflict with my social life. I've always been perfect in her eyes. She's convinced that men only have to see me to desire me. Therefore, according to Barbara, the divorce is completely James's fault, he's never been quite good enough for me, it's just as well he's out of the picture, her daughter was destined for greater things and better men. Hasn't Barbara always said so?

I allow Barbara to continue in these faulty assumptions. At least someone thinks me flawless. Easier than explaining that I have no social life. A few couples nearby, our friendships based solely on convenience and propinquity, have dropped away through my neglect and their disinterest. Until the break-up, I thought James's honey Maureen was my best friend from several years back, whom I'd nursed through her own divorce.

"You're up early," Barbara says. She pulls off a denim baseball cap and fluffs out her short reddish-brown hair with her fingers. People often comment on the physical similarities between Barbara and me, adding, "You two could be sisters."

A not surprising comparison. Identical hair color and texture, golden-brown eyes, strong profiles, dark eyebrows, height pushing six feet. Except Barbara possesses a self-confidence and sophistication that I can never claim. Where she got it, I can't guess. Barbara was born in Clear Fork, Colorado, population five-hundred, to a rancher disillusioned by the Depression and the constant dust storms of the plains. Her father had eked out a living running a hardware store with dirt-encrusted windows and cluttered counters, selling nails by the gross, screws in pairs, and paint as unvarying as the colors of the grasses of the prairies. Although she was both valedictorian and Homecoming Queen, Barbara never progressed past high school and, like me, married a classmate.

However, Barbara must have cherished ideas of life on a bigger scale, nurtured by those old true-confessions magazines in Clear Fork's sole beauty parlor or paperback romances from the library.

Once my father left mother and daughter, perhaps because his wife challenged him in too many ways, Barbara simply marked time until I left high school and married. Then, as if detonated from a cannon, she cut out for the biggest city in the state and non-stop career jumps from administrative assistant to office manager to salesperson to unit director. Volunteer work supporting Opera Colorado, self-development classes in yoga and gardening and elaborate dinners for select friends based on Julia Child's recipes.

I automatically turn in the direction of the kitchen and the gourmet coffee brewing there, a favorite of both of us. Barbara breathes the aroma before she continues her imaginary version of my life. "You'll wear yourself to a nub combining late-night fun and sunrise chores. I called you about eight, but I didn't get an answer. Where were you? A party? A play?"

Thinking of my Saturday evening television movie and giant bowl of popcorn, I shake my head and change the subject. "I'm on a new regime. An invigorating exercise class every weekend. My energy's doubled," I cheerfully equivocate.

"That's good. You've let yourself go lately." Barbara touches my hair. "Like that ponytail. Not that your bone structure doesn't look great with your hair pulled back. But it's almost like you don't care."

"I've been miserable, Mom. I haven't felt like fixing my hair. But I have a goal now. I'm sweeping the remains of my husband from my life." Balancing the mug, I start back to the bedroom closet, Barbara close behind, and gesture at the heaps of clothes on the floor. "I'm converting his closet for off-season storage."

"About time, Joan," Barbara approves in the voice she saves for lectures. "You wasted more than ten years on James. He's a nice enough boy, but nothing special. Just like your father. You deserve someone special. Are you seeing a particular person now?"

"No, Mom. Only the regular run of promising actors and budding entrepreneurs with an occasional expensive attorney thrown in beating down my door. Why don't you give me a hand?"

Barbara reaches for a hanger. "You really should get rid of the house itself. It ties you down. Think of what you could do with the money, not to mention the free time. Travel to Europe, lounge on the Riviera. Or buy one of those fancy little sports cars. Bright red."

Barbara's eyes haze over as she indulges in a private daydream. I guess the sports car is a recurring character in my mother's fantasies.

"Mom, why don't *you* buy a sports car? You'd look great in it. Your hair would be tousled from the wind, your face tanned, your mouth wide in a silly grin." Then, with a sly touch, "A young, handsome millionaire sitting beside you? An oil baron who adores opera?"

"Joan, you're mad. James drove you around the bend." Barbara is flattered, nonetheless. She drapes a pair of my winter slacks over the hanger and turns to the closet. "I want you to have everything I didn't. Oh, I don't regret my life, staying in Clear Fork until you finished school. Everyone has to make choices, weigh one action against another. But it's as if you've been given a second chance now. Take advantage of it."

"I'll do my best, Mom, starting with this closet. And I *have* been considering selling the house. It's too big for one person."

We're making real headway into the task when the doorbell rings again. My ex-husband props his thin body against the door frame as if he lacks the strength to stand up straight, a woebegone expression that surely has taken hours of practice to develop plastered on his face.

"Hello, Joan. Got a few minutes? We've got a major problem."

My heart bounds despite my head's caution and my newly acquired determination to build a new life. Can this finally be a plea for a reunion? Will my defeat turn into a victory? I stand to one side and gesture a welcome.

James spots Barbara in the hallway behind me, pauses, shrugs his shoulders. He knew from the first disagreement over honeymoon location that he wasn't Barbara's favorite person. (Barbara thought a weekend at a suburban hotel an inauspicious beginning for her daughter's marriage and had no hesitation in telling James so). He goes to what has traditionally been "his" chair in the living room, an overstuffed corduroy recliner that still bears the imprint of his body from parking himself to watch television, year after successive year.

A breathy whisper comes out of my mouth. "How about an iced tea?" *Or something warmer, more intimate? A hug? A kiss?*

"Fine," James replies. Anything to stall until Barbara takes a hint and leaves, I'm guessing. But she ensconces herself on the couch and calls for a glass, too.

I have my own reasons for wishing my mother would leave. If James wants a reconciliation, how can I nudge him in that direction with my mother looking on? She'll never keep her mouth shut if she thinks I'm crawling back to James after all the humiliation he's put me through. Her inherent enmity is aggravated now by her belief that James is the same love-'em-and-leave-'em type as my father. I offer a subtle suggestion with the refreshments. "Here you go, Mom. I know you can't stay too long."

"I'm in no hurry," Barbara answers as she settles back into the cushions and pounds some throw pillows into a more comfortable shape. Nothing short of dynamite will shake her loose now. She assumes an attitude of intense interest consisting of lips pursed so tightly they wrinkle and eyebrows pushed together.

Under Barbara's eyes, as watchful as a broody hen's, James has to put up or shut up. Desperation or fear prods him past common courtesies of how-are-you and not-bad. He begins abruptly.

"I'm here about the house. You've got to put it on the market immediately."

The delusion of a reunion splinters, shatters, and falls in shards in my mind. This isn't an attempt at a settlement complete with soft, yielding embraces and pleas of forgiveness. It smacks of the concrete-hard-headedness of a man sent on a mission by a determined woman, an *other* woman, bent on feathering a nest for her mate.

Disappointment clutches me right about the level of my diaphragm and chokes out my response. "No. Not now."

I don't know what I expect, but it's not James's leap out of the chair and his frenzied pacing back and forth like a caged stray dog. Nor is it the gush of his words streaked with desperation. "Be reasonable, Joan. I've got to have the money. A house, I've got to buy a house as soon as humanly possible."

"Use your ill-gotten gains from Power Ball," I toss at him.

James throws his hands in the air. "Gone. All gone. God knows where. But right at the start, wheet!" he whistles, "fifty percent to the feds. Then the new car. A few dinners out, some decent suits..." His voice trails off and his eyes get a far-away glaze as if he's trying to remember how his winnings disappeared.

"Guess you should have followed the advice you were always giving me about saving for a rainy day," I say without the least compassion and turn my attention to my iced tea.

"Joan, I'm begging you," bursts from James by the fireplace. He leans so far forward, he nearly falls. "You've got to be reasonable. Maureen is pregnant. Without my share of this house, I have no chance of buying a place for us and the baby."

"Pregnant? Reasonable?" I whisper. They sound like incomprehensible nonsense syllables. I hear an increasing buzzing in my ears and black spots appear in my vision, whirl, meld into streaks that threaten to block all sight. Maureen is pregnant? After I tried for so many months, years? Prayed, wished on stars and wishbones, subjected my body to the most humiliating and invasive physical procedures? Spent every spare nickel and a hell of a lot of un-sparable dimes on doctor visits? And Maureen turns up pregnant without even trying?

Something seems to snap in the vicinity of my brain immediately behind my eyes. "Reasonable!" I shriek back. Everything is happening too fast. My security, my wifely status, the definition of my "self," my hope for a child, my husband, my stability. All vanished, gone. Now, my home.

I no longer have control, no influence over the forces affecting my life. Well, I'm tired of being polite, frustrated with rationality, fed up with hopelessness. Maybe a tantrum will relieve my frustration. I leap to my feet and hold a cushion over my head, ready to throw it at James. "You walk out on me, destroy our family, and now you want to steal my home? That's reasonable?"

Taken completely by surprise by this show of aggression from his normally buoyant and complaisant wife, James cowers at the threat implicit in the dangling cushion. "Take it easy. You're right. No real immediate rush. Just think about it, okay? Has Kevin contacted you? He'll do a good job for you."

I look up at the cushion in my outstretched arms, then back at James, fearful of feathers. I nearly giggle but realize I'll lose my psychological advantage if I do so. Slowly the cushion lowers.

Tightening control over my emotions so I can react with dignity, I command, "Get out of my house."

CHAPTER FOUR

A shoulder hunched to ward off an attack, James spews, "Feeling out of sorts? What's the matter, haven't had a snack this morning? Maybe I should have brought some candy to sweeten you up."

"You bastard!" I have no defense against this line of criticism and James knows it from the ten pounds per year that had gathered around my hips, chin, thighs, arms over the past three years.

Then, in the swift reversal typical of his treatment throughout our marriage, James switches to little-boy begging. "Promise me you'll think about it," he says on his way out the door. "Talk to Kevin."

"I won't promise you a thing," I throw after him like an abandoned hat.

Barbara, who's dogged James's steps to make sure he leaves, closes the front door and calmly resumes her seat. "Well, that was quite a scene," she says, sipping her tea, flavoring her judgment with an undertone of pride.

"What a spineless nerd," I reply. "Afraid of a pillow." I drop the aforementioned pillow on the floor and sit on it.

"You can hardly blame the man," my mother answers. "You looked ready to stuff the cushion down his throat. You've always been emotional, sky-highs and dirt-lows, but I don't think I've ever seen you so out of control."

"I wasn't out of control. Just angry."

"I thought not. I knew you were doing it for effect," says Barbara, changing her opinion without a qualm, a technique she's perfected over the years to encourage me in the direction of self-awareness. She figures if she throws me off-balance, I'll be more open to considering all sides of an issue.

"And then he tossed in that comment about my weight. It reminds me of when Daddy used to make mean jokes about me looking like a brick. I've tried. I've really tried, Mom. Some of that medication I was on, especially the hormones, made losing weight impossible. And it's like my mouth has a mind of its own. Food just disappears down it. If I weren't fat, I never would have lost James." Wrapping my arms around myself, I curl into a ball and roll off the cushion.

Barbara scoots off the couch onto the floor next to me. "You're not fat, you're healthy." She slaps me on my not-insubstantial rear. "With your height, you can carry more substance. It makes you look...queenly. Any reasonable man would see that."

"But it hurts!" I bury my head in the cushion. "It hurts so bad when he says things like that."

Somehow Barbara gets her arms around me and the pillow, rocking me gently back and forth. "That's why he says them. To strike out at you to excuse his own behavior. Just like your father did."

I make strangled sounds into the pillow. "Don't cry, honey," says Barbara with a greater display of maternal concern than she's shown during my childhood, when her response more typically would have been a swift kick in the pants to get me going. "Things will get better."

I raise my head. "Did you see him?" I ask. "When I hoisted the cushion? He flinched, like he feared his heart was going to fail him at any second." The laughter I've been holding in comes billowing out. Nothing like the ridiculous to boost my spirits.

"How can you laugh?" Barbara drops her arms.

"Easy. He looked so stupid."

"What I'm saying is, shouldn't you be crying? Upset over losing your husband, not your house? Don't you agree?" She assumes the look of a perfect, concerned mother.

I eye my mother suspiciously. Was Barbara starting a sermon? "What's the moral?"

"No moral." Barbara rounds her eyes in innocence. "But maybe, just maybe, you were motivated to your extreme response by something other than love."

I give the matter my consideration. Why aren't I devastated by James's visit and subsequent betrayal? Why aren't I sad instead of angry? How can I be laughing now, not sobbing? "I'm ready to move on, past my wreck of a marriage? I'm ready to move on! You're too perceptive for your own good," I say to Barbara, throwing the cushion at her for emphasis.

Smug with satisfaction, Barbara easily catches the pillow. "I'm proud of you. I knew you'd finally realize he's an old habit you have to break. And I'll be here to help you in any way you want. All you have to do is give me a nod. A shoulder to cry on, a companion for a glass of wine, a timely loan. Whatever you need. Even a pair of hands to houseclean. Now, let's go finish that closet." Barbara returns to the bedroom, me tagging after.

"But how do I break the habit?" I ask with a plaintive wail.

"You substitute a better habit," my mother answers. "You used to sing in the choir. Why don't you take that up again?"

"In high school. Everyone does. Hardly a consuming pastime, Mom."

"All right then. Substitute a habit like cleaning. Cleaning away surplus detritus like clothes and houses. James is right about one thing. You should call a realtor."

Barbara now crouches on the floor, the better to dig through shoes, I note with alarm. An old pair of Birkenstock sandals bounce into one corner, joined by screaming red stiletto heels that make my feet look like boats. Clearly the discard pile is taking shape. Once Barbara really starts an organizing job, she's like a runaway train hurtling along until out of fuel. Nothing can halt her. My entire wardrobe can disappear into a donation bag.

I forcibly restrain my mother's hands by gripping both. "That's just what I'll do, Mom. After you run along. I can't discuss business details with anyone else around."

With this excuse, I manage to deflect Barbara from the task and wave her out the front door. I really should contact Kevin. I've let several days drift by without taking any action. Remembering the movie I was glued to on Saturday night, I ask myself, is this what Saint Joan would do? No! She'd seize every opportunity to move forward to her goal. If my goal is to create a new life, connect with good friends, develop new habits, I must make the most of my time. And that includes breaking all those old rules for good girls. The ones that say, "Behave yourself at all times," or "Don't take too many chances," and "People won't like you unless you're nice." Really, being a good girl has gotten me absolutely nowhere so far. I'll try being bad or at least a little daring.

Damn it, I am going to call Kevin. Might be a little delicate, a trifle disconcerting at first to admit I need help. I imagine a few mumbled words from me and Kevin, further expressions of sorrow over the breakup of a marriage, a sad shake of the head from Kevin. Well, the possibility of a fat commission will smooth over any awkwardness. I reach for the telephone.

A sultry voice answers.

"I'm sorry," I apologize. "I must have dialed incorrectly. I was calling Kevin Bostwick."

"No problem," says the distinctly feminine tone. "Just a minute."

When Kevin picks up the phone, I blurt the first thing in my mind. "Who was that?"

"Who is this?" Kevin questions back.

"Joan." I gasp, recalling my manners. "Oh, I'm sorry. It's just that I've never thought of you as..." I frantically fish for an inoffensive euphemism for having sex, "...dating."

"Really, Joan, I passed puberty long ago. Did you assume that you're the only woman in my life?" Amusement and a hint of something else—perhaps satisfaction, perhaps annoyance—underlies his question.

CHAPTER FIVE

Amusement always marked Kevin's demeanor toward me. From algebra class in high school when he poked fun at my faulty assumptions and erroneous equations to his hysterics at my Christmas kazoo band only last year, Kevin never takes me seriously.

He'll have to now, I think. Nothing is a more serious occurrence to an individual than divorce. Unless it's making a living.

"I never thought I was 'in your life' at all. And I apologize again. But let me get to the reason for my call. I've decided to go ahead and list the house."

"I thought you might. But I didn't want to pressure you the other night, so I left," says Kevin.

"Cut the baloney, Kevin. You were afraid you'd get caught in the middle of an embarrassing scene. I understand. But what I need at this minute is a real estate agent, not a friend. Interested?"

"Certainly. Should I come over now?"

"That's rather rapid in view of your company, don't you think?" I imagine the owner of the sultry voice lounging naked in a king-sized bed rubbing Kevin's bare back as he talks. "How about two hours?"

"You're right," replies Kevin with a self-conscious chuckle. "Two hours then."

I switch on the radio for background noise and, although I'm not in the mood, get tidying the house, which differs from cleaning. "Cleaning" means removing dirt and chaos, scrubbing, organizing, losing fingernails and taking hours. "Tidying," on the other hand, connotes making the visible parts of the house appear in order, a matter of stacking magazines neatly on shelves and jamming dirty dishes any which way into the dishwasher and for this moment, include kicking the remainders of the winter-clothing project abandoned by Barbara behind some cardboard boxes on the closet floor.

A golden oldie blares from the radio. *Just start dreaming about what's coming...*

I find myself singing along to the song and moving, dancing really, in time with it. "The past's no more, the past's no more..." the refrain echoes. I turn the sound up as loud as it will go. The song's a catalyst. It captures the major jump forward I've made in taking control of my life, all the strength and optimism I've won through standing up to James. This is going to be my theme song from now on, I tell myself.

The buoyancy boosts my hope for the house. Although Kevin has visited often enough to be familiar with the its design and structure, putting its best face forward could help establish a better asking price. Next, fresh coffee for Kevin. As for myself, I'm starved as usual but need to do my makeup. Nope, not enough time for makeup and a sandwich.

I shrug. Heck, why do I need makeup? I'm not getting ready for a date, only old pal Kevin. I'm constructing a triple-decker turkey and cheese when the doorbell rings. I apply a little force to the slice of bread and press the contents into the sticky mayonnaise spread on the insides.

Kevin, complete with casual briefcase, otherwise known as a messenger bag, continues the conversation from his previous visit as if no time has passed. "Yeah, it sure feels strange without Jim here. You think this situation is all some weird seven-year itch on his part? Has he fallen and hit his head? Run a high fever? Maybe this idea of his to sell the house is an excuse to worm his way back in here."

"He won't," I say sharply. "Never again if I have anything to say about it. Oops." I swallow a bit of sandwich and place the plate on the glass-topped coffee table. "Let me get you some coffee. It's all ready. Be right back."

When I return toting the pot and two mugs, I find Kevin resting back at his ease on the couch, but he straightens as soon as I enter. "You sound very determined," he says. "Quite a difference from last time. Then you were more bewildered at what was happening. What changed your mind?"

I concentrate on pouring coffee in a mug. "I'm not bewildered now. Now I realize that the marriage was over long ago. I really should thank James for walking out. He faced the facts before I did. Anyway, turns out his girlfriend is pregnant."

I don't want to look at Kevin. I fear the pity I think I will see. But the coffee is getting cold. I can't stand here forever with a mug in one hand. I have to turn to him.

"Coffee?" I ask shakily.

No pity. Sympathy softens Kevin's dark eyes. He ignores the coffee and speaks to me as openly as only men who are with a very close friend do. "But painful nonetheless. Especially the baby part. I wish you hadn't been hurt."

The mug starts to quiver in my hand. Kevin reaches for it and places it on the coffee table as my eyes fill with tears.

"Damn," I swear softly. "I thought I was over this."

To my amazement, Kevin doesn't avoid my eyes or change the subject to the house, or the weather, or even a pending football challenge. "It's okay, Joan. We've known each other a long time. You don't need to hide what you feel."

Kevin's quiet compassion is my undoing. I hold out a hand. He extends both arms and I move into them, curl next to him on the couch. Sobs shake me, but Kevin's solid body absorbs them. A never-before experienced comfort fills me. After a few short minutes, I quiet and lean back.

"That's the final cry," I announce. I duck my head and disguise wiping away the track of tears as if checking under my eyes for smears of makeup. "Truly. I don't know what came over me. Must have been sheer relief. I've accepted the end of a bad marriage and I'm ready to move on. The house is the first step. James and I agree to sell."

Kevin swallows some words he's been about to voice, gives my shoulder a final reassuring pat, and clears his throat. "Fine. If you're ready, let's take a walk through."

I've never seen this Kevin before. As we view the rooms, he's the total, objective professional. He runs his finger along the caulking by the bathtub, peers behind curtains, opens and shuts windows, thumps his heel on floors. Mutters to himself accompany his tour, verbal shenanigans that carry no meaning to me.

The circuit complete, we return to the kitchen where we sit at the wood table, bare except for the coffee cups and a plate of Oreos. Kevin opens the briefcase and pulls out some papers, which immediately brings the table back to its usual messy state.

"This is our standard contract. It's an agreement that you will work through me exclusively for the period of three months. If I can't sell your house by then, you're free to take the building off the market or change to a different agent."

"Three months! Do you think I'll need that much time?"

"Depends. How badly do you want to get out? What price can you accept? Are you willing to pay closing costs?"

Closing costs. That dreadful phrase. I remember it from the original purchase of the house, but I still can't figure out their purpose, except to add to the price. "I don't know what closing costs are," I say with a plaintive note.

Kevin opens his mouth to explain.

"No, no, don't bother." I shake my head. "Can't you take care of them? Add them, subtract them, multiply them, whatever? Just tell me what I reasonably can expect to make from the sale."

Kevin names a figure that makes me gulp. "If you're not in too big a hurry, I have to add."

"That's double what we paid."

"You bought at a good time. But that price is only a possibility. The market is bad for sellers right now."

I laugh. "A typical agent's disclaimer. When we bought, the market was bad for buyers. And everybody I've talked to in the last four years says the market has been bad for whichever side she was on. Is the market ever good for anyone? Other than realtors? You are the guys who always make out."

Kevin certainly isn't going to take this charge sitting down, although he is. Sitting down, that is. Like a gaping fish, he opens his mouth again. I immediately feel guilt and regret flooding me. Why am I acting this way, when Kevin's been so nice?

I hastily change the subject. "I can't believe that you're sitting here discussing real estate with me. We've hardly talked about anything serious before."

Kevin gives his head a small but definite shake, as if clearing it. "It's about time, then. And speaking of James, he'll have to be involved in the sale. Unless he gave you title."

"No, the agreement calls for us to pay off the mortgage and incidental costs, then split any profit. But could you, could you...?" I trail off.

"Talk to James? Sure. You won't even have to see him until the closing. Not even then, with some planning." Kevin drinks some cold coffee, picks up a cookie and puts it back on the plate.

"What about after you sell?" he continues. "Would you want to buy something smaller? And, no, I'm not looking to double-dip," he answers before I can ask.

"I thought an apartment or townhouse. A rental." I sketch a vague outline in the air. "I don't want to rush into a financial commitment. I'm going to put my share into a safe CD or something."

"I could get you a good deal on an apartment in my place. Close to Washington Park, shopping, buses."

"That's an idea. And I'd know someone there."

"I'll set up an appointment for you to see a model."

I bid Kevin goodbye and return to the living room for my half-eaten sandwich. Funniest thing, the excitement of pending change has eliminated my hunger. I return to the kitchen to wrap the sandwich to save for dinner.

A bad marriage, a worn-out habit. I ponder the terms that describe my failed union. I certainly never expected to be in the position of a discarded spouse. The feeling doesn't hurt quite so much now. Maybe I'm adjusting. Thinking back, I wonder when the marriage changed from an exciting doorway into discovery about ourselves as a couple into a routine. James and I became insulated in a round of individual, separate activities that intersected occasionally, like when we ate together or watched television. For several years, we hardly talked, never considered each other unless purchase of a house, the car, the furniture required a joint decision. It was as if the trappings, the externals, of our lives *became* our lives.

That must be when he surrendered to the constant temptations around him, the women with the mystery of the unknown, showing only their carefully manicured, polished and accomplished business personalities, eager to play flirty games and to present sensual challenges. He always had a sharp eye for female beauty as well as that con-man kind of charm that can slip through a girl's instinct for self-preservation. But he was raised with small-town values that took him some time to shake.

And I'd thought a baby could save us. That quest only added to our distractions and detachment as we turned into separate little machines composed of the sum of our physical qualities—hormones, sperm counts, body temperature.

Strange that my realization dawned from this morning's trivial, embarrassingly juvenile brangle. I have to hand it to James—he understood the emptiness of our marriage much sooner than I. He had the strength to search for improvement. Now my turn has presented itself.

Something to revive my interest in life outside myself. Once I start thinking, the possibilities are limitless. Charitable works—tutoring, collecting litter, feeding the homeless. Cultural activities—gallery openings, symphonies, dance, poetry readings, even singing. The other extreme—a return to youth and the life of a swinging single indulging in rock concerts and motorcycle rides.

Each idea produces a little 'ping' of excitement inside me, as if I'm swallowing a slow stream of ginger ale. Hmmmm. Maybe change isn't so bad after all. And a new place to live. I'll have to downscale. As I survey the kitchen, wondering if I should pull together a garage sale featuring my superfluous appliances, I look at the small plate in my hand, the one for my sandwich. White with a turquoise band, chipped on the edge, it matches none of my other dishes. I drop it in the trash with not one twinge of guilt.

"I'm looking for a new habit," I announce to Dolores on Monday during my late-morning coffee break. The cafeteria is nearly deserted since the noon rush hasn't geared up yet. I raise my voice just a trifle so she can hear me as she wipes down the tables on the other side of the row. "Something constructive, interesting, all-consuming."

Dolores hardly pauses. Dip, wring, wipe, dip, wring, wipe. "Gotta keep on the schedule from the new super. Fortunately, I can talk and work at the same time. A habit? Like brushing your teeth?"

"Not quite. A hobby, an interest. Something upon which to build a new life."

"Sounds like you've given up on James."

"I suppose so," I answer. "I don't have much choice. His girlfriend is pregnant, he kindly informed me on Sunday morning. Anyway, I think I've outgrown him."

"Oh, no." Dolores throws the dingy dishrag on my table and sits down, regardless of the new super's schedule. A slight ammonia smell wafts around us. "I'm so sorry. I know how much you wanted a baby. What a pain in the butt that James and his girlfriend managed it in a snap."

Must be the ammonia that's causing my eyes to water. "I'll tell you what it did. Made it impossible for me to fool myself that he's ever coming back. And a blinding revelation that I truly don't want him back under any conditions." I sketch in James's Sunday morning visit and conclude, "When I realized my reactions were either to hit him or laugh, I knew I wasn't in love anymore."

"Way to go, girl! You're making progress. An interest..." Dolores frowns, either at a smear of dried ketchup on the counter or in thought. She stands to collect the salt and pepper shakers from the tables and brings them to my location to refill. The frown remains frozen on her face until slowly replaced by enlightenment.

"I've got it! Bingo!"

"What? What is it?"

"Bingo! It's fun, you meet new people, you even can win if you're lucky."

"I don't know," I say, confused and doubtful. For me, bingo is a kid's game that I outgrew decades ago, although I'm vaguely aware adults can play it for money. "Sounds pretty boring. And don't you have to pay to get in?"

"You have to pay for anything. Everything takes money. You pay for a movie or a dinner out, don't you? Hobbies like stamp collecting or sewing can cost a fortune. Tennis? Skiing? All those clothes and equipment to buy. With bingo, you can relax, wear your old clothes. It's a thrill a minute. And a twenty will set you up for the evening."

"Wellll..." I hedge.

The warning bell tinkles and Scott Clark enters the cafeteria, his russet hair gleaming like a new copper penny, his pinstriped gray suit screaming "expensive." My jaw drops.

"What now?" asks Dolores. She spots the customer, gives a small snort, but sets down the shakers and trots off to serve him.

I sip a diet soda through a straw and study the man from under lowered lids. I note the way his slacks mold muscular thighs, the slight wave to his hair, his careless yet graceful manner of balancing the food tray. He sits down at a booth across the room, his back to me. He can't look more the opposite of James than if I had him made to order. A small moan escapes from around my straw, fortunately disguising itself as bubbles in the liquid.

Dolores flops down on the booth across from me. "I can't believe you. Lusting after a guy like that."

"Don't give me grief. Just give me facts. You hear people gossiping in here all the time. What do you know about him?"

"Probably gets his hair permed," says Dolores with disgust. "You have a lot of competition. He's an up-and-coming type, according to every giggling, dumb admin that comes in and makes eyes at him. He's the strut-my-stuff type, a different Armani suit for every day in the week, two-hundred-dollar ties, and makes sure everybody knows it. But if a real man came up to him, he'd cut and run. You don't need a wimp like him."

I close my eyes. "Spare me. You think any guy without a tattoo and a motorcycle is a wimp. Have you seen him with any women?"

"He changes women like he changes suits." Dolores pauses and leans forward to relate a confidence. "Goes for the skinny, sleek ones. Like that Kimberlee from your office. He's been with her a couple of times for coffee and sweet talk."

"Of course." I throw up my hands in defeat. "I'm out before I start."

"Not at bingo. A whole new world awaits you."

"All right, all right. I'll go."

The bingo parlor sits smack-dab in the middle of a run-down shopping center. Weeds grow through cracks in the sidewalk until even they die from lack of water and miscellaneous trash, the most innocuous of which is paper, moving up from there on the hazardous waste scale to you-don't-want-to-know, blows from one end of the parking lot to the other. Dolores and I pull up in Dolores' unstable, undependable Pinto. We see a stream of people, many of whom are over-weight, middle-aged women dressed in oversized, pastel, polyester pantsuits, pour into the entry.

"I think I've changed my mind," I say. "There is no way going into that decrepit building with those people who look like cartoon versions of my grandma is going to change my life for the better."

"Too late," responds Dolores, a cheery smile on her face and a glaze over her eyes. "You're a tiny bit terrified because you've never done this before. You're a virgin bingo-er. But you absolutely need to get out and try new things. Anyway, we're here and I'm not leaving until the end of the night. You can sit in the car if you want, but I'm going in."

The only thing that appeals less to me than playing bingo is sitting in a lonely parking lot for three hours, minus even the comfort of a radio, for that's broken. I square my shoulders and follow Dolores.

Total confusion greets us inside the warehouse-like structure. The immensely high ceilings bounce the echoes of hundreds of people calling excitedly to each other. These people stand five deep in front of a low plywood table heaped with thousands of bingo cards. All sense of decorum lost, the ones at the front paw through the brown and green pasteboard squares, tossing them back and forth to each other, passing them to those who can't reach the table, tussling with their neighbors for a card with particularly lucky numbers.

Shivers begin to run up my arms and spine and my breathing rate increases madly. I pause just inside the door by the concrete-block wall. Crowds give me claustrophobia. And this mob seems especially aggressive. Dolores disappears into the throng and I give a squeak. Nope, Dolores hasn't been trampled—there by the cashier flashes her florescent orange lounge dress decorated with rows of contrasting yellow and green rickrack.

Now I begin to perceive some order. You run through the door, dash *first* to the cashier's line to pay, turn immediately to battle your way to the cards, push back out, then careen with your elbows forward for protection to a second plywood table. That table bears a hand-lettered sign over it, "Pickles."

"Pickles?" Why would all these people want pickles to eat? I edge my way to the pickle table where I see folks thrusting their hands into large glass jars filled with green objects. In a random rhythm, up and down, back and forth, their hands move over the objects, then drop something on the floor. Cardboard with printing on it.

Dolores finds me by the pickle table and tugs me toward a break between two unpainted, drywall barriers marked with soot and palm-print smudges. "Relax, relax," she says. "You're going to have a great time. At the very least, the excitement of the game will churn up your blood and you'll forget your problems. Then, once in a while, a great looking man turns up, and boing-bingo!"

I hardly find this an incentive since all the men in sight match the women—overweight, senior-aged, and dressed in polyester pastel slacks. The only difference as far as I can tell is that the men also sport wide suspenders bearing cartoon figures like Donald Duck or Goofy or insignias of sports teams. Still the sight of a well-rounded, colorful crowd around the second table, like a heap of huge Easter eggs decorated by a particularly non-artistic child, piques my curiosity. "What are they doing?" I ask. I have to crane my neck around to get close enough to Dolores' ear so she can hear. "What are 'pickles'?"

"Another way to win money. Kind of like the lottery. You scratch off the covering to see if you've won. I don't like 'em. No skill involved," answers Dolores.

"Bingo doesn't take skill," I respond.

Dolores bristles. "Of course it does. You've got to be really alert to spot the numbers as they're called."

I don't think reading a few numbers will tax my talents. Until I sit down next to Dolores at a long table perpendicular to a stage and Dolores commences dealing bingo cards to me. One, two, three, four.

"I'm starting you slow because this is your first time," explains Dolores. She now has eight cards on the table in front of herself.

"You mean, I have to watch all these for one game?"

"Sure. You'll catch on fast. And you can keep them for the other games if they've been lucky for you. When one of your numbers is called, you pull down the little red plastic cover over it."

"I can't. I can't read four cards at once."

"Four's nothing," Dolores explains patiently. "Look around."

I look. The huge room is filling up as the players take their seats. Some have as many as sixteen cards held on specially constructed racks. Food appears to be almost as popular as the games, and diet Pepsis, Cheetoes, Snicker bars, and nachos (heavy on the cheese and jalapenos) are grouped a hand's reach from cards. I see numerous heads wearing sunshades inside, with green and blue translucent cellophane brims pulled over foreheads and florescent highlighter pens in yellow, pink, blue, green drawn from purses and pockets. Clearly bingo is a world unto itself.

"They certainly look serious," I say. "What are the shades and pens for?"

"They are serious. You can win up to five hundred dollars. The shades are to block the glare and reflection from the overhead lights. The markers are to keep numbers straight. Now, let me explain the rules. Remember bingo when you were a kid? You had to get all the numbers in a straight line? That's one way, but here you can win with a blackout —covering all the numbers —or a round-robin, covering all the numbers around the very edge.

"If you think you're a winner, you raise your hand and yell for a checker. He'll come over, give you a little red flag and read your numbers to the caller. And if you want to exchange your cards or play specials, you ask the checker, too. Got all that?"

"I suppose so," I say doubtfully. Still five hundred dollars *is* five hundred dollars and nothing to sneeze at. A surge, a tingle moves down my arms, and I catch my breath as I think of what fun I could have with the winnings. I can almost see my hand holding a stack of bills, ready to pay for a new hair style or a box full of new CDs or fuzzy Ugg boots for winter. *Someone has to win,* I think, *why not me?*

No more daydreaming is possible because a man is mounting the stage to sit at a small card table next to a wire cage full of plastic balls bearing numbers and letters. "First game, first game," he announces, turning the cage's handle. One ball bounces out. The man picks it up. "O-71," he intones over the microphone. "That's orange-seven-one." The competition commences.

At first I frantically track numbers and letters called against the ones on my cards, too busy to pay attention to my surroundings. Once I discover a method (moving my eyes vertically up and down the rows of all four cards works best for me), I notice a strange silence in the room. Except for a low murmur and an occasional call for new cards or a check for winning numbers, the players concentrate totally on the game. No laughter, no chatter.

The game has me in thrall. I rivet my attention totally on my cards. Each time I near a bingo, my heart beats faster, my breath comes more quickly, my hands grow damp. But each time I'm disappointed.

"Time for a break, folks," the caller announces, and I feel close to collapse, quickly replaced by intense relief.

People stand, stretch, and their conversation surges into a roar. Many of them head toward a small room off to the side, this, too, unpainted drywall. Dolores and I join them in the snack bar, sidestepping an old woman with an aluminum walker on her way out, the bag hung over the arms bulging with her food supplies.

"That was a great win," says a woman with her hair in curlers, adjacent to them in the ragged line that runs next to three long tables loaded with packaged desserts. "How did you do it?"

"It's all in the cards," answers her friend. "When I choose my hard cards, I close my eyes and rub my fingers along the edge. The right ones seem to call to me. I've won three weeks in a row."

Dolores hands me a soft drink and several candy bars as we walk to a small, round, super-tall table mounted on a single metal leg. Designed for speed, an eat-and-run approach, five of these are scattered in the snack bar, and people amiably share standing room around the tables.

"Thanks," I say. "I'm hungry." Two men approach our table and motion an unspoken question about joining us. I nod amiably.

Dolores and I tear into the snacks. Between bites, Dolores asks, "What do you think of the game?"

"There seems to be a technique to selecting the cards. Did you pay attention to the edges when you picked them? Did you feel any positive vibrations?"

"Naw. I just look for my lucky numbers," answers Dolores in all seriousness.

"I've found that choosing little-used cards gives me an edge," says one of the men. "There's an affinity between those cards and the number balls, a baffling attraction."

Because a stranger has addressed me, I assume this is customary at bingo games, like conversations with spectators at a basketball game or chats about the weather in grocery store lines, and paste a half-smile, neither welcoming nor sarcastic, on my face, although I prefer not to be bothered tonight being polite. "We'll certainly take that into consideration," I mouth without any real thought, and turn back to Dolores.

"Yeah, just like there's a baffling attraction between us and you two," adds the second man, breathing deeply enough through his mouth to stir the air around them.

Dolores and I exchange looks. What next? In unison and in the silent communion single women share when out together and confronted with potential contenders for their attention, we focus on our would-be suitors.

Tweedledee and Tweedledum. Short, rotund, foreheads gleaming from the exertion of building up each other's confidence to approach women. Aggression posturing as assurance.

"So, you ladies want to find real winners?" asks the first, slightly taller and with hair considerably more shellacked than his companion. "Stick with us."

"Ummm, thanks, but my friend and I are here just to relax on our own," I murmur, straightening up at the same time.

"Ain't you a tall drink of water," says the second, staring at me. My height beats his by six inches.

"Well, yes," I answer. Quips about my near-six-foot height fail to raise my ire or interest, so commonplace were they when I was a teenager. His hackneyed pitch simply irritates, yet I feel a tingle of delight at the masculine attention, something that has been missing from my life recently. "Too much for you, I'm afraid. Time for us to get back." This is delivered with a super-brightness designed to repel all advances, like Wonder Woman's magical bracelets. I stand and move several steps toward the main room.

Dolores takes a few seconds to get the hint, time she fills by freezing the men with her glance, dissecting them as if they're bugs, searching for any sign of suitability that she might have missed in her first survey. After all, as an experienced veteran of sexual skirmishes, she doesn't need to be nearly as picky as I. Maybe one has more money than is apparent, or connections with a band, or a fine vehicle, or even, unlikely as it is, a sense of humor. Through some extrasensory perception, she realizes they fall short on every scale, snaps her fingers in their direction, and catches up with me. "Boing-less," is all she says.

Back at the table, Dolores picks up her cards, shuffles them into a different order and lays them on the table again. "Now, my special numbers. My birthday, social security number, that sort of thing," she said, pointing to a square with an eight and another one with a forty-five.

"Those wouldn't be lucky for me," I answer.

"Try your own numbers when you buy a special."

"A special?" I echo.

"The colored, paper sheets. You're ready to try them. Come on, the game's about to start."

I purchase two specials. Specials, Dolores informs me, pay more than hard cards. I select my favorite colors, blue and yellow. Maybe they'll be winners. After all, a man has paid attention to me, even if he isn't a Prince Charming. Maybe my luck is changing.

As the night wears on, I wear down. Game succeeds game and the checker carrying a red flag to declare a game to be a winner never comes my way. The little gaming fever I possessed deserts me, leaving me lethargic, mechanically shutting plastic covers or crossing out numbers on the paper specials. I wish the evening were over. I could be home washing my hair or packing up worn towels to be donated to a thrift shop. Anything would have been more productive than these endless bingo games.

So inattentive am I that I almost miss Lady Luck. Dolores pokes me again. "Just one more, Joan!"

I straighten and struggle to focus on my cards. Without much hope, I listen to the caller.

"B-9. That's Banana-ny-een."

"I think that's me," I whisper to Dolores. "It is. It's me." My voice increases in volume. "It's me! Bingo! Bingo!" I screech.

A checker rushes over to me, thrusts a small red flag in my hand, and runs down my numbers carefully. The caller echoes each.

Yes, they confirm. I've won. And not just a measly twenty-five dollars. I'm now the proud possessor of one hundred big ones.

"I can't believe it," I keep repeating on the drive home. "I won. I won. What a great game."

"See, I told you," says Dolores. "Got any plans for the money?"

"I don't know. Buy some clothes. Get a facial and a manicure. That's not important. This win is an omen that things are changing for me. No more losing. I don't have to sit around waiting for excitement or good fortune. I'm a winner. I knew when we set out this evening that something good would happen."

Both of us ignore the truth that Dolores had to practically drag me into the building.

"That's the spirit. And you even flirted with some men. True, they were boring and short."

"And may have been married, for all we know."

"And were generally boing-less, but they *were* male. Proof positive that we're not past our prime. So what's first on your list?"

We're approaching my suburban bungalow, a sole light shining in its front window. A house, no longer a home. The symbol of what's finished and over, not the future.

"Sell the house," I announce. "Get rid of the last tie to a dead past."

Kevin meets me at the doorway of the apartment building, a modern brick tower with well-tended grounds.

"The first thing you should notice is the security system," he says, opening and closing the door several times. "You need a key to get into the lobby itself. Guests can buzz you directly. Otherwise, no annoying sales calls or unwanted drop-ins. And you saw the reserved parking, didn't you?"

"Yes. What about amenities—laundry room, swimming pool? Not that I swim."

"Right this way," says Kevin, with a sweeping gesture like a tour guide's.

The tour covers the common areas. A glassed-in swimming pool welcomes the outdoors in. The exercise room with a

Stairmaster, a stationery bicycle, dumbbells in varying size, also includes a sauna and whirlpool. Laundry room, snack machines, nothing is missing. The crowning touch is a giant party room partitioned for a conversation area around a stone fireplace, a billiards table, large-screen television with DVD, and small kitchenette.

"I'm impressed so far," I admit. In fact, I'm overwhelmed. And yet the building and common areas are somehow institutional in their appearance, as if passersby fear leaving a fingerprint on a door or smooshing down a track on the carpet. Wood paneling, if it *is* wood and not some manmade approximation, which seems highly likely, reflects the glow from oversized ceramic-based lamps with elaborate Chinoiserie tracings. Huge reproductions of museum-type landscapes, clouds and trees and lakes overwhelming miniature humans, hang in gold-tinted frames on every wall. I've never been in such sumptuous surroundings, can't picture myself living here comfortably.

"Come on. Let's look at the apartment." Kevin whisks me up a chrome and mirrored elevator to the sixteenth floor, down a plushly carpeted hallway hung with lithographs, and into an empty apartment.

The view of Washington Park captures me immediately. Framed by a large picture window, leafy green trees wave in the breeze far below. I can see joggers, bicycle riders, mothers pushing strollers in the placid scene. In the distance lies the recreation center, home of the dreaded exercise class. Even that doesn't destroy the beauty of the panorama.

"Don't stay glued to the window," urges Kevin. "Go through the rest of the place."

A compact, well-equipped kitchen lies adjacent to a combination living-dining room with a fireplace. Two bedrooms are arranged on either side of a short hallway, the smaller guest room next to a large bathroom. I breathe a sigh of relief to see carpet and paint in light neutrals and not an ornate mirror or gold leaf light switch plate in sight. Maybe regular people can live here.

"Plenty of closet space," says Kevin, throwing open the twin doors to a narrow pantry. "Storage throughout, including lots of kitchen cabinets. I know it's not as big as your home, but it will be easy to clean. And carpeting is part of the package."

"Do you get a commission when a tenant signs a lease?" I ask with a sarcastic twist to the question. "You're awfully eager for me to move here."

Kevin draws up in mock offense. "Certainly not. I'll admit it would be nice to have a friend nearby. I don't know many people in the building."

"What's the rent?" I ask. He names a figure that approaches my current house payment, and I gasp. "I can't afford that until the house sells. There's no way I could handle rent on top of my mortgage."

"It would only be for a few weeks, while you're closing on the sale of the house. Don't you have some savings?"

I think of my pitifully tiny bank account and shake my head. Then a ray of light appears. My mother. She'll help. She tapped her contacts to find me my job. She offered not long ago to make me a loan. There's no reason for me not to plan to move if the accommodations suit me.

"Where's your apartment?" I ask.

"Several floors down. The view's not as good. Want to see it?"

"Sure."

Kevin's floor plan is almost identical to the model. Its furnishings are as warm and comfortable as he—leather couch, lots of pillows, a wall of books. The kitchen is spotless, too spotless. Not a crumb on the counter, not a stain on the stove.

I sidle over to the refrigerator and swing the door open. A few microwave dinners, a piece of fruit, a half-empty carton of milk. "Ah-ha!" I exclaim. "Now I understand. You want me around so I'll cook for you. You obviously don't have many skills in that area yourself."

"You caught me," admits Kevin. "The only time I ever got a home-cooked meal was when I visited you and James. I've lain awake nights dreaming of meatloaf and roast."

"You'll have to dream on. I need huge meals the way I need an extra leg. Part of my new lifestyle is losing weight."

"Losing weight? Why?"

"In case you haven't noticed, I have a spare tire around my middle. Not to mention the extras hanging from my thighs and other miscellaneous body parts."

"Well, you're not skinny. But you're certainly not fat. Big-boned, I'd say."

"Thank you for that supportive comment. But one of the reasons James left me was neglect of my physical condition. That won't happen again. I'm determined."

"No buttered popcorn as we watch a movie? No waffles on Sunday morning?" says Kevin without hope.

"Nope. Maybe some carrot sticks or a bowl of oat bran."

Kevin visibly droops. But he perks up as he says, "I wonder..."

"Wonder what?"

"How long this will last. You aren't the type to punish yourself for something that's not your fault. Your marriage didn't work out. So what? Lots of marriages don't these days. Particularly when the people involved tie themselves down at such a young age," says Kevin. "And you like to live life to its fullest. You enjoy everything, including food."

"Why, Kevin, another revelation about you that I never knew. You're an amateur analyst, probing beneath the surface of personalities."

Kevin flushes. "Just with my friends. And now, let's stop this seriousness. Time for fun. Shall we grab a hamburger?"

"Food again?" I groan. "Okay, I'll start my diet tomorrow." But as we exit Kevin's apartment, I'm not thinking about food except in relation to Maureen. I can't help wondering if her pregnancy is causing her to gain weight and I'm envying her ability to make that discovery.

With the sale of the house underway, I decide to tackle my list of new interests. Dismally brief, consisting to date of two items— bingo and exercise. Bingo, although lucrative for one time, is, on the whole, a bore. You sit in one spot all night, never talking to the person next to you. With the exception of Dolores, whom I already know, the people don't seem to be especially congenial with my interests, even if I'm not quite sure what my interests might be.

Exercise as an interest rather than an obligation is tolerable, just barely, but I lack the frenzied commitment of a true fanatic. No, I need mental stimulation as well as a way to occupy my time. I call Dolores, who has had more experience in the quest for a single's lifestyle.

"Sure," says Dolores, in reply to my question about activities that combined sociability along with fun. "Too bad the bingo scene didn't work. I still say those two weren't the only men around. We didn't mix with anyone else, so how do we know if they were freakazoids? But I can think of lots of other possibilities for action. Salsa dancing, singles' bars. I've met people at Broncos' football games and basketball games and baseball games. Supermarkets, those are excelleeeeent. Especially by the fresh fruits and vegetables. For some reason, the sight of all those dewy skins throws men off balance. They're desperate for advice. And you can tell by the contents of their shopping carts if men are with someone or not. Speeds up the process."

"No," I say, thinking about Dolores' initial suggestion of that stereotyped method for mixing. "I should break out of my 'wife' mold gradually. It's scary to be a whole again rather than a half. I don't want to plunge right into some frantic meat market like a singles' bar, let alone a real meat market in a grocery store."

"There's another method. I don't go very often because I find too much of it's boring, but it's free, with food, and masses of people, most of 'emteachers or lawyers or students. Art."

"Who's that?" I ask.

"No, no, not a person. Art, pictures, paintings."

"I don't have much talent for drawing." I think of the exercise class, the ceramics class, the social milieu of bingo, wondering if Dolores is intent on improving me one way or another, mentally or physically or creatively, whether I want to or not.

"You needn't lift a pencil. I mean art openings. In little squirrelly places all over the city, run-down warehouses and cheap business buildings, they go through a regular routine every few weeks. They change their artists and exhibits, throw an open house, provide refreshments, sometimes even music. You trot from one gallery to another making smart-ass comments about technique and self-expression. After a while, you start to recognize people, strike up a conversation."

"You're sure I won't make a fool of myself? I can't tell one brush stroke from another."

"You don't need to. If you can't think of anything else to say, you lean back, press your lips together, squint your eyes, and let loose with something like, 'very interesting,' or 'somewhat derivative.' Then the man next to you, preferably tall, dark, and handsome, disagrees, and off you go."

"You'll stay with me, won't you?"

"Sure. I may get bored with posing as an art lover every week, but openings are fun occasionally, and they don't cost a penny. Sign the guest book and you're on the gallery's mailing list for life. You always know when the next fun-filled event occurs. A round's coming up Friday. I can meet you at six. My mom's watching the kids."

How do you dress for an art opening, I wonder on Friday. I take out then put back a black cocktail dress (too fancy), a pair of jeans (too casual), a skirt and blouse (too juvenile), a suit (too conservative).

I'll do my hair first. Maybe an outfit will jump out at me afterwards. I brush my straight, shoulder-length hair with hard, punishing strokes. How do you fix your hair for an art opening, I wonder, pulling reddish-brown hanks one way and other. I try a bun (too conservative), a high pony tail (too juvenile), several braids (too freaky), a French twist (too fancy).

Dolores's car roars up and I run to the door before she knocks. "You're not going like *that*?" gasps Dolores. The same question could be asked of Dolores, dressed as she is, or isn't, in a florescent pink tube top, tight mini skirt with a more colorful abstract print than any produced by Jackson Pollack, and dozens of glass bead necklaces that completely cover her neck and shoulders. Dolores looks down at herself at my unspoken query. "Oh, this is my hot Chicana outfit," Dolores explains. "No male artist can resist it, even the gay ones."

One hand still clutching my hair, I look down, too. I've forgotten I'm wearing a short, flowered bathrobe. "I don't have anything else," I wail. "You'll have to go without me."

Dolores marches me into the bedroom. "You're panicking over nothing. An art opening is not that big a deal. Let me look."

She begins throwing clothes helter-skelter out of the closet onto the bed and floor. "Nope, not that. Not that. Not that." From deep inside the closet, Dolores's voice resounds, "You're right. This wardrobe is a mess. Where have you been for the past ten years?"

"Married," I say gloomily as I lean against the nearby wall, my arms wrapped around my middle to prevent the bathrobe from gaping. "I didn't need glamorous dresses. I had a husband."

"We're not talking husbands. We're talking moderately stylish clothes to cover your body. Aaaah. Try this."

Dolores emerges holding the skirt to a suit and a loose, plaid pullover that I usually wear for yardwork.

"That's my grubbiest shirt," I point out, "and my most expensive skirt. I'll look like a fool."

"No, you won't," Dolores assures me. "You're going as a New Age hippie. Leave your hair down, wrap a scarf around it, add a bunch of beads and dangly earrings, and there you are."

An hour later, the two of us leave, decked out like an advertisement for a jewelry shop and clanking and jangling like a Christmas recording. I follow Dolores down the sidewalk to the first gallery, selected because of its reputation for appetizing hors d'oeuvres. This part of Denver recently has become popular with gallery owners. The historic brick office buildings, three and four stories high, glisten with new paint and large shiny windows that replace the original small ones. Canvas banners of mauve and pink hang from wrought iron bars over the entryways.

Before Dolores and I reach our destination, we see herds of people standing outside the galleries and trooping from one building to another, plastic wine glasses barely disguised within hands or held close to bodies, a perfunctory acknowledgement of city ordinances prohibiting open consumption of alcohol on the street. Shrieks rise from gaggles of girls as they spot their friends and throw their bare arms around each other's equally exposed necks and shoulders. Everyone seems to know everyone else well enough to parade around in the summer heat half-exposed in tube tops, miniskirts and strappy sandals. A chill runs up my spine as I think of striking up a conversation with a total stranger who has zero interest in me and wears the minimum of garments to cover her all too human—and usually model thin—flesh.

Then I realize that the acres of bare skin overwhelmed my senses. Clothes actually run the gamut from business apparel to short-shorts. I don't need to worry about standing out in this crowd. I'm more likely to be overlooked as run-of-the-mill. Well, that's all right. This first time I want to get my bearings and soak up the atmosphere.

Dolores leads me into the first gallery—a series of enormous rooms with high ceilings, painted stark white. Upon each wall hangs one huge canvas with swirls of color going round and round. To me, all the paintings appear identical, resembling Dolores' skirt and beads, and I get dizzy looking at them. I read the paper that was thrust in my hand as I came through the door, describing the artist's experience and his artistic intent for each of his works, trying to make sense of what I see.

"What does this mean?" I ask Dolores, who has reappeared at my side, two wine glasses in hand. *"The painterly mannerisms reflect the moral turpitude of society, its ennui with reality, its escapism to fantasy."*

"Who knows?" answers Dolores. She scarcely glances at the artwork, a collection of florescent pink and vibrant purple swathes that could be flowers or clouds at sunset or an alien space setting, for all I know. "Who cares? Let's go to the next gallery. I saw a man I've been tracking for months walk in there."

"What about the glass?"

"Take it with you. They don't care as long as you're not obvious."

I obediently follow Dolores into the next gallery. This one is devoted to photography. The male and female nudes are all right, at least not repulsively ugly, I think, but I can't make out the photos that consist of several layers of bodies overlapping one another.

Turning to ask Dolores a question, I discover she has disappeared. A young man in a tuxedo with slicked-back hair and thick eyebrows bristling in all directions notices my perplexity.

"What do you think?" he asks.

"I can't tell what the photo is. All those bodies."

"The image comes from exposing several stacked negatives simultaneously." He speaks the lofty phrases through his nose. "Then they're printed high contrast to drop out the middle tones."

"Oh." I can think of nothing else to add. "But what does the photo mean?"

"Mean? Mean?" the young man probes. "An image doesn't carry a meaning. It exists as itself, a separate entity."

"Oh," I repeat. "I was afraid it was an orgy." I laugh weakly.

"An orgy?" He actually rears back and raises his bushy eyebrows, as if the word is offensive.

"That was supposed to be a joke," I say in a voice that fades as the man whirls and walks away, evidently finding my conversation boring or childish. He takes himself and his tuxedo off to the next room. I wander around, lost in a maze of black and white images until I spot Dolores leaning against a wall, talking to a bearded man. She waves, squeezes the man on the upper arm in what seems a far more intimate action than a kiss, and approaches me.

"Contact!" Dolores crows. "I finally met him. We have a date tomorrow."

"Who is he?"

"A sculptor. Doesn't he look like one? Of course, he works construction to make money. Art's hard to sell."

"He's rather hairy, isn't he?"

"Men usually are. Oh, you mean the beard. I think it's cute. I'm tired of macho Latinos, like most of my exes. I'm experimenting with all different types. Tomorrow a sculptor, the day after a motorcyclist."

I consider the idea. Maybe I should experiment. James doesn't have the least trait out of the ordinary. For that matter, no men with whom I come into contact do. Lawyers, accountants, businessmen, real estate agents—suit guys. Men whose positions in life are more noteworthy, memorable, important than their true identities. Suddenly they all seem dreadfully identical and boring. I toss my head and feel my hair, earrings, and scarf brush my cheeks on either side. I'm dressed like a wild woman—maybe I should act like one. And maybe, just maybe, suit guys will view me as an irresistible temptation, an out-of-the-world experience that ultimately will carry more meaning for me than for them. From dull little suburban displaced homemaker into a Bohemian wild woman, exuding mystery and a touch of danger.

"Do you have something in your eye?" asks Dolores. "You're jerking your head around."

"No," I mutter. "Feeling my freedom."

"Well, we've scoped this place out. Let's go to the next gallery."

Across a street so clogged with people that cars have to crawl along to avoid running them down, stands the gallery featuring realistic works of art. I actually can tell what each picture contains. Western landscapes, detailed views of horses and dogs, several portraits, all framed in rough wood, hang on bare brick walls.

Dolores and I stroll slowly along the perimeters of the room. A burst of laughter lures me into turning my head. *My* lawyer stands in a small group of men and women, laughing and gesturing.

I grip Dolores's arm. "Look. Over there. It's Scott Clark from my office. The one we saw in the cafeteria. Remember? Isn't he gorgeous?"

"I still think he's a phony, but I have to agree he's not bad-looking for a lawyer. Not bad at all. Why don't you go talk to him?"

"I don't think he know me from Eve," I answer.

"Well, now's your chance to get noticed. He's walking around. Saunter in the opposite direction and stop when you get by him."

"Too obvious."

"Joan, you don't know the least thing about technique. Do it," Dolores commands. "It will work, I promise you."

In a deliberately casual walk, I take Dolores's advice. I glance at each painting as I pass, but I don't halt until I reach my lawyer. Side by side, we survey a sunset going down behind beige cliffs.

"Hmmm," Scott says and squints his eyes.

"Interesting," I say, turning as bold as an extroverted and determined used car dealer. "But rather derivative, don't you think?"

"I agree," he replies. "An attempt to capture O'Keefe's technique, but much too muted."

"Oh, yes," I echo. "Much too muted."

"Now if he had enriched his blues and violets, he would have approached her perspective. But still he'd have nothing original."

"Nothing original," I agree with enthusiasm because I realize how truly simple a conversation about art can be. The woman simply agrees with the man, just like conversations about sports, or cars, or national security, or stocks and bonds. No thinking required.

Scott turns his attention toward me. "You seem to know quite a bit about art. Are you an artist?"

"Oh, no. Just a self-taught, interested layperson," I reply with the modesty of a nun.

"You must have a natural eye," he says and adds, "This sounds like an old line, but haven't we met before?"

"Yes, we've seen each other. I'm the receptionist for Horowitz, Trimble, Hawkins, & Jones," I say. My heart is pounding so loudly, I'm sure Scott can hear it, and I place the flat of a palm on my chest."

"Ah, yes." Scott makes a motion with his fingers as if they are a revolver and clicks his tongue. "My landlord. Receptionist, hey? You must be the nerve center for the entire operation."

"Not quite. Although I do have to be familiar with all our cases and clients," I say with what I hope is becoming modesty.

"I'm pleased to meet you formally. Name's Scott, Scott Clark." He sticks out a hand with the assurance of a man whose acquaintance everyone is eager to make.

"Yes, I know. Nerve center and all that, remember?" I gingerly take his fingers, waiting for a bolt of lightning to shoot through me. I'm actually touching him! "I'm Joan Nelson." I feel a warmth, a tingle, but no electricity.

"Joan?" He cocks an eyebrow at me. "Smacks of hometown Americana. Mom and apple pie kind of feelings. That you?"

I'm horrified. Does my mere appearance advertise my background from a small farming community? "Oh, no," I fudge without going into detail. "I've lived in Denver for eight years. San Diego before that. How about you?"

"About two years. I moved from Boston. Studied at Harvard Law but decided I wanted the wide open spaces of the West. Now I've passed the bar and I'm ready to take on the world. And I'm especially glad to get to know you better. You're the one who keeps the law business going. You find lost files, placate irate clients, and always say your bosses are in court, even at eight at night. Right?"

"Right," I answer, even though the statement has been delivered with the practiced, subdued ease of a cliché.

"Now what about the paralegal in the office named Kimberlee? Petite, blonde, slinky? What's her story?"

My heart plummets to my feet. "Kimberlee? What do you mean?"

"Is she married, going with anyone?"

"Not that I know. We're not very close, though."

"She seems real knowledgeable to me. About the firm and practice of law. Lots of real interesting people in the office." Scott's eyes begin to move from his scrutiny of me to dart around the gallery, as if in restless search of another person more special than I am. "Listen, I've got to go. Catch you later." A flip of two fingers in a casual salute and he is off.

Scott's well-filled jacket soon is lost in the art crowd. I wander over to the hors d'oeuvres table. My stomach, clenched previously, has relaxed into an enormous void that has to be satiated.

Dolores reaches me after I've eaten through one round of three types of cheeses and four of crackers, but before I insert a fistful of nuts. Dolores slaps my hand. "You're on a diet, remember?" Dolores chides. "How did you make out with the attorney?"

"I managed to squeeze out a few words, thanks to you. The 'interesting' comment works very well."

"I told you so. Did he ask you out?"

I shake my head. "Once he found out I'm a mere receptionist, he got more interested in my co-worker."

"Don't give up yet. At least you've established contact," Dolores points out. "And you're on mailing lists for four galleries."

These small triumphs have to sustain me through a two-week spell during which absolutely nothing happens. Not a sign of Scott in the cafeteria or on the elevator. He simply sticks his head in the door of the office occasionally to change the instructions on the in-out board. Not a nibble of interest in the purchase of my house. Two Saturday exercise classes pass without an ounce of weight loss.

A minor catastrophe strikes Monday morning. I enter the office to see a huddle of lawyers and staff by a computer. Kimberlee motions me over to the group.

"The computers are down," says Kimberlee. "We don't know what caused the failure. Maybe a lightning strike. You didn't leave your terminal on when you left Friday, did you?"

"I'd never do that," I demur. "I'm still nervous with the equipment." Although the protest rises spontaneously, I frantically cast my mind back. Am I the guilty party? No, I'm sure I switched off the computer at closing time, both at the terminal and the surge protector. It's part of my regular routine.

At the Monday morning staff meeting two hours later, the office's standard calm shatters entirely. Mr. Horowitz, the firm's leading partner, stands and draws his dignity around him like a judge's robes. His moustache, a fringe of neatly clipped gray hair, wriggles over his mouth as he speaks with control.

"I regret to inform you that the computer failure does not appear to be the result of natural causes. We suspect someone tried to tap into our files without permission. We can only assume that he or she attempted to copy them. When the perpetrator was unsuccessful, he left a little present, whether intentionally or unintentionally, that created havoc with our records, freezing each work station as it opened."

A collective gasp circles the assembly.

Mr. Horowitz continues. "Fortunately, our system always backs up all files."

Kimberlee raises her hand. "How do we know nothing was copied?"

"We have a tight security system." He cocks an eyebrow at the staff. "We can be fairly confident the system is inviolate. Otherwise, why would the perpetrator wind up stumbling into a self-destructive circuit?

"But even though this attempt failed, I want to stress the necessity for absolute confidentiality about our files, our computer system. We can take this as a warning to be ever-vigilant. I trust each of you keeps your password strictly to yourself?" He fixes his eyes on the support staff one by one as he looks around the circle. "A word dropped in innocence to the wrong person, a cursory conversation in a restaurant, anything could have set this off. And it may happen again. Be attentive in your search for any clue as to how the incident occurred." Mr. Horowitz stops talking but continues what seems to be an inspection of the office personnel. Then he abruptly sits down, saying, "That is all."

The meeting breaks up and people head toward their desks. I can't shake a tremor of guilt, although I know I have nothing to feel guilty about. I stop by Kimberlee's place. As the senior staff member, she always knows more than the rest of us peons.

"Do you think it was someone in the office?" I ask.

Kimberlee shuffles the papers on her desk and avoids my eye. "I doubt it. Most of the people here have been around for years and know how important security is. But someone could have been careless without intending to be."

"Except me," I say, a hollowness filling my stomach. "I'm new. Does that mean I'm a suspect?"

"Any reason you should be?" asks Kimberlee, reaching for some envelopes but pausing with them in her hand. "Maybe a slip of the tongue somewhere?"

"No, no," I deny, backing up to escape Kimberlee's implacable gaze. I resume my seat and try to quell my disquiet.

I can't wait for coffee break. I want to tell Dolores about the attempted computer theft. Sliding a tray loaded with coffee, several donuts and a bag of caramels along the counter, I reach the cash register, pass over my money, and whisper to Dolores, "I need to talk to you!"

The crush in the cafeteria finally clears. Dolores approaches, putting all her energy into wiping off the table at my booth.

"I can't sit down. Supervisor's watching," she says in an undertone, the words coming through unmoving lips, a technique perfected under the authoritarian thumb of many supervisors. "What's up?"

"Someone tried to break into our computer system," I gasp.

"No!" Dolores halts her action. "Is that bad?"

"Of course it's bad. He ruined all our files. He could have gotten highly confidential information. But more than that, it's against the law just as much as stealing."

"Who do you think did it?"

"I'm the prime suspect," I answer, torn between a smidgeon of pride and a dollop of humiliation. "Because I'm the newest."

"You?" Dolores scoffs. "You won't even cross the street on a red light." She picks with a fingernail at a nonexistent smear on the table.

"You and I know that, but my bosses don't."

"Have they fired you?"

"No, not yet." Gloom settles on me, pushing my shoulders down. "But the way my life's been going these past months, it's inevitable." The emotion pulls me along a stream of depression. I see myself job-less, penny-less, friend-less, evicted from my apartment, living in my car, eating out of trash cans. Dolores breaks this chain of thought.

"Maybe you can catch the thief." A glint comes to Dolores's eyes. "Could be exciting. We could hide in your office after everyone's gone. Under a desk or something. Leap out and surprise him." Her cleaning rag moves in tight concentric circles as if her enthusiasm has to be expressed somewhere.

Fantasies notwithstanding, this is going too far. "Don't be crazy. How would we know when he's coming? Or even *if* he's coming? And we might be killed."

"But you'd save your bosses. They might give you a reward."

"Honestly, Dolores. Do you get these ideas from reruns of *CSI*? Forget I told you. I'm not going to catch the guy."

I wrap the donuts in layers of paper napkins and huff out. At the door I miss Scott by inches and nod a small hello. His blank look bounces from the messy, gooey packet in my hand up to my face, when recognition breaks.

"Joan. Sorry, my mind's on a case. How are things with Horowitz, et al?" he asks.

"I didn't see you at the staff meeting. You missed the commotion. Frantic today." I can't hold back my exciting news. "Our computers are down. Someone tried to break into them."

Scott's smooth countenance creases in concern. "Nothing of the firm's damaged, I hope."

"No, we're fine. Don't worry. I'm sure your files are safe, too."

"That didn't cross my mind. My files are separate from yours and my computer isn't networked. Remember, I'm the firm's tenant, not a member."

"Still, security is a top priority," I say.

"As it should be. If you want some tips, I'd be happy to talk with you," he offers and heads toward the cafeteria line.

"Why...why, thanks," I stammer, watching his retreat.

On the way up the elevator, I hug myself, heedless of the donut frosting leaking from the napkins onto my dress. Scott seems interested in spending time with me. The proposal to help me with computer security has to be an excuse—everyone knows passwords can't be revealed.

I nibble on a donut. As I reach my desk, a cold wave washes over me. Mr. Horowitz warned the staff against revealing anything. I'm not supposed to be talking about the system failure. A quick review of my conversations reassures me. I've revealed nothing confidential. Surely Dolores isn't included in the prohibition—she doesn't even know how to use a computer. And Scott's nearly a part of the firm. The two most harmless individuals I could have told. Neither stands to gain by my discussion.

I rub my hands down my thighs and feel a stickiness. How has that happened? The donuts. I place them gingerly on a corner of my desk and turn my attention to sponging the frosting from my skirt.

The crisis at the office nags at an edge of my mind all day and into the evening's labor. My self-assigned chore is to plow through the kitchen cupboards. I'm dividing the contents into dishes to be kept and items to be thrown out or offered to James (I don't care which). Now that I've made up my mind to sell the house, I can hardly wait to move.

A stack of mismatched plates—a white one with a blue band, two blue willow patterns, a yellow and a brilliant orange—remainders from the first year of marriage, are close at hand, and I transfer them to the counter. Friends and relatives gifted me and James with their discards to make do until the newlyweds could buy a complete set.

I don't need much concentration to complete the task and can worry with impunity about my future with the law firm. Finding a decent job was exhausting and humiliating, I recall. With only a high school education and a variety of low-paying, unskilled jobs on my resume, I met one rejection after another.

A persistent chime from the doorbell finally breaks through my musings. Who would come over unannounced? Tempted to ignore the summons, I sidle along the wall so the visitor can't see me through the window, put an eye to a crack in the curtain. "Kevin!" I throw the door open. "What are you doing here?"

No slob he, Kevin wears an impeccable business suit, pale blue shirt and paisley tie. Even more impressive are his freshly combed hair and congenial greeting. At the end of a long, grueling work day, Kevin bears no signs of fatigue or defeat. Unlike paranoid and depressed me, whose rumpled, dingy sweatsuit, faded from gray into a streaked greige, matches my attitude.

"I was in the neighborhood and thought I'd drop by to discuss several informal offers on the house," he says.

"In the neighborhood? Get serious. This is miles from your place. You're a sweetheart to worry about me after I wailed on your shoulder the other day. Come in and have some coffee."

Turning to go back to the kitchen, I catch just a glimpse of a flush that mounts Kevin's face. As I move from cupboard to sink to counter, chattering about the computer incident and my fears, I also notice his unusual reticence.

"So you see I'm working off nervous energy as well as preparing to move," I say with a gesture at the open cupboards and the cups teetering in stacks on the table where Kevin sits. "If I get fired, I couldn't bear having to pound the pavement again. My ego was totally destroyed. I don't know which type of rejection I preferred—the unanswering void of some potential employers who didn't bother to respond to an application or the politely worded rebuffs."

As if unfolding a letter, I pretend to quote. "We sincerely thank you for applying. Although you met the requirements for the position, we regret to inform you that other candidates were better qualified. Therefore we are unable to offer you the position of 'you-fill-in-the-blank'. We wish you good luck in your job search."

Kevin shakes his head so emphatically he destroys his combing job. "You can't let rejection discourage you. I get dozens of rejections every day. How could I ever close a sale if I allowed the no's to slow me down?"

I return to my cupboard. "Easy for you to say. I was desperate for a job. James had walked out and I had no income when my mother alerted me to the opening at the law firm. I was grateful for her assistance. Pride prevented me from asking James or my family for financial help. I found pride was the last quality I needed after seven weeks of hopeless, fruitless inquiry. I couldn't bear to go through the process again."

Three shelves in the cupboards are clear. I look at the stack of miscellaneous mugs heaped on the top shelf and decide to discard them. An array of assorted colors and sizes, they proclaim cute sayings on their sides such as, "If you think today was bad, wait until tomorrow," and, "Keep your paws off!" or "Mondays are God's punishment for weekends."

I shudder as I climb on a stool for a better look. James and I used to exchange the mugs regularly on birthdays, a kind of contest to see which one could find the ugliest or rudest. Until two years before the break-up, I suddenly realize. Another subtle sign of the disintegration of my marriage. I don't need them as reminders.

Kevin's voice breaks into my thoughts. "You won't have to worry for long."

I poke into another assortment that has been hidden at the very rear of the cupboard. "What do you mean?" I ask.

"About supporting yourself. Surely you have a *very good friend* waiting in the wings."

Whirling around on the stool where I stand, I nearly fall over. I hook five or six mugs firmly over my fingers, clamber down, and advance on Kevin while brandishing the dishware. "Listen, mister, James is the charmer, the con man, the one with the sweetie-pie, not me. Was that way in school, remember? Every time I turned around, I had to pry him out of the hold of some adoring females, after a basketball game when he'd made a winning basket, hanging out in the park during the summers. Evidently, no difference after he finished college and started in business either. *Don't ask, don't tell* was my philosophy. I didn't probe or spy. And I never was unfaithful to him, before or during marriage, and I resent your implication."

Kevin recoils and leans back as far as possible in his chair. "Sorry. I'm the best one to know you weren't. I don't know why I said that."

"What do you mean, you're the best one to know?"

"Don't you remember the pass I made at you just before you got married? The summer after high school?"

Thoroughly bewildered, I shake my head.

Kevin stands, puts his cup on the table, shoves his hands in his pockets, thereby disarranging his suited perfection. "Not an incident to be proud of, to put moves on a friend's girl. The party when James had to leave because his dad was out of town and his mom called to say his little sister was sick? He left and I got you in a corner to nuzzle?"

I lower my arms to my sides, still holding the mugs. The action matches my dropping jaw. "That was a pass?"

Kevin is motionless, as if my comment is sinking into his consciousness, until he throws back his head and laughs. "I don't know whether to be offended you found me so inept or grateful you haven't resented my action all these years."

"I thought you were just practicing. Everyone necked constantly with anyone in reach. They were like puppies or kittens squirming around to learn about their bodies. I didn't know you were serious."

"And if you had known?" Kevin asks. A silence stretch between us. I don't know where to look, so I stare at my toes. "Ah, well, now is not the time for what-ifs. We're all grown up. Like a brother and sister, right?" He reaches for some of the mugs to help pack them.

"If you hold it, you keep it," I warn. "These are discards."

"One. Only one," Kevin says, touching my hand lightly with all his fingertips. "So, there's no one in your life?"

Now it's my turn to flush. "Well, a guy in the offices at work is interesting. We haven't gone out, though."

Kevin's fingers grasp one particularly grotesque mug which resembles a stony gargoyle. "This will do as a memento. Time for me to take off."

"I thought you were going to tell me about some offers," I protest.

"Until earnest money's involved, an offer's not serious. No, don't bother," he says when I make motions as if to walk him to the door. "I'll find my way out."

I shrug and continue my chore. The cupboard is nearly empty. Piling the mugs on the counter, I think again about work. My mother would be crushed if suspicion falls on me. And if I were dismissed? Can I find another job despite a bad record and no recommendation?

A call from Dolores ends this dismal line of reasoning. I can hear Dolores's three kids screaming in the background.

"Quiet!" Dolores yells at her brood. "Sorry," she apologizes. "Summer hours set them off. They need space to run around, so I'm taking them to the band concert at the park tonight. Want to come? Make it part of your continuing search for a new interest."

"Sure," I reply with immediate enthusiasm, envisioning attractive couples at rest on checkered cloths, toasting one another with wine glasses, a rosy sunset over the mauve mountains, a full orchestra decked out in tuxedos, soft strains of violins broken by the crash of cymbals, a restful and idyllic finale for the weekend. "What shall I bring?"

We settle on the easy way out—fried chicken from a fast food outlet. I stuff myself into jeans that fit a year ago but are skin-tight now, a roll of fat at the waistband hidden under a loose shirt, and buy the food on my way to the park. Dragging along an old blanket to sit on, I meet Dolores at the park entrance. Dolores's daughter and two boys already run far ahead, down the grass-covered slopes to the concert area.

"Where do they get the energy?" I shake my head in disbelief.

"They don't work all day like we do. They piddle around at the child care center drawing pictures and playing games." Dolores shifts a giant red cooler from one hand to another. "All they need is junk food and soft drinks and they're raring to go again."

Carefully picking our way through the families already inhabiting the knoll in front of the bandstand, Dolores and I head for the kids' frantically waving hands from the middle of a small if prime spot about to be beached by a wave of newcomers. We stake a firm property claim when we spread our blankets and unpack the food, reinforced by the shrieking kids' water-bottle squirt-battle that clears the immediate area of the faint of heart. Complete comfort and quiet at last are achieved with the distribution of chicken encrusted with so much coating that the meat is scarcely visible and the diners' clothing becomes dotted with oily scraps. Still, we drink in the evening's cool relief along with our icy soft drinks.

I watch Dolores's little girl, the epitome of femininity, first lick her purple-tipped fingers one by one, then wipe them with great delicacy on a paper napkin. "Do you wish things could have been different?" I ask Dolores, who understands the real underlying inquiry.

"Sure. It's hard to raise three on your own. That's why I send them to their fathers whenever I can. *Revenge!*" Dolores laughs at herself. "Not really. With the first one, I thought two parents were better than one, no matter what. That's why I got married. With the second, I realized having a father around is nice, but not always practical. Then, with the third, this way is actually preferable. Not ideal, but superior to the life we had together. The arguments were terrible. The screaming, the threats, the dependency. It was as if I had an extra kid. Hmmm. Now that I look back, that's true of all the men I've lived with. What I wouldn't give for a real adult male."

"I wonder," I say. "I wonder if any father is better than no father. Oh, I know that's not always possible. But I grew up from the age of ten without a father. I felt like a discarded, useless bundle of rags. He disappeared—*whhhht!*—for no reason I could determine. There hadn't been lots of open warfare as far as I could tell."

"Then why did your parents split?" asks Dolores.

I answer slowly, feeling my way through old memories that I'd never considered before. "I think, I do believe, maybe another women? Hard to imagine in a tiny farming town, isn't it? But we'd get these strange phone calls at night for him and sometimes I'd see him on a corner downtown with different ladies. I'm beginning to guess the accusations toward my mother about her terrible housekeeping habits were his excuses for his own bad behavior. But, God, I missed him."

"Nope," says Dolores, briskly brushing her hands together to get rid of crumbs or the image of my father. "As a mother I can tell you that a stable home with the basics of food and clothes, along with a dependable parent, is better than the uncertainty you've just sketched out. Unless a man is willing to accept responsibility, the family's better off without him."

"What about the future?"

"Who'd take a woman with three kids? I can't find a lion tamer or mental patient to marry let alone a mature father figure. That type would run screaming the other way when he saw my crew. I've resigned myself to being alone. Maybe that's why I live out my fantasies on weekends with bikers and artists and an assortment of others."

I lie on my back to watch the clouds passing overhead. Faintly tinged with pinks and purples from the setting sun, they billow high, trailing streaks of vapor behind them like a train on a wedding dress. A bird soars so high I can't tell what kind it is. What an idyllic evening. Nothing bad should be able to happen in a world like this. But it does occasionally. Marriages break up, people get incurable diseases, murderers run loose. "Aren't you afraid to go out with some types? Bikers don't have good reputations. And artists aren't noted for their stability."

"A risk that has to be weighed. I'm careful," Dolores insists. "You and I both got married young. The sexual revolution passed us by at first. Now I'm experiencing what I missed. I see an interesting guy, I fantasize what he'd be like. Sometimes I take action. Although I've been burned so often, I've learned not to bring my fantasy home."

"What's your best fantasy? Your forever-after wish?" I ask, still studying the clouds.

A huge, upside down face imposes itself between me and the sky. "I thought that was you," says Kevin.

I sit up so fast I almost knock him down. He recoils back on his heels. "Kevin! What are you doing here?"

"The same thing as you, I presume. Waiting for the concert."

That makes sense. The park is right next to Kevin's apartment building. I introduce Dolores and Kevin. Dolores squints at Kevin with interest and offers him a piece of chicken. He rejects the food but accepts a corner of the blanket, sitting cross-legged with the ease and grace of a dancer.

"We were just discussing our fantasies," says Dolores.

"Have you just started your stories?" asks Kevin. "And what type?"

"Sexual," says Dolores, providing a clear opening for Kevin.

"But everyone still keeps his clothes on," I throw in hastily with a gesture toward the children. "A PG-rating. The if-you-could-make-up-the-script type. Dolores, for example, specializes in diversity. Others might select historical legends or athletic endeavors."

"My favorites are adventures. Pirates, fighter pilots, heroes rescuing cities from tornadoes. But if you've ruled out straight adventures, I can always throw in maidens being threatened," says Kevin. "You don't want to hear my overt sexual fantasies. Not appropriate subject matter for the audience."

"Kevin, another surprise about you," I say. "You're so work-a-day. He's a real estate agent," I explain to Dolores. "Not many wild times in that profession. I guess he must escape into his imagination."

"You'd be surprised. Few dragons, but lots of ladies in distress. Like Joan. A big house that she wants to get rid of. Plenty of empty beds and assorted challenging surfaces. A talented real estate agent who can help in every way possible. Presto."

Dolores leans back on her elbows and studies Kevin as if he's a mouse she's trapped. "My fantasies vary with the situation. Right now I'm visualizing being swept away by a blond, muscular hunk whose fathomless glance takes in every detail around him, who looks capable of handling any challenge life throws at him, and comforting every broken-hearted woman who passes. Say like me, who's been tortured by life's whims, sabotaged through lies from losers, imprisoned in a dead-end job."

I crow and push on my friend's shoulders until she topples. "Don't believe her. She'd do backflips to charm you, then drop you faster than you can blink. I'll warn you right now, Kevin. That's her style. She loves 'em, then leaves 'em."

"An intriguing thought," replies Kevin. "But what about you, Joan?"

I shut my eyes. "My fantasy? Tall. Trim but with those well-defined muscles you can see under his clothes. Reddish, wavy hair. Intelligent. Interested in the finer things in life, like art."

"Sounds very specific." Kevin frowns.

"Oh, that's her current crush," Dolores throws in. "Some tight-assed lawyer. Seems dull to me, but Joan doesn't take chances, even in her fantasies."

"It didn't take you long to recover completely from James," says Kevin. "The man from work, I presume."

"Now, what about you?" Dolores asks Kevin, before I can could reply. "Probably a Christy Brinkley type, well-built, with a tinkling laugh and long legs."

Kevin stands abruptly. "My fantasy is even more mundane than Joan's, I'm afraid. Hardly of interest to either of you. The concert's about to start. Dream on, ladies."

My head turns to follow Kevin's departure. "Now what on earth is the matter with him?" I ask Dolores.

"You are one stupid woman," answers Dolores.

CHAPTER SIX

"What brought on that comment?" I ask.

"You have a man like that sitting here eating you with his eyes and you're off in a make-believe world with a lawyer who doesn't know you exist," says Dolores.

I notice my plate of untouched chicken and slaw and feel a pang of hunger. I pick up a leg to nibble. "Kevin? He's an old friend, actually more James's friend than mine. We have a brother-sister relationship."

"I tell you, he's hot for you," Dolores insists. "I practically put myself on the blanket for him and he turned away."

"You mean if a man rejects *you*, the only possible reason is that he's in love with someone else. What conceit."

"Joan, Joan, look at him," Dolores begs. "Don't let him slip through your fingers." She points in the direction he went.

In the din and flurry of musicians tuning up, people taking a final stretch before the program, Kevin's solid figure walks without hesitation. His torso and legs, substantial but not flabby, could bear the weight of the world. Strength lies, too, in the broad bones of his face, in the straightforward way he surveys the crowd.

I smile at the familiar form and the grin increases as Kevin sits down next to an attractive brunette. "There, see? Why would he want me when he has her?" I crow. "Relax and take your mind off men. Listen to the performance."

Can daydreams bloom at night? Flutes twitter and their strains fill me with a buoyancy in which my life takes a new direction. I see Scott beside me, hear his low tones speak of fascinating topics, political affairs, say, or travel to mysterious places.

My conversation suddenly becomes facile and with articulate phrases, I express important thoughts. My body thins, my hair thickens, I move with grace and charm. Utterly captivated, Scott leans toward me, coming closer and closer.

Bam! Crash! The drums and cymbals of the band shatter my dream and shock me back to reality, which again bears little resemblance to the setting I imagined before we came to the park. No tuxes, but jeans. No violins, but horns. No wine, but soft drinks. Not even a heck of a lot of tranquility in a park crammed with thirty-thousand people, half of whom are cranky kids. During the final strains of the concert, Dolores and I gather blankets, cooler, and children to beat the crowd's rush. Too bad existence can't be like fantasy, I think, still caught in my dream, with transformation of someone's hitherto dull or dreadful life occurring in a heartbeat and according to a whim.

I change my mind about quick changes a few days later when Kevin calls with word that he has a firm and excellent offer on the house. The family, complete with two school-aged children to be enrolled in local institutions by fall, is pressured to find a place and wants to move in as soon as the papers can be signed. James has already agreed—do I have any problems with the deal?

No, but goodbyes are wrenching when made in a short space of time. I turn from the telephone to survey the structure I've called home for five years. Commonplace and cookie-cutter as it is, a fake-brick box identical to its five hundred or so neighbors, here James and I had come filled with hopes for a glowing future—a ladder of upward promotions and stimulating projects for him at the insurance agency where he passed his work days and children with wet bottoms and sticky kisses for me. In the kitchen, we prepared holiday dinners and invited our mothers on alternate years because the two women never moved past the carefully polite stage since the year they both had run for Homecoming queen in high school. I remember burning a turkey thoroughly on one early memorable Thanksgiving, then feasting on mashed potatoes, yams, and pie.

The living room furniture, chosen with such care and with an eye for soothing earth tones and sturdiness, so it would last through the growth pangs of several children, was purchased on time payments. I budgeted, earmarked a check each month, did without luxuries to make the investment. I run a finger over the back of the loveseat on my way to the bedroom, changing my mind as I consider. Maybe quick change, swift and sure as the plunging of a sword is better. No lingering, no time for regrets.

The bedroom. Soon others will lie and love in a different bed, look up at the ceiling. Will they like the color or repaint? Probably they'll make a fresh start by wiping out all signs of my habitation.

On the other hand, I'll never have to clean the bathroom tiles again. I've always hated them. They will not come completely clean no matter which cleaning product is applied, and the gray and moldy grout requires backbreaking scrubbing sessions. The apartment bathroom has smooth sheets of plastic. Another unlamented chore will be shoveling snow from the driveway. And mowing the grass, a task that falls to me since James's departure. I can dump the associated tools, too, since the apartment maintenance staff takes care of these jobs with professional efficiency.

Dump them where? And what about the rest of the flotsam collected over ten years of marriage, now to be abandoned? I can't simply walk out and lock the door, discarding ten strings of Christmas lights, snow shovel, king-sized sheets (I'll never need a bed *that* big again), jelly jars, James's collection of *Sports Illustrated*, outmoded curtains and drapes, the matching sweatshirts that read "I'm with Stupid" followed by an arrow pointing to your partner, purchased in Albuquerque on a weekend trip. A garage sale is the answer for getting rid of all unwanted items. And summer is the perfect time for a sale, what with decent weather and people walking and riding bicycles around the neighborhood. Time, that precious commodity, presses its limitations on me. So much to do, so few days to do it in. I reach for the newspaper to look over the cost of a classified ad.

I feel born again in the new apartment. I've bought a literal fresh start, with recently painted ivory-toned walls throughout, clean carpet, empty closets spacious enough for my personal belongings. Although it isn't the model I was shown and it lacks the panoramic view since it's several floors lower, the suite lies down the hall from Kevin's. He, in fact, occupies a place on a kitchen chair as I unpack boxes.

"You're a big help," I jokingly complain. "I went through this exercise-in-frustration two weeks ago. Now I'm doing the whole operation in reverse. You promised to give me a hand. *And* you said that moving in would be half the work of moving out. It's double. Especially when I have to detour around a lump like you."

Kevin continues peeling the orange he holds. "I'm helping. Anything that goes too high for you to reach, I'll put away."

"Since I want virtually everything within stretching distance, you don't have to make much effort." I slam the plates on a shelf, lift one in my hand and threaten a throw.

"I'm also offering moral support. I'm the welcoming committee." He gestures toward the fruit basket on the table.

"You're plundering the gift you brought me. I'm beginning to think you bought it for yourself," I say, rinsing dusty glasses in the sink.

"No, I'm decreasing your tasks. Now you won't have to wash so much fruit." Kevin takes a bite, spraying juice across the kitchen.

I pick up a damp dishcloth and wipe table, counters, cupboards. "Thanks. I appreciate all you're doing. Especially the chair you're dusting and polishing with your ass."

"You'll appreciate me more when I drag you out of this apartment. You've done enough for one day. Look at yourself. You're drooping."

Standing to put his hands on my shoulders, Kevin turns me to the window on the built-in oven. The reflection shows my fine, fly-away hair standing out from my head as if I stuck a finger into an electric socket and dirt smudges on my face where I've wiped away perspiration with a filthy dustrag. I see Kevin standing behind me, spotless as a just-scrubbed sink, blunt-tipped fingers on my shirt, looking at my reflection, too. I lean closer to the oven and squeak.

"The oven's dirty!" I exclaim. I peer more closely. "No, it's not. I'm looking at the broiler rack."

"That's it!" Kevin steers me back to the sink. "Wash your hands and face. I'm not taking a grubby thing like you into my clean place."

I throw up my hands in surrender and obey his command. I'm exhausted. Nothing stands out from the stream of existence in the previous two weeks. Constant rushing, packing, telephoning, and signing forms all blur together. I deserve a rest.

Kevin pushes me down the hall to his apartment and into a chair by the fireplace. A moment later, he places an icy glass of white wine in my hand. "Stay there. I'll show you I can cook."

Nose-tickling smells waft out of the kitchen along with strains of music from the nearby stereo. I tuck my feet under my bottom, feel my head droop, my muscles relax. I almost could sleep in the overstuffed chair. A hum rises spontaneously from my throat, my response since childhood to contentment.

The clatter of a tray and dishes on the coffee table snaps me back to the present. Kevin's serving a concoction that appears to be made of dark lumps.

"Black bean and chicken stew," he says. "Kind of Mexican, with chili, garlic, and fresh cilantro. I created it myself."

"Not bad," I compliment as I take a cautious taste. "If I keep my eyes closed." I reach for a flour tortilla to sop up the juices.

"I heard you humming with the music," says Kevin. "You have a pretty good voice. Do any singing nowadays?"

"Remember I was in the church choir when I was young? Now, just in the shower."

"I've got a piano. Do you play?"

I shake my head. "Piano. You never mentioned that. Did you play in high school?"

"No. I was one of those kids whose parents forced them to take lessons. In high school I gave it up. Not cool enough to fit the image. But after I got through my macho-football player phase, I went back to it. Want to see the instrument?"

I follow him to the back bedroom, converted to a study and music room. A compact, highly polished piano occupies a place of honor. Kevin sits on the bench and lifts the piano cover.

He poses his curved fingers over the keys. "What would you like to hear? Jazz? Ballads? Classical?"

"How about rock?"

Kevin smiles and breaks into "Rock Around the Clock," tossing his hair back and forth like Jerry Lee Lewis. I merge with him by belting the lyrics with a heart-felt beat.

Completely winded, I sink on the bench next to Kevin. "I'm bushed. I guess piano players have it easier than singers."

"Don't kid yourself. You're out of shape. A brisk walk in the morning around the park would get you going."

I groan. "Not you, too. My friend, Dolores, is always dragging me off to exercise."

"How can you resist?" Kevin walks to his window and I join him to look at the park that spreads from the street below us. In the panorama outside, small lights surrounding the lake reflect their shattered selves in the mini-waves, bounce their rays off the rippling water. The moon sails through the sky and backlights the clouds. On the path that winds for miles, curving in and out as if to embrace the earth, some evening joggers pass a few strollers.

"Look at that park," Kevin says. "Night or day, summer or winter, it's constantly changing, yet it's always the same. Aren't you tempted to explore the reeds by the lakes? Watch the toddlers try to climb a slide? Breathe air unhampered by walls and windows?

Besides, you'll need to build your stamina if we're going to launch careers in show business."

I lean my head against the window. "What would we call ourselves? The Dynamic Duo's already taken. The Mile High Singers? The Lost Souls?"

"How about Lost and Found? Kind of describes us, don't you think? When you and James first split up, we lost touch. Then we found each other again," says Kevin.

"Has possibilities."

"We can sing as we walk around the lake in the morning. Let's discuss our plans while we finish dessert."

"I'm more bushed than I am hungry. I think I'll head home now," I say.

"Okay. But I'll beat on your door at six-thirty tomorrow," Kevin warns.

The next morning sets the pattern for our following weeks. I fall out of bed at six, throw on shorts and tee-shirt, splash my face, and am ready when Kevin knocks. We ride the elevator and walk to the park in silence, still half-asleep. By the time we get to the lake, where ducks converge by our feet, quacking dictatorial edicts for moldy bread crusts or stale popcorn or handfuls of cereal, we're mumbling a few words. "Nice morning," or, "Boy, I'm tired."

At the lake's east shore, Kevin usually starts a song. We go through old favorites, musicals, folk tunes, children's nonsense verses. When we forget the words, we make up lyrics, usually containing vulgarities or references to bodily functions. The walk ends in the apartment lobby where we warn each other to quiet down with loud and long-winded shushes. Another elevator back up, into my apartment, and juice and cereal for breakfast. Then we split for our respective offices.

I'm not bursting with happiness, but I'm content. Kevin has made the transition between house and apartment easy. I nearly forget I'm supposed to be finding fresh interests.

My mother reminds me. Barbara appears at the apartment one night to "do something with that hair of yours." "Something" includes a trim and a body permanent.

"You've wallowed in misery long enough, Joan. The move here was a good idea. Now you need to get back on track with your looks." Barbara's magic fingers sooth my scalp as they snip and curl the baby-fine hair into a free-swinging, short style.

"How are the new interests going? You've tried bingo and art openings. What's next on your agenda? This music thing with your neighbor?"

"No, that's just fun." I watch my mother in the mirror, fascinated with her confident movements as the scissors flash and curlers wind. Where did she gain this skill as a hairdresser? As far back as I can remember, Barbara has been the mother all my friends came to for advice on style, color, length.

"I don't see why," Barbara says over the growl of a hair dryer. "You've always had talent. You could try out for a dinner theatre musical."

"Forget it, Mom. I have enough trouble with one job, let alone two."

"Just go to see one. I happen to have a spare set of tickets. You could take Kevin."

Awareness hits me like a slap on the forehead. Barbara is plotting. She met Kevin last weekend when he barged in to borrow some detergent. Her eyes lit up like little Christmas bulbs and increased in illumination when she discovered he sold real estate and wasn't married.

"Mother, I've been single less than six months. Let me enjoy myself," I scold. "Kevin is perfectly happy as he is. If I stalk him, he'll disappear so fast you'd jump. Besides, he's a nice guy, but not my type. Romantically, I mean."

"What do you mean? The guy's gorgeous. If I were single, *I'd* make a play for him. But okay, okay." Barbara jerks a little on my hair to calm me down. "Continue with the interests."

"Nothing great. Sometimes I think I should go back to school. Paralegal training only takes a few months. Or maybe I should aim higher, for law school."

"You'd be a wonderful attorney—sharp yet compassionate, determined yet flexible. But I didn't know you found your job so fascinating."

I frown. I hadn't meant to mention work. The computer puzzle still hasn't been solved. I brush my mother off. "More training equals more money, that's all. But a fun project's come up and it includes music. Some of the staff are getting involved in the annual Bar Association Revue. Each firm produces a skit with music and dancing. We won last year. Maybe I'll work on that."

"Work" isn't an adequate description. Neither is "fun." The Bar Association Revue mixes the two in a hysterical combination, requiring more effort than pure amusement, less seriousness than real labor. Plus a strong helping of creativity, I discover, when I go to the first planning meeting.

Jones, the youngest partner in the firm, is in charge. He begins by instructing everyone to call him Harold. "I'll remind all of you that I majored in theatre in my younger days," he says. He smoothes thinning strands of black hair back from his forehead as if drawing attention to a classic, Roman-nosed profile.

"Not to mention being a ham," murmurs Kimberlee, who's sitting next to me. I jerk in surprise. I've never heard Kimberlee make a joke before.

"You can have every confidence in me," Harold continues. "I led you to victory last year. I'll do the same this. Let's begin by brainstorming a theme. Anything related to the legal profession will do."

Harold excels at pulling ideas out of the group, encouraging strange twists in concepts that lead to new ways of looking at familiar situations. He paces back and forth at the front of the room, making a fist and jerking downward with a verbal "Hey!" when one person shouts out a phrase—"torts" or "trials"—and another builds on the notion.

I notice during the discussion that each thought ultimately relates back to the computer, indispensable as lawyers themselves. I hesitate...should I suggest computers as a theme? Although nothing has been said recently about the questionable activity around the office's network, the mystery remains. Will a mention of computers throw suspicion on me?

The idea's too good to pass up. I raise my hand. "What about a skit based on computers? We depend on them completely. We search citations, format documents, do billings, even duplicate language. When they break down, we're as lost as Hansel and Gretel. No matter what your legal specialty or your job position, computers impact you. And—" I take a deep breath for my ultimate selling point and continue, "it's easy to make up rhymes with *computer*. Refuter, saluter, neuter, cuter."

Kimberlee darts a disdainful look at me, but the others respond with enthusiastic cries.

"Perfect. The audience will crack up," a junior attorney says. "We could do a segment on computers replacing lawyers."

"Everyone can relate to computers," says Mr. Horowitz's admin. "They're convenient scapegoats when messages and appointments get garbled."

"How about a mock operetta? Hero, heroine, computer?" throws in someone else. "Learn every program, punch every key," he warbles to the tune of "Climb Every Mountain."

"But would the computer be the villain?" asks the office computer expert with a worried frown. "It shouldn't be. It's labor-saving."

I wave both hands. "No, no. This could resemble science fiction. The computer starts out threatening the office, like an out-of-control robot. Then the hero, a dashing and distinguished attorney, masters it properly, saves the heroine, a beautiful intern assigned to the office, by showing her."

Kimberlee objects. "Why can't the heroine be the one who harnesses the computer's power? After all, the paralegals and admins in this office use the systems much more than the lawyers."

The sole female attorney disagrees. "I use mine all the time."

"That proves my point," says Kimberlee, flouncing as she turns back in her seat to face the front.

"Ladies, ladies," Harold interrupts. His head tilts at an angle and his eyes glaze, as if he's intent on an inner vision. "We don't need to decide the particulars now. The passion of your response settles the matter. Computers it is. At our next meeting, we'll consider the libretto. This meeting is adjourned."

I hum songs from musicals all the way home, mentally rearranging words and adding new phrases. Oblivious to the stares of my fellow bus riders, I slap my knee in a syncopated beat. The rhythm continues in my head as I ride the elevator up and open the apartment door, accompanied by a burgeoning desire that I can help write the show and maybe even win a part. I'm sure Kimberlee will try for the female lead—even in my mind, the heroine should be blonde and thin. But what kind of voice does Kimberlee have? Her speech is low and a little breathy. Does she sing like a foghorn? A shriek?

In the midst of fixing dinner, thumping a wooden spoon on the counter in cadence, I hear a different sound, a kind of soft gurgle even when the water in the sink is off. Cocking my head, I follow the noise down the hall to its source—the closet housing the hot water heater. I fling the door open.

Ominous rusty wet streaks dribble over the top of the heater, run down the white sides, puddle below the bottom. I crouch on my haunches to peer underneath. A good inch of water lies under the appliance. The liquid spreads by the second, fast approaching the hallway carpet.

Even as I watch, the water touches the carpet and is sucked instantaneously into the sponge-like carpet pad. I stick a cautious toe onto the carpet and hear a definite "squish." Leaping back as if I've been burned, I gasp, raise a hand to touch the heater, pull the hand back, lean down to look at the gas flame that heats the water, shake my head.

What am I to do? If the water hits the gas, will the liquid douse the flame, leaving the fumes to creep throughout the apartment? Or will they spontaneously combust into an inferno? I flash on the scene from *Joan of Arc* when Ingrid Bergman succumbs to the final explosion of flames. I know I can't be as brave as she. I panic, follow a frantic trail of thoughts. How do you turn the gas off? If you don't turn the water off, will it keep pouring out, flooding the floor? How do you turn the water off? How do you get the water out of the heater once you turn the incoming water off? If you do nothing, will the entire contraption explode, rocketing through the ceiling to the apartment above? Or simply fall through the weakened floor to the apartment below?

Call the manager, that's what I should do. With shaking hands, I dial the office. No response except a taped message. Now what? Run into the hall and scream for help?

No, help is more immediate if Kevin's home. I sprint down the hall to beat on his door with my palms. "Kevin, Kevin," I beg at the top of my lungs. "Are you there? Please answer."

A hurried thump of bare feet and the door swings open. Interrupted in mid-bite, Kevin holds a sandwich in one hand and a napkin in the other. He wears a ripped undershirt and the most disreputable pair of ragged cut-off jeans I've ever seen.

"What's wrong?" he asks.

"Come with me. Now!" I drag him back down the hall to my apartment and toward the closet. "Look!" I announce in a drama-laden voice.

"Uh-oh." Kevin steps on the carpet, which makes a sucking sound as he moves his foot. "Looks like you've got trouble." He tiptoes down the passage.

"What should I do?" I implore.

Kevin's movements are quick and confident. "First the water." He reaches above the heater to a faucet and twists it. "Next, the gas." He stoops and again twists, this time a lever. "Now we need a pail or a large pan."

I dart to do as he bids, returning with an aluminum turkey pan. I crouch next to him. "Why do you want that?"

"Doesn't look like the heater's leaking from the bottom. But to reduce the flow from the top, we'll drain some water." Kevin turns the faucet near the heater's base. Hot water gurgles into the pan. "That should be enough."

"How about a towel to soak up the remains?" I ask.

"Good idea." He grabs the one I offer and stuffs it around the heater's legs.

We both stand and I let loose a sigh of relief. "I was terrified," I admit. "I thought the whole place would flood or else the heater would explode. James always handled situations like this. How did you know what to do?"

"Just one of those things that men understand instinctively," he replies with a twist of humor. "Makes you women depend on us. We've got to be good at something. You're all so independent in other ways."

I grin but twine my fingers together in agitation. "How am I going to get ready for work? I can't take a shower."

"The manager will replace the water heater tomorrow. You can use my bathroom in the morning," Kevin reassures her. "Will you be okay tonight?"

"Oh, yes, now that you've handled the crisis."

But my sleep is disturbed. I keep dreaming I hear water running or see flames licking the walls, forcing me into wakefulness. I'm astounded how Kevin knew exactly what to do to stop the crisis and I can't quite believe I have nothing to worry over. Several quick trips to the closet prove that nothing is wrong. Still, the next day a drooping body and strained face bear witness to my long night.

"You should have come over to my apartment if you were concerned," Kevin reproaches me on our morning walk.

"I couldn't bother you again." In the light of day, the sun so bright already that I have to squint, fear seems a mere shadow or a cobweb I should be able to brush away.

"That's what friends are for," he says. "Anyway, look at it this way. Maybe you didn't know what to do to resolve the problem, but you kept your head and got help. You met the challenge and won."

"I guess I did," I say with a touch of surprise. "I can feel proud about that." Maybe I'm more like my namesake than I think.

"Don't let your head swell too big. You won't be able to get into the bathroom first when we get back."

"I'll control myself. And I'll cook breakfast while you're showering."

"You got it," he answers. "I deserve eggs today." He quickens his pace to a near-run as if suddenly hungry.

That day the manager responds promptly and installs a new hot water heater. I show it off to Kevin after work. We admire its gleaming white sides and test the hot water in the kitchen and bathroom, sending steam billowing to the ceiling. We fight through the clouds to meet by the front door.

"Looks fine," says Kevin. "Guess you won't need my services any more."

"You sound almost disappointed."

"Just because it's back to the cereal-and-milk routine for breakfast. If you're not asking me for favors, like bathroom privileges, I can't make requests for special catering." He hesitates before opening the door.

"Wipe that frown from your face," I say. "I'll get the sugared variety on Saturday. Now scoot, so you can get enough sleep to take a walk."

Luxuriating in a surplus of hot water, I soak in a bubble bath that puts me nearly to sleep. I wrap myself in a cotton nightgown and fall into bed.

Somewhere around one in the morning, I wake from a sound sleep with a sense of foreboding. I've been dreaming of water, not a placid lake nor a turbulent sea, but water in pipes in a house. More like a mansion, an immense brick structure painted white. I've been in the basement with the pipes over my head. One by one holes appear in the pipes, springing leaks too numerous for me to hold my fingers over.

I roll on my side to go back to sleep when I hear a faint hissing that reminds me of the water escaping in the dream. Sitting bolt upright in bed, I concentrate on the sound, trying to block out the refrigerator's drone and the clock-radio's hum. I even hold my breath. The hiss still is there.

With a speed born of fear, I vault out of bed and run down the hall to the closet. I put my ear against the door. The hissing increases in volume. I open the door.

"Oh, no," I moan as I lean against the wall.

Steam rises from the top of the new water heater and circles out to the ceiling of the hall. Condensed drops run down the side of the appliance, hissing as they hit the hot gas that converts them to more steam.

I back down the hall, grope behind myself for the front doorknob, edge along the wall to Kevin's apartment. I beat a faint tattoo on his door. When there is no response, I knock louder.

Kevin staggers to answer my call. This time he doesn't even wear shirt and cut-offs, only undershorts. Prying open his sleep-drugged eyes, he moans, "What now?"

"The new heater's leaking. Truly it is. I'm sorry to bother you, but I'm not making this up," I answer.

Kevin waves a limp hand. "Okay, okay," he mumbles and starts toward my apartment.

"Kevin, put something on," I chide. "What if someone sees you?"

"Who? Where?"

He tries in vain to focus.

"Never mind. Just come on!" Taking his hand, I lead him back to my apartment and the water heater.

At the sight of this, Kevin blinks, shakes his head, opens his eyes wide and comes fully awake.

"You must be cursed," he says, reaching immediately for the controls. He goes through the same routine as previously—turn off the incoming water, shut down the gas, drain some liquid. "I think the connections simply need tightening. But call the manager in the morning. Good night."

"Wait." I catch at Kevin's hand. "I don't want to stay here tonight with that *thing* in there. Can I stay with you?"

Kevin crosses his arms over his bare chest. Is he trying to keep warm or has he realized the paucity of his clothing? "I don't know if that's a great idea. A man and a woman alone? Temptation."

"You and me?" I scoff. "We're friends, not lovers. And I'll sleep on the couch."

"The couch is lumpy as a gravel road. Sure you don't want to share my bed? It's large, soft, comfortable." Kevin watches me through narrowed eyes.

"And listen to you snore all night? The couch will be fine."

The third time is bound to be lucky, I think the next evening as the manager checks the water heater. He knocks on the connections with his wrench and confirms that they simply needed tightening.

I wish that Kevin could be there, but he has a date. I still find the idea of Kevin dating strange, as if he doesn't have a real existence outside of the times I see him.

When I was married, Kevin's appearances were pleasant interludes, but otherwise he never cropped up in my thoughts. And nowadays, he and I seem to spend most of our free hours together. If we aren't walking and having breakfast, we're swapping dinners or grocery shopping or watching television. When I envision him doing anything in my absence, I see him in an office, behind a desk, talking on a telephone.

I wonder about his date. Is she tall or short, talkative or restrained? What does she do for a living? From there, my mind wanders to Kevin's love life. He isn't celibate, that's for sure. I saw a box of condoms in the bathroom cabinet once, then shut the door quickly on my own accidental snooping.

"All done," says the manager, breaking into my thoughts. "You won't have any more trouble, I guarantee you."

He packs his tools and leaves. I don't want to tempt fate by filling the bathtub again. I'm tired, too. Kevin told the truth when he said his couch was lumpy and hard. I got scarcely a minute's sleep the previous night. So I go straight to bed.

The dream returns. This time not only the pipes leak. The basement's walls bulge, water starts shooting out from spots all over from ceiling to floor. As fast as I place a palm on one hole, another yawning gap appears with water spurting out of it. A pool gathers on the floor, rising higher and higher, to my knees, waist, neck.

I wake shrieking. Without a pause I bolt out of the bedroom, through my door, down the hall to Kevin's. Thump, thump, thump on his door. Will he never come?

I hear Kevin's steps drag, as if he hasn't the strength to lift them. His door opens a mere inch and one brown eye looks through the crack.

Kevin's groan is muffled. "This is a nightmare. It must be a nightmare. The water heater again, right?"

I nod, speechless.

"Is it spewing water? Is the gas leaking?"

"I don't knoooow. But I can't sleep for fear something will go wrong. I keep having nightmares about floods."

"Joan, please. Spare me. I know we're neighbors and friends and all, but I've had a rough day. Drink a glass of warm milk and go back to bed."

Kevin still hasn't opened the door any further. A rough day, I think, and an even rougher night? Maybe his date's inside. Maybe I've interrupted a seduction. I gulp.

"Sorry," I say in a tiny voice. "I shouldn't have disturbed you. I'll leave." I turn, my head hanging low.

"Don't go!" Kevin steps out from behind the barrier. He wears a bathrobe for a change. "You're really upset. I'd feel like a louse if I drove you away. You can stay here again tonight."

I swing back, make my eyes plead. "I have to learn to stay in my own apartment, not avoid it. Can you sleep over at my place? Please?"

Kevin exhales a gust of sheer exasperation. "All right. Let me get my keys."

He returns, keys in hand, rubber thongs on his feet. As he locks his door, he grumbles, "It's no wonder James divorced you if this is how you react in a crisis."

Anger at the accusation sparks my temper. "We never had a crisis until our marriage ended. If you're going to be a jerk, just stay here." I start marching down the hall.

Kevin double-paces to catch up with me. "I didn't mean that the way it sounded." He catches my door as I swing it in his face.

"Hold on. Let me check the heater first." He ducks inside before I can stop him.

"Everything looks fine," Kevin says, after a quick survey of the hot water heater.

I haven't moved from the front door where I continue to glower in Kevin's direction. He stands, starts to walk toward me, but his steps slow when he realizes I'm fuming.

"Just how *did* you mean it?" I prod. "Your statement about James and me?"

"Come on," groans Kevin. "Give me a break. I was half asleep and pissed at being woken up for the third night in a row."

The irritating kernel of truth in Kevin's words about my marriage rubs me raw and looses a barrage of reaction. "I was a child when I got married and James kept me a child. He wouldn't let me make major decisions. He discouraged me from continuing my education. He harped continually on my appearance. How could I grow up? Become a real adult? And for the last few years, after I became what he thought he wanted, he was giving into temptation with real adult women. "

"Whoa." Kevin holds up the palms of both hands. "You sure have a short fuse."

"No, I don't. Yes, I do." I wilt. Defenses vanish like smoke on the wind. "I'm making excuses. I don't want to admit that I could have changed my life earlier if I'd tried. But worst of all, now that I have some perspective, some insight, I can't think what to do to improve. It's like I went from an absolutely clear map of where I was headed into total chaos. I can't make out the roads and even if I could, I wouldn't be able to figure out how to get from one point to another. Or why I'd even want to bother making the trip." An enormous sigh escapes from my lungs.

Kevin leans forward and rubs my arms. "That's because you're pure emotion. You always have been. Euphoric and high as a kite one second, lower than Hades the next. And I've always thought that was your most endearing quality. You feel so deeply, with every pore. You're not guarded, masked by false sophistication. For you, every moment is worth living to its fullest."

Open-mouthed, I listen to each of Kevin's words. "Well, thank you soooooo much. Even if I don't think you're describing me well. What you see as deep feelings is simply continuing confusion over my life. But you're helping me put myself in order by staying here tonight. Thanks."

"No problem," Kevin mumbles. A yawn catches him unaware.

"Now, to bed. Where do I sleep?"

"Well, there's the couch."

"That's all? Your couch is a loveseat. My legs would be off one end and my head off the other."

"You've seen my furniture. I don't have anything else except my bed or the floor," I say, thinking Kevin and I are back to squabbling like children quick as a flash.

"I'm *not* sleeping on the floor." Kevin heads into the bedroom.

I freeze where I am. "But I sleep there."

"So what? *You* can use the couch or the floor if you don't want to share the bed."

I weigh the alternatives. Kevin is the guest, has come at my specific request. But I need rest badly and I'm sure not to get any unless I sleep on a bed. I look down at my nightgown, a fairly sturdy, concealing affair. I'll do it, I'll share. The bed is king-sized. We're both so exhausted that nothing will happen. I'm also so tired, I don't wonder why I need a rationalization to sleep in the same bed as Kevin.

After switching off the other lights, I sidle into the bedroom. Kevin appears to be asleep already. I douse the remaining lamps and slide into bed as far from Kevin as possible. As I slip into slumber, I remember one last item.

""Kevin? Kevin? Thanks." I don't know if he heard until he answers, soft as a sigh.

"Sure. Any time."

Work at Horowitz, Trimble, Hawkins & Jones is becoming almost superfluous. From inertia, normal activities continue. In the bright florescent light pouring from overhead, I hold up my end of telephone calls and typing, the paralegals range at desks behind me whisper urgently to one another, the attorneys dash in and out from court hauling files and spewing directions. Billings never stop going to the mail. But the real spirit of eight-to-five focuses on the skit.

The conference room is transformed into a rehearsal area, its stuffed armchairs pushed into makeshift rows, the walnut table banished to a back wall for the duration. Coffee breaks and lunches serve as excuses to spend five minutes or an hour practicing or re-writing a song. Computers fill duel purposes by storing scripts and lyrics as well as legal documents.

The amateur actors select a parody, "The Sound of Muzak," as their plot line. Kimberlee turns out to possess a real flair for writing dramatic scenarios. She produces page after page, draft after draft, of dialogue crafted from extensive suggestions and resulting arguments among the cast.

The skit takes shape. Instead of a singing family of children in the Alps, a singing collection of lawyers, paralegals and secretaries in Denver. Rather than the menace of Naziism, the intimidation of computerization. No nuns, but technological experts lighting the way.

Of course, Harold commandeers the hero's role for himself. Fortunately he has a passable voice. He dictates several try-outs and people struggle without accompaniment through songs of their own choosing: "Home on the Range," hymns, "God Bless America," "When the Saints Come Marching In." I opt for "To Dream the Impossible Dream." Might as well base my audition on my philosophy.

One by one the characters are assigned to staff members. I wait and wonder why I haven't been given a part. I'm the only true soprano. Surely at least the motherly figure of the top computer expert should be mine.

Well, I'm the newest employee. I'll help any way I can. If that means wearing my fingers down to bloody stubs doing re-writes on Kimberlee's script, so be it.

Dolores complains that I have no time for food. She packs calorie-laden snacks and lunches to keep my energy up. "Another lunch to go?" she asks one day as she stuffs a cardboard container with sandwiches, chips, and brownies. "You're sure busy. We've never had a chance to go to that little country and western place I told you about."

"Maybe after the Revue," I beg off.

"The Revue?" Scott materializes at my elbow. "The firm's entering?" He signals to Dolores. "I'll have a ham on rye to go." Then to me, "Do you have time to sit and eat or is practice time pressing?"

My heart rate increases at Scott's proximity, but I manage to keep any sign of surprise at his sudden appearance from my face. "I have to run. We're not practicing but we're deep in rewrites. And, certainly, we're entering. We won last year. And by the way, why aren't you helping us?"

"I'm just a tenant, remember?" Scott waves my question away. "Not really a member of the firm. But I do know you'll have stiff competition. What do you have planned this time?"

"I can't tell you. Top secret. We don't want the competition to get a hint," I answer.

Scott raises an eyebrow. "I have my sources. A musical, right?"

I gasp. "What do you do, listen at the door?"

"Nope." Scott smirks. "You just confirmed my hypothesis. You're dealing with a lawyer, remember?" We leave the cafeteria together and pause outside the door, each carrying a boxed lunch. "Plus I'm working on the production crew, so I've seen the preliminary notes."

I huff and push his arm. "I know now not to trust you. But please don't tell anyone that you learned anything from me," I plead, as we walk to the elevator.

"You ready for first rehearsal in the hall?" Scott asks.

"I don't know. I'm a novice. What's 'first rehearsal'?"

Scott holds open the elevator door so I can enter. "Every participating firm registers for practice in the hotel where the Revue's going to be held. At that point, secrecy's moot. They're all so hell-bent on paces and timing, they don't care if others see their masterpieces. Starts next week."

"If that's the way things are done, I'm sure we'll be ready," I say.

Scott heads to his office with a, "See you then."

I float the rest of the way to my desk. Flirting, actual flirting, even some real communication with Scott. What do I care if I have a part? I can volunteer to be on production so I can be near him at rehearsals. We'll bump into each other casually, maybe have a chance to go to coffee. If I weigh love against hobbies or interests, love tips the scale every time.

As I'm busy weighing love against all other attributes, I walk smack into Harold, possibly because he stands in an unexpected location right next to my desk. Normally he hands me work from the front. I blink at his appearance.

Harold clears his throat and smoothes his striped tie down with one hand, his way of signaling a relaxation of his standard formality. "You may have been wondering why you haven't been given a role in the skit, Joan." His eyes dart to Kimberlee's vicinity. "I've, that is, we've been considering who should play the lead. I know this is your first year with us, but you have a good voice and I think you can handle the part. Will you do it?"

Stunned into immobility, I stammer, "Are, are you sure?"

A small nod moves Harold's head followed by a stronger, more determined one. "Yes, I'm sure."

"All right, then. I'll try my best."

"Fine," says Harold, as if he has to say something. He thrusts his hand at me. I shake it numbly. "Kimberlee will give you a script."

Kimberlee stands and extends a handful of papers, her face absolutely blank. Was she angry that I have the lead? I'm not the physical prototype of a heroine. Maybe Kimberlee thinks I'm incompetent, unfit to represent the firm. I become determined to show the paralegal up. You didn't need to be thin and blonde to sing and act well. With a mumbled "thanks," I take the papers and turn to my desk.

"First hall rehearsal is next week," Kimberlee says to my back.

"I know," comes out a peevish voice I hardly recognize as my own. I try to soften the tones. "I'll be ready." I begin mentally to block out time in my daily schedule to practice. Kevin and I can warble together over the lake on our daily walk without bothering anyone except ducks and geese. With his background in music, including piano, he makes a near-perfect coach.

Rehearsal comes before I feel prepared. The hall consists of a banquet room in a seedy hotel, stripped of most of its furnishings and all its former gilt glamour. I arrive alone but quickly spot my co-workers clustered by a sign on a round table. Groups from other law firms are similarly situated around the room. Harold is expostulating on the importance of projecting one's voice to the audience, given the unreliability of the sound equipment, which reliably breaks down every year.

He notices me and motions me to his side. "And here is our heroine." He puts an arm around my shoulder. "You've heard her informally in the office. Tonight we'll block out our steps on the stage and try the libretto. Kimberlee, do you have the cassette and the music?"

The blonde nods and holds up the equipment.

"All set then. Let's go to the stage."

We troupe up together. Most of the cast mounts the shaky, portable stage. Harold stays on ground level to guide our movements and shout directions. Kimberlee sits on a chair next to him, switching the music off and on as it's needed.

Even though I know my entire part, I feel as unstable and wooden as the portable stage. I mouth my words, move my arms stiffly, jerk my head in response to cues. An unreal haze fills my sight and I have trouble remembering what person is which character. It doesn't help that people from other law firms waiting for their turns drift into an informal audience.

"No, no," bellows Harold. "Joan, you're too stiff. Try closing your eyes when you sing."

Obedient as a well-behaved child, I shut my eyes tightly. While the action helps me concentrate on my singing, it does nothing for my movements. I open my eyes and stare straight at Scott, who's been loitering in the background, eying every act in its turn. He straddles a chair backwards, gazing at me but leaning close to Kimberlee, who's laughing and batting her lashes. The haze of disorientation swirls like a slow whirlwind.

"That's it for tonight," Harold announces, looking at his watch.

With sighs of gratitude, the company on stage starts breaking up. Thank God, I think. I've got to get to the bathroom before I'm sick.

In the restroom dingy with faded, flocked wallpaper, striped in once-regal purples and golds, I splash water on my face from a fingerprint-smudged peach porcelain sink. Check my eye makeup for smears and wonder. Could Scott have been lingering, watching because *I* was on stage? Hot and cold waves flow over my body. Is it possible he's interested in me?

I pick up my purse and walk down a narrow corridor that twists and turns back to the ballroom. Sounds of conversation drift from the large chamber, among them the voices of Kimberlee and Scott. I pause in relative darkness behind the wall.

"So, the fat lady sings," Scott is saying. "Looks like Horowitz, Trimble, Hawkins & Jones has a new star."

"Stay away from her," Kimberlee purrs. "She's not up to your speed."

"Don't worry," Scott replies, his tones dropping to match Kimberlee's. "You don't have any competition. She could be a looker, though, if she lost some weight."

CHAPTER SEVEN

There it is. Confirmation of what I've suspected, but somehow in my heart never could quite believe. I've gained so much weight no man could be attracted to me. Overweight, chubby, pudgy, plump, heavy, obese, downright fat. Never a chance with Scott. I've been feeding a fantasy in my mind.

I can't face the others. I turn back down the corridor and find a side way out of the hotel. The numbness that overtakes me possesses me all the way home. I park automatically, automatically ride the elevator up.

Once in my apartment, I switch on the radio in the bedroom, then strip off every piece of clothing and stand nude in front of a full-length mirror. I inventory each physical flaw—double chin, love handles along my sides, spare tire on tummy, thunder thighs. Then I take a hand mirror, turn around, and study my rear view— thick upper arms, flab hanging over my waist, droopy behind.

Although I want to throw the mirror against the wall, I set it down carefully on the bureau. Self-control stands me in good stead until I sink on the bed. Then that fortitude cracks.

I cover my face with my hands and sob. As I wail, I toss my head back and forth. During one of these turns, as I reach to turn the radio full-blast to drown the sounds of my breakdown, I open my eyes and see my tear-blotched face in the mirror across the room. See my plump shoulders shaking and the tremors gyrating down my body.

Standing and facing the mirror again, arms straight by my sides, I watch the tears stream down my features, my frame with its excess weight quiver. It's useless. I never can rival someone as trim as a model in a magazine or one of those upward-bound young women I've seen striding along the sidewalk in the financial district dressed in pencil-thin short skirts, or even Kimberlee. Solid as a brick, that's me, and I remember my dad's teasing nickname for me. Brick. No wonder James left me.

Drained of emotion, I drag on my bathrobe. I need comfort and I seek an ever-ready source in the kitchen. A snack will make me feel better. Left-over spaghetti, several pieces of bread and butter, half-dozen Oreo cookies, a diet soft drink, I line them up on the counter.

The feast makes my mouth water in anticipation. I grab a fork and prepare to plunge in. But should I? As if someone holds my arm and whispers in my ear, I freeze. How many calories does this food contain? What about carbs? Is this any way to lose weight?

It's hopeless, I tell myself. I've been trying to cut down for months. My metabolism simply burns energy too slowly. Anyway, I can start a diet tomorrow. My arm and the fork move toward the spaghetti.

You can start tonight, the little voice whispers. Avoid this food now and forever. Take a vow that you'll never eat again. Starve yourself. Be thin, be happy. You can do it. You can be thinner than Kimberlee, thinner than James' new girlfriend.

I see myself skinny, so skinny that my ribs can be counted. Like Joan of Arc, depriving herself of food so she can attain ecstasy. Her sufferings make her features incandescent. Mine can, too. I see my gaunt cheekbones, pointed chin. Hardship highlights each sharp surface. I see the admiration I know will come to Scott's face when he absorbs my slender new attractiveness. See Kimberlee gnash her teeth as I tempt Scott away from her.

I'll do it and I'll start tonight. Back the fork goes into the drawer. A frenzy of activity follows as I yank open refrigerator and cupboard doors. Sour-cream flavored chips, cookies with chunks of chocolate, popcorn, individually wrapped portions of snack cake with raspberry filling, old-fashioned grape jelly, and maple syrup fly into the garbage can. Leftover spaghetti, sauce red and thick as blood, and fried chicken mingled with Rocky Road ice cream and flavorful dips—onion, bean, ranch—into the sink until they can be ground up in the disposal.

I dig deep into the cabinet and pull out packages of brownie and pancake mixes, throw them on the floor. Bread, crackers, pasta join them. A large plastic trash bag will hold the items until I can dump them down the trash chute. The plastic sides stretch ever bigger as I add peanut butter, home-style soups, frozen waffles, cheeses, gourmet sauces, salad dressings thick with buttermilk and fragrant with herbs.

With the shelves nearly bare, I slump on the floor. The open refrigerator shows a pathetic head of lettuce, wilted celery, carrots, and a few slices of lunch meat. The kind I don't like. Salami. Purchased solely because Kevin adores it. Cupboards are similarly empty with a half-full box of granola cereal and rows of spices I rarely used because James favored mild flavors. Food overflows the counters and lies heaped on the floor.

In my right hand I clutch a stale mini-donut, the sole survivor from yesterday evening's emergency run to the nearby 7-11 to quell a craving. I watch as my hand moves automatically toward my mouth. My jaw drops, my lips open, my teeth take a bite and chew as if they're possessed by an evil spirit.

From the bedroom floats the sounds of a golden oldie. *Just start dreaming about what's coming...* The melody pulls me from my robotic action. I find myself singing along to the song and moving, dancing really, in time with it. "The past's no more, the past's no more..."

"No!" The strangled sound rises out of my throat and I jump up and run to the sink where I spit the donut out. What's wrong with me? I turn on the water and rinse my mouth again and again. Finally satisfied that not a crumb remains, I turn back to study the room. It's a disaster.

Did I create this mess? I must have gone crazy temporarily. Do I expect to nourish myself on air? What if someone, like Kevin or my mother, walks in? They'd commit me for treatment of a mental condition.

Envisioning Kevin's stunned reaction at the sight of the kitchen stripped bare and myself standing here with a bathrobe flapping loosely around my nudity, I start to laugh. The hilarity builds and builds until I have to grip the sink to hold myself upright.

With laughter comes a return to rationality. I begin picking through the food, returning most things back to storage, leaving the sweet and salty snacks in the garbage, singing at the top of my lungs, "Just start dreaming about what's coming." Yes, I'll start cutting back on food immediately. But I won't go overboard. And tomorrow, I'll get information on diets and exercise.

Luckily the library is open late the next evening. I walk to the section containing books on diets and find hundreds. Likewise, the volumes on exercise number too many to count. Figuring that a woman author has more knowledge and understanding of what an overweight woman faces, I first eliminate all books written by men. Then I go by date, selecting those published within the last two years.

Through this process, I wind up with about a dozen in each category. Hauling the load home, I stack them on the kitchen table. Dinner is to be a green salad, no dressing, and four crackers. I rinse off the lettuce as one book is propped open on the counter next to me.

Cottage cheese and toast for breakfast, cottage cheese and fruit for lunch, cottage cheese and more cottage cheese for supper. Sounds boring. With one wet finger, I slam that book closed. Ten wet fingers carry the salad to the table where I alternately eat and page through more treatises.

All the books feature photos of thin model-types prancing around in leotards. They all claim that their approach to dieting will leave the reader feeling full and satisfied while shedding pounds at an amazing rate. One advocates eliminating all carbohydrates, another removing all protein. Some depend heavily on yogurt. Rice and nuts compose the meal plans in a brown-covered publication. I get more and more confused. How can all these guides be right when none of them agree?

Kevin's distinctive knock hammers at the door and I go to answer it, nose still buried in a book. "Come in," I invite, standing to one side.

A plastic bag bulging with small cartons swings from Kevin's arm. "I brought Chinese," he says as he walks to the kitchen.

I follow him. "None for me, thanks. I'm on a diet."

"I can't eat all this myself," says Kevin. He sits at the table, opens the cartons, and motions to me. "Dig in."

I resume my seat. "I'm serious. I'm cutting back. A salad's enough." I grab a bite and chew enthusiastically, smiling as if pleased with my choice. With each chew my anger grows. But what am I angry about?

Kevin frowns. He finally notices the stacks of books crowding the table. "What's up? Are you taking a class?"

"Nope. I'm trying to find the quickest and easiest way to lose weight." I force myself to swallow the mushy goo in my mouth and realize I'm angry at Kevin for not noticing the theme of all the books.

"Not again?" Kevin groaned. "You're obsessed."

Maybe I'm angry at him for always pretending I'm not overweight. Resentment joins anger. "No, I'm not obsessed. I told you about the practice last night during our walk. But I didn't tell you everything that happened." I summarize my eavesdropping on Scott. "So I'm determined. No more excuses. Twenty-five pounds or bust, so to speak." Now I think I'm angry at Scott, at the injustice of a world that judges women solely on their looks.

"You're really serious about this guy," states Kevin as if finally realizing my fascination. "You want a man who won't accept you as you are. He must be an absolute jerk. Doesn't sound like a great match to me."

"That's because you've never met him. He's worth any trouble."

"Convince me."

"He's great looking."

"That's a good reason." Sarcasm drips like honey from Kevin's falsely sweet words.

"Don't interrupt. He's tall, has these piercing eyes, is a lawyer."

"Even better reasons to lust after him."

"Do you want to hear or not?" I voice exasperation.

"Sorry. Continue."

"He's very smart, charming, interested in art and the finer things. I know that we'd get along if he'd give me a chance."

Kevin balances his chopsticks on his fingers and eyes them like they are scales of justice. "So," he intones in a voice like a television announcer's summarizing plot developments for an audience, "On the one hand we have Joan, young, brimming with life, eager to reach out. On the other we have Scott, handsome, successful, with stringent standards. The problem is how do we bring the two together? Even further, do they deserve one another?"

With a twist of his wrist, Kevin sends the chopsticks spinning in the air and catches them as they descend. "All right. I've made up my mind. Not my business if this guy is good enough for you. You deserve a chance and I'll help you. There's no denying that the outside of a package always affects what someone thinks the inside contains. So it's worth a shot to lose weight. Not that I think you're overweight, by any means. But I know the fashion is to be as thin as humanly possible while still maintaining life."

Laughter releases the lid on my anger, allowing it to dissipate, and I realize I've been furious with myself, no one else. I scoff. "How are you going to help? Sew my mouth shut?"

"I'll start by removing temptation." Kevin dumps the multi-colored and textured contents of the cartons—orange, green, red, beige, white...sprouty, smooth, crunchy—together into one container and shuts the lid firmly. "This goes back to my apartment. Now for the books."

Two hours pass while we thumb through the volumes. Then Kevin slams the last book shut and calls for paper and pencil. He thrums the eraser end on the table.

"Most of this stuff is junk," he says. "The advice is contradictory. But they contain a germ of truth. To lose weight you must either eat less or burn more energy. Seems logical that if you do both, you'll shed pounds faster."

I nod in agreement.

"A pound is comprised of about thirty-five hundred to four thousand calories. To lose two pounds a week, you've got to get rid of seven to eight thousand calories. Now, how can you accomplish that?"

Kevin bends his blond head over the paper. His pencil scribbles columns of figures as he scans calorie and exercise charts. Adding, subtracting, totaling, shaking his head, erasing, re-figuring. He seems to have entered the bizarre state of mind that accompanies a higher level of consciousness—say when Bach created a symphony or Einstein sought the answer to relativity. I, who might as well not be present, shift on the hard kitchen chair, feeling hungrier and hungrier.

Finally Kevin holds up the paper, pointing with the pencil to several circled numbers. "One method would be to walk or jog seventy miles a week or ten miles a day. Probably unrealistic at this point since you're not accustomed to that level of energy expenditure. Another would be to eliminate a thousand calories a day."

"I can't do that," I complain.

"Why not? Do you eat an ounce of potato chips daily? That's about 150 calories right there. How much butter? Five pats? Ten?"

I nod and shrink back into my chair.

Kevin shakes his head and sighs. "You're right. I can't force you. But how about this? Try to cut out five hundred calories. Then we'll add some activities. A few workouts at the gym, a bike ride or two, a tennis game, and you'll be set." He leans forward with a look of such delighted self-satisfaction that I can't disappoint him.

"Sounds good," I say with forced brightness. "Thanks."

Kevin stands to leave, tucking the left-over Chinese meal carton under his arm. "If it's Pygmalion you want, Pygmalion you'll get." He rejects my offer of coffee and refuses my company to the door.

With an ever-increasing schedule of performance practices, I find my time for exercise limited. Rehearsals run smoothly except when I'm forced to talk to Kimberlee or when Scott drops by to observe. I initiate no conversation with either one. Toward Kimberlee, I become distant and professional. I ignore Scott even to the extent of overlooking his casual greetings.

But I notice that Kimberlee and Scott are together with increasing frequency. This only multiplies my determination to whip myself into shape. Such sights as the afternoon when Kimberlee and Scott walk into the office arm-in-arm from lunch don't have a chance of throwing me off-balance.

I focus on my keyboard as Kimberlee clings to Scott, type frantically as Kimberlee flutters her eyelashes at her companion. I don't wince when Kimberlee murmurs to me, "Sorry I'm late. I couldn't tear myself away."

No, scenes like these don't bother me much. Out-and-out snooping does. Such as the time I return from coffee break to surprise Kimberlee standing by my desk, hands poised over the computer. Kimberlee stammers a lame excuse about searching for some data, but the same information is available on Kimberlee's computer. Or the way Kimberlee has started going through the mail piece by piece even though someone else is responsible for sorting it.

Kimberlee also launches a campaign of false friendliness accompanied by subtle probing. How is my divorce going? (I recall I've never mentioned James in the office.) Do I date frequently? (It's none of Kimberlee's business, I think.) Aren't tall men attractive? (Only one nameless man, I muse.) To each of these inquiries, I make a noncommittal answer. What is Kimberlee up to? She appears to have Scott firmly wrapped around her little finger. No way she can view me as competition.

Or can she? As the days pass, exercise and diet start paying off. Ounces, then pounds, begin slipping away. I check via scale and measuring tape daily. And although the results vary widely up and down, the overall trend descends.

I'm considering this state of affairs with satisfaction the day that Kevin introduces me to a new form of physical abuse—weight lifting. The weight room's metal and leather accessories could have been transported from a medieval torture chamber, while strange oils, streaks, and effluents smear surfaces and handles. A smell of pungent body odors permeates the air. At the entrance, I recoil behind Kevin and wrinkle my nose.

Dressed in baggy shorts and tank top, Kevin turns, puts his hands on his hips. "You're not backing out now?" he accuses. "You've mastered volleyball and jogging's finally coming easy. Weights trim and tone, add that final sculpting to your body."

"It stinks in here," I complain.

"Good, honest sweat. You'll get used to it. In fact, you'll soon find the smell has its own natural fragrance, like new-mown hay or damp earth. It will mean more, too, because you'll have added your own effort to creating it. First I'll give you a tour of the equipment and demonstrate each piece."

Kevin drags a reluctant me from station to station (that's what the various machines are called, I learn), lecturing as he goes. Triceps, biceps, quads, lats, the list of muscles apparently is endless. Each requires a special maneuver. Extensions, curls, lifts, presses, squats. All using particular equipment—small weights, big weights, bars, pulleys, straps, benches.

"Now that you're familiar with the layout, we'll start creating a routine for you," Kevin announces, his obvious fervor equaling that of a religious prophet.

"I'll never remember what to use for what," I complain.

"Sure you will, once you've made a few circuits." At my puzzlement, he adds, "A circuit is one go-round through your routine." Kevin is determined to submerge me in this strange world. "Now, watch me and try a few reps. Repetitions."

Holding a small dumbbell in either hand, he flexes his arms toward his chest. He passes them to me, motions the movements he wants me to copy and counts off three sets of eight. My muscles clench in protest.

Kevin beams, sadism writ large on what I used to think as a pleasant face. "You're doing great."

"Thanks. Well, let's save the rest for next time." I turn to head to the locker room.

"Hold it." Kevin blocks my exit. "Not until you've completed all the exercises."

"I can't just ease in?"

"You are easing in. I'm using the smallest weights possible. Now for the bench press."

Kevin continues as harsh taskmaster, running me through my paces until I'm ready to drop. He isn't even breathing hard although the weights he lifts are enormous. I compare our physical conditions in the full-wall mirror. My plump body, hidden within layers of clothing, droops and my hair, in short damp tendrils, straggles.

Funny, I've never noticed what good shape Kevin is in. His body, although big, bears not an ounce of flab. Perspiration molds the tank top to his torso and gilds his skin all over. Broad shoulders bulge, thighs swell as he works out. No gut hangs over his waistband.

His muscles have muscles, I marvel. How do they feel? Full of curiosity, I poke Kevin's upper arm just as he lifts the handles of a weight machine. He yelps and drops them.

"What was that for?" he demands.

"I wanted to know if your muscles are as hard as they look."

"And?"

"And they are." Kevin beams. A new horror crosses my mind. "Say, I won't wind up built like you, will I?"

"Nope. You'll resemble her." Kevin nods at a woman in the corner, busy with her own routine. Slender and firm, she embarks on an endless stream of stomach crunches with effortless ease.

"Time to hit the showers," says Kevin, tearing his eyes away from the woman reluctantly. "We'll be back day after tomorrow."

"I'll try to restrain my enthusiasm," I throw out and snap my towel in the direction of his retreating bottom. Still the glow coating my body owes as much to self-pride as to hard work.

Yes, despite basic laziness, aching body, and hunger pangs, my physique's showing amazing results from the strenuous regime. The change makes itself felt in small ways at first, a casual glance from a passing man, an unsolicited, "You look different, have you cut your hair?" from a co-worker.

Dolores is blunt. "Girl, you're shaping up. You're wearing your clothes, not hiding in them. Seems to me it's time to try your new self out. Let's go dancing."

I make a face at the cup of black coffee I hold. Sugar and cream have gone the way of chips and butter—out of my life. "Where? At a singles' bar? I don't know. Aren't those places meat markets? You're judged solely on your physical appearance."

"If you're developing something to show, then learn to strut your stuff," Dolores replies.

"What about weirdoes?"

"You're just dancing with them, not going home." Dolores studies me. "What are you really afraid of?"

I consider the question. "That no one will ask me to dance. I'll be lost among all those gorgeous women and wind up sitting at a table in a dark corner all night."

"The shape you're getting into now?" Dolores hoots. "Besides, most people are ordinary looking. Why do you think bars are dark? Hides all the flaws. *You* can imagine your partner could be a movie star. *He* gets off on his own fantasy. So come on, Saint Joan. Buckle on your armor and proceed into battle."

~ ~

I find myself the next evening once again driving with Dolores to an activity for which I feel no desire. Dolores has managed to pour herself into a skin-tight shiny dress with bright red sparkles that accentuate each over-abundant curve. Her hair, smothered in gel, sticks straight up in the air as if she's received a permanent electric shock. Black makeup circles her eyes.

Next to her, I feel drab as a dog even though my new dress is two sizes smaller than my old clothes. Slightly heavier mascara and eyeliner, along with an unusual touch of violet eye shadow, hardly are obvious.

As we approach the layered cubes and flashing neon lights that herald the dance club, Dolores pulls me to a halt and draws a comb from her purse. "Let me do a little something to your hair," she begs. Without waiting for a reply, she rapidly flicks the comb through my curls, expanding them to twice their natural volume.

"There," Dolores says with satisfaction. "Too bad I didn't bring my hairspray, but you look tough now."

Dolores shakes her own head, smooths her dress over her stomach, sticks out her bosom, and minces up the stairs in spike heels. Her round bottom sways from side to side with the gentle, hypnotic rhythm of boat on a calm sea. I shadow her, trying to blend into the background.

I succeed, for the periphery of the barn-like room is dark as a cave and cloaked by smoke. Since virtually nothing on me swings, dangles or glitters, nothing draws the eye. Dolores's busy elbows poke men and women indiscriminately until she reaches her goal— a waist-high counter overlooking the dance floor. Standing there, a line of sharp-eyed, razor-tongued guys and gals toy with drinks and exchange blunt comments on one another's physical characteristics.

Dolores slithers into the queue, smooth as a drop of water down a glass, immediately striking up a conversation with a short, dapper man with a fedora. I signal a waitress and order a wine cooler. I pass the time by dunking an ice cube into the liquid with one finger to see how far it will rebound.

All my fears are realized. Tune succeeds tune, my neighbors wax and wane, Dolores boogies her heart out, her hair switching directions as she twirls, her dress reflecting shards of light from the disco ball revolving overhead. I stand. And stand and stand. Not that I'm complaining, I realize.

Most potential partners carry an indefinable air of greasiness about them, with their hair slicked back or dangling in curls, their black and white suits slightly shimmering from synthetics. I can't imagine close dancing with any of them. The fast numbers don't require contact though, creeps a tiny, wistful thought in my mind.

My toe taps the beat of its own volition. I sigh and push an ice cube down with extra vigor. It pops back up all the way out of the glass, ricocheting off the chest of the man next to me. A wet stain spreads on his shirt front.

"Oops. Sorry," I gasp.

The man stares down at the stain in disbelief. "My new Lauren. Ruined." A crystal pendant dangling on a chestful of wiry hair points to the spot.

I grab a paper napkin and make ineffectual dabs at the stain. "It's not that bad. Really. Some lemon juice will take that right out." I fish in an abandoned drink for a lemon slice and lean forward, squeezing the fruit between my fingertips.

"No!" the man shouts as he leaps backwards. "Don't touch me."

In so doing, his vigorous action knocks over a chain of people down the line, sends glasses and bottles crashing to the floor, handbags and cigarettes flying, legs thrashing in the air. I freeze in horror at the chaos I've created.

A hand seizes me; a voice murmurs in my ear. "Time for a strategic retreat." I feel myself being drawn to the dance floor although all I can see is a tall, sweater-clad back.

As we worm our way to the center of the polished parquet, music and voices rise in volume until my eardrums throb. My companion turns and gestures to me to dance, accompanying it with a command.

"Dance," he yells. "Otherwise you won't blend in, and that lynch mob you created will hang you from the spotlight."

I comply, all the while studying my partner. Hardly what I'd expect here. Body thin to the point of skinniness and clad in tan slacks, brown sweater, and light blue shirt. Homely face overshadowed by a beak of a nose. Wide mouth curving up in a comfortable grin.

"Surprised to see someone like me in such a groovy place?" he asks.

"Surprised to find someone sensible," I correct. "You don't have a sparkle or a sheen on you," I add.

"You either," he says with approval.

The song ends and the tall man grips my hand again. "You can't go back there. Your victims are still upset."

Yes, a cluster of people cling together by the counter, alternately sponging each other and moaning into their beers. They definitely look dangerous. Walking back in their midst would be like flying into a hurricane.

"Where?" The word comes from my diaphragm on a whisper.

"I'm at a table on the other side." The man jerks his head sideways.

"What about your friends?"

"They're busy dancing. You might as well fill a chair."

When no one runs screaming after me, pointing and calling names, I allow myself to relax. I accept a drink, then ask, "Why did you rescue me?"

"I'd been watching you for a while. I noticed you looked as awkward as I felt. You kept tugging on your skirt to cover more of your legs and you didn't eyeball any of the guys who strolled by. I wondered how you'd been strong-armed into coming."

"A friend."

The man nods in sympathetic agreement. "Me, too. Reminds me of that old saying, with friends like these, who needs enemies?"

"I'm recently divorced and she thinks I should circulate. I'm just not sure these are people I want to circulate with. There's someone I'm interested in, but he wouldn't come here."

"My fiancée's out of town and the guys thought I should take this last chance to be a swinging bachelor. Guess I'm not a dancin', drinkin' fool."

"Me neither. "

We smile at each other in complete understanding. Now that we know neither is a romantic threat, we can relax.

"You do stand out in the crowd, though," he continues.

"I thought I blended in. Into the background."

"Never. Your dress may be more subdued, but here that draws attention to you. And your height, your bearing, make you distinctive," my companion says. "By the way, my name's Davis, Davis McIntosh."

"Like the computer?"

"Nearly. No 'a.' I guess I was fated, though. I'm a computer programmer, commonly known as a computer geek."

"Where do you work?"

He names a major financial firm based in the 17th Street financial district.

"I'm Joan Nelson. May I call you 'Dave?'"

"I'd rather you didn't. I'm so ordinary that I prefer a name that's a little different. I go by 'Davis.'"

"You're no more ordinary than I," I object. I collapse back in my chair with a small shriek. "What a thing to say. I *am* ordinary."

"Let's compromise and say we're both extraordinarily ordinary. Or ordinarily extraordinary," quips Davis.

"You must be if you work with computers. They're essential at the law firm where I'm employed, but I only know enough to push the right button. You must have quite a responsibility at your job. Guarding against thieves who are continually trying to get into financial records and steal money or identities?" I'm thinking about the situation at the law firm.

"Always a challenge," he admits. "But you're not afraid of them, are you? They're actually very stupid machines," Davis says.

"I was too dumb to be afraid of them at first. Now I am. We've had files simply disappear."

"Impossible. Something caused it. A power surge, electrical failure, something."

"Nope. The equipment was fine and none of the programs disturbed." I ponder. Maybe help is here. "We came in one morning, called up a particular file, and it was gone, along with several other critical documents. Kaplowie. Zip. Nada. The person who passes as our techie said someone had erased things. We still don't know if it was accidental or deliberate."

"Were the files backed up?"

"Yes. Fortunately. We had all our passwords changed afterwards."

"That doesn't present a barrier to a talented, persistent hacker. Could be sabotage, not an accident." Davis nods like a judge. "Your firm competing with anyone for clients?"

"It would be unethical for an attorney to go to those lengths to land an account!" To me, such a situation is as incomprehensible as lying to a minister.

"You *are* an innocent. Any disgruntled clients? Dismissed employees?"

"Not as far as I know. The worst part is the suspicion that's brooding behind every gesture or word. Everyone's trying to be nonchalant, but you can't help but feel guilty or look over your neighbor's shoulder."

"But only the one incident?" Davis probes.

"Yes. About a month ago."

"Hmmmm." Davis holds a stir stick from his drink between his hands and stares at it so hard his eyes cross. A new song, which has no melody, thrums its beat among the yells of the vocalists. Davis puts forth his decision in a voice that conquers the noise. "Biding his time to put you off guard. You should take measures."

"What kind?"

"You could set up false files. Track by dates and times. Do a reverse trace. I assume you're networked in the office."

I nod.

"Faxes from terminals?" By now, Davis' unfocused eyes show he's lost in a cloud of computer possibilities.

"Just one central separate machine. Lawyers are not cutting-edge. Their entire profession is dedicated to preservation of the status quo."

"So many ways to damage your information," mutters Davis. He gathers his straying ideas. "The first thing is to inspect your software programs." He nods and twitches in my direction as if barely restraining himself from leaping up to dash to my office.

"I'm sure that's not necessary," I say, suddenly aware that in the sheltering dark of the club and the relief of making a human connection with someone interested in more than physical appearances, I've again violated the confidentiality insisted upon by the law firm's partners. I give a little laugh that sounds artificial even to me and put a restraining hand on his sleeve. "The most likely situation is that an employee blundered and erased the files and either doesn't remember or is afraid to admit the error."

"Well, if it happens again, give me a call," Davis offers.

Dolores materializes at my shoulder. The black spikes of her hair, having undergone a beating from extended physical exertion, draggle down into parentheses framing her face and dark makeup smudges circle her eyes like a mask. "Where you been?" she demands with a suspicious glance in Davis's direction. "We agreed not to leave each other."

"I've been right here," I respond and to assuage my guilt about not mixing, seek Dolores's approval by introducing Davis.

He obviously flunks Dolores's "babe" test, for she neglects to flash her toothsome grin. Instead she wriggles her red sequins into a chair and blows one wayward lock of hair off her forehead. "How'd' ja do?" she asks and adds without the least regard for Davis's sensitivities, "Any good potentials? I gave my number to three or four guys."

"Yes. I told you," I answer while directing at Dolores the piercing gaze women use to convey unspoken warning to other women. This consists of a simultaneous raising of eyebrows while squinting the eyes. "I met Davis. He's a computer expert."

"Oh, yeah." Dolores grabs my drink and takes a swallow. "Well, it's after midnight. I've got to be up at six. Time to take off. If you're ready, that is."

I make a special point of taking a careful farewell of Davis in case he's offended by Dolores. He stands, winks his eye on the opposite side of Dolores, and assures me the pleasure has been his. "Don't forget my offer," he reminds me.

"What offer?" Dolores asks as we hurry to the car through the chill of the fall night. "I hope you're not going to see that geek again."

I can't suppress a chuckle at the word Davis used to describe himself. "I might. He said he'd help if we have more computer trouble. But don't worry. He's engaged."

"Engaged?" Dolores's irritation peaks. "You spent the night with an engaged man? Especially one who looks like he irons his underwear. What a waste of time."

"He's very nice," I object. "I didn't come tonight to hustle dates."

"What other reason could you possibly have?" Astonished, Dolores halts in the middle of the parking lot

"To get out of the apartment, to dance, maybe to make new friends. I did all three."

Dolores throws her hands up in disgust. "I give up. You're hopeless. If you're not mooning over some smooth-talking phony, you're passing the time with a geek."

"You're right," I agree as I climb in the car. Much as I like Dolores, our ideas about social activities clash every time. Bingo, singles' bars, bowling bore me to tears once I recover from the initial culture shock. I let Dolores down easy. "I'm a stay-at-home at heart. I appreciate all you're trying to do for me, but I just drag you down."

Dolores pulls out of the parking lot before she speaks, taking great care handling the wheel to make a U-turn and just maybe allowing a little awareness to permeate the sense of unreality spawned by a combination of loud music, alcohol and three hours of flirtatious dalliance. "Oh, Joan, don't mind me." This said with a touch of regret or guilt. "I worry so much that you're too innocent and shy for your own good. That you'll become one of those cat ladies. Do you know what I mean? The kind that are hurt by a man and spend the rest of their lives taking care of strays, feeding them, combing them, collecting donations to *fix* them, and finally at age eighty, all wrinkly and skinny, they die in a dirty room surrounded by hundreds of cats? But I think it's too soon. I've pushed you into running around before you were over your divorce. Let me know when you're ready. Still friends?"

"Friends," I affirm and we smile at one another over the car seat. "But you don't need to worry. I'm more of a dog person myself."

Punchy from lack of sleep, I skip the morning walk with Kevin and stagger into work with my hair barely combed. Fortunately the day is quiet. A few phone calls, some filing, a round of typing. Clients move in and out on time, legal documents pass over desks, smooth and regulated disturbance-free as an atomic timepiece. Until, that is, Kimberlee steps over to a five-drawer filing cabinet in a bank of similar equipment next to the far wall. The drawer slides out smoothly.

"Oh, no," Kimberlee breathes. She reaches for another drawer and performs the same action. "Oh, no," she echoes.

I stop mid-document to see Kimberlee slumped and leaning against the cabinets. "What's wrong?" The woman looks like she's violently and suddenly ill or has received horrendous news about a loved one—face drained of color, lips pulled into a rigid line, hands clenched to prevent their shaking. I stand at her desk and call again. "Is anything the matter? What can I do?"

Kimberlee takes a deep breath and pulls herself together, straightening up into her normal perfectly erect posture. "No," she snaps. "Nothing's wrong. Mind your own business." With one smooth move, she slams both drawers back into the cabinet and hurries off toward Mr. Horowitz's office.

"Of all the..." I mutter, then shrug. Who can explain Kimberlee's arrogant attitude? I sit and turn back to the document I'm working on.

A few minutes later, Kimberlee reappears, Mr. Horowitz at her heels. They head directly for the filing cabinets, where Kimberlee, speaking in such low tones no one can overhear, pulls drawer after drawer out with dramatic flourishes. Mr. Horowitz copies her actions. Then, grim-faced, both disappear in his office again.

The two other paralegals, who share the back area of the front office, crane their necks to watch the duo, exchange puzzled looks, turn in my direction. I raise my shoulders in a shrug of bewilderment. Answers, or at least explanations, are shortly forthcoming when one-by-one the women are beckoned by a phone call into Mr. Horowitz's presence. I'm the last and I watch as paralegals Tiffany Marez and Amy Chung step smartly to the summons, but on their returns have traded their professional demeanor for hang-dog looks of persecution and suspicion, much like what can be seen in news photos on the faces of people resident in stern, violent dictatorships.

Then it's my turn. By this time, I'm restraining my fear only through superhuman effort, repeating to myself a silly refrain my mother used to chant to me in childhood. "Never trouble trouble until trouble troubles you. Never trouble trouble until trouble troubles you." The phrase freezes in my mind when I enter the sanctum of Mr. Horowitz and find him and Kimberlee, heads together over the desk, until they turn and stare at me without a blink.

"When did you leave last night?" barks Mr. Horowitz without preamble.

"Quarter to five, as usual," I answer. My knees feel as if they can't bear my weight and I lock them to prevent myself from falling down.

"Was anyone still in the office?"

"You mean from the support staff? Yes, everyone. Including Kimberlee," I make it a point to state. "I'm the first to leave because I used to have to catch an early bus. No longer. Do I have to catch that bus, I mean. I've moved. Closer. Maybe you knew that." Stop babbling, I warn myself. You're babbling. You'll look nervous. But why not? The atmosphere is clearly one of mistrust. But why?

"And you never came back?" he snaps.

"Why on earth would I?" I ask, now completely bewildered.

"We can check your story against the video taken at the main door." The statement, flat, emotionless, lies between Mr. Horowitz and me like a line over which I'm being dared to cross. It forces me from trembling misapprehension to self-righteous indignation. No fears, no regrets, I remind myself, thinking of Saint Joan's attitude when facing her judges. Calm yet passionate. Inquiring yet firm.

"Am I being accused of something? You can't just initiate some antiquated reign of terror and not tell us what! Isn't that illegal? Against the Bill of Rights or the Constitution or whatever? And how about the attorneys? How many of them were working late? Or do you automatically trust them because they're the professionals and we're not?" Oops. Probably shouldn't have let that opinion slip, I think.

The outburst, however, clears the air. Mr. Horowitz halts his harangue, seems to fold in on himself, and looks ten years older than his actual age. "No, we're attempting to determine the exact sequence of events from about four-thirty yesterday until eight this morning. Kimberlee found the filing cabinets unlocked. You know we have a strict procedure that they are to be secured every evening as a safeguard. Kimberlee complied and Tiffany and Amy confirmed her action. It would have been a relief to discover someone had been careless, but it appears we may have suffered a breach of our system again."

"Oh, no," I breath as I sink down in a chair without asking permission. "What now?"

Mr. Horowitz rubs his palm over the length of his face. "Now we call our technical consultant to see if any inroads have been made into our computers as well as notifying the authorities."

An hour later, a grim-faced Mr. Horowitz orders an all-staff meeting. For the first time in memory, he gropes for words. Hands clasped behind his back, he stares for some time out the full wall of glass that overlooks downtown streets twenty stories below. Finally he turns to the assembled group.

"We appear to have a major problem," he says in blatant understatement. "I can't go into details for obvious reasons. And I won't believe that anyone in this firm would deliberately undermine our work. But something has gone wrong somewhere. The technician confirms that obvious and unskilled attempts were made to access our computer files. And you all know the locks to the filing cabinets were jimmied. I'll be meeting immediately with the other partners to determine what steps must be taken.

"The door will be rekeyed. Until alternate directions are given, no one is to be alone in the office at any time. If you have to work overtime, do so in pairs. I regret these measures and I'm confident that by working together, we'll soon eliminate our trouble. That is all."

Mr. Horowitz turns back to the window. Without a word, the staff file out and take their seats at their various desks, avoiding each other's eyes. This aversion doesn't apply to subtler tracking. When an admin stands to make a photocopy, her co-workers with hawk-like attention note each action. If a lawyer goes into the coffee room, others watch the clock to determine how long he's gone.

I detest the atmosphere that permeates the firm as quickly and thoroughly as water from my apartment heater soaked my rug. What has been a team working for the same goals is on its way to becoming a tyrannical state, with people searching for clues, ready to turn each other in for unknown crimes and treason at the drop of a hat. I imagine that the perpetrator will find it easy to pin the crime on some innocent, say, even myself. Or a collective hysteria could grip the employees and label someone, anyone, even the most recently hired person a scapegoat.

My fears materialize. As the day goes on, I notice that I become the object of attention of an increasing number of the staff. Kimberlee doesn't hide her interest. She quite openly asks me where I was the night before.

By four-thirty, I'm shaking. No dawdling to finish a task tonight. Even putting on a coat is a major effort. And the cold wind outside can't match the office's chill.

After arriving at the apartment, my first act is to phone Kevin. He isn't home, his message announces, but the machine would be happy to take my news. I gasp a plea for help and hang up.

The wait is agony, knotting my stomach and tightening a band around my head. I slip off my high heels and change into casual clothes, but that doesn't help. A scrap of paper on the dresser catches my eye. I smooth it out. Davis McIntosh's name and phone number leap out at me. I hurry back to the telephone.

Yes, Davis can come right over. His fiancée returned today and he doesn't want to desert her, but my panic is so pervasive that I take precedence. While I wait for him to arrive, I make a platter of sandwiches almost unconsciously, my stomach sensing that food will help me pass a nerve-wracking time. Peanut butter and jelly always are particularly good—a comfort food, its fragrance and taste emanate sensations of childhood snacks at a gingham-covered table, not a cliché in this instance, as Barbara truly made gingham tablecloths standard decorating at home. She favored them in off-beat colors, however—lime green, sun yellow, freesia pink.

In twenty minutes, just as I'm slicing the bread into triangular quarters, Davis knocks on the door. I burst into an anguished recitation of the chaos engulfing me at work as I show him into the living room.

"I should have listened," I mourn. "You warned me. We should have taken steps to prevent this. I know I'm in trouble. I'm the newest employee. Sometimes I forget to officially log out. I'm the one everyone's sneaking accusatory looks at."

"Calm down," Davis tells me. "This is not unsolvable. Of course the best option would be to find the culprit himself. We may never accomplish that. But your firm can safeguard your system against future violations."

"How?" I plead.

"Give me some paper, a pencil and a few minutes," answers Davis.

"I could use some coffee and food," I say. "How about you? I made sandwiches. I'll get the paper and pencil, too."

I'm rummaging in the desk when the doorbell buzzes. "Answer that, will you, Davis? I'm having trouble locating any paper."

Success comes in the corner of the bottom drawer where I find a half-used tablet. Fanning it in my hand, I hurry back to the living room. Davis and Kevin face each other in the middle of the floor, Davis looking puzzled by the antagonistic set of Kevin's tensed shoulders under a light khaki windbreaker.

"Kevin! I thought you were out," I say to break the mood.

"Well, I'm back. You said you needed help. I didn't even stop to take off my jacket. But I didn't mean to break up anything," he retorts.

"I do need help. That's why Davis is here. Did you introduce yourselves? Kevin, this is Davis. Davis, Kevin."

Davis sticks out his hand, which Kevin ignores. "I'll be going since the trouble's under someone's control," Kevin says. He tugs his jacket collar up and reaches for the zipper.

"When I couldn't get you, Davis was kind enough to desert his fiancée and come over," I say.

"Fiancée?" Kevin's head swings between Davis and me. "Fiancée. She probably wasn't thrilled with that. We'd better get down to business then. Sit down and tell me about the problem."

The instantly affable Kevin waves us to seats as if the apartment belongs to him. I comply, curling up on the flowered sofa, although his responses confuse me.

Davis executes his role—justifying his presence, with or without fiancée—with the speed of a man being hounded by a rabid dog. "Yes, Helen was unsympathetic, to put it mildly. But there's major trouble in Joan's office and I promised to help." He quickly outlines the recent developments and his ideas to safeguard the computer system.

"Joan could become the fall guy in this scheme," says Kevin slowly. "When you consider the physical layout of the rooms, the assignments of various staff, her lack of seniority, she's the obvious scapegoat whether that is the thief's intent or simply because everyone else will be rushing to cover his ass. Not a good situation for her." He rubs his upper lip with a finger as he ponders the issue.

"Maybe," Davis says. "I can't tell yet. But there's definitely a weak link in the office somewhere. She needs first to guard herself, then take steps to eliminate the problem if she can."

"But if she proposes to the partners that you get involved, will they accept her advice? She doesn't have much credibility. Maybe we should go with her."

"Whee-ee-t," I whistle from the couch, waving my hands over my head. "I'm here, guys. Remember? I'm an adult. You don't need to run interference for me. And you do need to consult me, not make decisions." The men turn in my direction.

"Oops. Guess we got carried away," says Davis.

"No, we didn't," Kevin disagrees in a cool, flat tone. "In a crisis, Joan doesn't have the sense she was born with. First she panics, then she goes to emotional extremes."

Where has that attack materialized from? "I resent that!" I glower at Kevin. "I've come through lots of hard times."

"Like when you couldn't decide to sell your house? Or the time you were determined to lose weight through starvation?" Kevin raises his eyebrows at me.

His imperturbable attitude ignites the bonfire of frustration always ready in my mind since my split with James. I vowed never again to be a naïve timid follower or a passive victim of other people's maneuverings. And while Kevin's support has enabled me to make major changes, often improvements, in myself and my actions, not even for him will I calmly accept some negative interpretation about me. "Kevin Bostwick, how dare you imply I can't handle my own life!" A flush mounts my cheeks to match my increasing rancor.

"Let's just say you need someone with experience to keep you grounded, give you perspective." His face assumes that smug smirk men get when exercising a patronizing attitude toward women.

I grind my teeth and try again. "I'm sure you mean well," I say, tight-lipped. "But I need to make my own choices. I'm the one affected by what's happening. I'm the one whose job's on the line."

"Whoa there. Don't declare war on me." Kevin holds both palms up in surrender. "It's time to calm down rather than letting your emotions run away with you as usual."

"That's it." I jump up and point to the door with my index finger." "I say it's time for you to leave."

CHAPTER EIGHT

Davis clears his throat, bouncing his Adam's apple up and down. "I believe I'll be going now." He shrugs his jacket on, turns toward the door, then interjects a final observation. "And, yes, the decisions have to be Joan's." With a nod, he hustles away.

Kevin, in poker-backed conflict with the overstuffed chair, has the reluctant grace to avoid my eyes. "I apologize. I don't know what came over me. You've been asking me for help so frequently that I assumed strong measures were called for on your behalf."

Regret sweeps me as I realize I'm battling with my best friend, the guy who's supported me through pretty terrible times lately. I relax my stance and my arm drops to my side. "I'm sorry, too. For blowing up at you." Head drooping to hide the strength of my remorse, but determined to be honest, I step next to Kevin's chair. "You really can tick me off. And I get maddest when you're right. I do tend to panic or react blindly. So I guess I had those humiliating comments coming to me."

By bending a bit at the waist and peering up, Kevin sees under the fringe of my swaying hair. "Hey! This is new for you. *Mea culpa?* Pitying yourself? I prefer the shouts and screams, whether of anger or joy, to whimpers."

"More criticism." A flat statement, not a question.

Kevin reaches up and pushes my hair away from my face, holds it at the side in a firm grip. "This thievery business at work is warping the rest of your life. Fight back, Joan, or cry. You're letting yourself become paralyzed. Unblock yourself."

I jerk my head away. "I am not. You don't know everything about me."

"Maybe not. But I do know you need this." Kevin quickly pulls down and back, knocking me from my feet. I collapse in his lap whereupon he sticks his fingers in my ribs and tickles.

No use to try to escape, wriggle though I might. Those gym-strengthened muscles make efforts futile. Kevin takes pity on me after a minute and allows me to capture his hands.

"Feel better?" he asks.

I stick out my lower lip and consider. "Yes," I say with surprise. "I do. Why is that?"

"Laughter is the best medicine, even falsely induced laughter." Kevin's face moves closer to mine, studying me for a reaction. When I cross my eyes and stick out my tongue, he boosts me from his lap and rises to his feet. "Now, how about something to eat? We didn't have a chance before."

"Maybe. I'm not very hungry now. But I could use some coffee."

I pour the coffee while Kevin samples the sandwiches, chewing vigorously if stickily when he first hits the peanut butter. Since he can't talk, he raises his eyebrows.

"Full of protein," I say without a trace of defensiveness. "Easy to make, tasty, and reminiscent of a protected childhood."

Choking down a too-hot swallow of coffee, Kevin manages to croak a suggestion. "You need to get away from the stress of your office. Why don't you come camping with me this weekend? I'm going with a couple of college friends."

"I've never been. I wouldn't know what to do," I demur.

"Nowadays the equipment's so good that you hardly feel you've left home. Everyone pitches in with dishes. So your only unusual test of character will be sacking out in a sleeping bag. I guarantee that the scenery and fresh air are well worth the hardship. And there are no computers. Think you can meet the challenge?"

"At least camping would give me new things to worry about—bears, forest fires, bad water."

"Don't forget outdoor toilets," adds Kevin. "They can be dangerous. The insects, the pit far below you."

"All right. Anything to get out of town for a while."

I manage to beg off work a few hours early despite fears that this will put me in a bad light. For the first forty-five minutes of the trip, my mind continues to tussle with office matters, ignoring the pine-clad slopes that loom higher and higher around the highway. I don't have a thought to spare for the upcoming trial.

As Kevin turns off the paved street, my worry mushrooms, but now it centers on physical surroundings, not emotional turmoil. More a path than a street, the dirt road twists around hairpin turns, reels up and down mountains like a roller coaster.

Barely wide enough for two vehicles, in some sections it narrows even more. An occasional pool of water on the right-hand side forces Kevin to drive on the very edge of the road. Over his shoulder I spot abrupt drop-offs, cliffs with junipers clinging for dear life, just as I cling to the door handle. The car bounces and jounces over the washboard surface dotted with rocks.

I grab the side of the seat. Foolish, I know. We're perfectly safe. We're not the first to travel the road. Someone constructed the path, rough though it is, and went as far as the campground to build the tent sites. I also recognize tire tracks of vehicles that preceded us.

"How far to the campground?" I ask through clenched teeth.

"Just a few miles," answers devil-may-care Kevin with not a worry in the world.

I wish he wouldn't look at the scenery so much. He should keep his eyes on the road. Watch out for obstacles, like that immense hole we're about to drop into. We miss it by an inch.

We rattle along for what seems like hours. An occasional wooden sign flashes small but steadily decreasing mileage amounts to the campground.

"Isn't this great?" Kevin crows. "All this fresh air, the mountains, the trees?" He waves one hand out the window.

I squeal. "Two hands," I beg, "two hands on the wheel."

"We're perfectly safe," says Kevin, echoing my own thoughts. "Hundreds, thousands of campers come here every year."

How many crash? I wonder, but do not voice. Another sign comes into view. "Betty Gulch Campground" it says and I spare a thought for the unknown Betty. A mother, a sister, a daughter, a mule who perished in the canyon's confines, perhaps?

Kevin makes an abrupt turn left and plunges down an even narrower dirt road past several vacant sites consisting of flat areas scraped from gravel, fire pits and grills in the ground, and logs to indicate parking spots. A pump for water, a real outhouse complete the amenities.

Just as the road curves by a roaring creek, a small group of people stand and wave their hands and cans of beer. This, evidently, is the goal. Kevin coasts to a stop and bounds from the car, answering their cries with his own, like geese welcoming a member of the flock. Overcome with relief that the trip has ended (the return still must be faced, but I put this idea firmly out of my mind), I sag in my seat.

The passenger door opens and Kevin thrusts a beer in my hand. "Time to unload," he says. "Only a little while until sundown." With every appearance of good cheer, he reaches behind me to the back seat and tugs out the tent, adds bundles and boxes until he can't see over the top. He staggers off toward two other tents.

I climb out of the car and look around. It's really glorious up here. The creek burbles and sings over a snagging waterfall of logs and rocks. Sage-green pine trees point their branches high into a sky the color of a robin's egg, dotted with only a few powder-puff clouds. Underfoot, gravel and sand mix with earth that seems clean compared to the dirty ground in the city. Around the campsite, barely held in check by the passage of humans, grows a multitude of varicolored wildflowers borne on tall, delicate stems. I take a deep breath to fill my lungs.

"Now you're getting into the atmosphere," says Kevin, returning to my side. "This is just what you need to forget the office for a while. Come and meet the others."

Kevin's gang of college pals exude health and good cheer. Men and women alike wear khaki or tan baggy shorts and flannel shirts. Collectively they're so clean-limbed and appealing, they could pose for one of those slick, mail-order catalogues in which the models always seem to be having a great deal more fun doing common activities than ordinary people do. I look down at my own body to reassure myself that my improving physique comes close to fitting the role.

Red-haired, petite Randi whose quick movements resemble a hummingbird in motion, lanky Evan with an intellectual's glasses and overgrown, tousled hair, and elegant Katherine, a model-thin body clothed in starched and ironed coordinates. I catch a quick impression of each, but I can't determine relationships yet. Maybe they all are just good friends. Good enough to share tents? I hope so—I don't want them to get the wrong impression about me and Kevin.

Some of the group begins to unload more of Kevin's gear. Kevin crouches down to lay the tent out. "Where's the fire? Dinner? I thought you'd have the food ready. Joan and I will be ravenous by the time we're done," he calls to Randi.

She bends over a two-burner cookstove striking match after match as she tries to light a flame. "You have the ingredients for tonight's meal. Why do you imagine everyone's being so helpful?"

"I thought because I'm such a great guy. Joan, give me a hand," Kevin says.

I hurry to where Kevin is smoothing out the tent fabric. He motions me to stand opposite him across an expanse of cloth. I don't see how the wrinkled mass can ever become a shelter.

"Ready?" Kevin asks. He pokes a series of short rods held together on a thick elastic band through a flap in the tent. Somehow it moves to emerge at my end, holding part of the tent in a curved arc in the air. In no time, two identical sets of rods perform the same magic, and the tent stands up, apparently by sorcery or sheer will power.

Kevin crawls around the tent's periphery to pound in stakes. "Take the sleeping bags and mats inside, will you?" he directs me.

I obey. Once within, I drop my load and study the interior. Very intimate, almost too cozy, I think. "You said this was a four-man tent," I call through the fabric.

"It is," comes Kevin's muffled reply. "Tent designers lay people out like sardines. Comfort is secondary to protection from the elements."

I spread the mats on opposite sides of the tent, unroll the sleeping bags, and place my pillow at the head of one. I don't think Kevin would put moves on me, but I won't put temptation in his path. From somewhere, an image of him in his gym shorts and tee-shirt flashes through my mind. Why has that happened? I shake my head to banish it.

Emerging from the door, I nearly bump into Kevin. He presses a flashlight in my hand. "Put that between the sleeping bags. In case we need it at night." To answer my puzzlement, he adds, "If nature calls."

Hamburgers sizzle in the fading light and the group begins to move quickly. Tasks seem pre-assigned with Randi flipping the meat, Evan setting the table, Katherine making a salad, and Kevin hauling water from the pump down the road. Only I stand empty-handed, my occasional awkward movements toward the supplies or food waved away by the others.

"All set," Randi announces. "Grab your drinks out of the cooler."

The invitation is a prelude to a period of camaraderie for everyone except me. Unaccustomed to camping, I move with misgivings, hesitant to help with dishes or pack leftovers. When tasks are complete, I isolate myself at the very edge of the firelight, sitting on a rock so hard it makes my bottom ache.

Oh, I try to join in. But Kevin knows these people from college, not high school. They share memories of good times and bad—

together they comforted each other through love affairs gone sour, supported one another on their climbs up career ladders. I have nothing in common with them, not even a college degree or the experience of camping. Eventually I stare up at the night sky, begin to count the minutes until I can gracefully excuse myself for bed.

Kevin tries, too. He offers me toasted marshmallows, teases me about the dangers of bears in the wild. Then he hits on singing. "Joan and I croon a mean duet," he brags. "Let's do moon songs."

We start with "By the Light of the Silvery Moon," segue into "Shine on Harvest Moon." The others join in as they know the lyrics or melody. The word "sailing" in "Moonlight Bay" leads me to initiate "Sailing, Sailing," which spins into a medley of boating and sea songs. From there I go into the Navy's theme, the Army's, Air Force's, Marines,' patriotic ditties, and "God Bless America" as a grand finale.

I'm marching in place, one hand clenched in a fist above my head, waving it in time to the music, as I direct the chorus in the final stanza. The group breaks into spontaneous applause and whoops.

"You know all the words," Katherine exclaims.

"Not all," I say modestly.

"Try her," Kevin challenges. "Give her a word, a phrase, or part of a melody."

Suggestions fly thick and fast. Sometimes I have to break down to humming, but usually I succeed. In the course of the evening, I learn Randi and Katherine had been Girl Scouts ("Make New Friends, But Keep the Old"), Evan loves his childhood Protestant hymns ("Rock of Ages, Cleft for Me") although he can't carry a tune, and Kevin has a secret desire to be a cowboy ("Home on the Range").

Finally their voices grow so hoarse they can sing no longer and the firewood supply is depleted. "I'm bushed," says Evan. "What say we go to bed?"

I watch to see who goes to which tents. Katherine strolls to a miniature pup tent, while Evan joins Randi in larger quarters. I still can't tell if anyone's romantically involved, but at least my sharing a tent with Kevin will go unremarked. He's dawdling by the fire, poking it with a stick to make sure the flames are out.

"Go ahead," he says to me. "You can wash up in the leftover rinse water. I want to make sure all the food's packed away. Bears, squirrels, chipmunks, wolves, that sort of thing, you know."

I do as I'm told. Inside the tent, I struggle in the dark to don a sweatsuit for warmth, then slip into the sleeping bag. Through the tent flap I see Kevin make a final check of the site, turn off the lantern, and grab a flashlight to pick his way to the tent.

The ellipse of illumination bounces around the interior as Kevin juggles the flashlight while unzipping his sleeping bag and removing his outerwear. He flicks off the tool before he crawls between the covers.

"How do you like camping so far?" comes his disembodied voice, through dark as thick and heavy as a stage curtain.

I consider. "It's strange."

"In what way?"

"In every way. I mean, here we are, eating burned or half-raw food, washing our dishes in tepid water that we also re-use for our faces, going to the bathroom in a hole, sleeping on the ground in our clothes, little bugs and who-knows-what crawling around us, maybe even in our hair."

"You hate it," Kevin deduces.

"No, I don't."

"Yes. You hate it. I thought it would be a total change for you, away from the trappings of civilization, isolated from everyday problems. Kind of us against nature. A new setting to test ourselves in."

"I don't think it's quite like landing on a virgin planet. And I don't hate it. I'm just not used to it. Give me time."

The tent walls billow and a wind whips the door flap back and forth.

"What's that?" My voice has a definite quiver I can't suppress.

The sound of zipper precedes Kevin's shadowy bulk crawling to the flap where he closes the rain cover and tent door as well as the screen. "The wind always forecasts a change in temperature. Ignore it."

Kevin stumbles back toward his sleeping bag, falling over my feet in the process, creeping the rest of the way. "What about my friends?" he resumes.

"What about them?"

"Do you like *them*?"

"They seem nice enough."

"Nice enough!"

I hear a rustle indicating that Kevin's sitting up. A beam of light hits my face and I squint. "Turn that thing off!" I demand. The light never wavers. I feel like a political prisoner undergoing brainwashing.

"They're the greatest bunch in the world."

"I'm sure they are. But I don't know them any more than I know these mountains."

"They made you welcome," Kevin accuses.

"After a few hours, when we were singing. Before then I could have been a tree stump for all the attention they paid."

"You sat there like a tree stump. You didn't lend a hand with anything."

"I didn't know what to do. And you didn't help me."

Kevin clicks the light off. "I never thought of it that way."

"Give me time with them, too. Now, fill me in on them. Are Randi and Evan a couple? Or are they like you and me?"

The silence grew so long that I think Kevin isn't going to answer. I hear his in-and-out breathing before he answers.

"No," he finally says. "They dated some in college. Actually, I dated her first. But somehow we all wound up being good friends, not lovers."

"Were you disappointed?"

"Not really. You can tell when some things are inevitable."

"And Katherine?"

"Part of the crowd. At this point, if one of us hit on another, we'd feel like we were seducing a relative."

"Yeah, I can see that. Randi's the mom, organizing things and bossing you around. Katherine's the sophisticated big sister and Evan, the baby. What are you? Oh, you must be the dad. Leading the way, ever dependable, doing the chores no one else will do."

"Is that how you view me?" Kevin sounds insulted.

"You've certainly rescued me often enough," I answer. "And told me what to do."

"Only when you asked," he points out.

"I admit I've been amazingly incompetent. But give me a break. I was going through a rough time. *And* I lacked experience with taking responsibility for myself and my home. Remember, I got married right out of high school. This is the first time I've ever lived by myself. I think I'm making amazing progress. I'm straightened out now. I've lost weight, I'm dealing with the office crisis, I'm paying my bills."

"God's in His heav'n, all's right with the world?" Kevin asks.

"What's *that* supposed to mean? Are you playing a mind-game with me?" I probe with caution.

"No, no," protests Kevin. "It's part of an old poem. Refers to life being perfect."

I sniff, an easy action in the increasing chill of the air which rushes up my nose and freezes my sinuses. "Showing off because you're with your college friends?" I ask, knowing full well that Kevin knows full well I never had the opportunity to go.

A choking noise that sounds suspiciously like a smothered laugh comes from Kevin's direction. "You can't be serious," he gasps. "Now you're searching for something, anything to take offense over."

Kevin's response snaps me out of my petulance. "Oh, Kevin, I'm sorry. I don't know why I said that. You've never acted superior because I lacked your education. I guess you're right. I really needed a break from the pressure at work." I roll from my back, where I've been lying, into a curve on the side facing Kevin. In the tent interior, I can barely make out the dark mound that is he. "I couldn't have asked for a better friend than you during this tough period. I've wanted to tell you a hundred times, but somehow it never came out of my mouth."

A hand grasps mine. I try to shake it off. "Ummm, a friend, I said, a good friend." The hand squeezes. "Come on, Kevin," I protest, although so low I barely can hear myself.

"Shussssh," Kevin breathes.

"Don't embarrass both of us," I way.

"I told you to be quiet. Listen." He pulls his hand away.

I fall silent. The wind's stopped and a soft staccato patter is hitting the roof.

"Rain," Kevin explains.

Why on earth did I suspect Kevin of putting moves on me, I wonder. I must be going crazy. Thank goodness the dark hides my blush.

We lie for a moment absorbing the soothing sound. Although rain often presages a thunderstorm this time of year, my usual stomach-churning at the thought fails to appear. Instead I catch the indescribable whiff of mountain-scented, damp air, bearing traces of pine, earth, and plants. The sprinkle changes to a shower.

"You now are encountering what makes camping worthwhile," Kevin says in a hushed tone. "You'd never experience this in the city."

"You're right," I admit.

We fall asleep side-by-side, to the cadence of raindrops.

I rub my sleep-swollen eyes, wishing, despite the magic atmosphere I imbibed during the previous night's rainfall, that camping had a few more luxuries like bathrooms. Kevin's nowhere to be found, but the others cluster around the picnic table.

"Hi," Randi greets me. "We've set up a washing area over by the rocks."

A small mirror hangs on a tree branch above a basin. I peer at my reflection, shudder at the sight. I splash the cold water on my face and shiver as it increases the morning's chill effect. Near the table, a fire's beginning to catch on the logs left from last night.

Hurrying back to the group and warmth, I come up just as Kevin approaches, carrying yet another container for water.

"Hi, Dad," I joke. "Working again already?"

He feigns offense at my humor. "Someone's got to in this crowd of weaklings. Bet you can't tote a full jug half-way back," he dares. He thrusts the large thermos in my hand.

"Pooh! In a second." I accept the challenge. The thermos holds five gallons in a garish, lime-green, plastic casing. The handle doesn't seem flimsy on the way to the pump. I have a little trouble lining the thermos by the pump, still water flows easily enough once I position the thermos correctly under the faucet. When the container is full, I search in vain for a lid, shrug, and start off. Somehow the combination of water-filled thermos and wobbly handle make the trip back endless.

Liquid slops over the edge with every step, soaking my jeans and shoes. My left arm aches down its entire length, numbing my fingers. I stand the pain as long as I can, then switch to the right side. It throbs immediately. Back and forth I pass the thermos, with the time I can carry the load in either hand steadily decreasing.

I add breaks for resting the thermos on the ground. When I notice Kevin and the others checking my progress, I grasp the handle with both hands and make the final stretch at a gallumping jog.

"There," I crow as I swing the thermos to the table. "Told you I'd make it."

"You're so successful, you can fetch the water all the time," Evan offers.

"It's a well-known fact that men have more upper body strength than women," I say. "I wouldn't dream of competing with you regularly."

From that point, I feel accepted by the group. No more hiding myself behind Kevin. I pitch in with the chores and accept an invitation for a "ladies only" sunbathing session.

The women head upstream to an isolated sand bar, clambering over hills composed primarily of huge boulders and fallen tree trunks to reach our goal. Surrounded by the beginnings of the creek that babbles and tickles our toes as we wade across, the tiny island basks in the day's heat.

Towels—striped, monogrammed, faded or plush, according to the tastes of the owner—snap in the air and float to the ground. Bodies—sleek, tanned, muscular, rounded, according to the habits and genetics of the possessor—hit the blankets. A bottle of wine makes a circuit, loosening confiding and curious tongues.

Randi starts the round. She smoothes sun block over every exposed, freckled inch of skin, seeming to address her comments to her bare midriff. "So, Evan's endless wanderlust's finally satisfied?"

I examine my companions, hoping for a clue about where the discussion's going. Katherine's pulling her hair back into a ponytail. When she finishes, she answers.

"Appears so. For now, anyway. He's back from India with eleven filled notebooks and no new plans."

"Evan's still working on his doctoral thesis," Randi explains to me. "It's about comparative religions. He believes in on-the-spot research. So far he's been to Mexico, China, Italy, Egypt and India. Unfortunately he doesn't realize someone back home would gladly travel with him."

Katherine raises her head and shoots a malevolent glance at Randi, who continues unabashed, "To help him take notes, of course."

"There's something between Katherine and Evan?" I ask. "I thought you were just friends."

Katherine sighs. "You might as well know. It's pretty obvious."

"To everyone except Evan," Randi interjects.

"Add Kevin to that category," I say. "He doesn't have a clue about Katherine's feelings."

I find the pairing strange myself. Katherine and Evan? Impossible. Two people more dissimilar can't imagined—worldly, urbane Katherine and head-in-the-clouds Evan. One with casual elegance, the other with total disregard for whether his socks match.

Sitting up, Katherine pushes her long dark hair behind her ears, crosses her arms over her knees. "It's been years since I've thought of Evan as a friend. But he's oblivious. His research consumes every minute of his time. He probably even dreams of it."

"Could he be interested in another woman?" I ask.

Randi laughs. "Only if she's dressed in the trappings of a religious order. Or is responsible for student grants."

"The trouble is," Katherine continues, putting her chin on her arms, "we've been friends for so long that he can't see us as lovers."

"That's supposed to be the best basis for a relationship," I say to bring some comfort to Katherine.

"Yes," Randi agrees. "Otherwise passion gets in the way. You can go years without discovering if you have anything in common. And disagreements get magnified because you don't know how to talk to each other. I'm the voice of experience. I was briefly, very briefly, married after college to a guy I'd known for a week. He swept me off my feet."

Randi stands up and brushes the dirt off her bottom as if ridding herself of a creepy-crawly, then steps to the stream to wriggle her toes in the water. "For the past ten months we've been plotting ways to put Evan in mortal danger and have Katherine rescue him," she continues, exposing the state of Katherine's heart without a qualm. "Or vice versa. A situation where he can be forced to face his true feelings."

"This trip would be perfect," crows Katherine, apparently nonchalant about the blunt confidences. Maybe she thinks I will be a source of inspiration or assistance. "A bear could rip into the tent. Or I could fall down a mountain where I'd cling to a tree limb."

"Food's another option. I could give Evan a small case of food poisoning. Maybe force a particularly large hunk of bread down his throat and Katherine could perform the Heimlich Maneuver," Randi suggests.

"All those sound risky to me," I say, shuddering as I imagine the difficulty an emergency medical crew would have getting to the campsite. "Not only for the danger. What if his true feeling is only friendship?"

"Then I'll have to face up and accept it," replies Katherine with a fatalistic shrug.

The conversation dies in favor of quiet baking in the sun. But later, I spy the ever-active Randi deep in dialogue, first with Evan, then with Kevin. Is Randi meddling, trying to smooth the path of true love? I can understand the other woman's machinations with Evan, but why meet with Kevin?

Watching Randi's fire-drenched curls bob in tempo with her unheard words, I'm not sure if I like the woman. More to the point, I don't know if I trust her. Randi, a born organizer, also possesses that rare quality of willingness to work as well as to give advice. Her entertaining wit flames as bright as her hair. But her chatter holds sharp undertones and she lacks a woman's usual compassion for her friends' troubles.

I prefer people to be easy to read. People straightforward in their response to life, honest in their dealings. Having tangled with James' web of deceit, wary of Kimberlee's possible duplicity, I instinctively react now to complexity by shying away. No, Randi isn't simple. Still, she's one of Kevin's closest confidants and deserves my consideration for that reason.

When Randi invites me for a walk on an easy trail circling the campground, my suspicions stir. Curiosity as well as a lack of an excuse impel me to join Randi. Twenty minutes and a mile down the road, our casual chatter about the weather and camping experiences fades away.

After a few feints disguised as questions like, "How long have you known Kevin?" and "Do you live near Kevin?" Randi drops her attempts at subterfuge. "I'm worried about Kevin," Randi says. Her strong stride carries her swiftly along the path as if trying to keep up with her thoughts. "Here he is thirty-two and he's never had a serious relationship. He's a great guy, completely dependable, bright, charming, makes a good living. He deserves a woman who treasures him. The woman he winds up with will have a prize. Don't you agree?"

"Ye-ee-es," I stammer. "Although I never thought of him quite that way."

"We're both good friends of his, right?" Randi shoots a quick look from the corner of her eye. "We only want the best for him."

"Right."

"And you believe just as I do that friendship is a good basis for romance, right?"

"Right."

"So all we have to do is get Kevin to see a friend as a romantic possibility and vice versa, right?"

"Ah, I see." I stop dead in my tracks. Randi isn't sneaky or untrustworthy. She's in love with Kevin! But he thinks of her only as a friend. "I agree completely."

"You'll give it a try?"

"Certainly," I enthuse. "I'll do whatever I can."

Randi rolls her eyes. "I'm relieved. I don't know why I worried so much about your reaction. I should have known that anyone Kevin liked was bound to have outstanding qualities."

"Nothing extraordinary. I'd do anything for Kevin. I'm with you all the way," I say.

Right in the middle of the pine-scented, shadow-dappled forest, Randi throws her arms around me. "I knew if I explained, I could count on you." She retreats and wipes her damp forehead with the back of her hand. "Now, come on. Let's go back. I'm really not a hiker."

Once Randi planted the seed, I'm eager to see it bear fruit. But hope isn't happenstance and I can't figure out a method to bring Kevin and Randi together.

I watch them as they prepare dinner. They work together well as a team, passing salt and pepper between them as they flavor salad and steaks, joking about the swarm of flies that tries to settle on the table. But something's missing—the spark portending the flame of passion.

Avoidance. If I take myself off and refuse to get into extended conversations with Kevin, he'll be forced to turn elsewhere, maybe even open his eyes to Randi's charms.

My plan limits my conversations to snatches of sentences wafted to Kevin on the wind, compels me to inject myself between Evan and Katherine to eat, and prolongs my clean-up with Evan into dalliance.

After the first few rebuffs, Kevin shoots puzzled glances in my direction. He doesn't seem upset during dinner, calmly spearing chunks of meat and sharing an ear of corn with Randi. Following the meal he clears and scrapes the plates even though I ignore him.

The men are dragging large logs to the fire pit to build up the flames when the first raindrops splatter.

"Oh, no, not again," Katherine groans.

"Let's give up," suggests Randi. "We can all crowd into my tent."

The idea is accepted in a flash. Kevin drops the logs, Randi throws a tarp over the dishes, Katherine grabs a lantern, and Evan, lost in his personal fog, stares up at the sky.

The same thought occurs simultaneously to me and Kevin and we start for our tent from opposite directions, reaching the entry together. "Just came for the flashlights," I say on a false, cheery note.

"Me, too," responds Kevin. "And extra sleeping bags. We can unzip them for blankets."

He bows me out of the tent into the rain that now pummels us with cold globules, drenching our thin t-shirts to the skin. Sidesteps and dodges don't shield us from the shower, but Randi's tent entices us to an immediately warm shelter. The happy campers cheer our arrival and press metal mugs in our hands.

I take a cautious sip—brandy!—as I scan the tent's interior. Evan and Katherine sit on a sleeping bag folded the long way to provide a cushion and huddle under another one opened wide, while Randi half-sprawls on the remaining bag, clutching the brandy bottle.

Without hesitation, I slip beside Evan, leaving Kevin no place except next to Randi. Two birds with one stone. I can ease Evan toward Katherine and encourage propinquity between Kevin and Randi. Randi immediately bends her head to Kevin in a murmured, intimate conversation. What about? No business of mine since I want Randi and Kevin to become friendlier.

The brandy's warmth wards off the chill and the lantern and flashlights battle shadows. This tent has walls that slant upward to a point, restricting the space available for movement. In an enforced intimacy, the choices are to talk or drink. Or both.

Randi suggests ghost stories. I try to veto the idea, claiming, "If they're bad, they're boring. If they're good, they're too scary." I'm outvoted, however, mostly because everyone is primed to cull from childhood's personal collections.

As Randi breaks into the third variation of the man-with-the-hook tale and Kevin leans closer to her to assume the villain's role, I yawn and incline back on my elbows, exhaustion then forcing me to curl up in a ball and pull the extra sleeping bag over myself. I close my eyes to rest just for a minute. The last thing I see is Kevin and Randi, heads in intimate contact. Success, I think, and wonder why my stomach feels hollow as a beach ball. Still, sleep seems more significant.

CHAPTER NINE

Absolute quiet. No, there's Kevin's hushed in-and-out breathing. What? Two sets of breaths? My eyes fly open. The rain stopped during the night and sunbeams slide down slanting rays of light, pooling in swirls over mounded bodies. I'm still in Randi's tent. But who's with me?

I roll over on my side. Somehow, I crawled (or been put) into the sleeping bag. Two bundled hillocks on the other side of the tent rise and fall with their occupants' movements. I crawl out of my sleeping bag on all fours to peer into the depths of the other bed rolls. In one, down-stuffed material smothers Katherine's fine features. In the next, Randi's red curls tumble from between the layers. No Kevin.

I rock back on my heels. That means Evan went to Kevin's tent. So both romantic schemes came to naught. I shake my head and vow never to try to direct the course of true love again.

"So, now what's your opinion of camping?" Kevin asks as we load the car right after lunch. Thunderclouds threaten another storm and everyone has decided to forego an afternoon hike in favor of retreating back to the city.

I shove a bundle on top of boxes in the back seat, hammer with both hands to flatten it below window level. Then I answer. "Very interesting."

"That can mean anything. It's usually an excuse not to make an honest reply," Kevin complains over the top of the car upon which he's roping the last of the leftover firewood.

"Okay. Everything was so new, I'm not sure. The experience was worthwhile, but I'm not convinced I'd repeat it. I liked the camaraderie, the sharing, the food. I hated doing the dishes in greasy, cold water. And getting sopping wet in the rain. Satisfied?"

Kevin grunts. "Yes. I wouldn't expect that you'd get off on the entire episode. All set?"

"Let's go."

On the trip home, conversation dwindles, then stops. I try to concentrate on a brilliant move to get Kevin and Randi together, but the closer we draw to Denver, the more the weight of my problems at work press on me. I can feel the expression on my face beginning to match the gloom of the sky.

"I guess escape only works for as long as you run away," Kevin comments without moving his observation of the endless strip of blacktop road.

"I must be terribly obvious," I say.

"Transparent as glass. Have you decided to ask Davis for help?"

"Nope. I'll just take my job one day at a time, as always. I'll wait and see about crime-solving."

The decision's taken out of my hands. Mr. Horowitz starts lining up employees for personal interviews, one by one, as if they're being sentenced in court. Before their turns come, people gossip and wonder about the reasons out loud. After they leave the spartan but well appointed office, their lips are locked and their faces grim.

I discover why when I receive my summons. Mr. Horowitz dropped his typical avuncular expression in favor of a cold immobility. His gray eyes slide over me, leaving me shivering. This must be his going-to-trial face, I think, and pity his opponents, of which I definitely was not one. Nor would I cower or act guilty, I instruct myself, although I'm scared to death.

"Well, Joan," Mr. Horowitz said in a deceptively bland voice. "I haven't kept tabs on you since you started here. Your mother would be disappointed and I apologize. How do you like working for us?"

"I enjoy it very much. I appreciate the opportunity you've given me, Mr. Horowitz. I've learned so many things, running an office, dealing with clients, operating a computer." Ooops. I bite my lip.

"That's just what I wanted to talk to you about." Mr. Horowitz leans into the high-backed, over-stuffed leather chair. By not so much as a blink does he appear concerned. "The computer. You picked up on it very quickly. One could even say that you seem to have a natural ability. It's difficult to believe that you had no previous training."

"But I didn't," I say. The chair in which I sit is so low I have to look up at Mr. Horowitz. "I worked very hard to master the equipment."

"I hope so, Joan. I'd hate to think that the daughter of an old friend is deceiving me." His voice, smooth as vanilla pudding, doesn't change.

The metal seat of the chair digs into the backs of my legs. I shift in a vain attempt to get comfortable. With a bravado born of desperation, I speak my thoughts. "Mr. Horowitz, we both know why you called me and the others in. We also know that I'm the newest employee. You didn't experience any problems with missing files, broken cabinets or the computer before I came. So suspicion naturally falls on me. But I swear I've had nothing to do with the incidents."

Mr. Horowitz adjusts his comfortable position to lean over his desk, arms straight before him. His look of indifference evaporates, leaving the man's sharp, steady, gaze undisguised. "I rely on your word, Joan. There's no one with whom you've discussed our cases, even casually? No one you've lent an office key to or admitted after hours?"

"No, no." I squelch the tiny doubt that surfaces as I recall my slip of the tongue to Dolores and Scott in the cafeteria after the first incident. And my subsequent moans and groans to Kevin about the atmosphere in the office. And then there was meeting Davis. Hmmm, I've been guilty of a string of mentions, now that I think about it. Have I been indiscreet? Untrustworthy? Surely not, those were minuscule remarks, more along the lines of casual conversation to pass the time. Except the confab at my apartment when I realized what a treasure I stumbled across with Davis. A flash of brilliance! Reveal Davis' proposal to help them!

I lean forward and put both palms on the edge of the walnut desk to control the excitement brimming up. "Well, actually, yes. Two friends of mine. After last week."

"Oh, Joan!" Mr. Horowitz covers his eyes with his hand.

I jump to my feet. "After, after. They can't be the ones. They have no connection with this firm. The one, he's a computer expert, didn't know a thing about our problems until I talked to him. You need to, too. He can tell us how to safeguard our system."

Mr. Horowitz just shakes his head.

Now enthusiasm overtakes my sense of self-preservation. I scurry over, crouch beside Mr. Horowitz's chair and put one hand on the arm. "Truly. We've got it all planned. He can rig our system so that it backfires on any hacker and leaves a trail we can trace." I widen my eyes with the strength of my sincerity.

The lawyer's fingers massage his temples, but he finally evinces interest. "And how did this whiz develop his expertise?"

"He's a programmer with a big firm. They do projects all the time like this."

"What about charges?"

I frown. "We never talked about money."

"So he'd do the work for love?"

"Oh, no." I blush. "He's a friend."

Mr. Horowitz's bristling eyebrows nearly meet over the bridge of his nose as he peers at me, mentally weighing the validity of my claims. The muscles of his face don't move, but his eyes glitter. He makes a decision.

"All right. I have nothing to lose. I'll meet him. The technology consultants we have a contract with certainly aren't handling the problem. But not a word to anyone else, Joan. Understand? That's on pain of dismissal. We can't afford any more leaks. And I'm not promising I'll take his advice."

I clamber to my feet and seize his hand in both of mine, shaking violently. "You won't regret it, Mr. Horowitz. Davis is a genius."

I leave the room humming. Quite a contrast with the previous hot-seat holders. Obeying Mr. Horowitz's orders, I tap another admin on the shoulder and motion for her to beard the lion in his den.

Kimberlee's faking work at her desk, flipping through a stack of documents and struggling to suppress the questions that threaten to burst out of her mouth. But glittering from under her lowered lids shoots a look that should have knocked me from my feet. Having nothing to fear now, I stare Kimberlee down.

"Don't get cocky," Davis warns that night. "Nothing is fool-proof."

He and Kevin have gathered once again at my place to plot their strategy. Two empty spaghetti plates are pushed to one side of the table. Kevin still is working on his dinner, patiently winding pasta strands around his fork to ladle huge portions in his mouth.

Davis launches a three-way argument with his statement. With boundless euphoria, I maintain the way is clear to catch the culprit. Kevin stoutly defends his position that danger continues to lurk behind my every action, while Davis contends that safeguarding the system does not equal apprehension of the thief since the man apparently is waltzing through the office at will.

I set down my coffee cup carefully. "One point you've both missed," I comment and tilt my head as if revealing a great truth. "You've forgotten that I made this decision on my own. Last time we met, you doubted I could. Yes, even you, Davis. I think I deserve congratulations for that. Now I've convinced my boss to talk to you. My instincts have been good so far. Why don't you trust me?"

Davis comes close to pouting. "I didn't say not to trust you. I'm simply pointing out the difference between protecting the computer system and exposing a desperado."

"A desperado?" Kevin hoots. "Where did that come from?"

"We are in the West," replies Davis with dignity.

"One step at a time," I break in. "First, let's meet with Mr. Horowitz. Neutral ground where we avoid anyone from the office." I gather enthusiasm with each word. "Say the art museum. Also we eliminate any possibility of surveillance."

"You're not going without me," says Kevin.

"Absolutely not. You're not involved in this, Kevin," I answer.

Clenching his jaw, Kevin repeats, "You're not going without me. Who knows what might happen? Maybe Horowitz thinks you're guilty and will try to set you up. Maybe he's the one responsible and will do anything to quiet you. You need an independent witness."

I groan from deep in my throat. "What is this, a party? Mr. Horowitz will walk in to be greeted by an entire, suspicious-looking gang. He'll probably call the cops immediately." I'm hooted down.

So it is that three individuals skulk into the Denver Art Museum at its Saturday morning opening. Although they ride in the same automobile, after parking they don't enter the huge angular building together. First, a man lurks behind two children, bends forward, almost covering them with his long, flapping overcoat. But as soon as they pass into the lobby, the children shoot off to the elevator while the man goes the other direction. He pauses in front of a computerized information terminal and follows the instructions on the screen, although he must have difficulty in reading the text, for he's wearing sunglasses inside.

Another man can't disguise his breadth even with a bulky fisherman's sweater. He hides his height somewhat under a tall cowboy hat, incongruous above wrap-around sunglasses. Off he goes through the front part of the lobby to the hulking steel sculpture where he stands with his back to the piece, legs wide-spread, as if daring anyone to challenge him.

More people pour through the museum doorway, including the final member of the dubious trio. This tall woman moves with an awkward grace, not quite accustomed to the flow of a billowing, chiffon print skirt around her slim calves. Not only are her eyes invisible behind horn-rimmed sunglasses, but also her entire face is shadowed by the brim of a slouchy hat. She holds her chin high, marches directly to the sculpture right beside the hatted man, but doesn't acknowledge his presence.

Also among the opening crowd, a compact, solid, short woman swathed entirely in black—black turtleneck and black jeans that only accentuate her voluptuousness, thin long black scarf wrapped around her head and neck, black sunglasses—enters. She swings her entire body stiffly from side to side as if a handicap prevents her from turning her neck. Walks directly to an eight-foot stainless steel, abstract sculpture that gleams in the lobby. Squeezes between it and the wall.

If someone were watching closely, he would have seen the chiffon-draped woman's lips move slightly. He could not hear her voice, low-pitched as it is.

"Pssst," say chiffon-skirted I. "I don't see him."

"Give him time," says cowboy Kevin, his mouth nearly immobile, too.

"I'm starved," I complain under my breath.

Kevin sniffs. "You're always starved when you're upset. Where's Davis?"

"He's across the lobby doing surveillance. Just in case."

The huge overcoat drapes over Davis's bony shoulders like on a hanger. He's plunging his hands deep into the pockets and crossing them in front of his stomach, presenting the appearance of a derelict ready to expose himself in an unlawful fashion. He rocks back and forth on the heels of worn, muddy sneakers, his head pivoting in the opposite direction as he tracks the visitors who flow past him.

Suddenly he materializes right next to me, jostling my elbow so that my hand brushes the sculpture. Alarms immediately ring and a guard hustles over, a frown marring his face. On either side of me, Kevin and Davis step away to disclaim any acquaintance with me.

"Say, lady, can't you read?" The guard points to a sign that warns, "Do not touch the sculpture." He switches off the alarm.

"So sorry. An accident," I murmur.

I glare at my companions as the guard leaves. "You two are most helpful." I load the phrase with the maximum of sarcasm. "And you look ridiculous."

"I didn't mean to bump you, Joan," says Davis. "I can't see very well in these sunglasses. I wanted to find out if Mr. Horowitz has arrived."

"Obviously he hasn't or else he'd be here." A niggling suspicion that I'm captured in a poorly scripted version of the Three Stooges with two of the comedians crosses my mind. I reject the thought that I'm the third Stooge.

"We've never seen the man," Kevin begins to complain. "How would we know if he's here or not?"

An expensive, three-piece suit crosses my line of vision. "Mr. Horowitz?" At my query, the attorney retraces his path.

"Joan? I didn't recognize you." The older man peers through his glasses to double-check my identity. "Your friend?" He nods in Kevin's direction with a hint of disbelief.

"A friend. Not the friend. This is the friend, Davis MacIntosh," I reply. Davis ducks his head. Mr. Horowitz does not appear reassured.

"The other one is Kevin Bostwick, a friend who's afraid to let me out of his sight in case I get in trouble," I continue.

"A good idea," the lawyer says, "since you are teetering on the edge of a cliff of ruin. I thought we'd agreed to keep this discussion confidential."

Kevin bristles. "Joan needs someone on her side. I'm well able to keep my mouth shut, sir, as long as she's not threatened."

Mr. Horowitz rolls his eyes, as if praying for patience. "Don't take offense, young man. If Joan's not involved in this mess, she has nothing to fear. Now is there somewhere we can go to talk?"

"Yes," I say. "The cafeteria area."

I lead the file (Kevin, Davis and I still wear our sunglasses) and the quartet takes their places on metal and plastic chairs around a table in the middle of the deserted cafeteria. Sunglasses finally are removed and everyone waits for someone else to start the conversation.

Mr. Horowitz harrumphs. "Well? Your proposal?"

Loving to spin his theories and philosophize about his specialty, Davis seizes the opportunity. "As I understand the situation, your office's security has been compromised. In addition to unlawful entry and attempted theft, there appear to be infiltrations of your computer system. We're presented with two separate challenges. In priority order, the first is protection and the second, detection." Davis tussles and plays with his ideas like a dog tugging a leash.

Not understanding computerese, I tune out to drift in a daydream featuring myself as the heroine. First, I'm crouching over the computer. Then with a speed possible only in imagination, I fast-forward to the police hand-cuffing a faceless suspect, my co-workers standing in awe as Mr. Horowitz shakes my hand in congratulations.

A passing shadow breaks my reverie. It's the short woman in black, who has abandoned her hiding place behind the sculpture. She still wears her sunglasses and carries coffee from a vending machine as the ostensible excuse for sitting in the area. And not just anywhere, at the table immediately adjacent to us. I scowl in her direction, to no effect.

Caught up in the deliberations, Kevin throws out a suggestion. "How about having Davis come to see you for legal advice? That way no one will suspect what you're up to."

Mr. Horowitz gives up any attempt to make sense of the situation or the people involved and capitalizes on the counsel. "Good idea. I'll have to tell the partners, of course. We'll make it late in the afternoon so we can stall until everyone leaves. Then you can get at the computer system. How soon can you come, Davis?"

"Monday?"

"Suits me." Mr. Horowitz shakes hands all the way around. He whispers in my ear, "Say goodbye to the woman at the next table. I presume by her sunglasses and demeanor that she's with you." Then he straightens. "Thank you, my dear. I had my doubts about your loyalty. Now I only question your sanity. Just joking. I'll see you in the office."

The woman waits only long enough to allow Mr. Horowitz to get to the door before she joins us, pushing her sunglasses on top of her head to reveal—Dolores. "How thrilling. We're making real progress."

She bounces into a chair to the paralyzed astonishment of Kevin and Davis.

"What are *you* doing here? What is *she* doing here?" Kevin addresses the question to me. "I thought we were being as closed-mouth as possible about our plans."

"*You!*" The horror on Davis's face is even greater, perhaps because his only contact with Dolores has been the impolite, if not hostile, interaction at the club.

I answer, a hint of defensiveness tinting my response. "I thought it would be good to have an independent, objective witness. In case something went wrong. Kev, you're always telling me to think in advance."

"There's no way Joan could keep me out of this. I've been wise to the action since the beginning. And a girlfriend needs another girlfriend with her in times of trouble, not just men." Dolores strips off her scarf and folds it carefully.

"Gender has nothing to do with this situation. Look at us. What a collection of weirdoes. Why did we all wear sunglasses and strange clothes?" asks Kevin. "Horowitz must think we're mad."

I object. "This is the first time any of us has been in a tricky, potentially dangerous, predicament. We're not professional spies."

"But we *are* a lot of fun," Dolores slides in slyly. Her subtle poke surprises us into laughter and we leave the museum in convulsions of hilarity.

"Mr. Horowitz," I say into the intercom late Monday afternoon. "A Mr. Davis MacIntosh to see you." Not a blink reveals that I know the counterfeit new client. "I'll show him in."

When I return to my desk, Kimberlee has picked up on an undercurrent. In the normal routine, clients aren't escorted personally to a meeting. The blonde's irrepressible nosiness forces out a question and she looks up from several law books on the desk, keeping her place with her index finger. "Who's that?"

"A new client." I refuse to reveal anything more than the most mundane fact. Hmmm, I'm getting pretty good at this spy thing.

"Why's he here?" Kimberlee persists. "Must be very important if you walked him back."

I fix her with a steely eye. "I thought client information is confidential."

"Come off it. We're all familiar with the basics of our cases."

Kimberlee's right. Her suspicions will grow unless I squelch them fast. "Something about a business lease," I make up on the spur of the moment.

Before Kimberlee opens her mouth for another question, Scott sticks his head in the door. "Kimberlee, ready to take off for practice?"

Never has a mood changed so quickly, from a near-scowl to a beaming smile. Kimberlee's eyelashes flutter double-time. "Give me a minute. Let me comb my hair."

She slips away while I concentrate exclusively on checking tomorrow's court dates. Scott clears his throat. No response from me. He tries again and I look up, the picture of cool disdain.

"Going to practice?" Scott asks.

"Of course."

"Better shake a leg."

"We're scheduled after a bit. I've got plenty of time."

"Is the skit coming together?"

What's up? Scott's leaning over the counter that separates the reception area from the office help. He acts almost...interested.

"You've watched us rehearse. Are you trying to unsettle me? Won't work. I perform best under pressure. You'd do better assuring me that I'm perfect and don't need more practice. Then I might rest on my laurels," I challenge.

"I have to admit that if the firm wins, it will be due to you. Evidently, according to word-of-mouth, last year's skit by Horowitz et al was adequate, good enough to win. But your talent makes this year's whole performance spectacular." Scott now is poised at the end of the counter, as if ready to move closer.

I hold my breath. Could Scott be putting moves on me? I don't dare believe it. And, with Kimberlee's return, I lack the opportunity to debate the question with myself. Kimberlee shoots me a look so dirty, the mud almost drips from her face. The blonde seizes Scott's arm and tugs him out of the office.

By seven, everyone has left except me. I hang around until Mr. Horowitz escorts Davis from his room. Interrupting a hearty handshake between the two, I say, "You can cut the act. We're alone. Did you settle on a solution?"

"Patience, Joan, patience," says Davis.

"More than that, discretion, Joan," Mr. Horowitz chides. "We can't be too careful."

"Yes," Davis seconds. "We agreed to keep all details between the two of us. The fewer who know about our plan, the better."

"But I can demonstrate our computer programs," I protest.

Davis shooes me away from my terminal with a wave of his hands, taking my seat. "Really, Joan, don't you imagine I'm familiar with your system?"

I study Davis to see if I've offended him. Silly me—he's deep into a relationship with the computer already.

Mr. Horowitz pointedly looks at his watch. "Aren't you going to be late for practice? Scoot, young lady. We'll be fine."

The word of the boss is my command. I scoot to the hotel. Costume rehearsal is scheduled, the first time to try attire, makeup, music, the works all together. The ladies' lounge doubles as a dressing room, filled with chattering, half-clothed women whose jostling bodies push the heat up to sweltering level.

Like most of the other actresses, I intersperse attention to my own makeup and costume with side-long glances at my companions. Previous rehearsals have been chaotic with little chance to view the competition. But now I spot the flowing robes of a Supreme Court justice (a skit on the most recent controversial decision?), two women struggling into halves of a horse's or jackass's body, one lovely attaching a tiara to her upswept hair, and a simulated boxer. Quite a collection.

I'm gathering my own share of looks as I draw careful red circles on my cheeks with lipstick and fill them in. Eyebrow pencil dots on my nose make perfect freckles and false eyelashes fan my face. Obviously an innocent young maiden, although what people will make of that oxymoron in the legal field still is to be seen.

My outfit is anything but innocent. True, it has a skirt, if a skin-tight wrap of sixteen inches can be labeled one. This slides over sheer, black pantyhose and couples with a white ruffled blouse that looks demure until I pull it down over my shoulders. This reveals my bosoms courtesy of a push-up bra and bosoms they are indeed, with the lush, old-fashioned, over-flowing plenitude implied by that term, scarcely resembling the set that I usually hide decorously under a tailored shirt or knit top for work. Four-inch spike heels, a crimson cummerbund, a saucy scarlet hairbow to match, and a crystal necklace dangling into my cleavage, and I'm ready.

I study myself in the full-length mirror, run my hands down the sides of my body. Diet and exercise really are paying off. I should thank Kevin for being such a slave driver. I toss my crystal earrings so they brush my shoulders, throwing dancing, tantalizing shadows over the curves of my upper torso. I can hardly wait for the call to the stage.

Can I blame the high heels for the strange change to my stride? They make my hips sway and my legs strut. And is the footwear also responsible for the surge of excitement that courses through my body, the way my chin tilts up and my torso becomes positively exhibitionist in its carriage? I neither know nor care. As I walk to the stage behind temporary partitions that block off the audience area, I draw furtive or admiring attention from men, depending on the marital status of the viewer.

Backstage I join the cluster from Horowitz, Trimble, Hawkins & Jones waiting for their entrance. Jitters make their presence known in nervous pats to hair, bitten lips, tapped toes, gnawed fingernails. I hum lyrics under my breath, ignoring the others. I know from my time doing solos with the church choir, that's the only way I can force myself to overcome the stage fright that strikes me before each performance. If I can hold nervousness at bay, once I start singing, a wave of euphoria will encompass me and sweep me higher and higher. The audience will disappear for me, leaving only its response, escalating in its warm reaction.

The preceding act concludes in a roar from the actors and they rush to the wings, laughing and chattering, swerving to avoid the Horowitz troupe. Harold Jones comes up behind me and squeezes my shoulder.

"All tuned up?" he asks.

I nod. Harold signals to the file clerk who's doubling as general go-fer to turn on the taped overture. With a wink, he soft-shoes to center stage. I push an inch of curtain back so I can watch his performance.

Harold as hero warbles his distress with the computer—my first cue. I take a deep breath, pull in my stomach, and waltz toward him. Twenty minutes later, our skit completed with absolutely no hitches, the firm's cast makes way for the next competitor.

Snapping my blouse up over my shoulders to relieve the pinching of the elastic, I worry about the smoothness of our presentation. An old superstition says that a costume rehearsal should be a shambles. Doesn't this portend trouble with the actual performance? Elation drains from my muscles and mind as I think about everything that could go wrong with the performance— Harold stumbling and falling during his dance entrance, lights or microphone malfunctioning, and do I have enough lung-power to project to the audience without a sound system? The chorus getting off-cue...producing a mumbo-jumbo of discordant sounds...what couldn't happen? I nod vaguely in response to my co-workers' congratulations and hand-squeezes. Until I walk smack-dab into a man's sweatered chest.

My eyes travel upward. Scott! I take an instinctive step back and cross my arms in front of myself and my bosoms, projecting themselves like an offering of fruit on a tray.

"Didn't mean to startle you," Scott apologizes. "I just wanted to tell you what a great job you did."

"Thanks. But it was only a rehearsal. The real thing will be much more difficult." Scott's staring so intently that I unwind one arm to run a surreptitious finger under my eyes, wondering if my makeup is smeared.

Now his glance is traveling downward. "And your costume is mind-boggling. What there is of it."

"Just assumed for my character, I assure you." My nervousness grows. Whomp! The free arm joins its partner in front of my chest.

"Yoo-hoo!" A feminine bid for attention comes from behind me. Kimberlee makes her inevitable appearance known. "Scott, I've been searching for you. Ready for supper?"

Scott struggles to hide annoyance when an idea seems to occur to him. "Joan, would you like to come with us? We're headed to a restaurant to join some others for a late snack." He nods in the direction of the entrance where several would-be actors linger, pulling on jackets and hats to hide costumes.

I nearly laugh at Kimberlee's evident dismay. "Ah, no, I don't think so this time. I'm dying to get home, shower off this junk, and put my feet up. But thanks anyway."

Kimberlee swaps her customary air of competence for stereotyped feminine helplessness. "My coat. I must have left it in the other room. Scott, do you mind?"

Good manners require Scott comply. With a nod to me and a shoulder shrug to Kimberlee, he leaves. Arms across her chest, but in a challenge rather than my defensive motion, Kimberlee waits until he's out of sight, following him with her eyes. Still gazing down the darkened hall, she addresses me.

"For your own good, Joan, I strongly suggest you stay away from Scott. He is infinitely more experienced than you. Without a second thought, he'll chew you up and spit you out."

I draw a quick breath in. Skirmishes and snide comments are one thing. Open hostility is another. I can't allow myself to be cowed by threats like a timid third grader. Or like the apprehensive wife I once was, ready to trade self-respect for peace or at least lack of conflict. Some action is required, anything to move myself out of being a victim into taking control of myself. I blurt out the first thought that crosses my mind. "Does he need a woman as seasoned as he? As ruthless?" I query. "Don't worry, Kimberlee, I'm not in competition. I bow to your superior talents and leave the field to you. For tonight."

Scott appears at the end of the hallway, Kimberlee's maroon wool coat flung over a shoulder. With the insouciance of a man handsome from youth, tousled hair, five o'clock shadow emphasizing a strong jaw, he looks like a male model for GQ and certainly good enough to fight for. Hurriedly, and in an increasingly lower tone, Kimberlee wraps her discourse.

"I'm giving you advice out of concern for you, Joan. You're playing a game without knowing the rules. A game that could have dangerous consequences. Don't get hurt." Kimberlee ends in a whisper concealed under a welcoming smile for Scott.

"Thanks for your consideration, Kimberlee. Have a good time, you two," I call, wriggling my fingers in a parody of good will.

As they stroll away to join the others, Scott throws out a final inquiry. "Some other time, Joan?"

I nod, hugging myself as I watch them until they go through the hotel's double glass doors, Kimberlee clinging to Scott's arm like a piece of lint, Scott with head high as if accepting attention as his birthright. I spin around and around in ecstasy. No doubt about it, Scott noticed me. And partly because I refused to fade into the background, had stood up for myself, real progress for a woman who ducked her head and scuttled out of a dead-end marriage only months before.

As I scrub off my stage makeup and climb in to relax under a hot, steam-filled shower, I reassess Kimberlee's words. What threat underlies the altruistic warning? That of one woman to a rival, certainly. But is there more? Was Kimberlee involved with the break-in at the office? Had she been performing the role of an innocent victim when she discovered the jimmied locks, the computer log-ons? I soap my hair until the bubbles course down my body and billow around my toes unnoticed.

Until now, I muse, I've been concerned with convincing people that I'm not responsible for the trouble. I've given hardly a thought to the real criminal. Perhaps Kimberlee's the culprit. Only Kimberlee knows all the details, is thick as thieves with the partners. Kimberlee watches me constantly, is now working very hard to shake me up. Maybe Kimberlee hopes to force me into a panic to throw suspicion on me. I refuse to be manipulated, I vow as I rinse off.

I wrap a huge towel around my body to soak up the drops, grab another to fluff my curls. Better dry my hair immediately or it will flatten out. As I flick on the hair blower and bend over from the waist, the towel drops to the floor. The sight of my own taut thigh and calf muscles captures my attention and I flex.

I have to hand it to Kevin. After only a few weeks, intense and painful as they've been, the weight room workouts are having a drastic impact on my shape. I switch the blower off and study myself in the foggy mirror. I pat my only slightly rounded stomach, turn and run a palm over a dimpleless derriere. No wonder Scott and others have started staring. Although I'm not thin ("trim" being a better description), my figure curves in and out in near-perfect proportions.

And strangely enough, I've started looking forward to weight room nights. There's a rhythm, a soothing sequence, as muscles alternate in a contract-relax, contract-relax cycle that leaves various body parts tingling even days afterwards. Challenging myself is fun. My strength increases steadily as I strive to break my own records. I don't even mind the sweating, the stringy hair, the exhaustion, because they make the ensuing soak and shower so much more refreshing. No doubt about it, I owe Kevin big-time for dragging me, a complaining, whining witch, to the gym.

I take an energetic brush to my hair, projecting my vigor into the action. My locks crackle with electricity and fly out in a halo. Everything's falling into place, I think. I'm helping set a trap for the office thief, plunging into new activity with the skit, losing weight, toning up, attracting Scott's attention. But what's next? What if Scott actually asks me out?

The brush drops on the counter next to the sink. I lean forward on both arms to look at myself in the wall-side mirror. A sudden chill shakes me and I seize a gray sweatsuit, ragged at the cuffs and threadbare at the knees and bottom, hanging from the hook on the door. My practice in seduction scenes is woefully limited to a few struggles in the back seat of James's father's car more than a decade before, struggles I happily lost at the time. James and I were both virgins and the simple completion of the act of making love was sufficient for us equally at the time, dazed and dazzled as we were by adolescent hormones and illusions assembled helter-skelter from tasteless Hollywood romances and *Playboy*'s Playmate sections. And, looking back, if I'm totally candid, sex was all mixed up with my urge for stability, a move toward maturity and a family of my own.

And while my love life with James was, well, adequate, it hadn't resembled the descriptions in novels. How does a real woman show that she's ready for a romantic encounter? Once in bed, what kind of moves should she be familiar with? Or even, gasp, initiate herself? In romances, the man and woman somehow sense that the mood and time are right, come together spontaneously with a great resonance of passion. They appear indefatigable in energy and double-jointed as they make love on couches, wade through the surf at beaches, stand up in bathrooms and closets, even clutch one another on horseback. I'm woefully lacking in both experience and imagination.

The telephone intrudes on my musings. "How was rehearsal?" asks Kevin.

"Unbelievable. I knocked 'em out." Maybe bragging isn't polite, but false modesty doesn't go far with Kevin. Anyway, he deserves to know how much he's been behind the success.

"Are you too big a star for supper with me? I just got in and I don't want to eat alone."

"I'll never forget the little people who helped me get my start. I'll be right over."

Without bothering to change back into my clothes, I shove my feet into a pair of scarlet, fuzzy, mule slippers and scurry down the hall to Kevin's humming, "Just start dreaming about what's coming," under my breath as I remember my triumph. He won't mind my casualness or lack of makeup. Kevin greets me with a bottle of beer and a platter of hot dogs and buns.

I sing in his direction, "Just start dreaming about what's coming."

The blast of song is so loud, he recoils. "What's that?"

"My new theme song," I say, then motion toward his offering. "Hot dogs? Hardly gourmet or health conscious," I point out.

"But nourishing. Eat up."

I join him on the carpet in front of the television. Kevin flicks on a basketball game that fails to sway his attention away from food. We attack the meal like we've never eaten before. Immediate hunger pangs alleviated, we start to chat about the rehearsal. Kevin cheers my victory over stage fright.

"I wish you'd worn the costume over, though," he adds as he collects the dirty, empty plates and silverware. "I feel like every man you know has seen you in it except me." He raises his eyebrows and wriggles them.

"Believe me, you've observed me in more revealing garments. Like at the gym."

"I appreciate the sight of you in tight workout clothes, but I imagine you don't parade the way you do when you perform."

I flash him a smile. His outrageous compliments always make me feel like the most attractive woman in the world. "Come with me for the last rehearsal. I'll strut my stuff just for you."

Kevin nods in agreement. Balancing the ketchup, mustard, relish, and left-over buns, he heads for the kitchen. "Help yourself to another beer," he invites.

I slowly pour a beer down the side of my glass to keep the foam under control. Beer and hot dogs. Not great for the cholesterol but no better tasting meal, unless it's champagne and steaks with Scott. I can see us, me and Scott in his dim apartment, candles casting a warm glow over us as we sit side by side on a plush couch. His arm will steal around my shoulder, his full lips descend upon my willing and eager mouth.

And then what? Total panic, I guess. I don't have the faintest idea of how I'll react. My inexperience will disgust him, thin and well-dressed though I might be. With the grand total of the men in my sex life being one, how can I know what pleases men in the plural? I might even miss an important cue.

Kevin would know. He'll help me. While I've been mulling over a dream scenario with Scott, he's settled down on the couch to analyze the skills of the players on television.

The beer gives me courage to speak. "Kevin?"

Absorbed in the basketball game, he grunts. I sit up from a half-reclining position against the cushions. I reach for his ribs and tickle him.

"Kevin!"

He jumps but keeps watching the game. "What is it, Joan? Aren't you tired yet?"

"I have a favor to ask you. A big favor."

"What?"

"Do you find me attractive since I lost weight?"

I catch his attention now. "I've always thought you attractive."

"Well, I have a problem. You know how much I want to go out with Scott?"

Kevin grunts.

"I think he came onto me tonight. I really do. Your exercise and diet regime is shaping me up. And Scott's noticing. I want to thank you. But you have some responsibility for the consequences."

I've broken his concentration on the game. Kevin's eyes narrow with suspicion.

I rush ahead. "You think he's a jerk, I know, even if you've never met him. But I love him. That's the truth. But I'm afraid, if I do go out with him, that I won't know what to do. Sexually, I mean. I've only been with James."

Kevin leans forward. "Do you want advice? Hints?"

"What I really want is for you to go to bed with me. Give me some experience. Now that you've launched me, you have an obligation to see me through to the end."

Kevin's face mottles, turning the strangest colors of red and white. "Go to bed with you. For experience," he repeats by rote.

"Yes."

Kevin springs from the couch as if he's been burned. "Sex isn't worth a damn without affection and trust. Even you, witless as you are, must know that."

I don't know whether to be offended or defensive. "Don't tell me you've never gone to bed with a woman simply because she was good-looking," I reply with equal fervor. "I've known you for twenty years since you moved to Clear Fork at thirteen and I remember your tales."

"That was different. I was young. I had to learn."

"And so do I. The only difference is that you were a teenager and I'm not. But I never had the chance. Give me a chance, Kevin. I don't want to be a complete fool with Scott." I spare a thought for Randi. Would I be betraying the woman's trust? No, because no commitment would be involved if Kevin and I go to bed together.

"You are already a complete fool. Pea-brained. Totally nuts. I've never heard of anything so dumb."

I cross my arms over my chest and stick an offended nose in the air. "If you don't want to, you don't have to. Not such a big deal. I'm not going to hold a gun to your head to force you."

"Force me?" Kevin leans over me, puts an arm on either side of me. "You wouldn't be forcing me. But you'd be playing with fire. I'll show you."

Kevin's head slowly descends, taking on the aspect of a large, overwhelming power. I open my eyes wider and wider and they begin to cross as Kevin nearly reaches my face. Under my sweatsuit, my body feels more than nude, if that's possible. I think I want to change my mind, but I have no time to voice my objections. His lips are pressing mine.

A vortex begins to whirl, pulling me down and down into its depths. I'm losing balance, falling back into the cushions. Kevin's hands are slipping under the sweatshirt, rubbing my back. He's murmuring in my ear, words I can't understand.

CHAPTER TEN

What have I started? The faint question drifts across a corner of my mind while the sensations radiating from the movement of Kevin's fingers across my body strengthen the tow of the vortex. The sound of his voice quiets, then stills, to be replaced by the soft movement of his lips as they scatter kisses on my face, emitting heat in their wake.

Fiery waves pulse in crests across my shoulders and arms, down my torso, to my legs. Hot, I'm so hot. I've never felt such burning before. My head twists back and forth, seeking a coolness that doesn't exist. I pant for relief, push with my palms against his sides, but succeed only in pressing him nearer. Then I pluck at my sweatsuit, trying to get air under it, but Kevin's solidity blocks the movement.

He continues his attention to my face, first simply rubbing his cheek against my features, wafting soft breaths over every cell. In response my entire body wriggles of its own volition. I have no will power, no control over limbs or head, torso or toes.

I fade further from reality when Kevin covers my mouth with his, not really a kiss, more a capture, sharing the air back and forth between us. A lack of oxygen must be causing this light-headedness, this inability to make a decision to move away. I'm trapped, too, by the angles of Kevin's features, the slope of his nose (neither straight nor classic, but emphatic nonetheless), the definition of his cheekbones, the strength of his skull blurred by tawny, silky waves of hair.

Suddenly, blam!, I find myself jerked forward, then back, my head snapping on my neck, my shoulders gripped so tightly I can't move my arms. And Kevin—*Kevin!*—is yelling right smack dab in my face like a madman.

"Is this what you want? Is it? A dangerous game, Joan. You'd get more than you bargained for. And I don't know about you, but I value myself too highly to throw myself away on a night that would mean nothing to either of us. A physical connection with no emotional commitment brings humans down to the level of dogs or cats. When I make love, the woman I'm with knows she's treasured. So, no, I won't help you get experience."

With one last shove, Kevin pushes me against the couch, releasing my shoulders at the same time. I lie there staring, while he, jaw rigid with anger, looks up and down, right and left, as if searching for a way out of this mess. He finds one in the door to the hallway and he takes it.

Something's tickling my ear. I brush at it without opening my eyes. The tickle continues, bringing me from sleep to half-wakefulness. I push the blanket away from my ear and the tickle ceases. Now my pillow, squished under my head as I curl in a ball, needs rearranging. I thump the pillow, trying to bring it to a better location, but something lumpy and hard lies underneath it. I flip from my side to my back. My feet hit a barrier at the end of the bed and my arm dangles over the side.

This isn't my normal position. What's wrong? My eyelids are glued together and I pry them apart to see a ceiling and walls distinctly different from my apartment's. I run my palm along the side of the bed to touch a leathery texture.

Kevin's couch. Kevin's living room. Kevin's apartment. How could I have forgotten last night? I cried so hard after Kevin left that I passed into sleep without realizing it. I groan and throw an arm over my eyes to block the sight. Here on this very couch he refused to make love to me. How humiliating. I never heard of such a situation. In all the annals of films, television shows, ballads, and romances, has a man ever turned down a semi-attractive woman's offer of sex? Maybe if he were married or gay, but those are the only excuses. If I'm so repellent, how can I ever expect to win Scott? A guy like that, handsome as the day is long, an attorney with a brilliant future, women throwing themselves at him as he walks down the street, dangling who knew what sexual suggestions, intimations, and favors in front of him.

As a gleaming vision of Scott's rugged yet somehow sensitive countenance rises in my mind, a cheerful whistle breaks the apartment's silence. Kevin! Why am I lying here mooning over Scott when in a few minutes I'll have to face Kevin? And how can I face him? I forced him into risking a long and treasured friendship in a quest for sexual seasoning. Humiliating! Maybe I can gather myself together and sneak home. I throw back the blanket and stand just as the whistler portends Kevin's entry. A massive blush mounts up my throat to suffuse my entire face, even my ears. I can't brave him, so I whirl around and pretended an intense interest in smoothing my sweatshirt over my hips.

"Ready for some breakfast?" Kevin asks from behind me. "I know we haven't had our regular run, but I think we can take one day off."

How blasé! Probably this kind of thing happens to Kevin all the time, women making passes at him, foolish girls placing him in awkward situations. No avoiding it. I owe him an apology.

I slowly turn back. "Kevin, I'm sorry if I..."

He steps to me, cutting off my sentence. "Joan, no regrets. I've got none. No apologies. Sometimes these misunderstandings just happen."

I can't raise my eyes past the button mid-way on his shirt. "You're not mad? We still can be friends?"

"Sure thing. Let's chalk it up to both of us being asses. You, for making a dumb request, me, for overreacting. We're good enough friends to forgive each other." He turns me around by the shoulders and gives a pat to my bottom. "Now, scoot to the kitchen for a lip-smacking meal of yogurt and granola."

I comply. If he can be suave, I can be urbane. If he can ignore my bumbling moves, I can overlook his set-down. At the tiny table, sunshine spills, splatters on the polished wood, dapples over my robe, canceling the chill that lingers in my bones.

Kevin burrows in the refrigerator for the yogurt, resuming his previous, toneless whistling. For some reason, I can't pull my gaze away from his long bare legs in baggy shorts that accentuate the chiseled hardness of his thighs and calves. He carries the food to the table and I notice the gliding of sinew in his forearms. He stirs granola into yogurt, takes a bite, and I see the clean line of his jaw running squarely from chin to ear. What's wrong with me? Is the disappearance of regular married sex finally affecting me in a major way?

"Eat, eat," he says and waves a spoon in my direction.

I pick up my spoon obediently despite my lack of hunger. As I eat, the granola crunches in my ears like gunshots. Kevin grins at the sound.

"We could chew a duet," he says.

I smile back without a trace of ill will or embarrassment. He really is nice, I think as I thump my spoon into the bowl, doing everything he can to make me feel comfortable. I wonder why he's never been married. The women he dates must be stupid or crazy.

Uh-oh, Randi. One woman who wants more from Kevin. And I usurped the role that my new friend wants to play. I can imagine the pain Randi would feel if she ever learns of last night's episode. Well, a knife won't force a word from my lips; and I suppose the same is true for Kevin since he's so nonchalant about the occasion.

"What's on the schedule for you today?" Kevin asks, tearing me away from these morbid thoughts.

I focus on him. "A new hairdo."

"What kind?"

"I think I'll go auburn."

Kevin moans and throws down his spoon. "When are you going to give up these attempts to change yourself? Your hair's fine the way it is."

I purse my lips and blow upward where some wayward wisps dangle. "It's like baby hair. The color is average blah. My stage career demands that my hair makes a visual statement. Something that attracts and excites."

"Attracts and excites whom?" Kevin demands. His voice shows his disgust. "Scott again?"

My spoon dips up and down in my breakfast.

"You hold yourself too cheap, Joan," says Kevin. He cuts himself off abruptly, pushes back his chair and carries his silverware to the sink. "Hop to it, then," he directs. "I've got a busy day ahead, too."

I start to gather my breakfast things together.

"Just leave them," Kevin says without turning, his shoulders and back as uncommunicative as marble. "I'll finish up. Just go on your way."

I leave before Kevin's indifference isolates him further from me.

The final dress rehearsal proves to be less chaotic than any previous practice. Facing the inevitable, everyone relaxes and goes with the flow. Kevin has promised to accompany me, and I don't let a little thing like his reluctance stop him. I need him for an honest critique.

His awe at the sight of my short curls, rosy as a sunset, bouncy as a squirrel's tail, persists from home to rehearsal hall.

"I can't get over it," he comments as we walk from the parking lot to the hotel. "I thought I'd hate the change. But I have to admit you look terrific. I don't know quite what creates the impression. All I know is that I can't pull my eyes away from you."

"I always felt I should have been a real redhead," I reply with great calm and a hint of humor, although my heart beats like a child's tin drum. "Underneath this drab exterior lies the soul of an emotional, passionate artiste. This dye job has freed me to take chances, try my wings. Quite a bargain for only sixty-five bucks."

Kevin stops so short, his heels squeak. "Not too many chances, I trust." He studies me narrowly. "Still pinning your hopes on Scott, I see."

I put my fingertips on Kevin's sleeve. We stand in the hotel entry, half-way up the steps covered with worn red carpet that leads to doors with tarnished brass fittings. Attorneys and other staff from law firms stream past us, hustling to make the final rehearsal on time.

"You can read me without a pause," I say. "But for now, please keep your thoughts about my romantic leanings to yourself. I need your unbiased evaluation of my performance. You're always happy to criticize me in other areas."

"Okay, okay," Kevin grumbles. "I'll limit my comments to your presentation."

As fate or a mischievous gremlin would have it, the first person we spy as we walk into the ballroom is Scott. I gasp and grabbed Kevin's sleeve. "There he is. Don't look. Pretend you're watching the stage. The tall one with wavy, auburn hair. I said, don't look!"

Kevin, like any red-blooded male, ignores my command. "Now I understand where the idea for curly red hair came from. What were you aiming for, twin appeal?"

My embarrassment colors my face as crimson as my hair. Turning my back on Scott helps until Kevin cranes over my shoulder for a closer look. He mumbles something under his breath.

"What did you say? Not a criticism, I trust," I question.

"A comment only. I said that I bet he wears French-cut, burgundy bikini briefs."

"*I* certainly wouldn't know. Forget this. Let's find something to snack on before my skit."

Kevin returns his attention to me. "Hungry already? We only finished dinner an hour ago."

"I've got a tremendous hollowness in my stomach. Chalk it up to nerves." I head to the table marked off for my office where a potluck of soft drinks, chips, and fast foods clutter the surface. Before I can pig out, the master of ceremonies calls from the stage.

"Horowitz, Trimble, Hawkins & Jones. Final walk-through."

I leave Kevin at the table. This time the rehearsal, primarily designed to time each scene, goes as poorly as I could hope. Props disintegrate, back drops fall over, actors trip, microphones lose power. The team from Horowitz, Trimble, Hawkins & Jones seem cursed — none of this happens to the other firms.

I see the bad luck as a good omen. I bow to the imaginary audience with the rest of the cast at the end of our segment. We don't, can't delay (the next group already is lining up for their entrance), but I catch a glimpse of Kevin flashing me the thumbs-up sign and Scott standing immobilized, staring in stupefaction at my wonderful auburn hair. I shake my curls like a happy terrier and exit.

Back on the floor of the ballroom, I rejoin Kevin. "What should I do differently?" I ask breathlessly.

"Absolutely nothing. I knew you could sing, but this time you sounded like a professional. Like our own little Sheryl Crow or something. You're full of surprises tonight," he answers. "And your heart-throb noticed, too."

Here comes Scott, words full of congratulations and eyes glimmering with what I hope is lust since he doesn't look anywhere except directly at me. "Another great performance," he enthuses, his normal air of smooth superiority missing for the moment. "The scenery falling was a fluke. And your hair knocks me out."

Somewhere along the way Kevin's arm becomes draped loosely around my shoulder, giving Scott pause when he notices it. He waits pointedly for an introduction.

"Thanks. Scott, this is a friend of mine," I say, emphasizing *friend*, "Kevin Bostwick. Kevin, Scott Clark."

Kevin nods, neglecting the customary handshake. Some basic male thing is transpiring, I recognize, although I can't give it further definition for the life of me. Scott recognizes the line over which he can't pass without challenging the other man. He represses his concentration on me and retreats. "See you at work, Joan."

After Scott walks away, I whirl on Kevin. "What was that all about?"

"What?" Kevin answers, all innocence.

"Pretending I was with you by putting your arm around me."

"I was trying to help you. You become more desirable if he thinks he's got competition."

"My heart-felt thanks," I say. I see my dreams disappearing along with Scott's dwindling figure. "I'll give that comment the attention it deserves—precisely nothing. You owe me, mister, for interfering."

"Call on me anytime, Joan."

On my visit to the cafeteria the next day, I think longingly of Kevin's offer of support after Dolores alerts me to a new development.

"He's here," my friend says.

"Who?"

"Scott. He asked me what time you usually dropped by. He's been stretching out his soft drink so long that the ice melted. I guess your new hairdo did the trick." Dolores counts some coins into the register to cover the conversation. "Move your butt in there. And act surprised."

I obey, wishing I have Kevin's advice, too. Unused to strategizing to attract a man, I feel lost. Should I show eagerness? Be cool and distant? Just friendly? Hyperventilation prevents me from making a decision. It's all I can do to perform a slow, casual stroll out of the cafeteria line and into the dining area. Then fake a double-take as I spot Scott, giving him ample time to invite me to join him.

"I'm glad I caught you, Joan. I've had a hard time getting you outside the office. Either your 'friend' is with you or Kimberlee's dogging my steps," he says.

Immediately intrigued, I bite. I slide into the booth opposite Scott. "Dogging? I thought you and Kimberlee were a couple. You're always together."

"Not my choice," Scott denies. "We were friendly for a while, but we don't have much in common. She just won't let go."

My heart feels as if it's leapt into my throat. I sternly suppress any sign of excitement or enthusiasm. Even I know too strong a reaction could frighten a male into showing his heels, like a hunter flushing a game bird into flight.

"Enough about Kimberlee," Scott says. "I want to talk about you. I'd like to know you better. When can we get together?"

I want to scream and jump up. Or faint flat on the floor. The sequence of days in the week flip through my mind. I promised to attend another of Dolores's at-home sales tomorrow. The day after, I have to prepare for the opening of the Revue. Then, Friday, premiere night. What if I miss this chance to be with Scott? Can I back out of Dolores's party? Nope, my guilt over Kevin compelled me to invite Randi along.

My hesitation must show on my face, for Scott holds up a hand to stall my reply. "I know this is the final stretch before the Revue. You probably need to rest. How about opening night? You'll want to relax after the pressure."

Scott, uncertain about my response? Scott, minus his normal confidence? Scott, his façade of supercool cracked? Kevin was right, I muse. It doesn't hurt to stall. Hesitation piques Scott's interest and makes him unsure about my response. "That should work," I say slowly, "if we're not exhausted. I may have to take a rain check. Can we make it tentative?"

"If we must." Scott's intense gaze makes me dizzy. He covers my hand with his, nearly upsetting my coffee cup. "Any cancellation won't be due to me."

I manage a smile I hope is half-mysterious, half-promising, as I disengage my hand, stand, and say, "See you Friday, then."

Dolores's parties, a never-ending succession of attempts to supplement her cash flow, have included a parade of plastic ware (guaranteed to preserve deviled eggs for up to a week), cosmetics (requiring purchase from the skin outward), home decorations that emphasize the "country look" (lots of straw, gingham, ribbons, and dried flowers), customized paper products (stationery to fit every mood and need), and miscellaneous gifts (mice and teddy bears were dominant themes). Out of a sense of obligation, I purchase something each time, even educational toys for non-existent nieces and nephews.

This affair is different and holds a great deal of attraction for me. "Luscious lingerie" the scented invitation purred in an elegant script. I think of my rag-tag undies and the practical sweatsuits that comprise my winter pajamas and shudder. Absolutely nothing to entice Scott past the first button on my blouse or a rumple of my bedspread. Although unconvinced that my upcoming initial date with Scott will lead me anywhere other than an ending at my own front door, I want to be prepared. The feel of sexy underwear against skin has stood many a woman in good stead as she teetered on the brink of an affair, I believe.

The party also offers an opportunity to sooth my conscience about Randi's persistent efforts to build a friendship. The natural redhead phoned numerous times to suggest lunch, drinks, or coffee and I always put her off, having nothing to report on the Kevin front (in fact, all my attention had been centered on myself, but I don't want to admit this fact). I figure the gathering to be an excuse to get together without indulging in heart-to-heart confidences.

Randi waves from the lobby of a shabby apartment house, then trips down the sidewalk, adroitly skipping over crumbling concrete steps. As a struggling entrepreneur, she prefers to invest in her jewelry business rather than her residence. "I'm so glad you called," she bubbles as she gets in the car. "I've wanted to find out how Kevin's doing."

A guilty shudder runs up my arms, which Randi misses. "You see him, don't you?" I ask. "I'm sure he's mentioned that."

"Oh, yes. In fact, he's taking me to your debut on Friday. But he's so reticent about his feelings. I thought maybe he'd opened up with you."

"Nope. Nothing new to report," I reply, ignoring my one rather huge, if unintentional, misstep, the seduction gone awry.

"Maybe tonight will change that," Randi says. "I've never been to a private showing of lingerie. Makes me feel rather risque. This could change our lives entirely. Not to mention Kevin's."

Visions of yards of lace, red or black silk, plunging necklines fill my mind as I pull up to Dolores's. How would Kevin respond to the sight? Of course, Randi would be the one undressed to kill in that instance. Scott, I suppose, is complacently accustomed to women's underthings. I vow I'll buy something to complement my new image and boost my self-confidence, as well as literally knock Scott's socks off if the relationship progresses as I hope.

Dolores opens her door a smidge. When she sees me and Randi, she swings it all the way in welcome. A giggle escapes from her. "Had to make sure you were invited guests," she admits. "The evening's offerings aren't geared for men or for straitlaced women."

I wonder if the term applies to either me or Randi, but I enter anyway. Dolores's working class house wears a definitely seductive ambience tonight. No overhead lights, but lots of chunky candles. An intense scent of potpourri wafts through the air, accompanied by the soft strains of a romantic ballad. Randi and I follow Dolores to the living room where a small group of women perch on sofa, armchairs, and straight-backed chairs moved in from the dining room. Instead of being relaxed by the low-key atmosphere, they clutch glasses of white wine and make nervous small talk, looking for all the world like a collection of teenagers waiting to audition for a porn movie.

Dolores introduces us newcomers to several ladies, then excuses herself. Before enough time passes to force conversation to lapse into silence, she returns, dragging a full length mirror, which she props against the wall.

"So we can see ourselves in the flesh, so to speak," she says gaily as if she were a matchstick-thin anorexic. "The modest among you can simply hold the lingerie up in front of you. The more daring can model."

With that she stations herself in the center of the room on a small settee next to two suitcases. She unsnaps them and draws out an armful of pastel froth. In an obviously rehearsed husky tone, Dolores begins.

"Ladies, we're all desirable on the interior. Our passion, unbounded, our romance, unquenched. But sometimes we need assistance in showing our feelings on the outside. Lingerie is one way to indicate our emotions. Admittedly a prop, nevertheless lingerie can present us at our best. Tonight you'll see the most flattering, most luxurious in intimate wear. Let's begin with a mood of innocence."

Dolores shakes out a pure white negligee sheer enough to allow a glimpse of flesh through it. An "ooooo" rises from the group. She stands and holds the straight, pale column at shoulder height, setting it shivering with slight tremors.

"Yes, in this gown your virginity is miraculously restored. You can play the coy maiden, hide behind its folds, all the while tempting your man to action with the promise of things to come."

I shake my head. I don't need the appearance of chastity with Scott. I favor blatant enticement since I, newcomer to the adult dating scene, still am not sure of the correct pattern to take the offense rather than the defense I always practiced before I married.

Dolores's rehearsed monologue continues. Hyperbole succeeds exaggeration, word pictures as full of frills as the lingerie. Wine loosens the women's inhibitions and some of them offer to display themselves as well as the merchandise. I can't quite work up my nerve but I take a vicarious pleasure in their antics. Perhaps their figures aren't perfect, yet they exude a collective, chattering feminine charm.

A form-fitting red sheath slithers down an exotic brunette's svelte figure. Standing before the mirror, a plump blonde in a pale blue peignoir urges her friend into a matching buttercup yellow nightie. A woman on the better side of fifty looks down with a small smile at her figure disguised into midnight mystery by a stunning empire-waisted nightgown.

When all the lounge wear has been exhibited, Dolores calls the ladies back to order. "We'll progress now into more revealing items. The lovable teddy, trimmed with mesh so fine it looks like spider webs." Dexterous as a magician, Dolores extracts the flesh-colored fantasy. The women burst into enthusiastic, if rather satirical, applause. To exclamations of appreciation, a parade of tap panties, slips, and chemises pour from the cases.

No one seems quite as eager to try on these clothes. However, they are willing to hold the delicate pieces in front of one another, securing them with gentle fingers to a neighbor's shoulders, or crossing a forearm over their own waists.

Dolores insists they put these articles aside and take a few moments for another glass of wine. Drawing a breath, she embarks on her narrative again. "Now for the grand finale."

She reaches behind the settee for a hidden container. It flips open on all sides to create a self-contained show case, lined with velvet. All manner of dainty bras and matching panties flirt with the viewer's eye, some prim, some daring, flowered or patterned, glittery or shadowy, like exotic butterflies perched momentarily on the contrasting cloth.

By their thin straps Dolores lifts the bras to show off their curves and supports, the way they caress and mold the figure. One appears to be nothing more than a wide band with a couple of smaller ribbons to cross over the shoulders.

I finger the smooth satin. "Must be a convertible style. Where's the rest of it?" I ask.

"That's all there is," says Dolores.

"You mean it leaves your top bare?" I find the notion unbelievable. "What's the point?"

"It's erotic," says Dolores. "But wait until you get a gander at this other one."

The women shriek when Dolores withdraws the last flimsy bra and panty set. Strategically placed holes peek-a-boo in both the top and the bottom, leaving nothing to the imagination of the sharp-sighted.

"I wouldn't dare," one woman blushes.

"Yes," agrees Dolores. "You need a great deal of self-confidence to wear this outfit."

"Or a bag over your head," jokes Randi. "No one would be watching your face." The group roars in delight.

The contrast between the final lingerie set and the first, now pristine-appearing, gown gives the viewers a range of clothing and seduction styles that loosen checkbooks and purses. Everyone finds something to her taste, including me.

I opt for a moderate yet provocative duo—a short chemise pale and insubstantial as moonlight, coupled with a string bikini bottom. They can serve as undergarments or night things. No slap-in-the-face allure for me or Scott. Besides I'm still a little unsure of my figure's quality when compared to the women Scott usually dates, so it's best to cover up a bit.

The women wrap their packages and leave Dolores's house in twos and threes, their heads together and giggling. Lots of happy husbands and boyfriends tonight, I think. When Randi precedes me to the car, I pause to give Dolores a quick hug as she stands by the door saying farewell.

"I can't thank you enough for inviting me," I say, taking Dolores by surprise.

"Why?" asks Dolores. "I've noticed you come to my sales reluctantly and you usually buy the cheapest item there."

"You just may have started a romance with your goods," I say.

"You've finally seen the light and decided to surrender gracefully to that gorgeous hunk you call a friend?" Dolores guesses.

"Kevin? No," I deny without a blink, praying that Randi can't overhear the topic of conversation. "I can't imagine why you'd think I'm interested in him. You know very well it's still Scott I'm after."

"I must say that you're working to deserve him. You've really trimmed down."

"You can credit Kevin. He forced me into it."

"The man is gone on you. Why lose the male in your hand for one in the bush?" Dolores just won't drop the subject.

"Give up. He's protective of me because he's known me so long. He goes on automatic safeguard. Anyway," I drop my voice lower, "Randi's scheming for him. He'll realize they're destined for each other eventually. Scott, on the other hand, is my ideal. Sexy, romantic, charming, mysterious. I have a date with him on Friday," I say as I walk outside.

Dolores leans against the door jamb and shakes her head in disbelief. "Your choice. Have fun. You can't miss in the outfit you bought. With your height, you'll look like a long, irresistible peppermint stick, one he'll want to lick all night."

The entire office shuts down at two p.m. on Friday to prepare for the Revue. Like all the staff, I retreat home for an hour's attempted rest. But the darkened bedroom appears and reappears between blinks of my eyelids before I surrender and get up to concentrate on insuring that every detail in my costume is perfect.

So immersed am I in pressing the skirt, top, and ribbons that the timer on the oven buzzes me into shock with its sound. The first in a series of alarms I set to insure I won't be late. But the next ringing is the doorbell.

Somehow I expected Kevin to drop by. He'd never let me face this challenge without giving me a proper send-off. A big bunch of daisies waves in my face when I crack the door to hide my partially clothed body behind it.

"Hey. Aren't these supposed to come after the performance? When I'm taking my bows on stage?" I joke. But I grab the bouquet and let Kevin enter regardless, checking to make sure the top of the bath sheet wraps firmly around me and drapes a decent amount down my thighs.

Kevin tracks after me to the bathroom, props himself against the counter when I pick up the blow dryer to finish my hair. "They're to soothe your nerves," he says.

"I'm numb, not nervous," I holler over the blowing.

"What about the hundreds of eyes that will be trained on you? The idea of that doesn't shake you up?"

"Pul-eeeze," I protest. I turn off the dryer and pick up a huge jar of cold cream, slathering a handful on my face. "You're supposed to put me at ease, not terrify me."

"What on earth are you doing? You'll slide off the stage before you have a chance to perform." Kevin strokes a finger down my cheek.

I shake his hand away. "That's to prepare for the stage makeup. Otherwise I'd never be able to scrub it off."

With a final, satisfied pat to my face, I pivot to leave the bathroom and crash against Kevin's arm stretched across the doorway. He drops the limb with excruciating slowness, as if waiting for some kind of response.

I brush away the idea (where has it surfaced from?) and dart into the bedroom where my costume lays smooth and ironed on the bed. Kevin sticks his head around the corner but whips it back behind the wall as I drop the towel to reveal a bustier and thong underwear.

"Joan!" he protests.

"What?" Mid-way pulling the blouse over my head, I glance down at my exposed torso. "Oh, sorry. I'm so used to you, I always forget you're not a girl."

"Thanks," he mutters from behind the wall.

Now costumed, I frantically paw through closet and drawers. "I'm late, I'm late. Where's that damn dress." I tug a jersey shift off a hanger.

After a peek to check that I'm dressed, Kevin enters the bedroom. "If you're late, what are you looking for?"

"My clothes for afterward. Ah, here they are." I ball up my new lingerie and stuff it in a tote bag, somehow hesitant to let Kevin see the delicate pieces.

"You're joining me and Randi when you're done, aren't you?"

"Actually, no." I avoid his eyes. "I wouldn't dream of barging in on your date."

"Come on. With Randi? She'll be disappointed."

I make for the front door, automatically hitting each light switch on my way. "To tell the truth, I have an appointment," I throw over my shoulder.

Kevin hardly can keep up with me. I shoo him out to the hall to lock the door, then hustle him to the elevator, my tote bag swinging from side to side behind me like a tail.

"An appointment on Friday night?" Disbelief is evident in Kevin's voice.

A punch of the button for the parking level, a quick check inside the tote bag for makeup, an intense study of floor numbers as they flash by. I rub my throat with my fingertips. "Yes, with Scott," I finally admit.

The elevator doors part and I step out, expecting Kevin to follow me to my car. Instead, he holds a door back to prevent its closing. "Finally. You've achieved the summit of your ambitions. Acceptance by your idol. Congratulations. Let me know about his underwear." With a wave of his hand, Kevin steps back to allow the elevator to rise.

A rather abrupt departure, I ponder. I shrug—no time to ponder now. A few minutes drive brings me to the parking lot next to the hotel and a mad dash inside carries me to the large restroom serving as dressing room.

In the marble and porcelain retreat, where huge mirrors on every wall multiply each movement by a dozen, a kind of hysteria seems to grip women in the throes of final preparation. Shrieks, low moans, thuds as shoes and cosmetics are misplaced, then found, the cacophony of tempers on a short fuse ricochets from ceiling and floor until the stage manager knocks for the half-hour warning.

"The audience is starting to come in," a woman alerts the group at large. Some attempt is made to quiet down by the amateur actresses in differing stages of undress.

I ignore the chaos to initiate breathing and singing exercises designed to warm up my voice. I follow with careful stretches of every muscle group, twisting left and right, a few knee bends, hands clasped behind me to bow my back, head rotations. A final check of my makeup in the mirror ends the sequence. Do I look like a clown? A strumpet? This is one arena completely new to me. Singing in a church choir, even solo, takes vocal talent. As long as your hair's combed and your clothing decent, no one judges your appearance. But the Revue requires acting, at the minimum a smooth delivery of lines and lack of collisions with furniture. My body begins to ice from the fingers and toes inward.

A second knock resounds. This time, the stage manager sticks his head inside the room. "Fifteen minutes," he says. "Time to go backstage."

This is it, I think as I walk out between clusters of two and three women. I reject companionship—handclasps or brushing arms or even quick and light chatter—in favor of an enveloping stupor. It stays with me to cushion me against the disturbances of players from other acts tromping back and forth, allowing me to concentrate on my part. If I register their presence at all, I hear a faint murmur or buzz in my ears, see shadowy figures flit past.

As I breathe deeply and focus on a spot on the wall, Harold jiggles my elbow. Little that's truly lawyerly about him, that is, subdued and elegant, remains. The typecasting of melodrama configures his costuming—dead black suit buttoned high to the collar of a pure white shirt. He's applied his makeup more than generously and his black-encircled eyes glow in a pale, luminous face, while his hair is slicked back into a hero's style. He holds a thumb upward. I surmise from this greeting that our act is about to start.

A wild round of applause indicates that the performance now ending has won the audience's hearts. Can anyone else compete?

From the stage rings the master of ceremony's sonorous tones. "Thank you, ladies and gentlemen. Now the cast from Horowitz, Trimble, Hawkins & Jones, in 'The Sound of Muzak.'" Polite clapping frames Harold's entry.

Fifteen minutes isn't much of a period to make a great impression, but for the employees of Horowitz, Trimble, Hawkins & Jones, it's ample. As heroine-secretary, I warble optimistic advice to the staff on controlling and directing the office's threatening computer. Assisted by a dashing Harold (playing an eager-to-learn attorney) and Trimble's admin (in the role of motherly computer expert), I master the computer's complexities to release its potential for the good of all mankind and the legal profession.

The grand finale sees the assembled cast advising in song, "Master every program, punch every key, study every manual, till you learn like we." At this point, and on center stage, I feel building and rolling toward me a response from the massed crowd, an intangible yet encompassing approbation.

Gradually, from the dozens of rows occupied by audience members who all look interchangeable in their business apparel and lawyerly demeanors, I'm able to pick out individual members—my mother cheering, Kevin next to Randi holding his hands high, Dolores with several of her children woofing and circling their fists. Finally, ultimately, Scott who gives me a small, intimate wave.

The entire cast takes bow after bow and steps back to yield to the major players. Then I stand alone as the show's star, basking in the adulation from the audience. The curtain drops to prepare for the next act and my co-workers and I clear the stage.

Too keyed up to retire, the group clusters in the wings behind the threadbare makeshift curtains, hugging one another in congratulation. Only one more entry remains in the Revue competition—twenty minutes until the winner will be proclaimed. No one doubts that Horowitz, Trimble, Hawkins & Jones will take all honors.

Sure enough, our act is proclaimed the winner. Mr. Horowitz, calm, dignified, moves with measured steps, precedes the mob from the office to accept the award. Hard on his heels and constrained only until he says, "Thank you," come his employees, slapping one another on the back and cheering. They break to stream backstage and down into the audience.

Flush with success, I join my mother. Barbara squeezes my arm in delight. "I told you that a hobby would help. And now, here you are, ready to embark on a new career."

"Hardly," I demur.

I have no time to continue, for here come Kevin and Randi, followed by anyone else with an excuse to approach. Mr. Horowitz beams, shakes hands with my mother who beams, and congratulates her on her daughter's performance. Even Kimberlee politely puts in an appearance.

In the chaos, Barbara maneuvers me to the side of the group to say in an undertone, "I'm glad to see Kevin here. Any progress?"

"What kind of progress do you expect, Mom? We're neighbors and friends. We exercise together, sometimes eat together, he lectures me about my life, and generally makes a nuisance of himself."

"You're wasting time. If you don't wake up and smell the coffee, you're going to lose your opportunity," Barbara warns.

"I don't want an opportunity. Randi, the short redhead, is the woman for Kevin." My frustration with Barbara's matchmaking makes me terse.

"Oh, really?" Barbara cocks an eyebrow and stares over my shoulder. I turn to see Kimberlee wreaking havoc with her eyelashes on Kevin's psyche. Not that Kevin appears uncomfortable. He's beaming down at the blonde, and Randi's nowhere in sight.

"Well!" I take off for Kevin's side so fast that my skimpy costume gets wedged between my legs. I grab Kevin's arm possessively. "I see you've met Kimberlee," I say, never moving my eyes from the woman's face.

"Yes," says Kevin, grinning like a happy drunk. "She tells me you're the firm's mainstay when it comes to turning out work."

"How nice of her," I murmur. "Where's Randi?"

"Hmmm?" Kevin's distraction focuses on Kimberlee's lanky legs, encased for the evening in some sort of glittery, silvery space-age fabric under a skirt approximately thirteen inches long. Kimberlee smoothes the mini over her nonexistent stomach.

"Randi? The woman you came with?" I don't even try to suppress my sarcastic tone.

"She had to take off. Something about preparing for an early meeting. Kimberlee, how were you involved in this evening's triumph?" Kevin leans toward Kimberlee so far that he breaks the connection of my handhold.

Kimberlee launches into a long but humorous story about writing the script. I tune her out when Scott sidles up to the still-chattering horde of Horowitz-ites collected by the door.

"I'm glad I didn't lay any bets against your winning," Scott comments, taking my hand in both of his.

My insides promptly turn to mush. Striving to disguise the fact, I shoot back, "The team effort is responsible."

"But you are the key element. That's what made the difference." He leans closer and puts his lips right by my ear. "I can't wait to be alone with you. Let's go."

"My car?" I squeak.

"It's in a lot, right? Safe there overnight."

I nod and slip away to get my things, all thoughts of Kevin, Randi or Kimberlee evaporating like smoke. In the hallway, I join Scott, and its emptiness shows that our escape is unnoticed. Scott leads me to a fancy, low-slung car (I don't know the make), shining with metallic splendor, roaring with bridled power.

The ride makes no impression on me. The mush within me has turned into a churning mass. I struggle to control my clenching insides even as Scott and I park, climb a short flight of stairs, and enter his modern townhouse.

It seems Scott has three or four pairs of hands, for all at once soft music plays, a fire glimmers, candles flame, champagne chills, and I find myself propped against soft cushions. Scott offers me a flute of champagne as he seats himself next to me. One of his arms creeps behind me on the overstuffed sofa, and his fingers rub my shoulder.

"You've changed, Joan. You've become a total delight. You sparkle, you fizz like this champagne. I can't resist you," he murmurs.

My stomach pitches. God, I'm hungry. Feels like centuries since I've tasted a bite. "Got anything to eat?" I ask brightly.

Scott recoils. Does he take my statement as a rebuff? I can't help that. Without nourishment, I'll faint.

"I guess that's understandable considering the energy you expended on stage. I wouldn't want you to collapse on me." He exits to the kitchen.

"I'll go change and freshen up," I call.

In the bathroom, I open my tote bag. I shake out my dress, reach for the new lingerie, feel instead something moist and squishy.

"Oh, no," I moan. A quick tug reveals the peach-colored silk smeared with makeup. In my rush to pack, the lid of my foundation must have worked loose. Now I have no sexy underthings. How can I be seduced in the sweat-soaked bra and panties I sported throughout the performance?

A glimpse in the mirror reveals another miscalculation—stage makeup is too messy to retain in an intimate setting. My eyeshadow and mascara have been leaking down my cheeks. Scott will slide off my face, leaving a smeared mess on my skin behind him. I'll have to remove the cosmetics.

"Joan?" Scott calls from the cozy retreat of the overstuffed sofa. "I'm ready. Come join me."

CHAPTER ELEVEN

I stall. "Just a minute. I'm taking off my stage makeup," I call with false cheeriness. A quick swipe with tissues, a lick-and-a-promise with soap and water, and my face sports a natural glow. I cringe at the sight. Maybe Scott won't notice the flaws—a prominent nose, a blemish, a crooked front tooth—in the dim light.

I can't remain locked in the bathroom all night. Especially with the hunger that gnaws at my belly. With a palm pressed on my abdomen, I return to the living room to see a small plate on the coffee table. It holds skimpy, foil-wrapped packets of processed cheese and a few crackers.

"Come here, you gorgeous creature," Scott says. He pats the narrow place next to him, between his thigh and the cushioned arm.

Thankful that the lights are low and hide my shiny complexion, I obey. My hand shoots out to gather the insubstantial collection of snacks. In between bites, I chatter, "I still can't believe that we won. But the most wonderful thing was the way everyone worked together. We created something bigger than any of us."

I try, but fail, to eat delicately. Surrendering to the most basic of urges, I fill my mouth but hold a hand in front of my lips to hide the bulge in my cheek. Scott doesn't notice—he's intent on running a finger around the low neckline of my costume. I shift nervously. Will he get so low he'll feel the perspiration soaking my bustier?

"Ah, Joan, Joan, I've longed to be alone with you," he whispers in my ear. A warm breath of air follows, tingling from my lobe to my neck. "I've seen us away from the interference of work, the constant demands of others, the noise of telephones and machines, even the dictates of our own consciences."

I feel a damp kiss on my jaw, then, shockingly, a tongue tracing my ear, dipping inside. I jerk my head away and chew the remainder of the crackers in great haste. Like an awkward, twitching dance, we trade movements back and forth. Every time Scott leans forward, I reverse the action because I remember I failed to swab my ears when I showered.

"You sweet, shy thing," Scott murmurs. He wriggles one arm between the couch and me, throws the other one in front of me, until he encircles me in his grasp. His body presses me back in the cushions and he gazes deep in my eyes.

I know what's coming and dread it. I never imagined I'd frantically be trying to swallow a mouthful of food or hiding disreputable underwear during my first kiss with Scott. The setting and timing are perfect—I'm the deficient element.

Scott's embrace, strong yet gentle, invites me to surrender to all but his presence. It goes on and on, an interlude out of time. Yet the sheer physical nature of the act sends an echo in my mind and body, renewing my hunger pangs and my fear of disrobing. I break the clinch.

"I've...I've really got to go," I stammer. "This has been wonderful, but we have another performance tomorrow. I need to rest and so do you."

Scott leans his head against the couch, his eyes half-closed. "All right. I understand. Tonight's overwhelmed you. We'll have other times together."

Despite Scott's words, I worry all the way home, for he makes no attempt at small talk.

I keep imagining what might come out of Kevin's mouth when I tell him about the evening. "Is the guy so dumb he can't keep a conversation going?" Or, alternately, "Pouting, was he, because he didn't get any?"

Scott doesn't even accompany me to my lobby, instead reaching over me to swing the car door open. I hurry inside without watching his departure. As I ride up the elevator, I lean my head against the mirrored wall to consider the performance and the date. I can't say I'm disappointed in the evening's finale. I rationalize that I'm applying Kevin's advice to take things slow with Scott, play a little hard-to-get. The next moment, the thought of a frozen pizza waiting for the microwave obsesses me, overriding concern over Scott's remoteness on the ride home. I burst into my apartment with the thrust of a rocket, careening into the refrigerator in my desperate need. The pizza seems to jump into my hands and the microwave sucks the frozen treat into its maw.

While waiting for the microwave to work its magic, I flip on the radio full blast, strip off my costume and exchange it for baggy t-shirt and sweat pants. As if waiting for the signal of the music, Kevin's tattoo beats at the door.

"You're back early," I greet Kevin.

He closes the door before answering. "I could say the same about you. Wasn't Scott as fascinating as you hoped?"

"Oh, he was great," I call as I walk back to the kitchen. "But I was exhausted and hungry. Want some pizza?"

Without waiting for a reply, I pull the snack out of the oven and slice it. I continue my explanation as Kevin takes the seat across from me. "Anyway, give me time to recover my balance. Nothing could match the thrill of winning the competition. Anything would be a let-down after that." I take a liberal bite of crust, lavishly laced with cheese and pepperoni and sigh with satisfaction.

"I can see why," says Kevin as he helps himself. "Even though I'd been at a rehearsal, I wasn't prepared for the performance. It was close to professional."

I prop my chin on my palm. "I can't explain what happened. Some kind of spirit possessed all of us. Maybe men competing in sports feel it, but I never have. Working together as a team for a nearly unreachable goal. It gave me an unbelievable high." I shake my head. "My regular routine will be...routine now."

"Your mother expects different. You're destined for a stage career, according to her."

"You overheard? Barbara's dreams are rarely grounded in reality." I spare a thought for my mother's flagrant hopes for Kevin and can only pray he hadn't heard that part of Barbara's comments. "By the way, what happened to Randi?" I ask.

"I told you, she had to leave right away."

"And you didn't take her home?"

"I'm not her keeper. She's free to do what she likes."

"Randi's one of your best friends. She deserves a little consideration," I scold.

"And you're not her guardian or mine," Kevin continues. "Lay off me. You sound like a matchmaker."

I pick at my pizza. "Sorry." Now that the subject's broached, however, I plunge ahead to subtly prepare Kevin to consider Randi in a new light. "But don't you ever worry about Randi? About her future? Here she is twenty-nine, never married, no serious relationships. Is something wrong with her?"

"Heck, no!" Kevin bristles. "Not many men are good enough for her."

"Is that her opinion or yours?"

Kevin considers. "Mine, I guess. I've never heard her say that."

"So you actively discourage those you consider unsuitable?"

"You're putting words in my mouth again," Kevin complains, biting into his pizza with unwarranted intensity.

"Think about it," I press on. I wave a piece of crust in the air as if conducting a chorus of responses. "No one's good enough for her. You see her frequently. What's the logical conclusion?" There are, of course, several logical conclusions, including the one in which Kevin suddenly realizes his love for Randi.

Another piece of pizza disappears down Kevin's throat before he answers. "That I've been selfish. You're right. I should be introducing Randi to possible partners, not criticizing in the background."

I roll my eyes and give up for the present. "That's some progress," I mutter.

"If you want to make matches for me, you can start with the blonde you work with. What's her name, Kimberlee?"

A piece of pepperoni goes down the wrong way as I gasp. "You're not serious! That's Kimberlee, my deadliest opponent. She's the one convincing people they should be suspicious of me. Plus constantly hustling Scott."

"She's very attractive. Seems bright, too. How about setting up a dinner and inviting her?" Kevin suggests.

"No. I absolutely refuse to help you get to know her better," I say, slapping my fork on the table. "Now, inhospitable as it sounds, you need to leave. I'm wrung out."

"I'm still hungry," Kevin complains, eyeing the three-quarters of pizza remaining.

"I'll pack it for you." I reach for the pizza box.

"Don't you want any more? You've hardly had a bite."

"Nope. I guess I'm more tired than hungry."

I thrust the package into Kevin's hands and push him towards the door. "I appreciate your emotional support. Good night, good night, and good night."

Laughing, Kevin allows me to direct his steps, but stops at the entrance. His turn brings him into full contact with my body. I jump back as if scorched. He reaches for me with both hands, rubs my arms from shoulder to elbow.

He's going to kiss me...*is* he going to kiss me? I ask myself, with no thought of my threadbare underwear.

"Congratulations again on your success," Kevin says. He bends forward to press his lips on my forehead. "Have a good rest. You deserve it."

I close the door after Kevin, then lean against it. Why on earth had I felt he was about to embrace me like a lover? I have to purge my mind of such unsuitable ideas. Shaking my head, I take Kevin's advice.

~ ~

My unresponsiveness must have discouraged Scott, I think gloomily. During the second and final night of the Revue, he sticks strictly with the stage crew, barely waving to me in passing. Then into the next week, still with no word. Exhausted from the yo-yo between hope and despair, sometimes cursing myself for missing my opportunity, sometimes remembering Scott's promising yet unfulfilled words, I'm ready to give up on him.

This morning is another emotional low with cloudy, windy weather to match. I push the office door open and stalk to my desk. The first task is to pull the cover off my keyboard, then punch the terminal on. Then immediately I go to the coffee corner for some caffeine to wake myself up. I peer into the mug as if trying to find the meaning of life in its dark depths.

A woman's voice interrupts my preoccupation. Kimberlee's standing by me, wearing a smile so plastic it creases her cheeks. "How are you this morning?" she bubbles, pouring a cup of coffee.

For days since the Revue, Kimberlee has been greeting me like a long-lost friend. Why the sudden camaraderie? I'm suspicious but confine my response to a mumble and turn away to head back to my desk.

"Just a minute, Joan," Kimberlee says. "I'd like to talk to you. I know we've had our disagreements in the past. But I want to call a truce."

I lack the guile for diplomacy and the intelligence for deceit, traits that brought me misery previously, so I can't for the life of me think of a tactful way to avoid this encounter despite the potential for disaster. I opt for bluntness. "Why?"

Kimberlee shifts her eyes from side to side, tilts her head back as if considering. "Because, because we work together. We're part of a team, the performance made me realize that. No sense in having unpleasantness, right?"

"I guess so," I say slowly.

Kimberlee sticks out her hand and takes my limp one to shake. "Good enough."

We walk back to our desks together, to all appearances congenial colleagues. As we take our seats and shuffle through the morning's mail, Kimberlee asks with the utmost indifference, "How's your friend? The tall guy with sun-bleached hair who was at the first performance?"

Understanding dawns. "Kevin, you mean?"

"Yes, that's his name. You see a lot of him?" Kimberlee's hands are busy with anything and everything on her desk. A virtual tornado of papers flies up and around her.

"He's a neighbor *and* a friend," I say, trying to give an undercurrent of warning to the phrase.

"Involved with him, are you?" Still Kimberlee acts nonchalant, straightening a collection of files until they line up like little soldiers.

I can't flat-out lie. Still, I imbue the answer with emotional overtones as if I intend much more than the mere words. "Not really. I've just known him for ages."

"Is he going with anyone?"

"There is this one woman..." I let my voice trail off to avoid a deliberate falsehood. I owe Randi some loyalty.

"Oh." Kimberlee opens a volume of legal opinions. "Well, time to get to work."

I feel no compunction at misleading Kimberlee, I assure myself. If Kevin's crazy enough to be attracted to the blonde, I'll do what I can to save him. And maybe her focus on Kevin will help her forget about Scott.

As if my thoughts somehow conjure him up, Scott appears in the office mid-morning, entering while Kimberlee's on break. He scans the room, walks around the counter to perch on a corner of my desk.

"Hi, gorgeous. What's up?"

I hunch a shoulder in Scott's direction. He has nerve, sauntering in as if five days' lack of notice has evaporated, expecting to find me ready to swoon over his attention.

"I'm busy," I say, frost edging my words.

"Uh-oh." Scott mock-shivers. "Feels chilly in here. I'm in trouble for not calling, right?"

I flick a glance in his direction. "I don't recall you saying you'd call. So how could you be in trouble?"

"I have a reason," Scott coaxes. "I wanted to give you time to recover from your fifteen minutes of fame. I hate being trampled by an adoring crowd." He leans forward to take one of my hands and rub my fingers gently. "What do you say, am I forgiven? Forgiven for wanting to be special to you?"

How can I resist the silent appeal in those ice-blue eyes? I think I see a need there, a masculine isolation that Scott can neither articulate nor even admit to himself.

"Yes," I answer. "And you're already special."

"Then let's make our next evening together outstanding. A symphony perhaps? With dinner in Larimer Square? On Saturday?" Scott assumes my agreement as he stands, giving a final squeeze to my hand. Kimberlee, who has just come in the door, walks to the aisle by her desk, all the time avoiding my eye. With the smallest of hip movements, she blocks Scott's path on his way out, and he maneuvers past with a tiny grimace.

Apprehension taints the two days that follow. Every time I think of the symphony, the dinner, the entire outing, my stomach clenches in a knot as big as a fist. The only symphony I recall attending is "Peter and the Wolf" on a fifth-grade outing that consisted mostly of an agonizing bus ride, during which little boys incessantly yelled out the windows and a girl whispered constantly in my ear. Do people dress up for a concert? I have a vague sense of long velvet gowns and tuxedos, glittering diamonds, opera glasses. And dinner! To balance a wine glass, juggle several pieces of silverware, insure no food falls down the front of a dress, and simultaneously make entertaining conversation!

I face the rendezvous like a dental appointment, with teeth gritted and upper lip stiff. Not a particularly attractive combination, I realize as I pace the narrow space of the elevator after Scott buzzes the intercom downstairs to signal his arrival, and I ride down to join him. I turn to see myself in the mirror at the rear, grimace, rub my cheeks with my fingertips, scrunch the muscles around my mouth back and forth to loosen them. Plaster on a smile as the doors open.

Stunning Scott. Darling Scott. He's studying the list of tenants' names on the mailboxes. How can a man perform an action so mundane and appear the epitome of style at the same time? Tall, straight-backed, wearing a perfect, three-piece, pin-striped suit and subtly patterned tie. Even his shoes are impeccable, their gloss so bright that they reflect the lobby lights. With a murmured greeting and a kiss somewhere in the vicinity of the air above my left ear, Scott ushers me out the security doors.

No traffic jams clog the highways, a parking spot materializes miraculously on the second level of the parking garage. Scott's charm evidently transgresses the bounds of normalcy to affect even physical surroundings. Inside the concert hall, we climb a giant staircase, immured by dowagers in chiffon dresses and furs, identical suit-clad gentlemen, here and there a thin beauty trailing scarf and perfume. I feel as though I'm in a television commercial about people escaping the bounds of hum-drum existence.

The lights in the hall diminish as late-comers seek their seats. I wonder if Scott will grope for my hand in the dark and I wipe my palm on my skirt just in case. But the symphony isn't like a movie theatre where lovers seem to pay more attention to their physical proximity than the film on the screen, for no one's getting cozy. All eyes are trained on the musicians.

After the first few crashing strains from the orchestra, in the overpowering sensation of rivers of sound pouring from the stage, I forget the insistent pull of sensual attraction toward Scott. Harmony, melody, rhythm, music, magic. This is nothing resembling the best sound system and recordings. The performance is *alive*, like the difference between the photo of an iridescent dragonfly and the buzz and shimmer of the real thing. The enchantment sustains me through intermission, the second half of the performance, the finale, and the walk to nearby Larimer Square. Not until Scott and I are seated at a linen-draped table do I recover my senses. What on earth have I been doing during my bemusement, sitting dumb as a stone? Has Scott been trying to chat, only to find me unresponsive?

Evidently not. I must have at least nodded in the right places because here we are in the Russian Restaurant, separate shots of vodka (flavored pepper, lime, and garlic) lined up on the right side of the plates with the innocence and transparency of water. Scott's pointing out an interesting borscht soup on a menu the size of a door. I endorse his selections, then lean back in my chair and sigh.

"That was fantastic."

Scott chuckles. "I thought you were caught up in the performance. One of their better efforts although the oboe section was a trifle overpowering. Perhaps because several of the violas were missing. An affectation of this conductor's, I assume."

Lacking the knowledge or familiarity to comment expertly, I have nothing to reply. I'm a little embarrassed by my own enthusiasm, which helps suppress the faintest twinge of annoyance deep down at Scott's critical attitude.

A waiter bearing a wine bottle as heavy as his accent appears next to the table. I gain a sense of trim bulk, of dark solid safety, that somehow assures me I'm doing fine, making time, talking trash, cutting dash. Well, maybe not that hip, but okay, keeping up. With a twist of his wrist, the waiter shows Scott the label on the bottle of wine he carries, pours a splash in the glass for Scott to sample. As Scott sips, over his head the waiter surveys Scott's bent head, the table, finally me from mouth to fingertips. Is he judging my clothes? My manners? My annoyance swerves from Scott to the waiter.

He might be proficient and knowledgeable in a rugged, peasant sort of way, I think as I notice his broad hands and blunt nails, but no reason exists for him to be patronizing me. The man reminds me of someone. That half-glint of amusement in his eyes. Kevin! That's who! How dare he interject the idea of himself into my date! I can see him as clear as a shot of vodka, sitting at the table with me and Scott, smirking as Scott closes his eyes and swirls the wine around his mouth to savor it. The waiter's observing Scott with the same supercilious expression Kevin's perfected, disguised under furrowed brow, it's true, because he wants a tip.

Maybe Scott seems a bit affected, a little over-done in his tasting. But connoisseurs know the correct methods, focus on the right approach. A professional singer can appear phony in his expressions during a performance, too. Who am I to judge? I throw that last unspoken question in the direction of the illusory Kevin and he disappears.

A sigh escapes my lips. Now I can relax and enjoy Scott's company. Topic of conversation? What's around? Food, diners, posters about Russia, wine, vodka. Turning to him with what I hope is an entranced expression, I ask, "How is vodka made?"

"From potatoes."

"Really?" I nod my head. Why don't our dinners come? This evening seems interminable. I seize the first shot glass of vodka and down it, immediately choking in reflex to the strength of the liquor.

"Although the root word is 'water,' 'voda,' as in the water that's needed to sustain life. Quite common in primitive peoples to label a popular liquor with the name for the most ordinary liquid, 'water.'"

"This tastes like pepper."

"It's a flavored vodka. Try the next," Scott urges.

I do. The first of many tastes, of vodka, several wines, after-dinner liquor. "Dutch courage" I vaguely remember the state I'm seeking is called. Why "Dutch?" Irrelevant. Courage to seize the opportunity to prove to Scott I'm sexy, attractive, cosmopolitan. Somehow I find myself outside again, in Scott's car, driving or floating back to my apartment.

Scott doesn't wait for an invitation to accompany me upstairs nor to enter my flat. And it doesn't seem as if much conversation's going on. In my hazy state, I have a vague sense of a light or two flicking on and off, a candle lit, murmurs in my ear, lovely sensations around my ear and throat and up my back, deep hungry kisses, an erratic trip down the hall, even a careen off the wall, into the bedroom. Clothes flying this way and that as the two of us roll around on the bed.

A continuing sensation underlying the others is persistent stomach unease. Try as I might, I cannot quell the distress. I hear

Scott's accelerated rate of respiration, the sighs that he begins to introduce. They set a counterpoint to the churning in my abdomen. I moan. Scott interprets this as a sign of passion and increases the fervor with which he's stroking me.

Finally I have to bat his arms away and switch on the bedside lamp. I groan again. "No, Scott, I don't feel well. I'm terribly sorry, but you'll have to leave." I wrap my arms around my torso (somehow all my clothing is missing) and manage to peer in Scott's direction.

He must be convinced by my appearance, perhaps my complexion is slightly green, for he doesn't stop to argue or plead. A leap from the bed puts him on the floor, hastily stooping to pick up his pants and shove his legs in, to grab his shirt and tie. But not before I catch a glimpse of French-cut bikini underwear in a bright blue. I'll have to remember to tell Kevin about his error—not burgundy but blue. If I can remember a thing tomorrow. I sink back on the bed with a groan, ignoring Scott's shirttail-flying departure.

A night's rest brings some relief from my over-indulgence. But waves of nausea begin to reoccur in the afternoon. I manage to drag myself to work Monday morning by lecturing myself severely. "I will not get sick. Illness is a state of mind and I will not surrender."

Unfortunately my body does not comprehend. By mid-morning I'm clutching the computer keyboard more than operating it and I keep losing track of my assignment. For a number of moments, I stare at the screen, then gaze at a framed poster of the mountains on the wall, then turn back to the computer.

The lines on the terminal screen (the document mostly with a faint yellow tinge, the help cues in green, the curser blue) waver and blend together. A squint pops them back into their original colors, but it hurts less to let my eyes simply take their natural course, providing a kind of cloudy, multi-hued effect. The red warning keeps flashing off and on as I hit miscellaneous keys, and I become more involved with the colored rhythm I can create with my smallest movements than with the content of the document.

A wave of heat moves from my head downward, followed by an equally strong swell of cold. The extremes clench my jaw and I shake my head to release the spasm. Then the screen moves to my right, followed by the entire room.

Kimberlee's face balloons between me and the screen. "Joan? Joan? You're wavering."

I know I'm not wavering—it's the rest of the scenery. A not unpleasant feeling, rather like spinning around and around when I was a child. I slump in my chair. "I'm fine," I say.

Kimberlee has suddenly gone deaf. "What?" she screams.

"I'm fine," I yell back. The volume sets off echoes in my head and I cover my ears.

An enormous hand appears out of nowhere, approaching as if to smother me, but spreading instead on my forehead. "You're burning up," Kimberlee's voice reverberates. "You should go home."

I try to say, "No," but only a moan comes out.

Time slips by. I feel my coat around my shoulders, someone leading me to the elevator, then outside. The next awareness hits at my apartment door when that someone takes my purse and rummages in it. Finally bed and its cool sheets cradle me, the chalky taste and feel of aspirin, a long drink of water, and ultimately, uniform oblivion.

The homogeneity, to my annoyance, is disturbed by Barbara bundling me into a bathrobe and dragging me off to a white-and-steel office where someone thumps me on the chest and back...hot chicken soup forced down my throat to make me choke and jerk...a sharp, pungent, piney smell accompanied by a gooey feeling on my throat...sweet hot tea filling my mouth until I have to gulp...automatic swallowing of pills, pills, pills. In between, a sweet, safe stupor into which I sink, pulling it around me like a feather pillow.

"Phoebe, Phoebe, life without you is worthless."

A man's low, strong tones underlain by a high-pitched whine rouses me. Who's calling me "Phoebe?" What's a man doing in my bedroom? I try to draw deep, calm breaths, but the air is muggy and heavy. He's trying to smother me! I sit bolt upright in bed.

The voice continues pleading. "I hate forcing you here in front of this judge. I'd much rather we settle things peaceably."

The whine gurgles and chokes, then resumes. A stream of warm air wafts past my face. A vaporizer, I realize, along with the dialogue from one of those court reality shows on television, Barbara's favorite no-brainer pastime. Therefore, Barbara must be here. Bits and pieces of recall fall together. I've been sick, various people helped me, mostly I'd slept. Now I'm hungry.

"Mom?"

The pounding of a gavel answers me. Feminine shrieks from the defendant or plaintiff? I don't know who is who by the voices. The male half of the courtroom litigants grunt some sort of denial. Barbara can't hear my call over the pandemonium on television. Every joint in my body aches, but I force first one leg then the other to the floor, shuffle my way by pushing my feet along the floor to the living room.

I cling to the door frame, panting like an exhausted dog. "Mom!" If ever I needed sympathy and succor (whatever *that* is), it's now. The sound is more of a croak than a word. To add drama to the moment, I sway and hold the back of my hand on my forehead. When there still is no response, I open one eye.

In an overstuffed chair just in front of me, an immobile Barbara appears bound by invisible rope to the television. On the screen, a woman judge is lecturing a teenaged girl dressed in the tightest, lowest tube top I've ever seen. I wonder how anyone in the courtroom can focus on legalities other than decency laws. Barbara's mouth hangs slightly open and her eyelids don't blink.

By leaning forward, I can just reach in front of Barbara, which I do. I wriggle my fingers. "Mom, Mom, I need you." Illness has rendered me as vulnerable and feeble and dependent as a child. My plea gains the volume needed to break through the television's sound track.

"Sweetheart! You shouldn't be up." Barbara hustles me back to bed, stringing reproaches and wise words along the way. "Careful where you step. Lean on me. Now cover up. The doctor said you should be kept warm at all times."

I snuggle under the blankets. "Doctor?" I have a recollection of steel and linen, a curtained cubicle, someone in pale green medical wear.

"You don't remember? You were nearly delirious with fever, so we took you to the emergency room yesterday. I knew working so hard and singing in that skit would be too much for you. Thank God the prescription worked. Can I get you anything? Of course, I can. Chicken noodle soup and juice. Perfect. Just lie here and I'll bring it."

Barbara scurries out before I can ask any questions. I feel deserted as well as isolated. Somewhere on the road to recovery, I'm suddenly convinced I'll expire anyway, bereft of companionship, succorless, without a crust of bread, stinking of medicated rub, hair matted and stringy. I hope Barbara will use the one good photo of me, taken a year ago as a Christmas gift, in the obituary. Two small strands of tears leak from my eyes and I sniffle.

"What's this? What's this?" Barbara returns carrying a large plate serving as a tray upon which she's balanced a blue pottery mug with soup and a plastic glass filled with orange juice. As she sets the tray on the bed stand, the soup spills on the flimsy white paper napkin next to it.

"Feeling sorry for yourself?" Barbara asks. She grabs for a tissue from the box on the bed and gets four or five instead. My dripping nose is her target and she pinches and wipes firmly.

"That's a good sign. Part of the natural progression of convalescence. You should feel sorry for yourself. 'Why me?' you'll be asking yourself. The next step will be a gradual growth of hope."

Barbara's throat seems to cry out for throttling as the advice spews lava-like out of it. I grapple for anything to shut off her unquenchable optimism. Extra-strong blowing of the nose accomplishes the same thing by blocking out her chatter.

"I'll leave you to eat in peace," says Barbara. "I want to see the end of Judge Judy anyway."

With nothing else to do, I crumble a handful of crackers into the soup until it has the consistency of a sopping sponge. A favorite way since childhood to play with my food and extend the soup's saltiness to a lengthy, mouth-filling conclusion. I alternate the semi-liquid soup with gulps of tangy juice, swishing it around my mouth, hardly tasting either with my sinuses blocked.

The television's musical finale swells and abruptly cuts off. Carrying her purse and sweater in one hand, Barbara trips back into the bedroom and swipes the tray and empty dishes with the other hand.

"I learn so much from that show," she comments. "This one had a charming con man taking advantage of an innocent young girl. Reminded me of your father. Hardly a fair match and the judge agreed with me. Well, I'm off. Just remember to take your pills in a few hours."

"What? You're leaving me?" I can't control the panic that swells in me and edges my voice as I picture myself isolated and lonely in my bed. "How will I get to the bathroom? What if I pass out?"

"You'll be okay now. Kevin's taking the evening shift," says Barbara.

"Kevin? Why's he coming?"

"He's been here nearly all the time I couldn't be. The guy's head over heels about you. If you don't grab him, you're crazy."

"What about Scott? Has he showed up?" I ask.

Barbara shakes her head at once. "Nope."

"Telephoned?"

"No. Not a peep, not a sign, except a bouquet." She pauses as if to let the news sink in, then continues, "You want me to help you move to the couch before I go?"

"No." I screw up my face to set the scene for a good cry. "I'd rather feel sorry for myself as you instructed." I throw her words back at her, roll over on my stomach and bury my head in the mound of pillows. Although the physical effect is like trying to breath through a giant marshmallow, the pillows sop up a quart or two of tears along with assorted other liquids and gelatinous secretions from my nose and throat. My body is shaking with giant if silent sobs when I feel rubbing on my back and shoulders and I raise my head, snuffling and hiccupping simultaneously.

"Whatever is wrong? This is certainly an extreme reaction to my departure. You're usually more than willing to see me go," says Barbara. She stops rubbing and lowers herself to sit on the bed next to me.

"I...I feel so aloooooone," I warble.

"I haven't seen you this miserable since you were eleven and had the chicken pox. Remember?" She pushes some loose stringy locks of hair off my forehead.

"Yes. Just after Daddy left. I was devastated. The chicken pox isolated me. There I was miserable, spotty, hot as hell, not even my father around to relieve me from that boxy room that felt like a coffin."

"You had me. Just like now." This is said in such a tiny little squeak, so unlike Barbara's usual full-throated tones, that I think I've hurt her not-so-delicate feelings.

Fearful to let words tumble like marbles out of my mouth, I stop, thereby allowing myself the opportunity to think, move back in time, evaluate my experiences and responses during that period. Twelve, eleven, ten, as I regress, emotions I haven't experienced, and certainly have never explored since that time, rise like shadows. I let them take shape, solidify. I pick my way carefully among them, reporting what I'm experiencing so that Barbara as well as I can understand them.

I close my eyes and words form themselves. "You always were there. That's not bad, not a criticism. You were the bedrock. But Daddy was the lodestone, the magnetic center to all my wishes. He'd call me Brick and tease me about being pudgy, then turn around one-hundred-eighty degrees and praise me for my ladylike manners. I never knew where I stood with him. Everyone idolized him—me, you, my friends, all our neighbors. He could have beat the mayor in an election, hands down."

A pause so long it's significant makes me open my eyes. Barbara is staring at her hands, which are clenched together as if she's hiding something precious within those manicured and lotioned fingers. She speaks slowly, each word ejected with effort, torn from her throat. "You knew your father had a girlfriend, didn't you?"

"A girlfriend? He had lots of friends."

"No I mean a girlfriend girlfriend."

"Well, sure," I answer. "I figured that out when I grew up. And it would account for his desertion."

"I haven't been totally honest with you," Barbara says. "He didn't have just the one girl friend when you were ten. He was compulsive. Any time a pretty woman walked by, he had to try his luck. In such a small town, it made things difficult for me."

"That was just Daddy's way," I object. "He was totally charming."

"No. I mean, yes, he was charming. But no, it wasn't occasional harmless flirting. The first time was when I was in the hospital having you. And it continued over and over and over. It got so I was terrified to go to the market or dry cleaners in case he was getting it on with a clerk behind my back and she'd be smirking at me for my stupidity."

"And then, the ultimate betrayal. Daddy deserted us," I say.

Another lengthy pause from Barbara. Her eyelashes flutter until her eyes open extra-wide. She reaches for my hands and holds on tight. "There's more. That I never told you. I wasn't sure at the time if I made the right decision. And hearing you talk about your childhood, I wonder even more if I was wrong. But I need to confess so you have all the facts. So you can see how they fit into your life, your relationships." She takes a breath so deep it doubles the size of her chest.

"Your father didn't desert us. I kicked him out. Threatened him that I'd disappear with you, he'd never see you again, if he didn't give me a divorce. Then, when he died in the car accident a few months later, it was too late to change the situation. There," she releases my hands, "I've confessed. Blame me if you will, shout, swear, shriek, cry. I thought it was for the best. It certainly was the best for me. But maybe, I think now, not for you."

I'm flabbergasted, speechless, absolutely bowled over. Barbara the honest? Barbara the scrupulous? So forthright that she puts a

Girl Scout or a minister to shame? "But, but, you didn't just let me think he'd walked out on us. You actually told me that."

Barbara nods and a faint flush mounts her cheeks.

"You flat-out lied?" Anger gives me the strength to struggle to sit straighter against the head of the bed. "Then Daddy didn't want to leave me?" There is no need to wait for her answer. "How could you? I assumed he loved you. He left because of me, that I'd done something to make him despise me. I magnified every shortcoming into an insurmountable flaw. I was never smart enough for him, so I stopped trying in school. Not thin, so what was the use of dieting?"

"I'm sorry," says Barbara. "That's the decision I made at the time. Maybe, today, I'd do things differently. But you'll learn as you grow up—you just have to live with your mistakes sometimes."

I'm still furious. "Something like the disappearance of a father leaves a child feeling...hollow...with nothing solid inside...constantly hungry for a connection. I worshipped him. He was the center of my life even if he didn't mean much to you."

She reaches for my hand and tries to stroke it, but I yank it away and hide it under my cover. She continues as if I haven't reacted. "Your father was a manipulator. Charming, I admit, but a con man. Everything had to revolve around him, every woman had to adore him, every man got a slap on the back or a punch in the arm. There was no room for something as mundane as a family. That's the main reason I never liked James. Even in high school, he reminded me of your dad, the big basketball star, could have any girl he wanted, and he chose you...*you!* You were so thrilled. I wanted to shake you and scream that you were worth ten of him."

I lean back against my pillows and feel my face twisting into a grimace. "Come on, Mom. Wasn't it a simple matter of jealousy? Of you putting yourself first, before Daddy, before me?"

Now I've done it! Barbara jumps up and clenches her hands so tightly her knuckles stand out white. "That goes to show how little you know. He never broke his neck trying to fight the court order or even get in contact with you, so I always felt vindicated. After the car accident, you were so emotional, so upset about his death, I was terrified you'd blame me for that. You weren't the most rational, logical person when you were a teenager. But I should have explained the type of man he was to you when you were a child."

I sag back against the pillows. I don't know if I'm hurt or relieved or curious or disappointed over this astounding revelation. I do know that I feel distinctly ill again, as if I don't have the energy to twitch. This must show in my face because Barbara turns, grabs her sweater and shrugs it on.

"I'm sorry to spring this on you when you're recovering, but I couldn't stand the deception any longer. To hear you blaming yourself for our split, to think that over the years you continued to run yourself down, it was too much. Surely the truth, even this late, is better for you to know so you can put all this behind you and move on. Tell me I've done right." She wraps her arms around the dark blue wool of her torso as if fighting a tremendous chill.

I can't reassure her. I'm helpless against the anger that starts to mount. Still under the hold of my illness, my words tumble out with no censor. "What you did was terrible," I spit. "To lie like that to a child, to *me*."

"Our lives, your father's and mine, were the lie," she answers. "Pretending every day that he cared for us. We were nothing but a backdrop, the little details he needed to complete his picture of his perfect life in a small town. My words may have been false, but my actions were absolutely true."

As sudden as a gunshot I sit up. "That's a lie. He cared for me. Maybe not for you. Maybe you're the whole reason he couldn't stay faithful. You drove him away. You forced him to leave me and he loved me. He did, he did. Now get out. I can't stand the sight of you. Anyway, I'm exhausted. And turn that crap off as you leave," I toss at her departing back.

Minus Barbara and the television, the apartment is too quiet, a regular isolation chamber in which my thoughts can pursue one another like a puppy chasing its own tail around and around. Leaning back against the headboard, I slowly fall into a kind of a stupor. A series of images cycle—James, once the foundation of my every action and emotion, Scott, desirable yet distant, Barbara and Dolores, mouths flapping with advice, advice, Kevin, friendly as a big-footed puppy. Where does my father fit in, that ghostly figure so transparent after twenty years' absence I can't bring his face to mind?

I've no protection against Barbara's appeal, much as I wish I could sustain my anger. I feel it fading, slipping away even as I think. It was us against the world for so long before my wedding and since the failure of my marriage, when she stepped up again. I remember her words the day I tangled with James over the sale of the house. "I'll be here to help you in any way you want. All you have to do is give me a nod. A shoulder to cry on, a companion for a glass of wine, a timely loan. Whatever you need. Even a pair of hands to houseclean."

Kevin materializes by the bed and I let loose a scream and sit straight up. "How did you get in?"

He holds up a key. "Barbara gave me your spare." Kevin pulls a chair close to me. "You look better."

"My mother said you've been taking care of me." I don't mean to make my statement sound like an accusation, but it comes out that way, more like I'm attacking her than relaying a simple fact.

"You must be getting well," Kevin says with a grin. "You've regained your spunk."

I hate that word. Also "spirit," "moxie," "grit," "nerve," and "pluck." Descriptions for a sassy, back-talking woman who won't stay in her place. Also, frequently, an euphemism for a girl whose looks are only fair to middling.

I snap my fingers. "This for your spunk. I don't like the idea of your watching me in my pajamas."

"Why not?" Kevin's amused. "I've seen you in a lot less."

"Not virtually unconscious. Let it go. Fill me in on the past two days. They're a bit hazy."

The room begins to whirl and I close my eyes. With light fingers, Kevin pushes me down. "I'll tell you if you lie quietly. You picked up some sort of bug. You were run-down and it wiped you out. The high temperature made you delirious. You were out of touch off and on until the antibiotic took hold."

"How did I eat? Go to the bathroom?"

"You weren't hungry and you had help with the essentials." Kevin's grin reappears.

"I'd say you went beyond the call of duty," I respond.

"That's what friends are for. Now we have to build you back up."

He slaps my blanket-covered knees and abandons me to solitary confinement for half an hour. I pass the time by chewing my fingernails. Then, recalling a trick from childhood, I close one eye and hold my thumb up in front of the other to cover objects from the room in my line of vision, pretending that, like Alice, I've grown to giant size. An occasional bang or rattle proves that Kevin still is in the apartment. Finally he returns, balancing two plates loaded with grilled cheese sandwiches and cottage cheese and fruit salad, two wine glasses and a bottle of cheap red wine.

"This will put you well on the road to recovery," he says, pouring the wine from shoulder height. Not a drop spills.

I'm dubious about the benefits of alcohol. "Are you sure?" I ask even as I sip. The fruity flavor slides down my throat and seems to spread relaxation immediately to my limbs.

"No. But it will help you sleep."

"I've been sleeping constantly," I complain with a yawn.

"Don't pass out until you eat," warns Kevin. He follows his own instructions by biting into his sandwich.

The snack doesn't take long to finish, but a refill of wine extends the meal into a companionable silence which I finally break because the topic's been preying on my mind since Barbara let loose with her mind-blowing revelation.

"Barbara was here all afternoon," I begin mildly. Kevin nods. "She admitted to something she did to me a long time ago. Something terrible. Made me furious." The relaxed slope of Kevin's shoulders and back deserts him as he realizes I'm unburdening myself.

"She forced my father away when I was a kid. Made him leave. Then she lied and told me he deserted us." I hold my breath.

I don't know what I expect, but it's not silence. When Kevin doesn't respond, I answer for him. "That's about the worst thing you can do to a child, take her father away. Then lie to her. Isn't it? Isn't it?" I find myself sitting bolt upright again.

"It depends," says Kevin.

"On what?" I beg. Maybe I want a justification, a reason for Barbara's actions.

"On the alternative," he says. "Maybe the situation in your family was so terrible, that the split was an improvement. Maybe lying to you while you were little was a way to protect you."

I throw myself back on my pillow. "You're just trying to find an excuse for her," I accuse.

"I've found," Kevin says, "when I was younger, life was all blacks and whites. Rights and wrongs. But the older I get, the grayer they become. I see subtleties, distinctions never apparent before. They actually make life and people more interesting. I guess that's part of growing up."

He doesn't need to hit me over the head with a brick to drive home his point and I realize I'm rising on a tide of joy that Kevin is here with me. A thought occurs to me and I voice it as a question hidden behind another yawn hidden behind my hand.

"I've been wondering. You mentioned friendship. I always thought of you as more James's friend than mine. But it's nearly night and you've just spent several days taking care of me in the closest quarters possible. Before that, you found my apartment, helped me lose weight, stood beside me when James left. You never mention him. Did you feel you had to choose between us when we split up?"

Kevin looks at the clock as if checking my facts or avoiding the question. The shadows in the room have lengthened with nightfall and his eyes are pools of darkness. His head turns toward me.

"Nooo." He draws out the word until it becomes a sigh. "I have a confession. James and I were great friends in high school many years ago. Then staying in contact became a habit, a base I'd touch when I came back to town. Over time, though, I felt closer to you. I saw both of you change and grow in different directions and you and I seemed to have more in common. When your marriage ended,

I didn't face a choice. Even sick and throwing up, you mean more to me than James."

"I never guessed," I say, feeling humbled by Kevin's admission but not knowing what else to say.

"I know you didn't." He shrugs. "Many things in life take us by surprise." On this enigmatic note he stands. "Time for me to be going and you to get your rest. Call if you need anything."

I grab his hand before he can leave. "Kevin? Thanks."

His fingers tighten around mine. "You're welcome. I'll lock the door after myself."

As I drift away, thoughts of Kevin's friendship and kindness wrap around me. So different from James, who responded to any demonstration of my personal needs by barking like a drill sergeant, "Tough it out" or "Stop feeling sorry for yourself." Or my father, ignoring my requests or wishes unless they duplicated his. It's nice to be pampered once in a while.

The nature of my illness leaves me weak for days. Kevin and I fail to resume our walks or gym visits. I spend most hours napping, so even the occasions when we shared coffee or borrowed videos are eliminated. Mr. Horowitz insists that I take as much time as needed to recover. The news, delivered by an unexpected visitor, Kimberlee, is accompanied by a fistful of newsletter articles from law firms about the Revue as well as a framed copy of the program autographed by the entire staff from the firm and a fruit basket that immediately tempts both of us into a binge. Finally Kimberlee leaves, assuring me there is absolutely no need to scurry back the office.

That means time to be filled and no strength to pursue any activities except eating. "Comfort foods" many of them are called. Dishes that remind me of childhood or an emotional high point. Like tomato soup sprinkled with pepper, a mainstay after late night dates in high school. Spaghetti wolfed straight from the can. Hot and buttery popcorn for those long, classic movies on television and ice cream and sugared cereals from the box during Saturday morning cartoons. My loose-fitting pajamas disguise the pounds I'm adding.

Until my inevitable return to work. The first dress I try on hugs my torso like a glove. Must have shrunk in the wash, I think. When the second outfit is just as snug, I weigh myself. Nearly seven pounds have mysteriously returned, most of it residing on hips and thighs. Maybe no one will notice, I think as I select a looser skirt. After all, thirteen pounds still are gone.

Kimberlee observes and remarks. "Your furlough certainly made an impact," she says. "You look much...," she searches for a word, "healthier...than when you left."

My relationship with Kimberlee is tenuous enough to make me uncertain of Kimberlee's meaning. I decide to take the statement as a joke. "More of me to love. Thanks for rescuing me when I nearly fainted."

Evidently the right approach, for Kimberlee says, "No problem," and waves aside the acknowledgement. "Now it's time to get back to the grind. I'll catch you up on the files you're handling."

Kimberlee notices me flipping through the billing screens, a single finger tapping up and down. When I say with the enthusiasm of a squashed cockroach, "It appears I didn't need to rush back," Kimberlee hides a smile.

"To the contrary, we broke our necks on your behalf. We didn't want you to have to face a mountain of work on your first day. So we all stayed overtime yesterday."

"What a relief. I was worried that I wasn't missed. It wouldn't speak well for my future with the firm."

"After you won the Revue for us? I'm surprised the partners haven't put you on retainer just to perform. Now, back to work."

"Okay, slave driver." I return to my computer.

The morning seems to evaporate and I welcome the lunch hour like it's a happy hour in a bar. "I must be weaker than I thought," I confide to Dolores. "I can barely drag my feet in front of each other."

"You need nourishment," Dolores answers. "Here, try the apple pie."

I scream and hold up a palm to ward off temptation. "No, no. I've gained seven pounds at home."

"Good. You were too thin. Men like a little meat."

The rattle of silverware attracts our attention and my whole body energizes. Scott's studying the menu of the day's specials. Incandescence seems to emanate from him, his russet hair and skin glows, an aura surrounds his body. He turns, sees me, does a double-take, swings back to the menu. I wait patiently by the cash register where I block the passage of a line of impatient lunchers and catch a number of malign glares. A short woman shoulders me, narrowly missing drenching me with vegetable soup.

Scott receives his order, places it on a tray, and slides the meal down the counter with infinitesimal slowness, almost as though he's avoiding me. That's impossible, I counter to myself. Didn't he send flowers? He even called several times, mentioning how much he missed me, wishing I'd allow him to visit. Which I wouldn't, I remind myself sternly, not wanting to expose him to my bug. I resolutely refuse to think Kevin's unfaltering attendance.

"Hi," I greet Scott breathlessly.

"Hello, yourself," he says. "Back at work, I see."

"Yes. The doctor's pronounced me fully recovered." I step to one side, waiting to follow Scott to a booth.

"Uh, I've got to return to the office. Big case coming up. See you later."

Scott disappears faster than a blink. Slack-jawed, I stare after him. What's happened to his impatience to see me? I can't remember much about our date—it's all a haze at this point. Did I say something to offend him? Disgust him with my behavior that night? How can I know if he won't talk to me? Panic at the thought of his sudden desertion drives me to wolf down my lunch. To get back to my own little desk where work will keep my mind off Scott.

But there is Kimberlee with her enigmatic ability to sense tension even hidden layers beneath routine. The electric pencil sharpener sings for each of the twenty instruments I insert until their points look like miniature spears.

"Are you a witch?" I ask after Kimberlee nags and nags for a response to her inquiry about what's bugging me.

"No," says Kimberlee. "If you sharpen a handful of pencils down to nubs, something's obviously bothering you. Are you sick again? Worried about the office break-in?"

I shake my head silently. "I don't think I can tell you."

"Why not?"

"It's about someone we both know." I sniff back a surge of emotion but don't dare glance at Kimberlee.

With humor dry as dust, Kimberlee says, "One guess. A certain tall attorney who sub-leases an office from us, right?"

I nod. "I know you dated him," I begin. Then thoughts and feelings come tumbling out ramble-scramble. "Maybe you even still care for him. But I really thought he and I were starting to....I mean, I went out with him twice, he called when I was sick....then I saw him today, and he, he avoided me. Like I had chicken pox or v.d. I started getting sick when we were out, so I must not have been very good company. He's probably given up on me. Are you two back together? Have you seen him with anyone else?" I hold my breath, torn between wanting news, any news, and avoiding an answer I prefer not to hear.

Kimberlee shuffles and stacks the papers clutched in her hand before she responds. "No, I'm interested in another man. Scott and I never were a couple, no matter what you think. We had coffee a couple of times is all. But, Joan, you don't really know this guy. You're infatuated with an image you've created out of air."

"Now you sound like Kevin," I accuse. Something flickers across Kimberlee's face, but she says nothing. "I'm not naive. I'm not a scared virgin waiting to be seduced by the evil villain."

"That's what you might think, but there's something icky about him. I can't put my finger on it. Something not quite right."

I refuse to believe her remarks since they must come from jealousy. "I just want a chance at the first good man that's come my way since my divorce. Looks like I won't get it."

My sniffle turns into a sob in my throat. Not again. Unable to disguise my emotions since my illness, I'm on the verge of crying. I hear the door to the office open and Kimberlee thrusts the papers at me.

"Here. Take these into the back office," Kimberlee says.

Grateful for the escape, I flee. In the room I stack the papers on a cabinet and cling to the door. Scott's voice drifts in, reminding me of the previous time I overheard a conversation between him and Kimberlee.

"So our little friend's back." A faintly patronizing sneer colors Scott's voice.

My knees feel weaker, I think. And my stomach's lurching, too. Is the flu reoccurring? No, my fear about Scott's opinion toward me, and a sinking sensation that I've revealed myself too clearly to Kimberlee, are responsible.

Papers rustle. "Yes, she's returned. Still somewhat frail," replies Kimberlee. "You're seeing her?"

"I see a lot of people," says Scott, "including you."

"She's not used to your games," Kimberlee warns.

"That's why she's so refreshing," replies Scott.

His voice grows fainter, stops, and then a door closes. Kimberlee enters the back office. "You heard everything?" she asks.

I nod, feeling as low as the hardwood floor. "Doesn't sound like he's much interested."

"I don't know about that. I think he's intrigued but doesn't want to admit it. You're not exactly a duplicate of his normal type."

"What's that? No, don't tell me. Like you. Sophisticated, pulled together, unshakeable. Wearing sleek, black gowns or the latest, high-class fashions."

Kimberlee folds her arms across her silk suit, squints one eye in my direction, checks me out up and down. "There's some truth to what you say. I don't mean you dress poorly or strange or so passersby point and laugh. You look...normal. It's more a matter of making fashion a priority. Featuring the unexpected like that!" Kimberlee snaps her fingers together.

I open my mouth to speak. Close it. Bite my tongue. Need and a tentative trust loosen my jaw. "Would you, could you help me? Give me advice?"

Kimberlee straightens up and smoothes the nubby stone-colored material of her skirt down her legs. "Why, Joan, I'm flattered. But I think you're better off staying who you are. There are real disadvantages to the alternative."

"I can't imagine what those could be." I step back and restack the papers to give myself some time, thonking them up and down until the edges are absolutely uniform with one another. Should I be completely honest or will I risk revealing a weakness? I think about Saint Joan. Total honesty guided her every confrontation and she did pretty well. Up to the very end, of course. I take a deep breath and proceed. "Why are you being so nice to me? Until the Revue, you acted as if I were a piece of litter someone dropped in the corner. Then you warmed up and now you're positively chummy."

"You want to know the truth?"

"I'd appreciate it."

A tapping of her toe precedes Kimberlee's words. "Hmmph. I was furious with you. You remind me of myself. When you started here, you crept in the office, poked away at your computer, every morning and night hiding the pain and rejection you felt from your empty house. It hurt too much to see you. I've been through a bad divorce myself. When I saw you, I wanted to shake you and tell you that your ex isn't worth the anguish. Yell at you to toughen up. Well, maybe this exercise in futility with Scott will build your protective shell. Or maybe he'll surprise me and turn into a real human."

"I'd like a chance to activate the transformation," I say with a glint of humor that surprises myself. "Although I can't believe a guy so gorgeous on the outside can be terrible on the inside."

"He's not terrible, just a below-average male. Meaning all the tendencies toward self-centeredness, immaturity, and hell-bent pleasure-seeking are magnified," says Kimberlee with her own fillip of sarcasm as we leave the back office together.

I resume work on my computer. The thought crosses my mind that Kimberlee could be belittling Scott because she doesn't have any ties on him. Scott certainly would explain Kimberlee that way.

Well, none of my business. My concern is attracting Scott, not analyzing him.

Monday night should be gym night if I'm going to get back into my routine. The thought of pedaling a stationary bike, lifting my knees on a stair master, or lugging dumbbells around makes me cringe. But Kevin will come beating on my door in any case, if I don't show up, so I might as well drag myself along for a curtailed sequence, reconstruct the habit.

As we walk to the gym across the park, Kevin borders on the jovial, a strange state for a weekday evening with nothing more tempting ahead than a workout and maybe a television detective program.

He's whistling with great vigor when he breaks off to ask, "How was work? You didn't exhaust yourself?"

"No. Kimberlee and the others covered for me while I was sick. I saw Scott, too, but he acted strange. By the way, did I tell you he does wear French-cut bikini underwear, but in blue?"

Kevin stops so fast that I find myself several steps ahead. "You saw his underwear?"

"Yes. When the bug started hitting me. A rather passionate scene interrupted by my upset stomach. Not the most attractive sequence. Wine, candlelight, me groaning in pain."

Kevin throws back his head and guffaws. "I'm sure. Blue bikini, I knew it. You quite ruined his seduction."

"You maintained his underwear would be burgundy. And it's not fair to laugh at someone's clothes."

"It is if they're pretentious." Kevin resumes his walk.

In the gym the sight of myself and some new bulges in workout attire sends me wailing out from the locker room to Kevin in the weight room.

"Help. Help," I say to Kevin's broad back. He waves a hand in my direction without turning around, so I tug on it. "Help. I've gained weight. I need my coach again."

His body has been hiding something. Or someone. As Kevin swings toward me, Kimberlee's blonde head appears, carefully coifed as ever, not a drop of sweat marking her shiny Lycra outfit. Kimberlee struggles to smooth her face and assume tranquil nonchalance before she smiles a greeting,

"Kimberlee! I didn't know you worked out here." I've never seen her at this gym before. Despicable suspicion rears its wavering specter in my mind. Kimberlee has made her interest in Kevin obvious, but to pursue him in this fashion is inexcusably predatory. What is he, a squirrel under the eye of a hawk? A deer stalked by a mountain lion? A bit of cheese to lure a mouse? Why does my every thought turn to food? I shake this off to stare at Kevin.

Kevin's bland affability reveals nothing of his attitude. No, it's more of a smirk. Unforgivable, the immensity of the male ego.

Throughout the evening, I have to endure the bizarre sight of Kimberlee asking Kevin for directions on the equipment as well as the equally unnerving appearance of Kevin complying with apparent pleasure. Kevin hadn't expended this much effort teaching *me* the routines. The woman's attempts to attract Kevin are so blatant, I can't understand how Kevin can succumb.

The gym is closing down, lights flickering to signal all-clear-out, when I wave Kimberlee in front of me toward the locker room, so I can loiter by the hall to attack Kevin.

"What is she doing here?" I hiss behind my hand in Kevin's direction.

"She asked about a good gym. I thought you and she were getting along recently."

"We are. Much better than before. But I don't want to be haunted by the sight of her day *and* night." With that parting shot, I march smartly into the locker room.

Wanting to avoid girl-talk with Kimberlee, I swamp myself in the shower. Steam clouds billow through the tiled corridors before I drag myself, limp-boned and glowing, from the water. A survey of the locker room shows no Kimberlee, thank God. It takes only five minutes to get dressed, a fortunate occurrence because Kevin gets impatient if he has to wait too long for me.

I needn't have worried about the time. As I exit from the building, I spy Kevin and Kimberlee in the farthest corner of the concrete terrace in front, plastered against one another in a passionate embrace. My heart feels like it stops for about ten minutes, then races madly.

CHAPTER TWELVE

Kimberlee spots me first because she faces the door. Her eyelids flutter open and she jumps back out of Kevin's arms. "Hi, Joan. I was just asking Kevin if he wanted a ride home."

"I can see that. You'll have a little difficulty driving with two of you in one seat. However, he can choose for himself, but I certainly don't want one. I need the exercise."

I ignore the paved pathway and set off straight across the grass, knees and elbows pumping high, breath swelling out of lungs that work overtime. I move so quickly I'm under a stand of trees before Kevin starts after me.

I hear his faint goodbyes to Kimberlee and his calls of, "Wait up, wait up!" Then the sound of his panting closer and closer. Feel his hand grab my arm and pull me to a halt. I whirl around to face him.

"What's the idea?" he says.

"Funny thing, some particularly acute perception on my part told me I'd be interrupting." Damn that instant sarcasm!

"I wouldn't have left you to get home on your own, you know that."

"I didn't know. You couldn't have gotten a dime between the two of you, so absorbed you were in your activity." I continue to shoot myself in the foot with my sharp words.

There, on a clear black autumn night, in the beginnings of a teeth-chattering chill, under branches whose leaves are just beginning to fall, Kevin and I shout through our first real argument. You-could-have's and I-should-have's deteriorate into petty accusations and head-tossing denials.

I win the award for worst behaved when I expose a confidence. "And what about Randi?" I say this with great triumph as if I hold the winning hand in a poker game.

"Randi?" Kevin looks around. Is she hiding somewhere? "What about Randi?" he echoes in bewilderment.

"You'll break her heart, that's what."

"Randi has no heart," Kevin replies with confidence. "She has a little calculator ticking away in her chest instead."

"That's what you think. Her dearest hope is that you and she will...that someday she and you can...she wants the best for you," I finish lamely, eventually realizing I shouldn't be revealing someone else's secret.

"You've finally done it, gone completely bonkers. Me and Randi. You are so desperate for romance, any romance, that you're fabricating attachments in your mind."

"Me, desperate for romance?" My voice rises to a shriek that echoes across the open space of the park. "Anyone who'd put moves on that skinny cold stick of a woman is the desperate one. Haven't gotten much lately, Kevin? Or do you need a constant stream and variety of women to satiate you?"

Never before have I seen the ugly sneer on Kevin's face which now distorts every feature. "That's what really bothers you. She's thin. You're jealous because she looks the way you'd like to."

So angry the words build up behind my tongue, I sputter. "You're...you're despicable. A worm. Less than a worm. The ground beneath a worm."

In the incandescence of a streetlight flickering between the shuddering leaves, Kevin and I stare at each other across the small but unbridgeable space of a foot. I feel like a steel rod passes through my entire body, immobilizing me. What are we doing to each other? What am *I* doing? This is my good friend, *best* friend, Kevin who's stood by me through divorce, a move, illness. In the shifting shadows I think I see a quiver run across Kevin's jaw, then he passes his palm over his face, hunches his shoulders inward, finally straightens.

I want to touch his cheek with my fingertips, coax a smile back, heal the hurt between us. "Kevin?" I choke out and step across the gap to put my arms around him and offer comfort. For a second I fear he'll push me away, but he relaxes and hugs me back. "That was really stupid," I say into Kevin's shoulder. "You're such an old friend, I want more than anything that you wind up with the right woman. I'm sorry."

"I'm sorry, too," he says. "More than you can ever know."

We stand silently holding each other. Beneath my hands, surrounding my body, I feel Kevin's solidness like a wall guarding me. I lean into him to increase the sense of security. A slight tang of soap from the shower, the piquant autumn-tinged fragrance of damp wool, the blessed warmth and toasted hint of skin scent envelope me in a miasma dangerous for its associations. Unbidden memories of the other time when we pressed together gather at the edges of my consciousness. Kevin's large hands moving over my body. His kisses, soft and hard.

Am I going crazy? So sex-starved I'd allow these thoughts to disrupt my affinity with Kevin again? I should be thinking of Kevin's well-being. He deserves a great relationship—stable, loving, exciting. I step back to break the embrace.

"Let's forgive each other and get home before we turn into icicles," I joke.

We each shoulder our separate burdens—me, a tote and he, a gym bag. We walk, separate but equal, through the knife-sharp chill of wind. I continue to ponder Kevin's condition as an attractive man with a strong sex drive who's not interested in pursuing a relationship with an equally appealing woman (Randi) because she's too much a friend, but who clearly requires some sort of female companionship because he's searching for it. As a woman, I have a responsibility to my compatriots. I draw a deep breath when we approach the apartment's front door.

"One last suggestion, Kevin," I say. "Then I'll be quiet on the subject forever. Kimberlee's not good enough for you. You don't have to settle for what's at hand. If you'd just make a small push, get out and meet more people. If you're not interested in Randi, I can go places with you so you can see the singles scene. Or fix you up with some real great women." Who those might be, I have no idea, but I'll locate them if Kevin agrees.

Kevin's prior emotion was mere irritation compared to the thrust of anger I now hear in his tone, although his body is as controlled as ever. "I have no intention of becoming seriously involved with anyone. Kimberlee, Randi, Paris Hilton. Don't try to change me, Joan," he says. "I don't need or want your help. Do you understand?"

More ominous than yelling or threats or accusations is this flat command. Wordless, I nod, happy that the elevator appears to whisk us to our separate apartments, away from tension so tight it could recoil instantaneously to destroy us both.

On our floor, each of us goes immediately to his own door. No lingering, no casual invitations or even words of parting. I'm left to dwell on the whys and wherefores of the evening, most of which reflect poorly on me. What possessed me? I cloak myself with the wounded obsessions of a rejected lover. Friendship could not excuse my interference, nor affection, my meddling. With friends like me, Kevin doesn't need enemies. Perhaps tonight was an emotional residue from my illness and Scott's unresponsiveness. Did Joan of Arc behave in this fashion when the Dauphin needed her? No! I resolve to be stronger, self-sufficient, more supportive of Kevin's desires even if they don't center on Randi.

Several days later, flat out of edibles, I'm forced to make a visit to the local market. The grocery store's lights promise refuge from a sleeting rain that's been fluctuating between drops and flakes all day, as if the weather can't make up its mind what to do. I slam the car door, duck my head, and run like hell to the entry, dodging streaks of ice-dripping water. The slippery tile floor, ankle-deep in muck, makes balance tenuous. I could hang on to a grocery cart, but since all the ones I see are coated with frosty detritus, I prefer to push with fingertips only.

Humming under my breath in accompaniment with a sanitized version of "Louie, Lou-aaa" over the store's sound system, I browse the fruit and vegetable section. Carrots a bit woody, onions and potatoes in their prime, broccoli over-priced, squash perfect. Eyes on the bananas, I turn the corner without full attention and succeed in banging my cart into an innocent bystander. I plaster on an automatic smile of apology, jiggle my head to focus, and take a moment to recognize Scott. (Thank God I kept my makeup on after work!) He's now in casual clothes—chino burmuda shorts and pullover. But the pullover is clearly cashmere in the multi-hundred dollar range.

"Oh, hi," I stammer. "I didn't expect to run into you here. Literally run into. Sorry. I never imagine people I know doing regular-old things, like grocery shopping."

Scott bends over my cart and pokes the contents. "Kind of heavy on the veggies. On a diet? You have added a few pounds." He grins as if he's made a witticism, smooths his hair with a hand and flashes his perfect white teeth in a grin.

Preparing to shrink away in shame of my newly re-plumped figure, I instead notice that Scott has something stuck in the corner of a tooth. What is it? I can't quite make out the color. Tomato? Chocolate? Whatever it is, it draws my attention so totally that I struggle to tear my observation away from Scott to look somewhere, anywhere else. But isn't it a universal law that you can't pry your eyes away from a horrifying sight? And maybe because we're standing in the produce section, I'm reminded of all the hackneyed jokes about the unromantic nature of food in one's teeth. I start choking down the giggles. Should I tell him or keep quiet? I really have no choice. I simply must make my escape before I collapse on the floor. I mumble an excuse about my frozen foods and take off, guffaws trailing after me.

The laughing spell dispels much of the romantic ambiance that normally fogs my vision of Scott. Doesn't the marriage ceremony say "for better, for worse, for richer, for poorer, in sickness and in health?" If the idea of Scott-flawed turns me off, maybe I'm not in love with him. I have to admit I've never said, even thought, I'm in love with Scott, only that it would be nice to be in love with Scott. Or with anyone.

What about when I was sick? Was Scott repelled by the concept of my illness, like I'm repelled by his teeth? Is that why he hadn't visited? Still, some people stood by me. Did Kevin have to struggle against an initial squeamishness? Did I turn Kevin's stomach? All that moaning and groaning, delirium, sweating until my hair stuck to my head in strands, and worst—actual vomiting! No, I'm sure I hadn't repulsed him. He's my oldest friend, has seen me fat and thin, crying and laughing, young and not-so-young. Sounds kind of like the marriage ceremony. Although what the status of our friendship is at this point, I don't know. I may have put serious strain on his typical patience and affability.

I survey the produce section. Greens wave their leafy fronds toward me, bacon bits and ready-made croutons tempt. I think of the spaghetti I can throw together in a few tasty minutes and vow to redeem myself with Kevin by inviting him over to dinner tonight. The conditions between us can't be as bad as I fear.

No, Kevin isn't busy that evening, although he hums and hahs around the fact. Yeeees, he can come to dinner, even though he's obviously reluctant. Yes, he's both hungry and polite. No, he isn't approachable and friendly. Still it's a beginning, a resurrection of cordiality, I think as I pour us both a second glass of wine.

This serving fulfills its purpose by tinting the walls, ceiling, stoneware and glasses, the streaked wood grain of the tables, even the insides of my eyes with a roseate glow. Or the glow may emanate from inside me as I relax into an overstuffed chair. Kevin's done the same on the companion sofa beside me.

In fact, he's stretched nearly full-length, his fingers locked behind his head, head braced on the low back of the couch, eyes closed, legs propped on the coffee table. I watch the slow rise and fall of Kevin's chest and wonder if he's fallen asleep.

Light from the lamp falls in an uneven pool over Kevin's face and chest. I make no effort to rouse him or to fill the silence with conversation, music, or television chatter. It's kind of peaceful here, I think, protected and sheltered from the agitation at work and the emotional turmoil of social relationships. I don't have to pretend with Kevin, act like he's God's gift to me, or that every word is something I'll treasure. I don't need to wear makeup or put on fashionable clothes. I can just be me.

Kevin opens his eyes slowly and blinks. In those first few, unguarded seconds when he surfaces from sleep to awake, a slow, easy smile creases his face. No hint of rancor or resentment lingers, although a clump of tomato sauce drying at the corner of his mouth bears witness to his enthusiastic dining habits.

"Sorry, I dozed off," he says. He stretches his left arm high above his head and rubs his face with his right hand, leaving a smeared trail of scarlet spaghetti sauce behind.

The smudge draws my attention utterly. I can't tear my eyes away. Should I tell him? Ignore it? It's, well, it's endearing. This doesn't make sense. Scott's imperfection repelled, Kevin's defect appeals. I stare so hard that the edges of my vision constrict like the murky blur around the circumference of the eyepiece as you focus through a microscope. A kind of pulse seems to throb around, within and from Kevin. It delves, reaches, for something far inside me, a response, a reverberation, which it meets and mingles with, moving to, then expanding within my chest until I feel it will burst.

Instead the sensation erupts from out of my lungs through my mouth as a whoop of laughter. I actually roll on the chair doubled over. The joke is on me. Somehow I've been hiding an affinity for Kevin behind infatuation with Scott. Affinity? More like obsession. Why else do I dislike Kimberlee's interest? Feel a strange pang of resentment twist my insides when I think Kevin has a date in his apartment? Hesitate to go camping where I'd be subjected to lying next to him in the intimate shelter of a tent? Finally, most revealingly, catch a glimpse of paradise that one unforgettable night when he kissed me with such intensity? Not because I'm sex-starved or afraid or lonely or maternal. Because I'm in love with Kevin.

"What's so funny?" Kevin's frowning at me.

Ooops. I forgot my revelation is one-sided. Between chuckles I open my mouth to tell him but snap it shut again. After years of friendship, I can't just blurt out my emotions. I have no idea how he feels—whether he's ever imagined us as lovers or experienced the sweet surge of sexual attraction. Longed to run his hands down my arms or nuzzle my neck to inhale the scent of me, as I now want to do to him.

"You have spaghetti sauce smeared all over your face," I offer instead.

Kevin sits up and scrubs at his mouth with a fist. "Guess that shows how much I enjoyed the meal." With his forearms resting on his knees, he leans forward, relaxed, tranquil. "I'm glad you invited me over. We've been friends too long to let a difference of opinion come between us."

"I agree," I say. I can't quite catch my breath. Is this the moment to tell Kevin of my discovery?

"I'd better take off." Kevin stands up. "Can I give you a hand with the dishes?"

"No, no. Not a problem," I say.

"I don't mind at all. In fact, I insist," he insists.

"And I insist you don't. You did so much for me when I was sick. Dinner was a small thank-you."

The frown returns and approaches a scowl. "You're under no obligation for that."

I gulp. Kevin never would have misunderstood my gesture of appreciation before our squabble. And he certainly never would have politely offered to help with the dishes. He either would have simply taken charge of the task or, more likely, tried to sneak away before he was pressed into service. We're not back to our original comfort level. Every word we speak seems inappropriate and each action, awkward.

Kevin's at the point of scrambling for an excuse to cut out. "Umm. Gotta go. Got to give Randi a call before too late. She's trying to set up a New Year's Eve thing. She wants you to come, too, of course."

Nothing like recalling the claims and complications of a friend or two to jerk your chain, I think as I accompany Kevin to the front door. I lean against the door frame to watch him go down the hall and wonder how a person, myself, can plunge from bliss to despair in seconds. Randi adores Kevin and while I've seen no sign of reciprocal affection from Kevin, certainly he's never shown any weakness for me either. Evidently the path of love never runs smooth with stranger *or* friend, I think gloomily as I shut the door.

My new perspective on love influences my interactions with Kimberlee. Rather than the anger I felt first following the incident at the gym, that stiffened my back and put a sour taste in my mouth, I soften and grow sentimental with sympathy for a fellow sufferer. The pain of unfulfilled desire, the loneliness of separation, the frustration of constant aspiration are physical realities, upsetting to my equilibrium although I refuse to let them impact the high quality of my performance on the job. We are two women in an office carrying on under the same adverse circumstances of love from afar, I imagine. My eyes mist slightly as I covertly scrutinize Kimberlee. Ever the polished professional, Kimberlee doesn't appear to labor under an emotional burden, but I *know*. Bad luck that both Kimberlee and I are hung up on the same guy.

Maybe more of the office staff also are victims of emotion. Probably not the men. I have an idea that men don't allow love to take control of them. Lust, yes. Love, no. But maybe the admins, the paralegals, even the female attorney struggle inside to maintain some sort of balance. Day after day, they come to work, push themselves to answer questions, prepare legal documents, eat lunch, respond to "How are you?" with politeness, all the while hiding their inner grief. I become indignant at the concept. Why should women be the ones to suffer so?

"Joan?" Kimberlee's voice holds a note of uncertainty, as if she's not sure of her reception. After meeting with several days of rigid disdain and cold shoulders following the meeting at the gym, before I made my major discovery about being in love with Kevin and became a casualty myself, Kimberlee has been approaching me only when necessary.

I turn a high-voltage smile on Kimberlee. I can't articulate my empathy, but I can try to hint at it. "Yes, Kimberlee, what can I do for you?"

Kimberlee blinks in astonishment, recovers, holds out a file. "Mr. Jones wants me to start training you on parts of the Globe Investment enterprises. The account's too large to be covered by just one office person."

Impressed in spite of myself, I promptly forget to be in the state of love in favor of the challenge of complex legal matters. "Aren't they the ones you read about every day in the newspaper? Fingers in every big financial transaction around? Oil, real estate, stock market, construction?"

"Yep. They're new clients. Oh, we're not handling the day-to-day stuff. We'll be pulled in on issues that have the potential for court action," says Kimberlee. She pulls a chair up next to my computer. "Now let me show you what we've already got on file." Screens and menus flip by at top speed until Kimberlee arrives at the selected document. She pauses mid-motion. "I don't need to remind you that this information is absolutely confidential. If anything leaked, it could be very expensive for our client, not to mention us."

That old bugaboo again! "I should be grateful I'm being allowed to work on Globe. At least it shows I'm no longer a prime suspect in the break-ins," I say. "We've all got our new passwords now, the locks have been changed, and other safeguards have been installed. I assure you, any leaks will not spring from me."

"No, no," says Kimberlee hastily. "I didn't mean to imply that. I know you're completely trustworthy."

Establishing document formats and procedures consumes the entire morning. I'm glad to escape for a late lunch. Like a kid let loose from the confines of school, I nearly race down the hall to the cafeteria.

"He's here again," whispers Dolores, under cover of making change. "He's been hanging around. I think he's waiting for you to show up."

I scoff at the idea. Not that I care anymore, but I haven't had the chance to confide my change of heart to Dolores. Still, Scott dangling after me? That will be the day.

The day evidently has arrived, for upon seeing me enter with my tray, Scott stands and motions me to his booth.

"You've been scarce lately," he says as he slides in right next to me.

Why did he do that? He's making it difficult for me to pick up my fork and eat my tossed salad. I feel like my elbow sticks out from my body about six feet, threatening to poke Scott, that my feet suddenly double in size and shift under the table.

"Actually it's only been a few days since I ran into you at the grocery store," I say.

"Back on a diet, I see," he says.

"What do you mean?"

He picks up a plate from my tray. "Plain salad. No chips."

I shiver. How did I ever imagine myself in love with a guy so insensitive to the feelings of someone else that he makes personal remarks in a public place? A guy, come to think of it, so self-centered he doesn't care if he hurts me, like James used to do? Or, come to think even more, like my father?

"Guess you've been busy in there in Horowitz, Trimble, Hawkins & Jones," Scott continues without noticing my recoil.

I concentrate on chewing and swallowing calmly. When I don't answer him, Scott adds, "What with the Globe Investment account. They are *biiiig* time."

"I guess so." I warm up a degree or two from the excitement of my new duties. "I get to work on some of it. Lots of responsibility and the chance to learn."

Scott smiles and nods his interest. "Isn't it strange that Globe's going outside their own staff of attorneys?"

"Not really." I speak with the assurance of the informed. "We'll be handling our specialties, litigation or taxes and that sort of thing. But look at the time. I've got to go."

Rising at the same moment as I do, Scott protests, "Not yet. We haven't really talked yet."

Talked about *you*, you mean, I think. Again the difference between Scott and Kevin strikes me. Kevin's always interested in my activities and opinions. Weird. For months I longed for Scott, treasured a word, a glance, like some empty-headed teenager. Now the minute I'm no longer interested, the roles reverse. Kimberlee is right. The guy's into manipulation games.

"What say we catch a bite to eat tonight after work? Nothing fancy. Italian? Mexican? Give us a chance to relax."

I consider. I'm not thrilled with the idea, but Kevin and I have dropped many of our old routines, and I face a boring night. "Well…" I fudge.

"Come on. You don't have any better offers, do you?" Scott pushes.

Scott or a television rerun? Scott or doing my nails? I might as well stay busy so I don't dwell on Kevin. "All Right. Seven."

By the time seven rolls around, I'm glad I agreed. Work was especially intense and I'm ready to let down my hair, put up my feet, go limp, just not think for a while.

From Scott's description, I expect Al Dente to be low-key, a casual neighborhood spot. Instead, a waiter in impeccable tuxedo helps me out of my five-year-old ski parka. Glittering crystal, bone-white china, gleaming silver, golden candles reaching for the ceiling, long-stemmed orchids arranged with artistry, oil paintings on the walls, even a supercilious maitre d' with a narrow mustache surround the guests in elegance and pamper them into feeling a counterfeit (at least in Scott's and my case) superiority.

"I can hardly relax here," I mutter from behind a three-foot high menu whose selections are written in a nearly illegible if stylish scrawl.

"What?" asks Scott.

I poke my head around. "I said I can hardly relax here. I'm too busy trying to figure out what fork to use."

Scott breathes out a sigh of absolute contentment and surveys the room with its discreet staff and debonair diners, as if congratulating himself for being part of the select.

"You don't need shabby to achieve satisfaction and *cheap* never pampered anyone. This, Joan, is what you deserve, what I deserve. Expand your ambitions. Now we come to places like this occasionally. Eventually, we can make luxury the cornerstone of our lives. If we plan right."

A waiter creeps close and Scott nods to acknowledge we're ready to order. Fortunately for him, he takes charge, probing into the type and quality of the ingredients for each dish, insisting on the most expensive wines, because I teeter on the edge of a collapse into giggles. Scott sounds so, so pompous, even pretentious. He's talking like a character from a Depression-era movie, like I'm the little girl from the slums and he's the big bad cutthroat businessman. What a phony. Every word, each twitch of his eyebrow makes him a caricature of a successful attorney. People nowadays don't have as their sole life's ambition the mere accumulation of wealth. At least not the people I know and like best.

As we wait for our drinks and continue throughout the salad course and entrée, Scott harps on the same theme. "We're both young, bright, talented. The world should be our oyster, with a priceless pearl right smack dab in the middle, ready for our plucking. All we need is an opportunity. You know, I've waited and worked hard, looked long for that opportunity. It just hasn't happened, not in the big, open-sesame way it should have. But I for one refuse to go deaf trying to hear opportunity's knock." Occasionally he does have to pause to insert a forkful of food or take a sip of wine, but he's able to construct a veritable tower of accusations, exhortations, and incantations that sway and twist and threaten to tumble down around our ears.

He gives up eating in favor of talking and doesn't even pretend an interest in the food. "The ways of the world are not fair," he continues, expanding on some cryptic personal logic. "Some people wallow in inherited riches. Like a lot of the diners here tonight. Doesn't mean a thing to them to drop three, four hundred dollars on a bottle of wine. But others of us must grab for what they want. Like me. I have plans. Big plans." He leans back, crosses his arms over his chest and tries to look mysterious and superior simultaneously, which produces a visual effect of irrepressible gastrointestinal distress.

I nod and smile, chew my lasagna, surreptitiously spread a drop of tomato sauce into a swirl on my plate, and wonder what in the hell I'm doing here. Why did I never notice that Scott only talks about himself? And that he's boring to boot? He acts like I'm supposed to be an adoring fan, treasuring his every stupid word. Again I get this weird sense I've lived a similar scene before, only the male in the picture was James talking about his view of some stupid politician. Even earlier, my father, extending a tidbit on how *he* could have saved a bankrupt business if only the owner had asked. What bull!

Then Scott bends forward so low he has to prop his arms on the table and switches topics so fast I nearly miss the change. "Ever think how easy it would be for one person to affect the outcome of an important event? Like the domino that sets in motion a chain reaction? Or a lynchpin, pull it out and *wheeet*, the structure collapses? Like the way one voter in each precinct can change who's elected or what taxes we pay. We can do the same in lots of situations, take us at work, you could lay your hands on important information. Tidbits of facts and figures that might make a major difference in the sale of a piece of property, for instance. Or a stock purchase. A lawsuit."

"I never have," I say. "I guess you're right. The discoverer of penicillin was one man and he made an enormous impact on health care. We're so accustomed to seeing ourselves as little cogs in big wheels that we forget what's possible."

"Right. And people who take the initiative and aren't afraid to go out on a limb a ways are the ones who strike it rich."

"I don't know if that's always true," I frown. "Think about prospectors. Lots of them died poor. Or speculators in the Roaring Twenties."

"I'm considering the hypothetical level. And dealing in information, not searching for gold or oil." Scott, his fingers interlaced prayer-fashion, elbows on the table, rivets his attention on me. Gone is the languid, self-indulgent survey of the room.

I can't suppress a surge of pleasure. Now this is fun, talking about something interesting, having Scott pay attention to my opinion. Unlike Kevin, I spare a thought for him, who frequently seems to have no regard for my judgment at all.

"I see," I say. "Coincidence plays a role. Like a woman has no idea her husband is cheating on her and then she finds a lipstick-stained handkerchief."

Scott frowned. "Maybe. I'm thinking of deliberate action, not coincidence."

Captured by the line of inquiry, I forge ahead. "How about an adult who sees a kid going wrong and times his lecture just right to prevent the kid from a life of crime? Or if I'm late paying my utility bill and the heat gets turned off on the coldest day of the year and my cat freezes to death? My gosh, I never realized how we're all part of interconnecting rings or links like a chain. What one person does can affect many."

The conversation is speeding away. Scott poises between frowning and laughing at me as I contemplate the vagaries of fate. He holds up a palm. "Stop, stop. You're as erratic in your reasoning as a car steered by a drunk driver. Hold on. You're taking the global view. It's true we're all inter-related. But we can hardly affect that condition—it's universal.

"I was referring, hypothetically of course, to 'what if's' on an everyday scale. What if you take a class in painting and discover you have a real talent? Your life's improved, right? What if you have the opportunity to invest in a company and you get rich? Your life's improved."

Scott takes my hand from where it lies on the table and captures it between his palms, gently rubbing my fingers. "What if someone asks for a few facts and figures from you and you build a closer relationship? Your life's improved. Right?"

I wish Scott would stop mangling my fingers. He's making me feel shivers up my spine, creepy ones not delicious frissons. And what's he driving at? "I don't understand," I say, pulling my hand away from him.

"Let me give you a hypothetical situation. You have access to information that can be critical in legal matters. I know men who would pay well to have certain proceedings weighted in their favor. You get the information, give it to me, I pass it along to them. Voila! Our common interests make us more comfortable and, at the same time, bring us closer together. We become better friends, not the least attractive part of the scenario." Scott gives me a sly wink.

"I don't see how I could know about anything that crucial. Anyway, isn't that against the law?"

A question for which Scott has prepared. "What is the law? A set of rules we've agreed to operate under. They come, they go. Sometimes they're even unfair, discriminatory, or bad. Each person has to decide which rules he'll live with."

I frown. "There are penalties for breaking the law. I don't think I like your hypothetical situation. Anyway, I respect the people I work with and I wouldn't want to hurt them." I drain my wine glass and set it as far from my plate as I can reach so the waiter won't assume I want a refill.

"Relax, relax," Scott protests with a chuckle. "This was a mental game of 'what-if.' You are such a child sometimes. That's one of the reasons why I adore you."

Adore? The evening's getting stranger and stranger. What's next, Scott as sycophant, me as goddess? I'm definitely not comfortable in that role.

"Let's go. I'm tired," I say without preamble. I stand and grab my old parka, ready to take it and myself back to familiar and comfortable surroundings.

Scott's forced to stand, too. He takes my parka from me and holds it for me to slip into. At the same time he leans forward and murmurs in my ear, "You know our talk was harmless chatter, don't you? I wouldn't want such a good friend as you to misunderstand."

At this moment I will agree to anything in order to get home. "Sure, sure, a let's-pretend."

The drive only increases my sense of unreality. Scott continues to act the enthralled lover with a touch on my arm, a smoldering glance, a whisper of praise. Relieved to pull up in front of the apartment, I leap from the car before Scott can park.

"See you, see you. Thanks for the dinner," I call over my shoulder.

"Wait," Scott leans over the seat and responds through the door I left open. "How about Friday night?"

"No can do," I lie. "I'm busy. Maybe some other time."

By this point I'm at the entryway and headed toward the elevator. The damn mirror in the elevator doesn't hide the blink of an eye or the twitch of an emotion. I can't face the confusion and, yes, the isolation I see reflected there in my own face, so I turn my back to the glass, wrapping my arms across my chest.

Seems as if my dearest hope from just a couple of weeks ago came true tonight, but as someone once warned, "Be careful what you wish for because you might get it." Scott appears enthralled with me just at the time I've discovered his superficiality, his selfishness.

I can't help but wonder if Barbara felt this way when she discovered what my father was really like. Only worse, because she married him and had a baby with him. She must have felt betrayed, stripped of all support, wondering what in the name of Heaven that she was going to do. No wonder it took her more than ten years to make a break, scant surprise she wanted nothing to do with him afterwards, or for me to, either.

Yes, all three major male interests in my life prior to Kevin have been the same self-centered, immature type. My father, James, and Scott. Oh, granted, they also were charming and had an indefinable zing. But compared to Kevin's reliability, warm friendship, wide-ranging interests, and honesty, as welcoming and unassuming as a

Sunday chicken dinner, Scott, James, and my father were about as deep and stiff as a cardboard cut-out and as appealing.

Hold on. I know that a list of superior character traits never makes a woman fall in love, though. Always, always a chemistry between man and woman is required, a touch that tingles, a yearning that draws the sexes together. I've been fortunate to discover Kevin's attraction before I made a mistake with Scott. Still, being in love by yourself, on your own, is a very lonely state.

Wish I could knock on Kevin's door, tell him how right he is about Scott, laugh the evening off. But the discovery of my affection (what a quaint, timorous term) for Kevin hinders me. How humiliating if he should discover my feelings without returning them.

My stomach growls in rhythm with my thoughts. How can I be hungry now? Must be because I rushed so at the restaurant to get away from Scott. Once inside the apartment, relief descends on me along with my pink flannel pajamas. Cinnamon toast and hot tea next. Comfort food, I think. Well, I need comfort. Seated at the kitchen table, I dunk the toast in the tea and turn the pages of this morning's paper from the back forward. A small item about auditions for the city choir. Maybe I should try out. I have nothing else to occupy my empty evening hours.

A front-page article about a foreign dictator brings Scott back to mind. Scott's absolutely mad, on some kind of power-hungry trip. Not only do I feel disinterested in him now, he actually repulses me. *Ick.* And this situation with Kevin, or rather this non-situation with Kevin, what to do about that? A wave of irritation sweeps over me. It isn't fair, if Kevin's not interested in Randi, that I have to take a back seat. Even if I did promise Randi to help her cause and nudge Kevin into seeing her as a romantic partner. I'm going to call Randi right now and back out of our agreement.

Although slow to respond, Randi finally picks up the phone. Surprise is apparent in her greeting, for she and I haven't spoken lately. First there was my poor health, then my embarrassment over the fight with Kevin, now my attraction to him. Randi cuts through the casual preliminary chit-chat.

"I've got company, Joan. What can I do for you?"

"I was just thinking about this situation with Kevin." I stumble for words, thoughts, phrases to delicately probe Randi's feelings. "It doesn't seem to be progressing. Are you still of the same mind you were?"

"Of course, Joan." Randi's voice instantaneously rises to a near-wail. "We can't abandon him now."

"But if no one's feelings have changed substantially, isn't it time to back off?"

"No." The answer is absolute. "Most men are like babies. Persistence, firmness, and gentleness are required in dealing with them. As for women, logic eventually shows them what's in their interests."

"But, Randi, you can't force someone's affection. If you're not successful after a while, it's best for all involved to step out of the picture."

Randi's voice drops very low.

"I've known Kevin for nearly ten years. He's part of my heart, my soul, my mind. He deserves to be truly happy. I can't believe we're going over this discussion again. I thought we'd agreed."

"Yeeesss," I stammer.

"Well, then," Randi returns briskly, "That's that. Now I've got to go. You've heard about the New Year's Eve party, haven't you? See you then?"

"Yes, yes." I replace the receiver with a sigh.

The future stretches before me, empty of purpose, forlorn in feeling. My infatuation with Scott dead, my desire for Kevin unattainable, life's pleasures seem to consist solely of eating and work. My eye falls on the newspaper and I recall the notice for choir auditions. Perhaps I should try out. No, I *will* try out. I'll let music fill the void, challenge and sooth me, just as when I was a child.

"I made it!" I crow at top volume over the phone several days later to Barbara. I haven't talked to her much since our heart-to-heart about my father weeks ago when I was recovering from my illness. But I can't hold back on this achievement. Barbara's always been my biggest fan and anyway, I've missed having her around with her ready-if-superfluous advice, her cheerleader enthusiasm, and her readiness to battle the world on my behalf. Perhaps I've been a trifle hasty to sit in judgment about her relationship with my father.

"I called to tell you I made it," I return to the topic foremost in my mind. "I made the city choir."

It's typical of her that she's ignoring my recent antagonism toward her. I don't know if this offends or pleases me. Is she a bigger person than I by disregarding our differences or is she so self-centered she doesn't remember the incident? In any case, she's obviously captivated by her handywoman work, because she murmurs, "That's nice."

"The city choir, Mom, remember the choir?"

"Oh, yes." Now enthusiasm enters Barbara's voice. "Just what you needed, a hobby. Is Kevin involved, too?"

"No. Mom..." I linger, tempted to ask my mother's advice. "Kevin and I aren't as close as we were. We had a disagreement and then, and then, I discovered. I mean, you know how you've always been pushing Kevin on me? Well, I agree now that he's a pretty great guy. But it's too late."

Barbara perks right up and takes notice of this. "What a momentous occasion. My daughter admits I was right," she teases, with an undertone of insecurity. Can she be hoping I'll confess she was right about lying to me concerning my father? In any case she plunges forward. "Don't fret, Joan. He'll come around. I saw how much he cared for you when you were sick. He knows what a paragon he'd be getting."

Proclaiming to a mother my achievement in the audition doesn't produce the same satisfaction as bragging to a lover, I discover. Even a call to Dolores, where I coincidently also catch Davis, who's giving her kids a hand with their homework, fails to inflate my sense of accomplishment. I try one last time to contact Kevin, finally leaving a forlorn pathetic message on his telephone when he doesn't answer.

"Kevin, I thought you might want to know that I just got in the city choir. I hope you'll come hear us perform sometime." I set the receiver down gently, not expecting any response.

I've never felt so alone in my life. Maybe I should apologize to Barbara, Kevin and the world in general for my bad attitude. I don't even try to hold back a flood of tears tonight as I sit next to the silent telephone.

Third times are supposed to be lucky and the maxim holds true for the office thief. On this occasion, the intrusion is so subtle that no one suspects trouble until Amy Chung, the math-whiz paralegal, double-checking a corporate financial statement, can't get the same figures in her head that appear on the screen. She calls Kimberlee over and together they compare each and every digit from the original document to the computerized version. When they're finished crouching with their heads together, they sit back in their chairs, rigid with dismay.

"I'll go tell Mr. Horowitz," Kimberlee finally says.

Although the parties immediately involved in the discovery make no comment on it, the buzz spreads through the office, mouth to ear. So I'm not surprised to see Davis stroll through the room around lunchtime, headed straight for Mr. Horowitz's office without even pausing to check with the staff.

The door to the inner sanctum remains obdurately closed throughout the lunch hour and sometime thereafter. It flies open with a bang! at about two-thirty when Davis marches out in front of Mr. Horowitz, straight down the aisle between the work stations to my desk. Paralyzed, I sit with my fingers arced over the keyboard. Davis jerks his head to one side and I roll myself away in the office chair, fingers still curved.

Davis begins a methodical search of the top of my desk, turning over the keyboard, flipping through messages and notes, looking under the telephone and pencil holder, emptying the file holders. Nothing. The inspection continues. Now he opens the drawers, with special attention to the insides. Again nothing. Finally he pulls out the auxiliary leaves that usually remain pushed into the desk itself. He flips one over.

"Ah ha!" Davis accuses and points dramatically with his index finger at the scrap of paper taped to the bottom of the leaf. Mr. Horowitz joins Davis by my desk and peers down at the paper.

"What's this, Joan?" he asks in a mild tone.

"My computer password, Mr. Horowitz. So if I forget it."

Mr. Horowitz motions Davis to replace the leaves. "Join me in my office, Joan," he says. He walks away without checking to see if I follow.

I gulp, stretch my fingers and shake my hands, cast an anguished look at Davis who remains absolutely blank-faced. I have no choice but to comply.

When Davis and I enter Mr. Horowitz' office, the partner shuffles through some papers on his desk, not bothering to look up. "This is difficult for me to say, Joan," says Mr. Horowitz. "Your password is the one associated with the current rash of computer hacking."

"No."

"Yes."

"No. Mr. Horowitz, it can't be." The words gush out of my mouth like a waterfall of denials and rationalizations straight from my brain. "You know I'm not involved. I wouldn't do anything to jeopardize the firm. I'm the one who brought Davis to you." I squeeze my hands together to control their shaking. Nothing can stop my knees knocking. Quit babbling, I upbraid myself. You look guilty as hell. But what else can I do, another part of my mind wails. I'm never going to be believed. I'll be fired, charged with a crime. Never work again. My name and face spread all over the news. Not fair, not fair. The first half of my swiftly deteriorating brain jumps in again. Act like Saint Joan in front of her accusers. You're as innocent as she! I stiffen my backbone as I wait.

Mr. Horowitz finally looks up, straight at me. "Relax. We know it's not you. The entries that fouled up our records were made during non-business hours. From your workstation, evidently," says Mr. Horowitz. "Not that you couldn't have come back after hours. But it's simply too unlikely that you would get up in the middle of the night and use your own password to make the changes when you could be traced so easily. That's someone else."

Davis's enthusiasm for the chase compels him to break in. "But it's probably someone who knows you, a person familiar with your work habits and personality. Unless you've given your password out indiscriminately?" He cocks an eyebrow at me and I shake my head. "Users frequently write their passwords down in a somewhat hidden location, which anyone with any smarts can figure out immediately, rather like a mother hiding a key for her kid under the doormat. That's why I poked around your desk.

"Anyway, only two possibilities exist for someone to get your password—either by discovering it at your desk or through connection with the one person in the firm who has everyone's code. Kimberlee."

I gasp. "You think *she's* trying to frame me?"

"I don't want to believe so. However, we can't totally rule her out." Mr. Horowitz waves his hand in the air in negation. "She's susceptible to the same process that could have gotten the password from your desk. An inadvertent slip of the lip, slight carelessness in guarding the master list, whatever.

"We have to notify the police, too," adds Mr. Horowitz. "This situation can't be written off as an amateur attempt at a practical joke. The welfare of our clients and the firm's reputation are on the line. Someone is deliberately attempting to sabotage them both. I only hope the culprit is not an employee. I'd hate to believe one of our own could do this to us."

"Now comes the hard part," says Davis. He pulls back a chair that faces Mr. Horowitz' desk. "Have a seat, Joan." He takes the chair opposite me.

"Catching the criminal," Davis continues his thought around his own interruption. "We need to set up some false files that duplicate those of actual clients with some critical substitutions of facts. You'll be working on them intermittently as a decoy with a new password. And you should make sure you put a copy of that password in a hidden, but logical, location. Not the same one as before, of course. After today's very visible unmasking, the entire staff will be speculating about what happened. Which leads me to a difficult consequence. Difficult for you, that is."

"What?" I can hardly wait to hear. After all, the way my life has been going recently, with one guy turning out to be a real creep, then my realizing too late who my true love is and being set up as the patsy for a crime, a depressing downward spiral is in motion.

Davis leans forward, elbows on knees, and clasps his hands loosely as if in supplication. "We'll try to protect you, Joan. But it's probable that suspicions will surface. In fact, we want to encourage speculations to flush the real culprit out. He should be thinking of one of two possibilities—either today's crisis will panic him into trying to finish up his espionage or he'll become overconfident that all doubts are directed toward you. Either way, he should move into action again soon. I told Mr. Horowitz that you're strong enough to endure a cold shoulder or sidelong glances or gossip. Aren't you?"

I don't want to disappoint my friend or myself. My automatic response is positive. "Yes. Of course." Then I wonder, "But how will using my password catch the culprit?"

"We know someone is entering the office after hours to search the files. I'm setting up a system to catch him in the act. You don't need to know more than that. In fact, you shouldn't," says Mr. Horowitz.

Because they hold some lingering suspicion toward me, I think, my stomach clenching. I'm well and truly trapped. Although the intrigue, with myself cast as prime suspect, now throws me into a dark depression I only want to run from, that's the last thing I should do. Unless I cooperate fully, I'll compromise my own innocence. Another horrifying thought hits me. "Was... was any damage done from the last intrusion?"

Mr. Horowitz grimaces as if suppressing a sharp twinge in his intestines at the thought. "Minimal, we hope. The files you've been working on heretofore are routine—divorces, personal injury. No big surprises, little confidential information. The file broken into was a Globe Investment one but not a critical piece. Another reason for the urgency. The thief will soon try to locate other passwords if yours proves unproductive of any substantial information."

Davis breaks in. "That's a very nice combination of utter panic and despair on your face. Think you can maintain that outside to entertain the troops? We don't want them thinking we've been sitting around having tea or something."

I somehow summon a smile that looks more like I've tasted a lemon than contains any humor. "That will be no problem at all," I say as I exit, mentally preparing for a battle to equal any Saint Joan faced.

My verbal compliance is all that's required. Once I agree, I set in motion a sequence of unalterable activities—phonied-up financials, surreptitious consultations. For me, though, they mask an idea I fear to voice. Who has an excuse to hang around the office regularly? Who ignores the implied barriers of desks and reception counter to make himself at home in the work areas? Who possesses an endless curiosity about the firm's cases?

Scott.

Still I can't just jump up and accuse him. I don't even feel comfortable mentioning his name to Davis or Mr. Horowitz. The suspicion taints my attitude at work and drives me to seek refuge in snacking to calm myself. But nothing soothes me. Only the fraternity of friendship holds a promise of solace. I wish I could call Kevin, but I feel so damn awkward trying to maintain a pose of mere camaraderie.

Davis provides the initiative, setting up a strategy meeting to discuss the ramifications of the new developments. The original troublemakers gather at my apartment again. Davis once more includes Dolores, saying he's been using her as a sounding board for some of his ideas. This time, Davis and Dolores share the small couch while Kevin and I sit in armchairs with the distance of the living room between us.

Davis, euphoric and bursting with excitement because victory in this strange quest seems very near, outlines recent developments and sketches the bare essentials of upcoming plans. "You shouldn't know more details than you absolutely have to," he warns me. "We want you acting naturally."

It would be nice if someone could act naturally, I think. Kevin has been sitting in the darkest corner of the living room, not a word passing his lips, as if our spaghetti dinner never occurred and no step toward reconciliation had been made. I, morosely concentrating on the chaos of my life, stare off in space while Davis continues his blow-by-blow description of the strategic planning conversation (that's what he actually calls it) with Mr. Horowitz. Dolores tries to cover the big, silent nonresponses in conversation by leaping up and passing around pizza over and over in a never-ending circuit, like a horse harnessed to a millstone.

"Think you can handle this, Joan? You seem remote. Are you afraid?" asks Dolores when she pauses by my chair, a giant piece of three-topping pizza held like an peace offering or protection between us. "You don't have to worry about the end Davis is handling. He's got fantastic ideas."

I blink. What's up with the enthusiasm over a mere man, I wonder. But I simply answer her question. "No, it's not that," I say. "I mean I'm afraid, but not of physical danger. I wake up in the middle of the night with a hollow feeling in my stomach that nothing ever will go right. That somehow I *am* responsible for the breached files at work, we'll lose all our cases because of me, everyone hates me and turns away when I walk by, Kimberlee sneers in my direction and says she always knew I'd screw up, the partners go broke and the staff are fired, Mr. Horowitz informs my mother, I have to try to find a job in a field where no one knows me or anyone connected with the firm—say cashiering at Wal-Mart, but, no, lots of different people shop there, I'll see friends and acquaintances—then I'm too humiliated to face the members of the choir, I try to sing and only a squeak comes out. Do you ever feel like that in the middle of the night when darkness is all around you and your only sensation is the sound of the furnace as it rumbles on?"

Davis and Dolores stare at me in surprise or sympathy, I can't tell which. Kevin's face, absolutely immobile, doesn't change, but his upper torso goes rigid.

Oh, God, I think, why did I let loose with that stream of nonsense, true though it is? I'm being overly emotional again. Men especially don't let themselves undergo these qualms. I look like a complete fool.

"Yes," says Kevin without at me. "I call the sensation the midnight willies. Or despair. Poets and drunkards and lovers suffer it the most honestly, but the rest of us undergo the pain without voicing it, sometimes without labeling it. Fortunately, the next morning without fail, the sun rises, you have to take a leak and eat breakfast, the newspaper arrives, and you forget until the middle of the following night."

"Joan, that's completely unreasonable," says Davis with a scientist's illogical logic at the ready, for who can explain emotions? "No one can hold you responsible for the problems at your work. Mr. Horowitz assured you of that."

"Not the point," I counter. "I didn't say this was a rational belief."

I'm relieved that Davis broke in so I don't have to respond to Kevin. Astounded that Kevin holds a fellow feeling. Who would have suspected that confident, strident Kevin ever endures discouragement and gloom? This sign of weakness—and maybe the midnight willies isn't weakness, merely a normal psychological state—makes Kevin more human, approachable even. I lack the fortitude to pursue conversation, but a hopeful notion takes root in my heart after weeks of partial estrangement and painful politeness from Kevin.

CHAPTER THIRTEEN

When I open the envelope, a shower of shiny, multi-colored sequins cut in the shape of teeny champagne glasses sprinkles my lap and the floor. I pull out a heavy, folded piece of paper.

"Come alone or with a date, come short or tall, come with a good will and a cheer, or don't come at all" the invitation reads. A drawing of frantic stick-figure people toasting one another, standing on their heads, passed out on the floor, or kissing, illustrates the request. The long-anticipated New Year's Eve party finally has materialized. The invitation presents an opportunity to resolve matters with Randi over Kevin. I ring her.

"What is this about alone or dates? I'm not seeing anyone that I'd like to bring."

"You think I am?" Randi's voice has a tinny quality. I can't tell if it comes from a portable phone or from frustration. "I'll have to drag some guy from work. I think he's gay. But that's okay. Preferable to being saddled with a jerk who thinks I owe him a roll in the hay for his kindness. I think most folks will be stag except those already coupled. We're old enough not to panic because we spend New Year's Eve with friends, right?"

"Soooooooo," I draw out the sound to make my inquiry casual. "You're inviting your whole gang?"

"More than that. This promises to be a real blow-out. I've asked everyone I know."

"Kevin?"

"Sure."

"But he's not your actual date?" I try to inject a tone of sympathy.

"No. Why would he be?" Now Randi sounds impatient. "Say, what's up? You want a guest list or something?"

"No, no. But I have something I need to tell you, as a friend. About you and Kevin and me."

"He's coming, I said. I've got to go and you need to get off this phone and write the appointment on your calendar."

I hang up the receiver and shrug my shoulders. If Randi won't take time to listen to revelations about my feelings toward Kevin, what can I do? This frustration is like trying to flag down a ride after a flat tire. Randi speeds by, intent on her own concerns, while I'm left in the dust, stamping my feet and clenching my fists. Yet something must be done. I can't live in this state of uncertainty about Kevin, Randi and me for long. I may have to throw myself in front of the vehicle that's Randi and force a confrontation.

Barbara, on the other hand, is surprisingly easy to face, probably because she's as eager for a reconciliation as I've become. Although we've resumed chatting and Barbara's even dropped by occasionally, we haven't had a heart-to-heart. Given the condition of my own heart, I need this. I need a resolution, preferably one during which I can valiantly hide my tears of regret, for I've come to learn that love can drive someone to almost any extreme. I know I'd do cartwheels, steal, lie, if I thought I'd win Kevin.

I can't practice the scene with Barbara in advance or I'll lose courage. Once again taking inspiration from St. Joan, I charge forward Sunday morning and knock on the bright blue door of her townhouse in Aurora. When she answers, sleep-tousled hair signaling her disbelief that any normal human would come calling this early, I thrust a bag of bagels in her direction.

"Thought I'd get you before you trotted off to some concert or the library," I chirp cheerily.

Barbara knows cheer and myself are mutually exclusive in the early morning, so she's suspicious but polite. "What's wrong? I mean, come in and I'll make coffee. Then tell me what's wrong."

Taking the ladder-back chair furthest from the sunny window, I waste no time in small talk. "I came over to apologize, Mom. I've discovered there's some truth to your comparison of Daddy and James. I seem to be attracted to the type—the fast-talking charmer. In fact, I nearly got involved with another one, the guy I may have mentioned when I was sick? Scott?"

Barbara sets a coffee cup and small plate in front of me and positions one for herself, busying herself with these small duties. "Yes, you hinted you'd expected him to drop by. The flowers were from him, right?"

"Yes. Well, he's pretty much like Daddy and James. But I'm over him now. Disenchanted, you might say. Like you must have been with my father."

Barbara sits, sips her coffee, and looks directly at me for the first time. "Then you've forgiven me for lying to you?"

"Yes," I nod. "I don't necessarily agree with that particular action, but I understand."

"Good," says Barbara. "I've wanted to apologize to you, but I didn't know if I'd thoroughly messed up our relationship."

"Oh, Mom, you could never do that. You've been my hero for years. The way you struggled to support us, then when you left to come to Denver and start a new life. Courage has always been your middle name." And with the swiftness of an electric shock, I realize where my infatuation with a brave woman must have begun. Not with St. Joan, but with Barbara. She set the stage, introduced me to the idea that a woman is capable of as many, if not more, balls as a man. It's all in how you decide to live your life—with control and understanding or at the mercy of every personal whim or chance occurrence that comes along.

A trifle shaken by this discovery, I gasp out another confession. "And you were absolutely right-on about Kevin. He's a great guy. I should have paid more attention to him before instead of treating him like a pet or a piece of comfortable furniture. Now I've messed up any chance I might have had with him." I give a self-pitying sigh which Barbara won't tolerate.

"Don't be ridiculous. You have as much nerve as I. Look at your final response to James, when you threw the pillow at him. Look at your job, your success in the musical. Take a risk with Kevin, tell him how you feel."

"I just might do that. Thanks, Mom," I wrap the topic of conversation.

The most placid Christmas in my memory comes and goes without an emotional quiver. Mom, turkey dinner, a trip to the holiday lights at city hall, a sprinkling of snow, sensible gifts like books and scarves. I feel life is holding its breath for New Year's Eve.

I certainly am. Looking back over the year, I see lots of changes, so many that I'm unable to decide if they've been for better or worse. The divorce that is for the better now, although at the time, I thought the worse. My job, for the better if I can hold onto it. My intermittent singing career, more of an avocation, brings me a great deal of satisfaction. Weight? Up and down, down and up.

When I turn to thinking of romance and the men in my life (or lack thereof), I cringe. An infatuation with a self-centered, dishonest, shallow charmer. Thank God I hadn't slept with him. Then the man I *do* want to make love with, my former best friend, currently the subject of my fantasies, no progress over the length of weeks.

I have plenty of daydreams. I think of Kevin constantly, his face a backdrop to any scene in front of me, his quick tongue whispering a comment in my ear. Even worse, what drives me to an insatiable physical hunger—the appeal of a big, rangy, blond body with a barely contained love of life, action, initiative, strength. I remember how, even at rest, Kevin seems to be anticipating that something will happen, preparing to leap up and move. See him in profile sitting in the park or sweat-drenched in the gym. Head thrown back to laugh at the dinner table. In disguise at the art museum. Singing a song from a musical at the top of his lungs.

I imagine kissing him, tracing, tasting with lips and fingers, tangling my tongue with his, rubbing body to body full-length.

Then the one fatal night that closed him off from me. One single night when, eyes closed, face intent, his fingers moved magically over my body only to finally and completely reject my advances. No, I realize now that that final incident was the culmination of a pattern of ignorance about my own feelings and a gross insensitivity to a special man's nature. How could I have been so stupid? Can I ever regain my friendship with Kevin? Sometimes it appears likely. How about a deeper relationship? Perhaps the party will present an opportunity.

Between Christmas and New Year's I bump into Kevin at the trash chute. With super-natural casualness, I address him.

"Still going to Randi's party?" I drop a load of papers down the chute.

"Sure. And you?"

"Yes." I hold the door for Kevin as a stalling tactic, hoping that he will suggest driving over together. When he adds nothing more, I say, "See you there."

From such small snippets of contact, I have to take comfort. Like an adolescent caught in the throes of a violent, mind-bending infatuation, I pass the hours before the party in vacillation between hope and despair. Should I ask Katherine or Evan about Kevin's feelings toward me? Flirt outrageously with him? Flirt with someone else to make him jealous—if he can be made jealous? Slip him a note for an assignation? The indecision extends to my clothing. Which outfit, innocent or sexy? The palest ivory satin gown, long-sleeved, high-necked, like an eighteen-ninety's society queen? Or rich, strokeable, plum velvet plunging past the bounds of decency?

So worked up am I that my hands shake while applying makeup. I have to wipe my face clean and start over four times, causing me to be nearly an hour late for the party.

Just as well, I think. Now I've missed the slow, awkward preliminaries where people stand around trying to make polite conversation. Instead I enter Randi's apartment with a small group of guests who cover my arrival. No sign of Kevin in the living room, which is beginning to be clogged with men and women chatting energetically and waving drinks in the air, nor in the uncrowded dining area where a gal in a very short red plaid skirt perches on the table with her arms draped over her date's shoulders. The kitchen revives the activity, for people instinctively head in this direction to be surrounded by familiar domestic appliances common to all homes as well as fast access to refreshments.

Here I find Randi shaking popcorn into a bowl with her left hand while she pulls crackers from a box with her right. "Hi. Here." Randi shoves the bowl at me as a greeting. "Take this into the living room, will you?"

I don't mind serving as maid. I have nothing better to do. I carry the popcorn into the next room, then assign myself a set of additional chores like collecting a load of empty glasses and cups and wiping spills off table tops. Wandering through the apartment, I notice Randi flitting from man to man. If she has an escort, he's faded into the background.

Still no Kevin. Katherine and Evan show up together. I've heard they've begun to officially date. They don't look especially lovey-dovey, don't hang on each other or gaze in each other's eyes. When I approach them, they welcome me enthusiastically.

"We're planning a trip to Africa this summer," says Katherine. "Evan has a grant and I'm tagging along as a volunteer."

"That's great," I respond. "Are you going to be able to keep up the travel?"

Katherine beams. "Evan's going to start applying for teaching positions. Then he'll have summers free. I'll join him for my vacations. I don't mind some separations as long as they're temporary. Any good marriage should be able to tolerate them."

"Marriage!" I shriek. "You're going to be married?"

Katherine can't stop smiling, in direct contrast to Evan who appears, as usual, to be thinking so hard about some abstract theory regarding the origin of the human species that he doesn't notice the people in front of him.

"Congratulations," I add, wondering to myself how this mismatched couple is going to survive.

Katherine pokes an elbow in Evan's side.

"What? What?" He surfaces from his reverie.

"Joan has offered her congratulations," says Katherine gently. "It's appropriate to thank her."

"Oh. Thanks." Evan, blushing like a girl, turns toward Katherine instead of me. The motion convinces me that somehow the couple will muddle through.

"Come on," says Katherine. "Let's say hello to Randi." She leads Evan off by the hand.

The evening's turning out to be a complete bust, I think. Big noisy parties don't encourage conversation. Not that I'm especially interested in talking to friends anyway. What's holding Kevin up? Rather than moping in a corner, I head to the bathroom, lock the door behind me, and look around the room. Mouthwash. I swish some through my teeth. Then I open the cabinet to poke in the contents. Randi has quite an array of makeup. I try a shiny eyeshadow and a new lip gloss, squirt a new perfume behind my ears.

Someone pounds on the door. "Hold your horses," I snap. "I'll be out in a minute."

What else? The towels are crooked, so I straighten them and rearrange a display of silk flowers on the counter. That completed, I look in the mirror, smooth my hair and exit. The first person I see is Kimberlee.

My initial surge of feeling is welcome relief at the familiar face, then unease (is Kimberlee stalking me because of the illegal business at work?), finally suspicion. What's Kimberlee doing here? She doesn't know Randi.

Suspicion turns to despondency when Kevin appears at Kimberlee's side, tucking her hand under his arm. "Hullo, Joan. How's it going?"

I wish I could sink into the hardwood floor, but that miracle fails to occur. I hope I'm hiding my shock and dismay behind a wooden smile that's a grimace inside. "Happy New Year, Kevin." The smile grows fixed and hard. "I didn't know you were seeing each other."

"Yes." Kevin puts his hand possessively over Kimberlee's. She looks up at him enthralled as a deer hypnotized by headlights. Goo-goo eyes, I think. Disgusting.

"I'd better go. Have to help Randi with the refreshments," I fib. Any reason will do to get me out of Kevin and Kimberlee's vicinity. I dart out of the bathroom doorway and back into the kitchen where I prepare a series of large, strong drinks—bourbon on the rocks, although I hate bourbon. Probably I should just go home, I think, gloomy as a stormy day as I set up the plastic glasses on the counter in a straight line, but I can't stand the idea of being alone right now—watching the festivities beamed from New York while the great bright ball of light descends in Times Square to mark off the seconds to the New Year...seeing through instant replay over and over the wrap-up of one humungus, garbage-level year. Fool, fool, fool, I tell myself. How can I be so deluded as to dream of a connection with Kevin?

Although it's never been the apex of conviviality and excitement, the evening goes steadily downhill from that point. Unbelievable to me, who supposes nothing worse can happen. Fortunately the bourbon throws a misty cushion around my feelings, so I escape being pummeled by pain. Later I will recall a series of incidents almost as if they occur to someone else...

The first couple of shots of bourbon jolt my stomach, then my head, with a sour twist...

Wandering from clique to clique throughout the apartment, trying to participate in the conversations, being ignored, feeling isolated...

Returning to the kitchen to find that a nefarious sneak has consumed several of my glasses of booze, yell accusations at some bewildered guy standing nearby...

Tucking a bottle of bourbon under my arm, the closest thing to an evening's companion that I get...

A wild, body-flinging solo performance to rock music when no one will dance with me, Kevin, perched on the couch, brilliant hazel eyes shooting condemnation...

On the balcony to cool down, discovering a cohort who flicks plastic glasses off the railing with me to determine the better shot...

Joining the screaming and yelling at the stroke of midnight, along with a deep-throat kiss with a total stranger...

In the bathroom again, upchucking as the consequences of my binge catch up with me...

Someone else in the bathroom—Kimberlee!—the two of us weep on each other's shoulders, me moaning my life's a mess, Kimberlee admitting she's damn lonely, Kevin doesn't love her, he's in love with someone else. Whom?

Finally, oblivion under the pile of coats on Randi's bed. I surface the next morning as if climbing from a warm cave. The pillows encircle me and a comforter even covers my head. I feel my forehead for a temperature and take my pulse. Normal. All things considered, I don't feel too wretched. I don't want to leave my cozy den, but I can't escape from the rest of my life. Time to face up to reality.

Randi's sacked out on the living room couch. Very quietly, I gather my things together, trying to exit without disturbing her. The attempt fails and Randi sits bolt upright.

"Joan? You okay?" Randi asks around a yawn and a stretch.

I pause by the door. "Yeah. Say, I didn't do anything to embarrass myself or other people, did I? The whole night's kind of hazy."

"No, not really, that I can remember. My eyes weren't glued to you and I wasn't in great shape myself. You did seem to go a little berserk. I never figured you for a wild and crazy type. You looked like you were having a blast when you performed that fake strip routine."

"I wasn't." I collapse on the couch next to Randi. "I was miserable."

"Why?" Randi tucks her legs up under her and leans forward to listen.

"Kevin. You must have noticed. You've got to be as upset as I am. I mean, I know how you feel about him and then for him to show up with Kimberlee. Although she told me he's in love with someone else, not her. Maybe that's you. It's sure not me. I'd prefer it to be you rather than Kimberlee. This isn't making any sense, is it?"

"Sure. You've finally realized you're hot for Kevin. It's about time."

I freeze, totally bewildered. "What about you?" I eventually get out. "I thought you wanted him."

"Whaaat?" Randi's jaw drops. "Me?"

"That's what you told me when we went camping. You talked about friendship turning to love and sometimes it took a nudge for both people to realize the fact."

"Kevin's already in love with you, he told me so himself up in the mountains. He let it slip in a sarcastic comment when I teased him about sharing the tent with you. He knew you were hung up on some other guy, sounded like you were interested in *any* other guy except him. Your responses to him kept getting clouded with this image you had of him as the boy next door. Kind of an overgrown benevolent cousin. When I mentioned nudges, I was referring to you."

"Me? I wasn't hot for him then."

"I know, you idiot, that's what I mean." Randi stands up, takes my hand and leads me to the sofa. "What a mess. For all these months, you've been staying out of Kevin's way because of me?"

I sink down on the sofa, clasp my arms around my bent legs, and rest my chin on my knees. "Not quite. You're right. He was right. My eyes were closed to how I felt until a while ago. Until too late. We had a huge fight, maybe he told you about it?"

"Nope. You know men. You have to tease the interesting things out of them. What was it about?"

"Kimberlee. Kind of. Mostly about his dating habits. Lack of long-term girl friends. I offered to set him up."

Randi roars with laughter. "I bet he hated that. I can imagine the look on his face when you lectured him. Was he utterly speechless?"

"No," I say, the weight of my error slumping my shoulders down. "He was furious. In fact he barely saw me or spoke to me for weeks. That was when I learned how much and in what ways I missed him."

"Then some good came out of the disagreement."

"Not really. He's forgiven me, but there's still a rift between us, still a self-consciousness, an awkwardness."

"Of course. Because now you're aware of each other sexually."

"No, no. I've lost any chance with him."

"I'm sure you're wrong. All through college, we knew that Kevin was hung up on some girl from high school. Then afterwards, it was like he measured every woman he dated against this unknown ideal. Must have been you all along. I could feel him out..." Randi lets her sentence trail off.

"No, absolutely not." I shake my head so hard my hair flares out. "If he's lost his feelings for me, assuming what you say is correct, that he had some sort of feeling for me in the first place, it can't be forced to return."

"Don't be such a wimp." Randi jumps up and starts to pace back and forth, gesturing wildly in the air. Each motion pulls her lemon-yellow oversized tee-shirt high on her hips, revealing thong undies. Somehow the sight strengthens her argument in my eyes. "These are modern times. You're entitled to take the initiative. Call him up and whisper obscenities in his ear. Jump his bones one night. Drop him a mash note."

"I tried." I blush. "I just about begged him to bring me to your party. He ignored the invitation."

Randi pauses in her pacing to consider. "And Kimberlee said he was in love with someone but not her. Who else has he been seeing? Who, who?" She brightens. "Still could be you."

I gnaw on a fingernail that somehow, somewhere was chipped the night before. "I wish. How can I find out?"

CHAPTER FOURTEEN

Slapping a fist into her palm, Randi exclaims, "The same way we got Katherine and Evan together!" She sits down on the couch again. "Remember when we went camping and we talked about creating an emergency that would bring Evan to his senses? That's just about what happened. Evan took off for another god-forsaken temple, got caught up in a minor political fray, and automatically his first thought for help was Katherine. She flew over, bugged the embassy and officials, pried him out of jail and carted him home. From gratitude bloomed love. All we have to do is set up a similar situation for you."

"And that is?"

"Listen, I can't be the only creative one here. You've got to come up with some ideas."

"I can't right now. I'm wiped out from last night. My head throbs, my throat's sore, even my hair aches. I'm going to crawl home and lick my wounds." And I do.

A devious mind is coming to life in the head of Davis McIntosh. Its presence astounds me. I never would have suspected that a very mild-mannered, calm, and courteous exterior hides the equivalent of a cunning criminal intellect, capable of twisted contortions and points sharp as broken glass.

Davis calls the gang of four back together for some plotting. We gather at a mall food court, unsuspicious territory, as Davis points out. He wants to avoid the law office, which might be under surveillance, and the noontime appointment makes a downtown location reasonable for everyone. Still, it's somewhat difficult to communicate or even pay attention when conversations are being screamed over and around our heads and our elbows are constantly jostled by fellow lunchers. And Dolores is breathless and late because her car's started acting up.

"This is all the better," says Davis with gusto as he attacks a huge plate of amalgamated Chinese delicacies. I can't tell if he refers to the food or the atmosphere. "All the better," he repeats, waving his chopsticks in the air. "No one can hear what we're saying because the background noise is too disruptive."

The atmosphere. Davis takes leadership of the discussion as he has been doing regularly, Dolores listens as if committing every word to memory, I pick at my salad, ignoring my hamburger and fries, wishing that I hadn't come, wondering what Kevin's thinking about, while Kevin, who hasn't bought a cup of coffee, let alone food, gazes over everyone's head. Yes, the atmosphere around us is noisy and jolly, but we look like somber study hall monitors from high school.

"We must precipitate a crisis," Davis announces. "This whole process is taking much too long. We've got to flush the villain out of hiding, create a situation in which he'll reveal his identity."

"Absolutely," agrees Dolores.

Kevin, seeming to address the ceiling light fixtures, asks, "Does Mr. Horowitz agree?"

"He doesn't know about my plan," says Davis. "I'd rather not inform him. It's easier to ask forgiveness than ask permission, you know."

Kevin finally lowers his focus downward to look Davis straight in the eye. "Is it dangerous? We can't put anyone at risk."

The plastic chair I'm sitting in feels hard as concrete and I shift, trying to get comfortable. "What does Helen think about you spending all this time away from her? She can't be happy her fiancé is gone constantly, wrapped up in intrigue."

"Oh, I'm not engaged any more. We broke up weeks ago," says Davis, chipper as a squirrel in spring. "I'm completely free to work on the set-up."

This news makes me lose my appetite completely and push the limp carrot curls in the salad to the side of the bowl. Icky things. I hate limp carrots. Carrots should be stiff and fresh, firm to the touch and sweet to the taste. The dissimilarity in carrot-hoods is rather like the difference between Scott's blubbery mouthings and Kevin's delectable lips. That reminds me that I should reveal my suspicions about Scott.

"I think I know who's breaking in," I say.

Perhaps because I appear to be talking to my disinterested salad, my companions pay no heed. Kevin, now intimately and personally enmeshed in strategy and protection, addresses Davis in undertones, while Dolores gives small distinct nods of agreement while chewing her mesquite-chicken sub rapidly.

I clear my throat and begin again. "I think I know who's causing the trouble." I rap my fork on the edge of my bowl for emphasis and speak like an announcer. "Attention, attention. The victim can identify the perpetrator."

"Wh-a-a-a-at?" The statement finally catches Davis's notice. "Who? Who?" he demands.

Lowering my voice to foil any eavesdroppers, I say one simple word. "Scott."

"Of course," says Davis. His eyes narrow to view infinity and his lips purse as he considers the matter. "He leases an office from your firm, has free rein in your offices, he's friendly with several of the female staff. That gives him opportunity. But what about motive?"

The expression on Kevin's face can only be described as a smirk. I hate giving him this satisfaction, but he's been right all along about Scott. Still, I can't bear for Kevin to gloat.

"Be a gracious winner, Kevin," I snap. "I admit you were right and I was wrong. Don't rub it in."

Kevin's eyebrows lift in surprise at my concession. He folds his arms across his chest and says, "I never thought you'd move out of that romantic cloud that you were wrapped in. I'm happy to learn differently."

"Oh, I gave up on that romance long ago," I answer in a flat tone, nary an emotion in sight. I return to the subject at hand. "Scott is an ego maniac and a manipulator. Although he disguises his interests through flattery, his conversations, with me at least, always ultimately lead to some perspective or information about the law firm. In fact, the last time I went out with him, he just about asked me to feed him details, names, figures, specifics on our clients. Kept blathering on about how we should and could be rich. That was shortly before the password episode."

"And you didn't inform anyone." Kevin makes a flat statement, not a question, as if passing a judgment that shows me deficient.

"Whom was I supposed to tell? He couched the proposal in the abstract, kind of an imaginary what-if, like asking what you'd do if you won the lottery. It wasn't until all this other stuff started happening, when my password was tied directly to the access, that I put the pieces together. All right, all right, I was naive." This is addressed to Kevin, who continues to mingle in his expression both disbelief and disgust. I raise my palms to the others in appeal. "Then when I realized I couldn't make an unsubstantiated accusation." I slump into discouragement.

My confession energizes Davis. "This is fantastic. Major progress. An actual suspect. Now all we have to do is catch him."

"I thought of a way to speed up the process," I volunteer. "Rather than waiting for him to snoop around and stumble on my password, I could, I could, drop a hint that we've been reassigned passwords because of our troubles. After a little talk, me depressed, him reassuring, I'd accidentally reveal my code."

"Are you still dating him?" says Dolores.

"No. The last time wound up being terribly awkward with me running out of the car and him at least temporarily disconcerted. But it wouldn't be difficult to bump into him at work."

"You'd raise his suspicions at once," scoffs Kevin. "You don't see him for a month, then suddenly you're weeping on his shoulder and babbling your new password? Get serious."

"When will you realize I'm neither a child nor an idiot, Kevin?" I say in an icy voice. "I won't be that extreme. I told him about the other incidents. It would be natural for me to mention this one. After putting up a show of resistance, I'll let my password fall inadvertently."

"I say she tries it," says Davis. "What do we have to lose?"

"I agree," Dolores says with no hesitation.

"And I say the guy could go berserk when he finds out Joan played a role in his capture," says Kevin. "It's too dangerous. I vote no."

"This is not an election." I direct my comment to Kevin. Why is the man so negative? Really, he can be the most irritating person in the world. He ignores me for months, then suddenly acts like he owns me. "I'm going to do it."

As if to dare one another, Kevin and I stare in open challenge across the table.

Kevin concedes first. "Okay, okay. But I insist that we bring Mr. Horowitz into the plan. We can't skulk around like poor excuses for spies."

"Like we did at the art museum?" I say. "All of us in disguises?"

At the reminder of the ludicrous picture we presented lurking through the statues and paintings, dressed in raincoats, hats, and sunglasses, one by one we begin to chuckle, laugh, finally howl, setting each other off in a chain reaction.

"At least we'll never be that stupid again," says Davis as we part company.

"No, we'll find a new way," I agree on a last note. "As the song says, 'The past's no more, the past's no more...'" I warble on the way out.

~ ~

No way around it, I feel nervous as a person with an impacted wisdom tooth at the dentist. Not only is my stomach tied in knots, but also my hands are damp, my heart beats fast, and my head throbs. And Scott's nowhere in sight yet.

I'm beginning to feel like I live in the cafeteria. All week I've loitered in its vicinity from eleven until one-thirty. Sometimes I drop by mid-afternoon, too, on the pretext of taking a coffee break. Good thing Mr. Horowitz is in on the scheme or I'd be called on the carpet for my absences. Trouble is, like my early days at the law firm, I'm wolfing down a huge variety and quantity of snacks. Well, I can't just sit at a booth staring at the wall, can I? Anyway, the food soothes stomach and nerves.

Now it's Thursday and Scott seems to have dropped off the face of the earth. He hasn't even appeared in the office during business hours, although his mail's disappeared regularly. Bored with the lack of progress in what I mentally label as The Case, I pick at a piece of lemon meringue pie, pulling the pudding away from the topping and squashing the crust with my fork. Dolores, swabbing tables, approaches, then perches on the end of the table.

"How's your car?" I ask, making conversation.

She makes a face. "My cousin's working on it. It may be terminal. But, *hija*, how about you? You been in here every day for hours. Getting fed up waiting for that Scott dude?" she says.

I check over my shoulder to make sure that Scott hasn't entered while I was lost to my surroundings.

"I am frustrated," I admit. I lower my voice to a near-whisper. "I'm worried he won't take the bait. Maybe he's lost interest in me. Or the project. Or he's the wrong person."

Dolores snorts. "No way, Jose. You got him pegged." Her eyes grow wide and round and she clasps her dish cloth with both hands. "Say, I have an idea. Remember when I told you we should hide out in your office to catch the guy? You wanna try that?"

"No." I shake my head. "We'll stick with the original plan. At least for now."

Dolores nods sagely as a cat. "I'll help you any way I can. Just give me the word." She stands up and returns to her duties at the cash register.

A short time later, I hear Dolores's voice ringing through the rooms. "Thank you so very very much, sir. Have a good day. I'm sure you will. Come again, sir."

What on earth? I raise my head to see Dolores twisting around and leaning off her stool until she's nearly perpendicular to the floor, waving her arms at me and mouthing, "It's him, it's him." Scott's just exiting the cafeteria line.

I draw a deep breath and summon up a huge smile. "Hi, Scott. Long time, no see. Would you like to sit down?"

I motion to the padded bench across from me while upbraiding myself. Long time, no see? What a stupid thing to say. I'm going to have to be better than that if I want to get this guy dancing fast enough to take some false steps.

The cheek-stretching grin concealing my thoughts probably isn't necessary, I soon understand. Self-centered as Scott is, without a doubt he easily could believe I now regret the friction we experienced weeks before. Aren't I flirting my hardest, like he's a gift I've mislaid under the Christmas tree? He sits down, as innocent of my ulterior motives as a seminary student who earnestly believes in his world as he's created it in his mind.

"How was your Christmas?" Another brilliant conversational gambit escapes my mouth. To disguise my words' vacuity, I purse my lips into what I hope is a seductive pout, gaze worshipfully upward, extend my hand toward Scott's pinpoint-striped arm and stroke my index finger gently over the cloth. I could swear he actually shivers.

It can't be this easy to bend a man to your will, can it? Look at him as if he were a god, bat your eyelashes, smirk and flutter and, finally, touch? I've wasted years, a lifetime, trying to figure out the complexity of relationships, always feeling at a loss, always scrambling to please my father, my husband, then Scott, fill some kind of template or mold of ideal femininity. Evidently I've been playing a solo game. I haven't had any competition except myself, any rules except my own, any judge except me.

These men who loomed so large in my life were all pressed from the same mold. Yet they're more pitiful than my wasted effort and years. That's the way they limit themselves. Their view of the world is so narrow, constricted to themselves and their self-interest. They never have the possibility to transcend themselves and be part of a greater whole, whether that's a real marriage, a true friendship, a worthwhile career, a cause as big as humanity. Unlike Kevin who proves his worth with every breath when he puts a friend first, extends a helping hand at every opportunity.

A surge like electricity floods me and I feel so powerful I know beyond any doubt I can make this covert venture succeed. This must be how Saint Joan felt when she first faced the British. Yes, the power of right was on her side...and mine.

"Fine, fine," replies Scott. The crease of puzzlement that appeared on his face when he spotted me gradually eases until his countenance resumes its customary plastic-like smoothness. "Guess you've missed me," he adds, "at least as much as I've missed you."

I nod. Whatever. I don't care what excuse he comes up with for my sudden cordiality, as long as he's hot on my tail again, so to speak. And, boy, is he. His nose nearly is twitching in his intensity.

He leans forward and clasps my hand in both of his, toying with my fingers in his habitual way, so annoying if mutual affection is absent. A stream of senseless chatter issues from his mouth. Or perhaps the words hold some meaning, but, intent on my own thoughts, I miss it. How can I steer the conversation to Scott's illicit proposal of some weeks before? Should I mention the most recent incident in the office? Manufacture a financial crisis in my personal life that would make me appear more amenable to revealing business information?

I needn't have worried, I soon realize, for Scott, avaricious as he is, never neglects close attention to his own interests. It requires only the slightest of hints on my part. A big sigh. "The worst thing about the holidays," I say, "is the bills afterwards. I'm flat broke."

A light enters Scott's eyes, a shimmer of concentrated awareness. "I sympathize. There's nothing worse than wanting to give your family and loved ones a really great Christmas and feeling too financially strapped to do it. You're not in too big a hole, I hope."

"No," I begin to contradict, hating to appear to be a fool with my finances, a woman who can control neither my desires nor my expenditures, then realize denial is counterproductive to entrapment. "I should be able to pay off my debts in several years. Only a couple thousand." I pull a face of such gloom I look like an inconsolable bankrupt.

Scott leaps to the rescue. "There are ways and ways to solve your problem. The one you've mentioned is slow and steady, but what do you do when the next Christmas rolls around? Hmmm?"

"I don't know. I just don't know." I actually manage to dredge up a dampness in my eyes, closely resembling tears but in fact the result of gritting my teeth to avoid my instantaneous revulsion when Scott moves his head so close to mine that they threaten to touch.

He's repositioned in order to keep our conversation confidential. "I hate to see you upset," he murmurs. "What if I help you out a bit?"

Where's this going? "You'd do that?" I ask, infusing my voice with a thrill of hope.

"Sure I would. For you." Under lowered eyelids, Scott casts a look of such longing at me, I feel like cheese baiting a mousetrap. Rat would be a better description for my intended victim.

"Oh, I couldn't allow you to," I half-protest while my body language shouts "Yes, yes, yes!" with a arching forward toward him, a lowered submissive head.

"I insist." He straightens, squares his shoulders, checks the knot in his tie. "What are friends for if not to give each other a hand?"

"Weeellll..." I tilt my head to the side and pretend to consider, tapping my fingernails on the table. "Okay. But only if it's understood that I'll pay you back eventually. I should be getting a raise next year."

"There's a simpler way," says Scott. "A way you can help me out and repay the debt without shelling out money or scrimping and saving." His eyes shift to the large window near by as if surveying the scene, as if completely disinterested in my reply.

Boy, he's good at this game, I think. I'll have to learn from him, the insouciance, the daring, the pure nerve, like a star quarterback stalking into a party after winning the football match. I begin practicing immediately. "Ooooo, what's that?" I gush back at Scott. "After your generous offer to me, I'd do anything for you. Well, almost anything." As I smirk and blink my lashes, I pray "anything" is anything other than making him think I'll sleep with him.

"I have a friend," Scott starts, "he's in a hard way. Made a few bad investments. Now his wife's been diagnosed with some major disease and he's got to raise money fast."

"What's that got to do with me? Unless you want me to wait for the loan you're making me?"

"I'm afraid his, er, problem is much larger than yours. However, it can be solved fairly easily."

"How so?"

"His investments are with Globe."

"And...?"

"If I could get a look at some of their memos or records, I should be able to steer him in the direction of a more stable venture. Just a quick overview should do it. Globe's a new client for you, right?"

"Yes." This guy's more than good, he's superb, the top rung of the con-man's ladder. I relax and let him think he's reeling in his fish. "And you'd just look at stuff. You wouldn't take anything."

"Oh, no. Nothing illegal." Scott holds up a hand, palm forward, as if pledging an oath.

"Okay. Let's go." I stand, take a last sip of coffee and pick up my purse, just to see Scott's reaction.

Immediate and negative. "Not right now. Not during office hours. Someone might wonder what you were doing. I wouldn't want the slightest appearance of misconduct to fall on you."

"When then? How?"

"We could meet back in the office one night. You could access your files and show me."

"Umm, no, I don't think so. You know how much on edge everyone is." I sit back down and prop my chin on a fist as if to mull a solution. "It's like we're in a prison or something. If I got caught after hours, I'm sure to be in trouble. And you can't sit next to me during office hours. Let me think. Let me think. How can you see my files when I'm not around?" I cast my eyes toward the ceiling and drum my fingernails on the table with more vigor. What's with this guy? Am I going to have to open my mouth and say the words myself? Why did I think he was so good at the con game mere minutes before? Password, password, I scream inside myself, ask me for my damn password.

"Your password," says Scott and I nearly fall out of the booth with mingled relief and amazement at my powers of mental coercion. "You could tell me what it's been changed to. Then you wouldn't have to be anywhere near me or offer me help."

"What a great idea," I enthuse. "You could just stay a little late or come in a tiny bit earlier, and kablamee, success. Okay. Here it is." I inhale deeply to add to Scott's suspense and he replicates my action. "Muzak-too. That's M-U-Z-A-K-T-O-O. I was still thinking about the Revue. Did I tell you that after we won the competition, I auditioned for the city choir and made it?"

"Wow. Cool," Scott throws my way with about as much sincerity as if he were applauding the antics of an especially boring child reciting "The Charge of the Light Brigade." He immediately gets to his feet. "I'll take off now. You wait a few minutes. Much better if we're not seen together," he says, fleeing so quickly the back of his jacket is the only thing in my view.

Dolores cranes around again from her seat by the cash register. When she sees the coast is clear, that is, the prime suspect no longer loiters in the dining room, she saunters to my booth, wiping her palms on her apron. "Did he take the bait?" she whispers. I dip one-two-three slow nods and Dolores claps her hands with the glee of the unrepentant waiting for an orgy.

CHAPTER FIFTEEN

The rest of the day I ponder, if pondering means thinking obsessively about the dummy password in between answering phones, greeting clients, and composing form letters threatening legal action against clients for whom legal representation was simply the most recent in a downward spiral of overwhelming debts and financial obligations. Since none of these activities requires more of me than one-tenth of my attention, I can consider what I now think of as the "Scott situation" from multiple perspectives.

It certainly appears that apprehension of the culprit is within reach. But what if something happens to prevent this? Scott is one slimy sneaky dude. He surely is skilled enough to cover his ass, most possibly with my skin. What a vision *that* brings to mind, I think, and quickly wipe it out. Maybe he'll figure out a way for me to take the blame after all? Maybe he's setting me up for a fall. An echo of Kevin's scorn from the last meeting of the Fabulous Four about my abilities drifts through my mind, followed quickly by his overdramatic, extremist appraisal of possible danger.

If I take a more active role in the proceedings, I'll never be in any real danger. Situations like that happen only in the newspaper or movies. I recall Joan of Arc. Was she content to sit in the background and let her troops lead themselves? No! She was in the front lines leading them on to victory. I'll show Kevin! I'll insure that Scott's captured and I play the heroine. Besides escalating my worth greatly to the firm's partners, I'll assume an aura of daring and bravery, a mesmeric combination of excitement and power, that will attract Kevin as inexorably as a magnet draws a nail. A metal nail, not one of those cheap, weak plastic ones used so frequently in shoddy workmanship nowadays.

I shake my head to rid myself of the extraneous thought. Pondering certainly is work, as exhausting as actually scrubbing a dirt-caked floor or hiking a rocky trail in the mountains. Thankful that only rarely am I compelled to ponder, I turn to the next task at hand—creating a plan whereby I will be transformed through my own sheer willpower into a heroine.

Obviously I'll have to get myself to the site of Scott's nefarious doings in the office. I place little reliance on Davis's guarantee that through some modern marvel of technology, Scott will be positively identified as the perpetrator. Who does Davis think he is, Superman? Without an eyewitness to his crime, Scott most likely will get away scot-free, so to speak. Therefore, I will have to be present.

But how can I know exactly when the crime will occur? Instantaneously tonight? That would be a disaster, for I have no plan. Might the surveillance continue for weeks? I can picture myself hiding in the bathroom at the end of every day or, worse still, crawling into the keyhole of my desk to escape notice when the last person leaves the office.

My goodness, this pondering consumes the hours, I think as I look at the clock and notice it's time to leave. With relief I also see the sign-out board where a number of the more athletic attorneys, including Scott, indicate their destination—their weekly basketball competition. That means no way Scott will be coming back to the office tonight. The games frequently last half the night and if they don't, the post-game visit to a bar certainly does, as reported the next day by the bragging participants.

I hurry home. A strategy's coalescing, taking shape like an apparition or a hope gradually materializing. I need someone to talk to, however, a reliable friend with strong common sense, off whom I can bounce ideas. Not Kevin—he's the one I want to impress. Dolores. Through thick and thin, highs and lows, Dolores has been a constant support.

I ring Dolores while dinner zaps away in the microwave. Naturally I reveal only the broadest strokes in the picture, a mere outline, sensing that even Dolores might object to my tackling a reconnaissance on my own. In addition, there's no way Dolores will tolerate being left out of an exciting development. So she'll have to be ignorant of details.

"I have the best idea," I announce without permitting Dolores to say more than, "*Hola.*" "Something to put that creep Scott away for sure. You know, I can't leave it up to chance that he'll be caught. Why, someone might think it's me using that password at weird times."

"What are you up to now?" sniffs Dolores with the bossiness of the eldest of eight children honed by the native suspicion of a mother of three.

"Don't you think he deserves to be humiliated in front of the world?" I continue, ignoring Dolores's question.

"Yeeees..."

"Well, I'm the one to do it. No more sitting around playing Ms. Nice Gal. I've come up with a way to force his exposure."

"And it involves...?" Dolores fades off, then completes her phrase, as she remembers our conversations over the months "...you hiding in the office and catching him in the act. Just like we talked about! Hooray!"

"Why are you so thrilled?" I put in.

"Because I'll be there with you."

"No. Absolutely not. This is my battle."

"No way I'm going to let you waltz off on your own. Just imagine yourself all alone in that big dark office. Skreeek. The door squeaks open. You see Scott in the doorway, huge and hazardous. He lumbers toward you, death in his eyes." She pauses for effect, then resumes in a normal tone. "And two witnesses are better than one. Right?"

I shiver off Dolores's melodrama. "Okay. You can come. But you have to do exactly what I tell you." After I give her the details and hang up, I expend my excess energy dancing through the apartment, first to the radio in the bedroom, then from room to room. When my favorite oldies group sings a refrain from my inspirational song, "Widen your eyes and look all around... You'll start dancin' to a different sound... Just start dreaming about what's coming," I take this as a guarantee.

I release a major strategy the very next day. As keeper of the phone lines, I know who's in when. So it's simple to track Scott's comings and goings. I can even leave a discreet message on his line suggesting he meet me mid-morning in front of the building. The cafeteria is an impossibility for a rendezvous. I don't want to take the slightest chance of Dolores interfering.

From behind one of the pillars in front of the office building, I observe Scott come through the door and scope out the concrete walkway and foyer. He's an attractive, even striking specimen of masculinity, I still must admit, but now I imagine the hair slicked back from his broad brow is oily not only with hair product but also with the natural sleaziness of the man's character. The blinders of sexual attraction are off my eyes entirely, I realize, and shudder to think how close I came to yielding him power over my life.

I step out into a square of blinding sunlight. Scott blinks, then smiles a toothy grin, somewhere between a leer and a salacious come-hither look.

"You needed to see me?" he asks. "Something to do with your *new client*?" Scott's voice italicizes the word as a substitute for Globe Investments.

I capture Scott's suit sleeve between my thumb and index finger and I tug him to the side of the foyer by potted plants that lend some camouflage. "Yes," I whisper, drawing the "s" out into a hiss. "I've heard that the partners are going to firewall some of our biggest clients so that no one but them can access the files. They are really really nervous about security. So if you're going to use my password, it had better be soon."

I nearly laugh out loud at the expression on Scott's face, but I choke it back into a sequence of heavy breathing, as if I've been running or terrified. Panic, pure and simple, pours down from his forehead to his chin in the space of three blinks of an eye, then disappears behind an immobile façade.

"Come, come," he says, reassuring and patronizing as a male physician. "I'm sure there's no reason to be concerned. Who told you this?"

"One of the paralegals," I gasp.

"Kimberlee?" he asks lightly, but between gritted teeth.

I cast around in my mind. If I finger Kimberlee, is Scott more or less likely to take the warning seriously? Less, I decide. Scott's overweening conceit will lead him to think Kimberlee started the rumor to get revenge on his rejection of her.

"No," I declare. "Actually one of the other two." To maintain my pose of financial desperation as my motivation, I add, "What now? This won't prevent you from lending me the money, will it?"

"Certainly not," Scott assures me. "But this changes the situation. Not in terms of my loan, but the speed with which I must act. I've got to go now." He begins to stride off. I half-cling to him and he nearly drags me in the direction of the elevators before he successfully shakes me off.

"Wait just a few minutes before you come up," he urges. "We still need to be careful about being seen together."

I release him with obvious reluctance and watch him enter the crowd of people headed up. Success! Not only do I possess a flair for singing, now I've discovered a wealth of acting talent, too. He's taken the bait, a foolish fish flopping at the end of my line of lies, nearly ready to be reeled in.

As for myself, now that I have the bit between my teeth, to change metaphors drastically, I feel power growing from the decision to take action. No fear. No hesitation. It's as if my path were marked as bold and brilliant as an airport runway at midnight. I've given Scott the best motivation for immediate action—self-interest. He'll come back to the office tonight, I'm sure. And I'll be there, too.

That evening, the power drained from my body and soul by three hours passed sitting on the floor next to Kimberlee's desk, only a tiny penlight to hold the dark at bay, I'm not so sure of my abilities. There's something about gloomy shadows and empty time that sap self-confidence. Did Saint Joan feel this way when she lingered in prison? Did she question her every decision, double-guess whether she'd been quite as smart as she hoped? I am, starting at the present and moving backwards in time minute by slow minute until I reach events like my divorce, separation, buying a house, moving back to Denver, accompanying James when he entered the service, marriage, high school graduation, my father's death, his desertion, even so long ago as the science project I chose in seventh grade, something to do with growing mold, as I recall, a disaster that convinced me to have absolutely nothing to do with science ever again, surely a life-altering decision. Maybe I would have been a wonderful nurse or pharmacist or doctor or microbiologist, whatever it was that people interested in science did. Now it's too late—I'll never be a nuclear physicist.

Speaking of late, where the hell is Dolores? She was supposed to be here within half an hour after I called her. If she doesn't hurry, she's in danger of running smack-dab into Scott. Even when she uses our secret code on the door to signal me—knock three times rapidly, then twice slowly—I might be opening the lock for her when Scott exits the elevator on our floor. I've tried both her home and cell phone. Absolutely nothing.

But I'm committed to this line of action. After spending this much time and effort to catch the sneaky fink, no way I'm going to abandon my post. Would Saint Joan? And like Ingrid Bergman as Saint Joan, I review my plan to make sure everything is set. Body, or at least butt, partly hidden in the kneehole of Kimberlee's desk—check. Telephone on the floor next to me—check. Finger hovering over the autodial for Security—check. Pen light clicking off and on easily—check. But I've been abandoned by Dolores.

Just as I reach this gloomy conclusion, I hear a scratching metallic sound by the office door. One tiny gasp and I switch off the pen light. Has to be Scott because there is no knock. I freeze, waiting for the overhead lights to go on. They don't. Instead a large ring of illumination bobs around the reception area walls, ceiling, furniture. Scott must be scanning to make sure he's alone. Bad move on his part, for anyone who may have spotted something irregular in the hall or the office would surely get suspicious to see a guy holding a flashlight in his hand like a burglar, I think, juggling my own flashlight from hand to hand.

Footsteps slap quickly from the seating area to the back side wall with the lighting controls. Now the overhead fluorescents activate and I wriggle closer to Kimberlee's desk for shelter. The footsteps move to the sector of the room reserved for office help. I hear the scrape of a chair being pushed, the creak as a body sits down, a soft sigh and distinctive ping-ding of a computer activating, the pulse of its screen coming to life, the tap-tap-tap of words being entered. Scott's hard at work breaking into the firm's files using *my* password.

Now comes the challenge, I realize. I've overlooked the fact that I can't tell exactly what Scott is accessing on the files, or when. Simply sitting at my desk and using my computer isn't enough to show he's the guilty party. He could claim he sat there for convenience. I have to catch him while he's looking through confidential files. Therefore, I'll have to peek out and watch him. I swallow hard and raise my head, slow and silent as a stalking panther or a curious monkey, to gaze over the edge of Kimberlee's desk. Yes, there he is, and the Globe Investments file is open! Now all I have to do is punch in Security. The office building is staffed with protection twenty-four hours a day. I move my arm carefully to Kimberlee's phone, remove the receiver and place it on the desk top, and push the nearly soundless button to connect automatically with help. Thanks to the speaker function, I don't even need to lift the receiver. A guard should be up soon to check on a call coming through at this time of night.

"Hello, Joan," says Scott. "I'm glad you decided to join me."

I'm paralyzed. How does he know I'm here? His back is still toward me. Maybe he's guessing. Maybe if I don't move at all, I'll blend in with the furniture.

"I can see your reflection in the screen," Scott continues. "I'm rather surprised, yes, and hurt, too, that you didn't alert me to your change in plans. What altered the situation? Decide you could get more money out of me than the measly several thousand to cover your debts? Think you'd strike out on your own and eliminate the middle man?"

"Nnnnnnnooooo..." I stammer as I stand. Then, putting some actual thought into a response to his question, I repeat with strength, "No. I'd never do anything that two-handed. Back-handed. Back-fisted. Whatever."

"Why not? Because it's dishonest? But you *would* give someone, me, maybe anyone, the password to your computer in exchange for a favor. Isn't that equally dishonest?" Scott swings around in my chair so he's facing me and pins a look of intense interest to his sleekly handsome face as if he can't wait to hear my explanation.

I don't disappoint him, but I hope I surprise him. "No. Because what you didn't know is I fed you a fake password just to trick you into using it. This has been a total set-up to trap you."

"Trap me?" He raises his palms upward and shrugs his shoulders. "I don't understand what you mean. I came back to the office to collect some papers and discovered you hard at work at your computer, digging through the Globe Investments file."

"Me? *You* are the one using the password," I say, fighting a sinking feeling that something's going very wrong indeed.

Now Scott leans back in his chair, legs stretched before him, ankles crossed, fingers laced behind his head, at perfect ease and in no hurry to respond. Finally he does. "Yes, but who could tell? Seems to me you're much likelier to be fingered as the culprit. And if you persist in setting me up, that's exactly what I'll claim. You bragged to me how you were going to make a fortune, I believed what you said. And I, defender of honesty and justice that I am, came back to the office to intercept you. Alternately, I just happened to stumble upon your nefarious doings when I returned for a forgotten document."

In a quandary, dilemma, predicament, impasse (no single word quite captures the situation), I struggle to make sense of the apparent reversal of my fortunes. From absolute euphoria at my successful capture of a sneaky thief, to being framed smack-dab head-over-heels for the evil deeds myself. What to do? What to do? Security hasn't arrived yet. Maybe no one is listening to the conversation. I might be getting framed for Scott's evil-doings. Another brilliant idea strikes me. I'll put the fear of God in Scott. I immediately open my mouth and let out privileged information.

"Security is listening in on this conversation via the phone. That will end this game without delay. Since I've reported the incident, I won't be a suspect." So there, I very nearly add. No sooner have the words taken flight from my lips than I immediately wish I'd controlled myself and left them unsaid, for Scott's face turns an unusual shade of red, bright and shiny like a tomato so ripe it's ready to burst. He bounds to his feet and lunges over Kimberlee's desk to wrap his hands around my neck. Nose to nose, he exhales his words on a stream of breath soured by intense anger.

"You smart-ass bitch. That cuts it all. No holds barred now." He's shaking me by the neck with such strength that my entire body flops like a rag. Then my words sink in and he recalls mention of a phone. He lets me loose, to scramble on the floor for Kimberlee's phone, pulls it out by the cord and flings it across the room. While he's occupied, I dart across the space between my desk and Kimberlee's, keeping the furniture between us.

Then he turns his attention back to me. The red has drained from his features, leaving behind a pallor and immobility that reminds me of a malignant corpse. "Don't imagine you'll have time to be rescued by Security or you're bloody crazy," he continues his tirade. "In fact, you'll be lucky to live another five minutes. I've tolerated you for months, chased after your fat ass, smirked and smiled and applauded your so-called talent, pitiful as it is, feigned fascination with your disgustingly naïve sexuality. If you think I'm going to let you ruin the biggest chance that's ever dropped in my lap, you're even more brainless than I imagined."

This is delivered in a voice so low that it's ten times more terrifying than a shouted rage. As he speaks, Scott rocks from side-to-side opposite me, stretching to reach me across the desk. I reverse his movements to keep out of his grasp, thinking we resemble a sequence in a cartoon. Humor, however, is not remotely included on Scott's range of emotions. His fingers are clutching and unclutching in a life-threatening reflex, eager to circle my neck again.

Now's my chance since he's stalled by the expanse of desk between us. I turn and dash for the office door, but Scott's even faster in his recovery than I am in my escape attempt. He grabs me by the arm. Instinctively, I struggle and Scott balances my action by pulling me to him until the weight of my body becomes unbalanced and I stumble, I tip forward, sprawled awkwardly against him. Scott releases me, only to grab my shoulders and throw me to one side where I stumble again, clinging to a chair in the reception area, trying to keep my knees off the floor, a vulnerable position. Rage seems to refine Scott's physical responses, slowing them down while magnifying them. He seizes me by the shoulders and hauls me upright, pulls one arm back to make a fist.

I find myself mentally praying, pleading, begging for help from whatever powers are superior to the human. And the strangest sensation comes over me. I've heard of a person's life passing before his eyes in a life-threatening situation. I've read about a change in time that can occur, a stretching and simultaneous slowing of movements and minutes. But I've never thought that a vision, perhaps a hallucination, is possible. Whatever the official term for the phenomena (and probably that's irrelevant), I see a blurry but inescapably feminine figure dressed in silver armor just behind Scott's dodging body. I hear the voice of Saint Joan or Ingrid Bergman addressing me. "Joan," she says, "Joan, this is the hour, now is the time. Strike, strike boldly." The exact same words as in the movie!

She holds a sword as long as her body and points its tip toward a marble-topped coffee table just to my right. I feel a kind of ecstasy, a strength filling me from head to toe, and at that moment I know I have the physical power to overcome Scott.

Somehow I know I've got to hold off until the last possible moment to make my move. I need something to throw Scott off balance, take him by surprise. And without any awareness, a song bursts full-force from my throat. The glass shade of the lamp on my desk rattles from the vibrations I've created in the air. "Just start dreaming about what's coming..." The hallmark tune that heralded my coming to adulthood.

I'm probably more surprised than Scott by what's coming out of my throat. But I'm accustomed to my own voice, so I don't jump as high as the desk, as he does, while he simultaneously jerks and releases me, shoving me into yet another stumble. As I recover, I move abruptly to the right and shove the coffee table as hard as I can in his direction. The flat plane and sharp edge of the marble top catch Scott smack in the shins. A hideous crack fills the air. He drops down to his knees with a pain-filled moan, still clutching my shoulder.

Blam! The office door flies open and rebounds off the wall. The unexpected noise compels a physical startle-reaction in both Scott and me. Instead of the blow Scott has been threatening, he plummets backwards, dragging me with him. As I fall, I look upward and see Kevin, hair standing on end and radiating from his head in a halo, looming over us like an avenging angel before all three of us wind up in a tangled heap together.

Kevin recovers first. Scrambling to his feet, he plucks Scott up by the scruff of the neck, pins his wrists behind his back, and focuses attention on me. "You okay?"

I nod, too breathless and overwhelmed by events to speak, at which point Kevin begins to wield Scott like a terrier with a rat.

The fall must have disoriented Scott, for he shakes his head as if to clear it, strains against Kevin's hold, and breaks loose. In the middle of the ensuing chaos, consisting of random swings, punches, grabs, most of which fail to make any connection but are accompanied by masculine growls, grunts, and threats, two uniformed officers appear in the doorway, guns drawn.

"Hold it," comes the command. "Just hold everything right there." Over the policemen's shoulders, Davis's head bobbles left and right trying to obtain a clear view from the hall.

CHAPTER SIXTEEN

The battling duo freeze except to swivel their heads toward the door. A tousled Scott, expensive business attire no longer impeccable, immediately raises both hands over his head in surrender and assumes his most charming demeanor. "Everything's fine, officers, now that you're here. I returned to the office to find this young lady busy at her computer in the middle of the night. We've had trouble with unauthorized access to files, so I imagine she's the culprit."

I'm immobile next to the two. I pale and imitate Scott, hands high. Is it possible that, after all I've done, all I've been through, I'll be sucked into the vortex of suspicion? Totally unfair. "No. You've got to listen to me. I didn't do anything illegal." I now know how much of a disadvantage holding your arms over your head puts you at. In this inferior, pleading position, I immediately feel guilty, regardless of circumstances, and wonder if I have any chance of convincing the police.

With attention focused on me and Scott, Kevin takes advantage of the perfect opportunity to haul back and punch Scott full on the jaw. While the satisfying result is Scott flat on his back, the complementary action consists of the police officers barking orders like neurotic watch dogs and forcing Kevin into a prone position next to a groaning Scott, who cradles his chin in one palm.

"No, no." Davis edges further into the room, waves his hands in the air and dances from foot to foot, gasping for attention. "You've got the wrong man. Him. Him." He points at Scott. Dolores appears from the hallway, clutching the back of Davis's shirt, and also moves into the room, her normal bravado conspicuously missing in this scene fraught with crimes of some tangible if indefinable type. Last to enter is the guard from Security, the one I counted on as first line of rescue. This guy resembles a starving mouse more than anything else, with thin gray hair combed over his pate, an even sparser moustache, small bony frame, and dun-colored uniform. He hugs the wall and twitches his nose in the direction of anyone who speaks.

In several minutes, authority is restored. The police pay heed to Davis's factual, objective directions to free Kevin and handcuff Scott, who still denies any involvement at the top of his lungs as he is escorted out, struggling. I look around the reception area while I massage my neck, thinking that the strength of Scott's fingers are surely going to create bruise marks. Not bad, I think, for a temporary war zone. During the struggles, my desk as well as Kimberlee's were swept clear of any small items, which landed on the floor in scatters like so many abandoned pieces of litter on a beach. A ficus tree, tall as a man, was upended and spewed its dirt and rocks in front of the brown leather couch where clients wait to be called into the august presence of their attorneys. Several office chairs joined the mess on the floor, their overturned legs thrusting small coaster-wheels toward the ceiling.

Into this scene, Mr. Horowitz steps, an anomaly with his hair combed, tie straight, pocket handkerchief bravely and fashionably fluttering. While he always seems to take life with equanimity, I think that having his every concern vindicated and resolved should bring a spark of enthusiasm to light his eyes and a twinge of satisfaction to quirk his lips. No. Simply Mr. Horowitz making sure, with a lawyer's precision, that i's have been dotted, t's crossed, and all is right with his world.

In unison and immediately, all of us in the room begin to talk. Who has done what, when, with whom, and why. What the repercussions have been. How well or poorly strategies have functioned. Mr. Horowitz seizes control. "Hold it! One at a time."

As the possessor of the most powerful voice, Dolores takes precedence. "So when Joan told me she'd found a way to force Scott's hand and he was coming here tonight, I promised to meet her and be a second witness and a safeguard. But then my car broke down. I panicked. I took a taxi to catch Davis."

"Yes and then I checked the cameras and saw what was going on, we could see Joan down by the other desk, and Scott at her desk, and we called Kevin and said we should contact the police to come with us," broke in Davis. "'Call the police? We can't wait for that,' Kevin said. 'This may turn out to be nothing or a minute may mean the difference between life and death. No way to tell.'"

Dolores takes up the recitation again. "And then I said, surely she wouldn't try to tackle a thief on her own, would she? And Kevin said, 'Oh, yes, she would. You don't know how pea-brained she can be if she gets a wild idea in her head.'"

Davis breaks in, "And he said, 'I'd better make tracks over there immediately while you call.' So that's what we did. Then we waited for the police and found the door open and we saw Kevin wrestling with Scott."

"Now just a minute," I say. "You may not know, but I'm the one who delivered the blow that brought Scott down. I shoved the coffee table into his shins." I conveniently omit my guide and mentor, Saint Joan, as well as the fact that I stumbled into my solution. "And I called Security. Plus left the receiver so Scott and I could be overheard."

Mr. Horowitz nods slowly, slowly, as if in final judgment. "Just as we thought. Well done, all of you, and especially you, young man, well done." This to Davis. "The video cameras you installed in hidden locations through the office will enable us to charge the culprit. What a shame it had to be someone associated with us." He shakes his head in mock dismay even while a huge grin of satisfaction finally occupies his face.

"Video cameras? You mean you saw everything that went on here? I'm not under suspicion?" I ask. "Why didn't you tell me about them when they were installed?"

"They didn't tell me either. Davis had the idea to install them," says Dolores, but for some reason, she sounds proud.

"We didn't tell you for the very reason that occurred," snaps Kevin. "We needed to make sure your innocence could be proven. Which we could hardly accomplish with you and Dolores running off half-cocked to try to make some secret, heroic capture on your own, which I suspected you'd do. Even if you managed through some fluke not to get murdered." He walks away to lean against the door and it's clear my bravery hasn't impressed him in the least.

"Hence, the cameras," continues Davis.

"Anyway, all's well that ends well," says Dolores. "I'm just relieved that you didn't get major hurt. I'm so so sorry that I let you down. That damn car. It's about fifteen years old and it breaks down every other week."

"That's something we'll take care of tomorrow," says Davis.

"I can't let you do that," says Dolores.

"You have no say in the matter," says Davis with a masterful demeanor I've never seen before.

What's going on? I expect Dolores to slap Davis across the face or scratch his bossy eyes out. Instead she flutters her eyelashes in a distinctly feminine fashion and caves. "Okay. If you really want to."

"What's going on?" I ask, then hesitate. Maybe not my business. What the hell, I've been through thick and thicker with Davis and Dolores. "What's up, you two? Have I missed something?"

"Nope. Happy endings always make me high," says Dolores. "Davis is boing-bingo!"

"Especially," says Davis, "since the happy ending is truly happy for me. Dolores and I are getting married."

"Whaaat?" This is totally unexpected, I think, watching in disbelief as Dolores buries her head in Davis's shoulder and apparently nods in agreement, although the only thing visible is her curls bobbing up and down.

"Yes, indeed," Davis says as he wraps his arm around her. "I know we must seem like a mismatched couple, but we actually fit together quite well. Balanced, as it were."

"Yes," agrees Dolores, nodding her head with so much enthusiasm her hair twirls. "See, he's tall, I'm short." She lays her head down again.

"I'm mental, cerebral..."

"And I'm physical and emotional," says Dolores, peeking out from her shelter.

"I've got a master's degree."

"And I've got a GED."

"My family's upper-middle-class."

"My family's working class."

"I've traveled the world."

"I've visited every fishing hole in the state."

"I hate to break into this joyful scene," breaks in Mr. Horowitz, "but it's past time to close the office. Unless you wish to continue discussing the incident all night. I, for one, need my sleep."

This announcement creates a general movement toward the door, disbanding the crew and disconnecting the exhilaration that naturally links our emotions. I don't dare to look at Kevin. He must be absolutely furious with me, I think. What a miserable mess I've made, when all I wanted was to convince Kevin of my finer qualities. Instead he thinks he has to drag me out of trouble like some ten-year-old child.

We all head out of the building and Kevin and I turn in opposite directions without exchanging a word, a reticence overlooked by the babbling happy couple of Dolores and Davis as well as Mr. Horowitz.

The short drive home is long enough for me to review my entire relationship with Kevin, from high school through the present. Most recently, month after month, he's spent the majority of his waking hours rescuing me from my own stupidity. If he held any tenderness for me before, my most recent escapade has surely convinced him I'm a hopeless cause. I need to stop depending on him to correct my mistakes, fix things in my crazy mixed-up life.

And I can no longer bear to be near Kevin when I lack the smallest chance of developing a romantic relationship with him. I have to take some sort of positive action. For Kevin's happiness and my own peace of mind, I have to distance myself from him. The best way to do that is physically, move away, get out of this apartment building where he's right down the hall, unavoidable in the elevator and by the mail boxes, a constant temptation to invite to dinner or out for a movie, take walks or watch television together. Too much companionship, not enough passion. Yes, that's what I'll do, find a new place to live, somewhere far out in the suburbs, preferably a residence filled entirely with maladjusted, rejected women like myself.

On automatic I park the car, enter the building, go up the elevator, open my apartment, switch on the lights, hang up my coat, and change into pajamas. I stand irresolute in the middle of the living room, unsure of my next action. A knock interrupts my gloomy musing. I shuffle my limp bunny slippers to the door and swing it open to reveal Kevin, who bursts into a tirade without allowing a second to pass.

"How could you? How could you take such a foolish, stupid, dangerous step? To waltz off on your own without any support, without even telling anyone? Are you a complete idiot or just training to be one?" His arms wave in circles through the air like a broken, helpless windmill, and his skin assumes that interesting mottled red effect common to angry, frustrated blonds. "That man is dangerous. He could have hurt you, even killed you."

I back up, drawing Kevin after me into the apartment, as if I were a magnet, and he, iron. "I know. I mean I know that now. I can't say how sorry I am. Not just for tonight. For the whole past nine months or so. Ever since you came back into my life." I keep retreating, Kevin continues to follow.

I know I'm nattering, chattering, just to give myself time to pull myself together. Is Kevin truly angry? Maybe I should play it humble. "I've gotten into one mess after another. So I made lots of mistakes. And, unfortunately, I dragged you into them, too."

"You are absolutely right," says Kevin. "You've messed up over and over." The flush is receding from his face and his voice drops into a lower register.

My mind is speeding, circling, about a thousand miles an hour, desperate to cultivate some sort of rationale for my irrational behavior, my childish attraction to Scott, my ignorance about Kevin's worth, my final recognition of how much he means to me. He deserves nothing less than complete honesty, even if I expose the depth of my feelings. "I don't know why I was such an ass. Maybe during my marriage I didn't mature. I was like a plant in a greenhouse, protected from anything that might challenge me. Once I was forced into the climate of the real world, I had to cram a lot of growing up into a short period of time."

"And have you learned anything? Anything at all?" he asks, but his question isn't shouted as an accusation. It's a gentle probe, like a blind man feeling his way with a cane.

"Have I ever!" I answer. In for a dime, in for a dollar in this game of life, I think, and continue shedding the layers of self-protection, the evasions, the hesitations, I've used to distance myself from Kevin. "I've lost my blinders about men. I used to have a soft spot for charming manipulators like my dad. Like James, like Scott. But they're self-centered and unreliable. Worst of all, they're boring because they never grow, develop, they never change."

"What do you prefer now?" Kevin says.

I avoid the question. "I, myself, have changed all out of my own recognition. I've made, make, a lot of screw-ups. In my own defense I have to say at least I'm trying. But I need to stop dragging other people into my messes." Tears well up in my eyes and begin to spill over, huge drops rolling down my cheeks uncontrolled. Still I talk, yammer, holding a complete loss of control at bay.

"So since I seem to be unable to stop involving you, just like tonight, it's past time that I learn to depend only on myself. I've decided to move away, find a new place where I won't be able to constantly call on you for help."

Looking as if he's suffering a delayed reaction from his tussle with Scott, Kevin's mouth opens and closes without emitting any sounds. He steps closer to me. I move back, hitting my thighs against the couch behind me, then sitting down with a soft thud. "Why?" he finally croaks.

"I told you," I say. "I'm sure you're tired of rescuing me."

"Did I ever say that?"

"No. But you've acted disgusted upon occasion. And you read me the riot act about not getting involved in your romances." A few more fat tears joined their fellows on my face.

Again Kevin is speechless, shakes his head back and forth as if words can't convey his feelings. This is succeeded by apparent paralysis, broken only by widening eyes and clenched jaw.

"What? What?" I squeal. No, dummy me. I'm witnessing the launch of a tirade.

"I know what's behind this fresh scheme," Kevin hisses as he leans forward and puts both hands on my shoulders. "You've discovered another romantic obsession, one that you're afraid I'll find fault with. Who is it now? One of the policemen? A new lawyer? Someone from Randi's party?" With each word he closes in, ending nose to nose with me.

How can he misunderstand me so? I hasten to disabuse him of his error. "No, no. It's you, only you. I mean I'm concerned about you." I scurry to throw dust in his eyes. "I'm concerned about you wasting your time taking care of me."

"Have I ever complained?"

"No," I admit. "You're a Superman. Absolutely flawless. That's the problem."

For long moments we stare in each other's eyes. I feel myself drowning in the cobalt depths of Kevin's, sinking into his soul. Soon I'll have no self. Only a thin, Joan-shaped shell will remain. I raise a palm to his cheek and murmur, "That's the problem. You're so much a part of me, I'm afraid I won't survive if you ever leave. So I've got to leave first." I raise my lips and press them gently against Kevin's, finally dropping every pretense, every excuse, every barrier to admitting my true feelings.

Always the perfect gentleman, Kevin wastes no time in wrapping his arms around me and deepening the kiss by a hundredfold. An awkward position? Yes. Kevin leans over me and tries his best to meld our bodies together. Within seconds we topple over on the couch, still locked together like, well, like two lovers, I have to admit to myself. And in true lover-like fashion, each of us murmurs nearly identical words, phrases like "I've wanted you forever" and "Don't ever leave me," "You make me complete" and "Only you, always you." Still we avoid the most banal of stereotypes, the immediate fall into a bed. We manage at last, after what seemed to be an hour or two, to resume seated positions on the couch to discuss the future with only an occasional nuzzle or squeeze to delay the proceedings.

"So you're not moving," Kevin states.

Surely he doesn't have a doubt? "No. Not as long as you want me here," I say.

"Now that we have that settled, I need to admit that you rescued yourself in the most recent episode," Kevin says. "I can't take credit for it."

"I didn't do it alone," I say, thinking of Saint Joan and the happy results of my stumbling around when Scott was trying to attack me. "You might say I stumbled into a solution thanks to my patron saint."

"Who? Oh, the Saint Joan obsession again."

"Not an obsession," I insist. "She was there, telling what to do, guiding my moves."

"Whatever works for you," says Kevin. "But in any case, I agree you've changed. Nine months ago you never would have attempted to save yourself. You would have curled up in a ball and cried."

I give him a mock-slap across the face that turns into a stroke. "Nice guy."

"There is one thing that will never change," says Kevin. "I've loved you since eighth grade. Fat or skinny. Rich or poor. In sickness or in health. It's about time I get rewarded for my loyalty."

"I'm a reward?" I ask, a blush of pleasure mounting my neck at the idea. "I'm a reward," I reiterate with certainty. "And you're my reward."

"Yes." Kevin gives me a hug. "No more loneliness for either of us. The misunderstandings and the trouble are over."

"No," I answer. "Don't you remember the saying? It's never over until the fat lady sings." I stand, belt out the "The past's no more, the past's no more" refrain from "Just Start Dreaming About What's Coming" and collapse into his waiting arms.

ABOUT THE AUTHOR

Bonnie McCune credits her tenacity for the successes in her life. She has been writing since age ten, when she submitted a poem to the *Saturday Evening Post* (it was immediately rejected). Still she was determined to be a writer. This interest facilitated her career in nonprofits doing public and community relations and also in freelance news and features. Her community involvement includes grass-roots organizations, political campaigns, writers' and arts' groups, and children's literacy. For years, she entered recipe contests and was a finalist once to the Pillsbury Cook Off. Her true writing passion is fiction, and her pieces have won several awards. *A Saint Comes Stumbling In* is her first published novel. For reasons unknown (an unacknowledged optimism?), she believes that one person can make a difference in this world. McCune lives in Colorado. Read more about her and her work at www.BonnieMcCune.com.

Thank you for your purchase.

We hope you've enjoyed your read and invite you to visit us
online for more sweet and inspirational romance titles from
Inspired Romance Novels!

www.inspiredromancenovels.com

Made in the USA
Lexington, KY
22 July 2012